Von der Fakultät Architektur, Bauingenieurwesen und Umweltwissenschaften

der Technischen Universität Carolo-Wilhelmina zu Braunschweig

zur Erlangung des Grades

eines Doktoringenieurs (Dr.-Ing.)

genehmigte Dissertation

Eingereicht am	23. November 2010
Disputation am	27. Oktober 2011
Berichterstatter	PD Dr.-Ing. L. Lehmann
	Prof. Dr.-Ing. J. Stahlmann
	Prof. Dr.-Ing. O. v. Estorff

ABSTRACT

The accurate prediction of ground deformations and ground failure is an important basis for the building of safe and economic constructions. False estimations can result in the worst-case scenario in the collapse of a construction. Hence, a reliable prediction of the bearing capacity and the deformation of the building ground is essential for the safety of the population.

This work presents a new method for the calculation of elasto-plastic building ground deformations and elasto-plastic building ground failure with included wave propagation in the ground. The presented procedure is a hybrid method, based on several common calculation methods. Included is the *nonlinear calculation* with the *finite element method (FEM)*, a *nonlinear HHT-α method* and the *scaled boundary finite element method (SBFEM)*.

Focuses of this work are the implementation of an *elasto-plastic soil model with isotropic hardening*, the derivation and implementation of a *nonlinear HHT-α method* with *full Newton-Raphson iteration*, and the implementation of these methods and the SBFEM in a *nonlinear overall calculation scheme*. Here, the *overall calculation scheme* represents a new calculation method in the time domain, because the combination of the named methods does not yet exist. Furthermore, the developed nonlinear HHT-α method with full Newton-Raphson iteration is a new extension variant of the nonlinear HHT-α method with modified Newton-Raphson iteration from (Crisfield, Non-linear finite element analysis of solids and structures, Vol. 2 Advanced Topics, 1997).

In the process of this work a general derivation of the FEM and the Newton-Raphson method is given, followed by an accurate and detailed derivation of the *cap model*. The cap model denotes the named elasto-plastic soil model. This soil model is then implemented in a nonlinear *overall calculation scheme*. The nonlinear overall *calculation scheme* is based on the Newton-Raphson method, in which the solution is calculated with equilibrium iterations.

In the further process the HHT-α method is derived for the nonlinear case for the including of dynamic excitations of the subsoil. The given derivation is based on a nonlinear HHT-α method from (Crisfield, 1997) with modified Newton-Raphson iteration. For better convergence the nonlinear HHT-α method with modified Newton-Raphson iteration is extended to a HHT-α method with full Newton-Raphson iteration. The previous *overall calculation scheme* is then extended by the nonlinear HHT-α method with full Newton-Raphson iteration.

Finally, the SBFEM is incorporated into the *overall calculation scheme* to include wave propagations to infinity. The now developed method can be used for complex building ground calculations in the time domain with the inclusion of elasto-plastic deformations and wave propagation. With it, occurring wave reflections in pure FEM calculations are avoided.

The applicability of the developed method is given with the help of several examples of different complexity. The examples are related to shallow foundations. But the method is also applicable to pile foundations, building pits and earthquake calculations.

Conclusion:

This work can be used as a tool for building ground calculations with non-negligible dynamic loading. The complexity of the calculation makes the application of the method quite extensive. But a further improvement of computer science will overcome this disadvantage.

ZUSAMMENFASSUNG

Genaue Vorhersagen für Baugrundverformungen und Baugrundversagen bilden eine wichtige Grundlage für den Bau sicherer und wirtschaftlicher Baukonstruktionen. Fehleinschätzungen des Baugrundes können bis zum Einsturz eines Bauwerkes führen. Damit ist eine zuverlässige Vorhersage der Baugrundtragfähigkeit unumgänglich, um die Sicherheit der Bevölkerung zu gewährleisten.

In der vorliegenden Arbeit wird eine neue Methode vorgestellt, mit der sich elastisch-plastische Baugrundverformungen und elastisch-plastisch berechnetes Baugrundversagen unter Einbezug der Wellenausbreitung im Baugrund berechnen lassen. Die vorgestellte Methode ist eine hybride Methode basierend auf mehreren Berechnungsmethoden. Sie beinhaltet eine *nichtlineare Berechnung* mit der *Finite Elemente Methode (FEM)*, einem *nichtlinearen HHT-α Verfahren* und die *Scaled Boundary Finite Element Methode (SBFEM)*.

Die Schwerpunkte der Arbeit liegen in der Implementierung eines *elastisch-plastischen Bodenmodells mit isotroper Verfestigung*, der Entwicklung und Implementierung eines *nichtlineares HHT-α Verfahrens* mit *voller Newton-Raphson Iteration*, und der Implementierung dieser Verfahren und der SBFEM in ein *nichtlineares Gesamtberechnungsschema*. Hierbei stellt das Gesamtberechnungsschema eine neue Berechnungsmethode im Zeitbereich dar, da es die genannte Kombination der Berechnungsmethoden noch nicht gibt. Auch das hier entwickelte nichtlineare HHT-α Verfahren mit voller Newton-Raphson Iteration ist eine neue Erweiterungsvariante eines nichtlinearen HHT-α Verfahrens mit modifizierter Newton-Raphson Iteration aus (Crisfield, Non-linear finite element analysis of solids and structures, Vol. 2 Advanced Topics, 1997).

Im Verlauf dieser Arbeit wird nach einer allgemeinen Herleitung der FEM und des Newton-Raphson Verfahrens eine sehr genaue und ausführliche Herleitung des „Cap Modells" vorgenommen. Bei dem *Cap Modell* handelt es sich um das genannte elastisch-plastische Bodenmodell. Dieses Bodenmodell wird dann in ein nichtlineares Gesamtberechnungsschema implementiert. Das nichtlineare Gesamtberechnungsschema basiert auf dem Newton-Raphson Verfahren, bei dem in entsprechenden Gleichgewichtsiterationen die tatsächliche Lösung berechnet wird.

Um Schwingungserregungen mit einzubeziehen, wird im weiteren Verlauf die HHT-α Methode für den nichtlinearen Fall hergeleitet. Die angegebene Herleitung basiert auf einem Verfahren von (Crisfield, 1997) mit modifizierter Newton-Raphson Iteration. Für eine bessere Konvergenz wird die nichtlineare HHT-α Methode mit modifizierter Newton-Raphson Iteration zu einer nichtlinearen HHT-α Methode mit voller Newton-Raphson Iteration erweitert. Das bisherige Gesamtberechnungsschema wird dann um die nichtlineare HHT-α Methode mit voller Newton-Raphson Iteration ergänzt.

Die bisher angesetzten Verfahren berücksichtigen noch keine Wellenausbreitung ins Unendliche. Um dem Rechnung zu tragen, wird in das Gesamtberechnungsschema die SBFEM einbezogen. Die nun entwickelte Methode kann genutzt werden, um komplexe Baugrundberechnungen im Zeitbereich unter Einbezug von elastisch-plastischer Verformung und Wellenausbreitung ins Unendliche durchzuführen. Die bei einer reinen FEM Berechnung auftretenden Wellenreflexionen werden damit verhindert.

Die Anwendbarkeit des entwickelten Verfahrens wird letztlich anhand von verschiedenen Beispielen mit unterschiedlicher Komplexität gezeigt. Die hier gezeigten Beispiele beziehen sich auf Flachgründungen. Die Methode ist aber genauso übertragbar auf Tiefgründungen, Baugruben oder Erdbebenberechnungen.

Fazit:

Die vorliegende Arbeit kann als Werkzeug zu Baugrundberechnungen verwendet werden, in denen kinetische Belastungen nicht vernachlässigbar sind. Die Komplexität der Berechnung macht das Verfahren jedoch recht aufwändig. Eine weitere Verbesserung der Rechentechnik wird diesen Nachteil jedoch zukünftig aufheben.

ACKNOWLEDGEMENTS

This thesis originates in the years 2006 until 2010, where I was an external doctoral candidate of the *Technische Universität Braunschweig* at the *Institut für Angewandte Mechanik*.

At the same time I worked as a structural engineer in *IBD Ingenieurgesellschaft* in *Schwerin*. In the engineering company part-time work was permitted to me during the process time of the thesis. With it, time was given to me to write this work.

My gratitude goes primarily to PD Dr.-Ing. Lutz Lehmann, who enabled me to write this work as an external doctoral candidate and who assisted me in enlightening scientific discussions or with helpful advice.

I also want to thank the colleagues of the *Institut für Angewandte Mechanik* for their friendly help and their efforts in terms of questions to the finite element program system, which was extended by me.

Furthermore, I want to thank Prof. Dr. Kersten Latz and Prof. Dr. Harald Cramer from the *Hochschule Wismar* for their assistance in particular questions to the thesis.

Finally, I have to express my gratitude to Thomas Bickel and Hubert Dierkes, which are the managing directors of *IBD Ingenieurgesellschaft*. They enabled the part-time work to me, despite inconveniences in the scheduling of the project management.

Martin Bransch

CONTENTS

1 INTRODUCTION

1.1 NUMERICAL CALCULATIONS IN GEOTECHNICAL ENGINEERING

The application of numerical finite element calculations in geotechnical engineering is attended by complex and extensive calculations. Therefore, standard cases in practice are mainly calculated with conventional methods of geotechnical calculations; given e.g. in (Simmer, 1994), (Türke, 1999). However, the increasing improvement of computer science and further specializing of technical knowledge will result in the application of numerical methods for structural geotechnical calculations. Nowadays, only special cases are calculated with the finite element method (Deutsche Gesellschaft für Geotechnik, 1991-2006). These special cases usually require an accurate prediction of the deformations.

Figure 1.1 (Muhs & Weiß, 1972) shows exemplarily soil deformation due to shear failure. The figure shows the settlement of the foundation (with $width = 2m$; $length = 0,5m$; $thickness = 0,3m$ and perpendicular central loading) after shear failure.

FIGURE 1.1. SOIL DEFORMATION DUE TO SHEAR FAILURE (MUHS & WEIß, 1972)

Advantages and disadvantages of numerical calculations in geotechnical engineering

An advantage of the numerical building ground calculation is that numerous influence parameters can be accounted for. These are not included in conventional calculation methods. Due to the numerous numbers of parameters, accurate calculations can be conducted. This is used especially for deformation calculations of the structure, including foundation and adjacent subsoil.

However, the application of the numerical calculation requires knowledge of the used material models and the employed static and dynamic solution procedures so that the results can be interpreted correctly. For the determination of the numerous parameters, a high laboratory effort is needed. Hence, many soil parameters have to be determined and transferred. The transfer of the material parameters in the numerical model requires a calibration and verification of the model, including the material parameters. In this connection, analytical comparative calculations with simple models can be very helpful.

Choice of the material model

The selection of the material model is carried out in accordance with the ground survey. The choice of the material approach must be appropriate for the calculated problem. The calculating engineer has to choose between numerous material models. The choice of material models ranges from simple to very complex material approaches. E.g., the following soil models are given in the order from simple to complex: linear-elastic models; models with varying Young's modulus (Duncan & Chang, 1970); elasto-plastic models(Drucker & Prager, 1952), (Coulomb, 1776),(Lade, 1977); elasto-plastic models with isotropic hardening (DiMaggio & Sandler, 1971), (Roscoe & Schofield, 1963); hypoplastic models (von Wolffersdorff, 1996).

In this work, the complex elasto-plastic *cap model* with isotropic hardening from (DiMaggio & Sandler, 1971) is used to conduct accurate deformation calculations of the subsoil in time domain. The used *cap model* is also known as the *hardening-soil model.*

Modeling of discretized part of the soil and boundary conditions

The dimension of the discretized part of the soil is chosen in a way that a further enlargement of the discretized part has no significant influence on the result of the calculation.

As boundary condition, the deformation on the boundary is set to zero in general. In order to reduce oscillation, damping spring elements can be included. However, spring elements implicate wave reflections under certain conditions. Therefore, the application of hybrid calculation models starts here. In these hybrid models wave radiation to infinity and an elastic deformation of the fixed boundary are included.

Application of hybrid calculation models

For the calculation of soil-structure interactions in time domain, the application of hybrid models is essential. Hybrid models include the advantages of numerical and analytical methods.

In general, the approach of analytical models is more precise and needs less computational effort. Nevertheless, the analytical model can only be used for simple application cases. Numerical models are usually applied if the problem at hand is more complex.

Static building ground calculations can be solved with simple boundary conditions. The problem of wave reflection occurs as soon as dynamic loading is applied to the building ground.

Hybrid models include a numerical calculation of the local soil-structure area, and an analytical calculation of the wave radiation to infinity.

1.2 Overview of the Research

In Section 1.2.1, two general approaches are summarized for dynamic soil-structure interaction. Section 1.2.2 outlines the state of research for specific dynamic soil-structure interaction models. In the subsections of this chapter the nonlinear finite element calculation and soil models are summarized. Only the common methods are presented.

1.2.1 Direct Method and Substructure Method

With the *substructure method* and the *direct method*, two general approaches are classified for the numerical modeling of dynamic soil-structure interaction.

The unbounded medium is subdivided into the irregular bounded medium and the regular unbounded medium, as sketched in Figure 1.2. The region of interest has finite dimensions and consists of the irregular bounded medium and the structure. This bounded part of the analysis can be modeled with the finite element method (FEM). The analysis of the bounded part is well-established. Nonlinearities can be included here.

For the regular unbounded part of the model a special treatment is necessary due to the infinite dimension. The regular unbounded part of the model is separated by an *interaction horizon*. The interaction horizon includes a boundary condition, which represents the unbounded medium.

There are two extreme positions for the interaction horizon. First, the interaction horizon borders the region of interest, which can exhibit nonlinearities. This leads to the substructure method, as sketched in Figure 1.2a. For the substructure method rigorous boundary conditions are necessary to achieve sufficient accuracy. Second, the interaction horizon is moved into the regular unbounded medium, so that the irregular bounded medium increases and a part of the regular unbounded medium is modeled with the FEM. This leads to the direct method, as sketched in Figure 1.2b. Now, approximate boundary conditions can be applied and a sufficient large finite element mesh results in a sufficiently accurate calculation.

Some special cases of the substructure method such as the *boundary element method* (BEM), the *thin-layer method* (Lysmer, 1970) and the *scaled boundary finite element method* (SBFEM) are summarized in the next chapter.

Moreover, the *FEM with damped boundary* and *infinite elements*, which are also mentioned in the next chapter, are classified as direct methods.

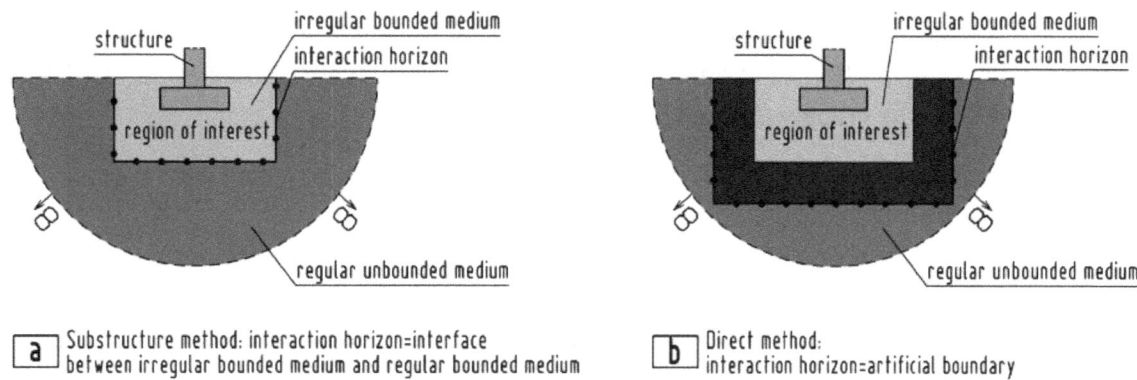

a Substructure method: interaction horizon=interface between irregular bounded medium and regular bounded medium

b Direct method: interaction horizon=artificial boundary

FIGURE 1.2. SUBSTRUCTURE METHOD AND DIRECT METHOD

1.2.2 COMMONLY USED CALCULATION MODELS FOR SOIL-STRUCTURE INTERACTION

The hierarchical diagram in Figure 1.3 shows the common variants for the calculation of soil-structure interaction in time domain. A fundamental problem is the treatment of wave propagation in the unbounded medium soil. This is approached in a different manner from the respective procedures. As illustrated in Figure 1.3 a multiplicity of combinations is possible. The different combinations are considered in the following.

<u>A single model for structure and unbounded medium:</u>

Finite element method (FEM) with damped boundary:

The calculation of the unbounded medium with the FEM implicates the problem of wave reflection. The FEM is developed for the calculation of bounded mediums. Detailed information of the FEM is provided by, for example, (Hughes, 1987), (Zienkiewicz, Taylor, & Zhu, 2005) or (Bathe, Finite Elemente Methoden, 2002). For the application of the FEM in the domain of unbounded media, a degradation of the wave reflections has to be included. The reflections at the fixed boundary can be decreased by an assembly of dampers in the form of spring elements. However, the wave reflection cannot be removed completely, which results in a conditionally suitable type of calculation.

As a precondition for the accuracy of the results, the radiation condition has to be satisfied. The radiation condition states that no energy is radiated from infinity towards the structure. In the FEM calculation with damped boundary the radiation condition is not implemented. However, all the following models incorporate the radiation condition.

Boundary element method (BEM):

A further possible procedure is the application of the boundary element method. Detailed descriptions of the method are discussed by, for example, (Beskos, 1987), (Banerjee, 1994) or (Brebbia, Telles, & Wrobel, 1984).

In contrast to the FEM, only the boundary of the domain is discretized here. Therefore, the number of degrees of freedom is less than in the FEM. However, the BEM yields a non-symmetric coefficient matrix with non-zero coefficients, which makes the final system of equations difficult to solve. This fact negates the advantage of fewer degrees of freedom.

The BEM satisfies the solution of the occurring differential equation exactly, while the FEM presents an approximation procedure.

With the BEM a calculation of the structure and a calculation of the unbounded medium can be conducted (Gaul & Fiedler, 1997). But problems with these calculations are the numerous restrictions of the BEM related to the properties of the modeled domain.

In the BEM, the so-called *fundamental solution* has to be known. For nonlinear materials the fundamental solution is not known.

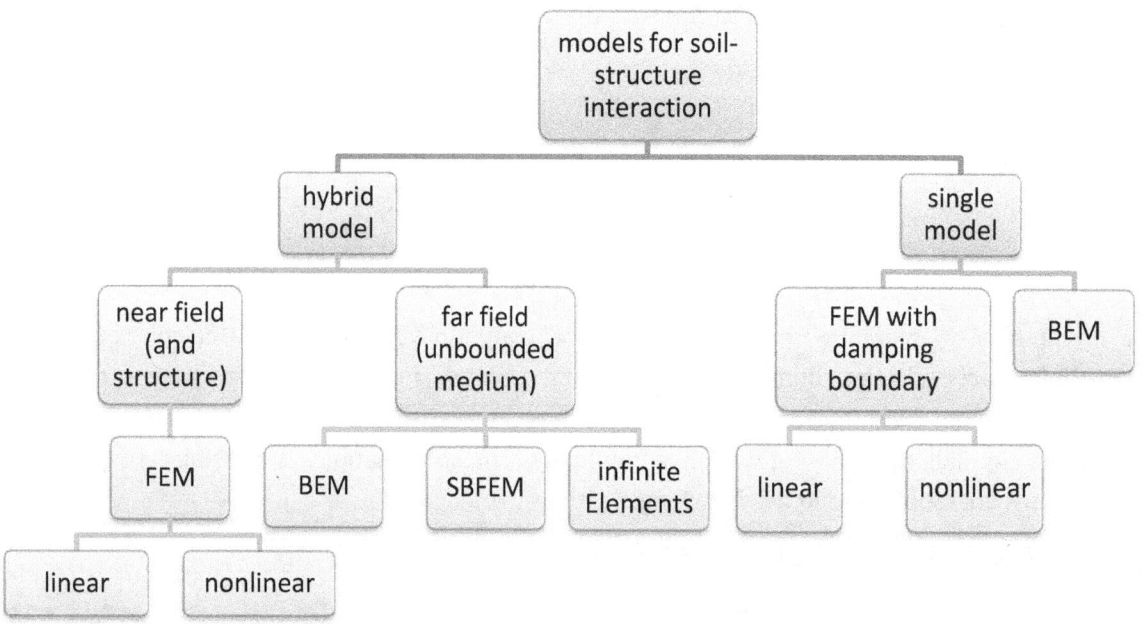

FIGURE 1.3. DIAGRAM OF CALCULATION VARIANTS FOR SOIL-STRUCTURE INTERACTION IN TIME DOMAIN

Further methods:

Furthermore, the thin-layer method (or consistent boundary formulation) can be applied as well. Descriptions can be found in, for example, (Lysmer, 1970) or (Lysmer & Waas, 1972). The method can be applied for horizontal layered unbounded media, such as soils. The formulation is given in the frequency domain and the displacements in horizontal direction are calculated exactly. An extension of the FEM is used in the vertical direction, whereby the vertical displacement is calculated approximately. The method needs no fundamental solution like the BEM. Therefore, it can be applied appropriately for vertical layered soil.

The finite difference method (FDM) can also be used for dynamic building ground calculations. In (Ang & Newmark, 1963) underground structures in connection with explosions are analyzed with FDM.

Hybrid models for structures and unbounded medium:

Normally, for the following hybrid methods the subdivision of the model to Figure 1.4 is applied. The soil is divided into *near-field* and *far-field* and the *structure* borders on the *near-field*.

The *FEM* is very suitable for the calculation of the *near-field*. The FEM has developed into one of the most widely used methods for structure analysis due to the flexibility of the method. Geometrical and material nonlinearities can be implicated and different boundary conditions can be incorporated.

For the *far-field* different methods can be used to account for dynamic excitations with wave propagation. In Figure 1.3 as common methods the *BEM*, the *scaled boundary finite element method* (*SBFEM*) and *infinite elements* are given.

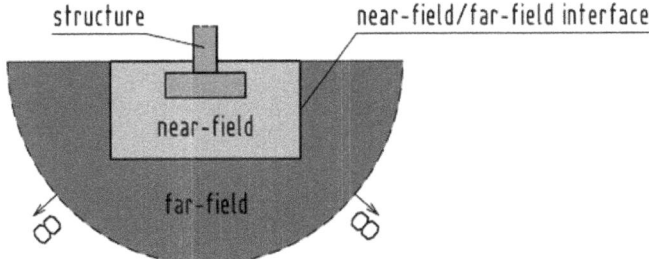

FIGURE 1.4. HYBRID MODEL FOR SOIL-STRUCTURE INTERACTION IN TIME DOMAIN

The FEM can be coupled with these methods due to the easy incorporation of different boundary conditions. With it, the wave propagation is included over the near-field/far-field interface in the FEM near-field and the structure.

A coupling to the named principle combines the advantages of the respective methods, and the disadvantages of the methods are cleared for the most part.

Coupled BEM/FEM model:

The coupled BEM/FEM model is the most commonly used model for modeling of the far-field and near-field. Detailed descriptions for soil-structure interactions can be found in (Estorff & Kausel, 1989) or (Estorff & Firuziaan, 2000) for example.

The coupled BEM/FEM model still incorporates some disadvantages of the BEM. So for anisotropic materials a fundamental solution does not exist, or the fundamental solution of a domain is very complex. Furthermore, the solution of the final equation system is difficult to find due to the non symmetric coefficient matrix.

Coupled FEM/SBFEM model:

In this work a coupled FEM/SBFEM model is used. The application of the SBFEM solves the above-named problems of the BEM. The SBFEM was developed by Wolf and Song (Wolf & Song, 1996), (Wolf, 2003). Improvements of the efficiency are conducted in (Lehmann, 2007) for example.

Most coupled FEM/SBFEM models which have been developed until now include only linear behavior. Another coupled FEM/SBFEM calculation with a nonlinear near-field is given in (Doherty & Deeks, 2005). The focus in (Doherty & Deeks, 2005) is the adaptive coupling of the FEM/SBFEM interface. For this purpose an ideal elasto-plastic Tresca material is incorporated for the near-field in (Doherty & Deeks, 2005). The material which is used in this study is essentially more complex and furthermore suitable for building ground calculations due to the three complex failure surfaces and the included isotropic hardening. This represents a new extension of the linear FEM/SBFEM model, which is essential for a realistic deformation calculation of the building ground.

Coupled infinite element/FEM model:

The far-field can also be discretized with infinite elements (Bettes, 1992). Infinite elements are an extension of finite elements. So a coupling with finite elements is easily possible.

The shape functions are assumed as decay functions here. The decay functions approximate the wave propagation to infinity. Infinite elements cannot directly be calculated in time domain. A calculation is only possible in the frequency domain. Furthermore, the calculation with infinite elements is not exact. An error remains due to the modeling of the unbounded medium.

1.2.3 Iterative Solution of Nonlinear Problems

Because the near-field is calculated nonlinearly, the state of research is briefly presented for this domain.

Solving procedures for one nonlinear equation:

A simple but robust procedure is the *bisection method*. For application the root has to be inside the assumed calculation interval (Corliss, 1977). In iterative steps the in interval is halved until the root has been founded.

In the bisection method the rate of convergence is low. The *method of successive substitutions* incorporates a secant approximation for new trial values within the current interval. This improves the rate of convergence.

The most common procedure for solving nonlinear equations is the *Newton-Raphson method*, which is also used in this work. With a quadratic rate of convergence the solution is found very quickly with this method.

A detailed overview of the named methods is given in (Kojic & Bathe, 2005) for example.

Solving procedures for systems of nonlinear equations:

In this work the *full* Newton-Raphson iteration is employed. The *modified* Newton-Raphson iteration is frequently used as well. In the modified Newton-Raphson iteration the stiffness matrix is calculated once only for every load or time step and not for every iteration, as in the full Newton-Raphson iteration. That saves calculation time, but can also result in convergence problems.

Other approaches are the *quasi-Newton methods* (Dennis, 1976). This group of methods is a compromise between the full Newton-Raphson iteration and modified Newton-Raphson iteration. The most effective quasi-Newton method is the *BFGS method (Broyden–Fletcher–Goldfarb–Shanno method)*. A detailed description of the BFGS method is given in (Matthies & Strang, 1979).

As the last group for solving nonlinear equations the *load-displacement-constraint methods* are mentioned here. These methods are particularly suitable for calculating the collapse load of a complete structure. The method was essentially proposed by (Riks, 1979).

A detailed description of all named methods is given in (Bathe, Finite Elemente Methoden, 2002) for example.

1.2.4 SOIL MODELS FOR NEAR-FIELD AND FAR-FIELD

Because of the adaptability of the FEM, several soil models can be applied in the near-field. The models can be used in different complexities.

Linear soil models:

In *linear-elastic models* stresses and strains are proportional. This material approach can be applied for the far-field and the structure. For the near-field of the soil the linear-elastic approach is too inexact. A failure criterion for the stress state is missing here. For the near-field the application of nonlinear soil models is appropriate.

Nonlinear soil models:

Nonlinearities can be incorporated in different forms. The simplest variant is a soil model with a *varying Young's modulus* as the *Duncan-Chang soil model* (Duncan & Chang, 1970). The Young's modulus is changing if a limit stress state is reached.

The complexity of soil models increases with the usage of *elasto-plastic soil models*. In these models the elastic domain is bounded. If the stress state exceeds the elastic domain and reaches the failure criterion the soil deforms plastically. Elasto-plastic soil models with failure criteria are the Drucker-Prager model (Drucker & Prager, 1952), Mohr-Coulomb model (Coulomb, 1776) and the Lade model (Lade, 1977) for example.

Extensions of the latter soil models are the *elasto-plastic soil models with isotropic hardening*. The limited volume expansion under hydrostatic compression is additionally included here. Therefore, cyclic loading with employed preload can be incorporated. The *cap model* (DiMaggio & Sandler, 1971) and the *cam clay model* (Roscoe & Schofield, 1963), (Roscoe & Burland, 1968) are examples of this. A usage of *elasto-plastic soil models with anisotropic hardening* is also possible (Abed, 2008).

Finally, very *complex hypoplastic soil models* (von Wolffersdorff, 1996) should be mentioned. These models are appropriate for the calculation of cohesionless soils, because an elastic domain is not included here. The hypoplastic material models include cyclic loading and a nonlinear material stiffness dependent on stress and density.

1.3 OBJECTIVES OF THE THESIS

The objective of this work is the development of an *overall calculation scheme* for the soil-structure interaction which includes the following influences:

- realistic deformation of the subsoil,
- dynamic effects and
- prevention of wave reflections at artificial boundaries.

Due to the various incorporated influences the *overall calculation scheme* is to be used for the calculation of realistic deformations and the stability of the soil and the structure. The incorporation of the three influences is described subsequently:

- According to *"Empfehlungen des Arbeitskreises Numerik in der Geotechnik"* (DGGT, 1991-2006) the following is essential: A *realistic deformation calculation* of the building ground can be achieved with *elasto-plastic material models with isotropic hardening*. The linear-elastic calculation is inaccurate. Elasto-plastic material models *without isotropic hardening*, such as the *Mohr-Coulomb* model or the *Drucker-Prager model*, are suitable to only a limited extent. These models cannot predict the plastic flow under hydrostatic compression. However, for stability calculations the application of the isotropic hardening is not important.
  Because the calculation scheme should implicate accurate deformation calculation, the *cap model* (DiMaggio & Sandler, 1971) is applied here. The usage of the cap model results in an *incremental iterative nonlinear calculation*. This is incorporated with the application of the *Newton-Raphson method*.
- Dynamic effects are included with the *HHT-α method* (Hilber, Hughes, & Taylor, 1977). The procedure is an extension of the common Newmark method (Newmark, 1959) and thus very flexible. The HHT-α method has to be used in a nonlinear form due to the elasto-plastic soil model. For this purpose the *nonlinear HHT-α method with modified Newton-Raphson iteration* from (Crisfield, 1997) is extended to a *nonlinear HHT-α method with full Newton-Raphson iteration* in this work. The full Newton-Raphson iteration enables the usage of larger time steps due to a better convergence rate.
- For the prevention of wave reflections a hybrid *scaled boundary finite element method/finite element method* model (FEM/SBFEM model) is applied. The model subdivides the discretized part of the soil in near-field and far-field (see Figure 1.4). The near-field is calculated with the FEM and the far-field with the SBFEM. The near-field includes the above-named nonlinear effects. The SBFEM (Wolf & Song, 1996), (Wolf, 2003) is very suitable for avoiding wave reflections due to the included wave radiation to infinity. This also prevents wave reflections at the *near-field/far-field interface* (see Figure 1.4).

An existing linear-*elastic FEM program system* is extended by the named nonlinear functionalities to show the applicability of the *overall calculation scheme*. The program system was developed at the *Institute of Applied Mechanics of the University of Braunschweig (http://www.infam.tu-braunschweig.de)*. It already contains an SBFEM calculation in the form of the program system *"Similar"* which was developed by (Wolf & Song, 1996). The implementation of the nonlinear parts and the coupling of the *nonlinear FEM near-field* with the *SBFEM far-field* (see Figure 1.4) results in the requested *overall calculation scheme*. After the implementation several examples are calculated to show the applicability of the procedure.

1.4 LAYOUT OF THE THESIS

After the introduction the thesis is divided into three parts. Part I describes the *theoretical part* and Part II shows the *applications* which are related to the theoretical part. All related appendices are given in Part III (A1 Nomenclature, A2 Mathematical Notation and A3 Elastic Constitutive Relations). The main parts I and II are described in the following.

Part I:

In Chapters 2 and 3 a general derivation of the finite element method and of the Newton-Raphson method is given. These methods are used as the basis for the Chapters 4 to 7.

In Chapters 4 and 5 a general valid elasto-plastic material model for soil calculations is derived. This cap model is included in an iterative Newton-Raphson calculation scheme in Section 5.3.

Furthermore, in Chapter 6 a new nonlinear version of the HHT-α is derived. An existing nonlinear version of the HHT-α method, given in (Crisfield, 1997) for the modified Newton-Raphson scheme, is extended to the full Newton-Raphson scheme. This represents a new calculation method in time domain. The developed HHT-α method for full Newton-Raphson iteration is then included in an extended calculation scheme for time domain in Section 6.4. With it, dynamic calculations of the subsoil are possible.

Finally, the total calculation scheme of Section 6.4 is extended for the SBFEM method. That includes wave propagation for the elasto-plastic and dynamic calculated soil section. This extended overall calculation scheme is given in Section 7.3. The combination of the mentioned calculation methods presents a new method for the calculation in time domains.

The calculation schemes, given in Sections 5.3, 6.4 and 7.3, are documented in detail, so that they can be easily adopted for other implementations in existing FEM program systems.

Part II:

Examples are presented in Part II of the work. An existing FEM program, which was developed at the *Institute of Applied Mechanics of the University of Braunschweig*, is extended for the calculation. The extension includes the elasto-plastic cap model, the HHT-α method with full Newton-Raphson iteration and the named calculation schemes of Sections 5.3, 6.4 and 7.3.

The examples are constrained to the calculation of shallow foundations. Other soil-ground calculations, such as excavations or pile foundations, need additional calculation features, for example interface elements. These additional calculation methods are not available in the existing program system and the implementation would exceed the scope of this work.

The Examples 1 to 3 are intended for the verification of the presented calculation method. Furthermore, they should clarify the influence of the presented calculation method. Finally, Example 4 shows a practical possible application.

The verification Examples 1 to 3 clarify the deformation behavior for simple geometry and loading. The deformations and stresses of these examples do not appear in the calculated magnitude in practice. However, the given comparison with the commercial program system ABAQUS®(2004) shows the accuracy of the calculated results.

The preload of the soil was neglected in these calculation examples, which results in greater deformations. This cannot be neglected for practical application, as also shown in Example 4.

In Example 4 the foundation of a commonly used bridge construction is analyzed. A load model for rail traffic, which is also used in engineering practice, is applied. The order of loading was employed in this example. The self-weight of soil acts at first, the self-weight of the bridge is then applied and finally the rail traffic operates. This order of loading is essential for an elasto-plastic soil calculation with isotropic hardening, because preloaded soil behaves differently to a not preloaded soil. Furthermore, the self-weight acts statically and the rail traffic dynamically in the calculation of Example 4.

I THEORY

2 FINITE ELEMENT METHOD

The *Finite Element Method* (FEM) is the most popular numerical method for solving engineering problems. It is used as a basic evaluation method in this work. Special cases or extensions, such as nonlinear dynamic calculations, of the method are considered in the following sections. The fundamentals of the FEM can be referred to in many descriptions, e.g. (Hughes, 1987), (Zienkiewicz, Taylor, & Zhu, 2005) and (Bathe, Finite Elemente Methoden, 2002). Therefore, a short introduction for the static case only is given.

For a considered engineering problem a differential equation can be positioned generally. This differential equation is solved analytically for simple problems. If the problem is more complex, an analytical solution of the differential equation is usually not possible. The fundamental idea of the FEM is to discretize the domain of the problem in many small domains (elements). The whole solution function of the differential equation is replaced by an equation system with simple basis functions of the elements. The basis functions have free parameters which have to be determined. This principle was first applied in the well-known *Ritz method* or the *weighted residual method*. Hence, the FEM can be seen as an extension of these methods.

2.1 STRONG FORM OF EQUILIBRIUM

The equilibrium conditions for the general spatial stress state are now derived. We take an equilibrium consideration for one partial volume V which is extracted from a domain D, as pictured in Figure 2.1.

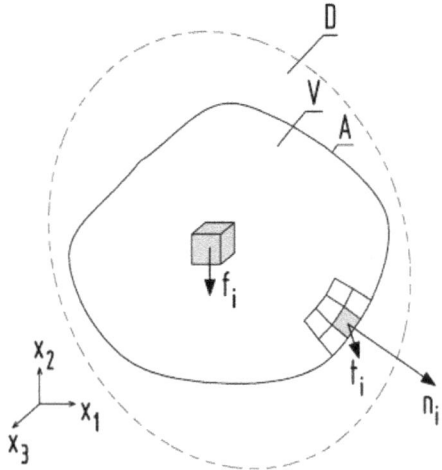

FIGURE 2.1. FORCES AT AN EXTRACTED BODY VOLUME

The partial volume V has the surface A and is loaded by the body load f_i and the surface load t_i. The normal vector n_i in Figure 2.1 is perpendicular to the surface A. The index "i" denotes the directions x_1, x_2, x_3[1].

---

[1] Indicial notation is applied here (including Einstein Summation); see Appendix A2

For equilibrium the sum of the external loads must vanish:

$$\int\limits_A t_i \, dA + \int\limits_V f_i \, dV = 0 \qquad (2.1)$$

With the known Cauchy formula:

$$t_i = \sigma_{ij} \, n_j \qquad (2.2)$$

(where σ_{ij} are the stresses) follows from (2.1):

$$\int\limits_A \sigma_{ij} \, n_j \, dA + \int\limits_V f_i \, dV = 0 \qquad (2.3)$$

Applying the Gauss integral theorem to the stresses:

$$\int\limits_A \sigma_{ij} \, n_j \, dA = \int\limits_V \sigma_{ij,j} \, dV \qquad (2.4)$$

Equation (2.3) is written as:

$$\int\limits_V \sigma_{ij,j} \, dV + \int\limits_V f_i \, dV = \int\limits_V (\sigma_{ij,j} + f_i) \, dV = 0 \qquad (2.5)$$

The volume integral in (2.5) is only equal to zero if the term in brackets is equal to zero:

$$\boxed{\sigma_{ij,j} + f_i = 0} \qquad (2.6)$$

This equation is a partial differential equation and it is known as the *strong form* of equilibrium. As denoted in Equation (2.6), equations of particular importance are framed in this work. If we relate (2.6) to D'Alembert's principle, it can be written as:

$$\sigma_{ij,j} + f_i = \rho \ddot{U}_i \qquad (2.7)$$

with ρ as density and $\ddot{U}_i$ as acceleration vector. Equation (2.6) is valid inside of the domain. On the boundary, the boundary conditions must be fulfilled. The boundary can be subdivided into one part with stress boundary conditions A_t and into another part with displacement boundary conditions A_u, as pictured in Figure 2.2. The stress boundary condition on A_t is given as:

$$\sigma_{ij} \, n_j = t_i^{A_t} \qquad (2.8)$$

and the displacement boundary condition on A_u is given as:

$$u_i = u_i^{A_u} \qquad (2.9)$$

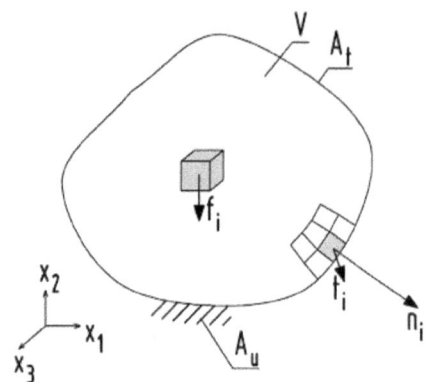

FIGURE 2.2. FORCES AT AN EXTRACTED BODY VOLUME WITH IMPLICATED BOUNDARY CONDITIONS

2.2 WEAK FORM OF EQUILIBRIUM

To solve equilibrium problems it is useful to introduce energy principles. Therefore, the internal and external forces are multiplied with the displacements $\boldsymbol{u}$. Furthermore, they are integrated over the volume of the body:

$$\int_V \left(\sigma_{ij,j} + f_i\right) u_i \, dV = \int_V \left(\sigma_{ij,j} \, u_i + f_i \, u_i\right) dV = 0 \tag{2.10}$$

Now we apply the product rule to $[\sigma_{ij} \, u_i]_{,j} = \sigma_{ij,j} \, u_i + \sigma_{ij} \, u_{i,j}$, this can be rearranged to $\sigma_{ij,j} \, u_i = [\sigma_{ij} \, u_i]_{,j} - \sigma_{ij} \, u_{i,j}$ and replaced in (2.10):

$$\int_V \left([\sigma_{ij} \, u_i]_{,j} - \sigma_{ij} \, u_{i,j} + f_i \, u_i\right) dV = \int_V \left(-\sigma_{ij} \, u_{i,j} + f_i \, u_i\right) dV + \int_V [\sigma_{ij} \, u_i]_{,j} \, dV = 0 \tag{2.11}$$

Applying the Gauss' integral theorem to: $\int_V [\sigma_{ij} \, u_i]_{,j} dV = \int_A \left(\sigma_{ij} \, u_i\right) n_j \, dA$ in (2.11) gives:

$$\int_V \left(-\sigma_{ij} \, u_{i,j} + f_i \, u_i\right) dV + \int_A \left(\sigma_{ij} \, u_i\right) n_j \, dA = 0 \tag{2.12}$$

When we now subdivide the surface A into the different boundary conditions (see Figure 2.2), Equation (2.12) yields:

$$\int_V \left(-\sigma_{ij} \, u_{i,j} + f_i \, u_i\right) dV + \int_{A_t} \left(\sigma_{ij} \, u_i\right) n_j \, dA + \int_{A_u} \left(\sigma_{ij} \, u_i\right) n_j \, dA = 0 \tag{2.13}$$

with (2.2), (2.8) and (2.9):

$$\int_V \left(-\sigma_{ij} \, u_{i,j} + f_i \, u_i\right) dV + \int_{A_t} t_i^{A_t} \, u_i \, dA + \int_{A_u} t_i \, u_i^{A_u} \, dA = 0 \tag{2.14}$$

For the term $\sigma_{ij}\,u_{i,j}$ the following is essential:

$$\sigma_{ij}\,u_{i,j} = \sigma_{ij}\,\frac{1}{2}\left(u_{i,j} + u_{j,i}\right) = \sigma_{ij}\,\varepsilon_{ij} \qquad (2.15)$$

with ε_{ij} as strains. Therefore, (2.14) can be written as:

$$\int_V \sigma_{ij}\,\varepsilon_{ij}\,dV = \int_V f_i\,u_i\,dV + \int_{A_t} t_i^{A_t}\,u_i\,dA + \int_{A_u} t_i\,u_i^{A_u}\,dA \qquad (2.16)$$

This is known as the *weak form* of equilibrium, because the stresses here are not differentiated as in (2.6). Therefore, σ_{ij} has a *weaker differentiation requirement*. The displacement field u_i can be an arbitrary displacement field, which does not have to be the actual displacement field. Furthermore it is noticed that the stresses, strains and displacements in (2.16) have to be static and accordingly kinematically admissible.

2.3 Principle of Virtual Displacements

Now the *principle of virtual displacements* is introduced. Virtual displacements δu_i are infinitesimally small, not really existing and kinematically admissible. Kinematically admissible means that the virtual displacements on the boundary A_u of the body are vanishing:

$$\delta u_i^{A_u} = 0 \qquad (2.17)$$

In the variational calculus u_i in (2.16) can be seen as a *compare function*. When we replace in (2.16) the virtual displacements with respect to (2.17) the weak form is given as:

$$\int_V \sigma_{ij}\,\delta\varepsilon_{ij}\,dV = \int_V f_i\,\delta u_i\,dV + \int_{A_t} t_i^{A_t}\,\delta u_i\,dA \qquad (2.18)$$

this relates to:

$$\delta W_i = \delta W_e \qquad (2.19)$$

with δW_i as *virtual internal work* and δW_e as *virtual external work*. Equation (2.19) means a body is in equilibrium when the internal and external virtual works are equal. For a linear-elastic continuum the work can be replaced by a *potential*:

$$\delta \Pi_i = -\delta \Pi_e \qquad (2.20)$$

If we introduce the total potential Π, Equation (2.20) can be written as:

$$\delta \Pi = \delta \Pi_i + \delta \Pi_e = 0 \qquad (2.21)$$

or:

$$\Pi = \Pi_i + \Pi_e = minimum \qquad (2.22)$$

Equation (2.22) in context with Equation (2.16) means the following: the body is in equilibrium with those kinematically admissible compare functions u_i which make Π to a minimum.

2.4 Finite Element Equations

Now finite element equations are derived. The body in Figure 2.2 is discretized as a group of many small non-overlapping elements, which are connected with nodes on the element boundaries. One typical 8 node element is pictured in Figure 2.3. The displacements in the elements are expressed as functions in the nodes. Hence, u is written as:

$$u = H.U \hspace{6cm} (2.23)$$

with H as interpolation matrix (interpolated with basis functions) for displacements, and U as vector with all displacement components in the directions x_1, x_2, x_3 of the respective coordinate system in the nodes (**bold** marked symbols denote a vector or a matrix; a dot (.) between two variables denotes a vector or matrix multiplication; see Appendix A2). The strains are determined with:

$$\varepsilon = B.U \hspace{6cm} (2.24)$$

where B is the strain displacement matrix, which is obtained by differentiation of H.

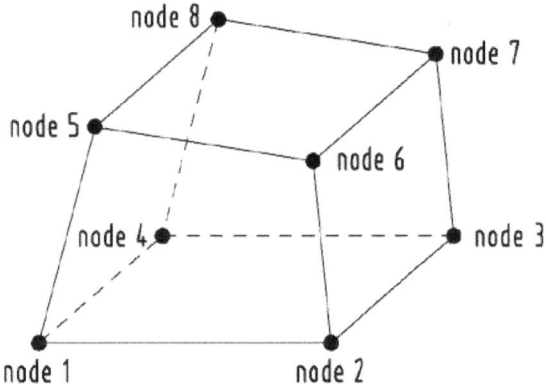

FIGURE 2.3. TYPICAL 8 NODE FEM SOLID ELEMENT

The stresses for a linear-elastic element are calculated with:

$$\sigma = C.\varepsilon \hspace{6cm} (2.25)$$

where C is the elasticity matrix (see A3). When (2.23), (2.24) and (2.25) are replaced in (2.18) the following equation is given:

$$\delta U^T . \left(\int_V B^T.C.B \, dV \right).U = \delta U^T . \left(\int_V H f \, dV \right) + \delta U^T . \left(\int_{A_t} H t^{A_t} \, dA \right) \hspace{2cm} (2.26)$$

The vectors U and δU are independent of the element, so they are written outside of the integrals. When δU is cancelled in (2.26), it follows:

$$\left(\int\limits_V \boldsymbol{B}^T.\boldsymbol{C}.\boldsymbol{B} \ dV \right).\boldsymbol{U} = \int\limits_V \boldsymbol{H} \boldsymbol{f} \ dV + \int\limits_{A_t} \boldsymbol{H} \ \boldsymbol{t}^{A_t} \ dA \qquad (2.27)$$

written in short notation:

$$\boxed{\boldsymbol{K}.\boldsymbol{U} = \boldsymbol{R}} \qquad (2.28)$$

with $\boldsymbol{K}$ as stiffness matrix and $\boldsymbol{R}$ as load vector. Equation (2.28) corresponds to the static case of equilibrium. For the dynamic case, inertia forces and damping forces have to be included. Then (2.28) is given as:

$$\boxed{\boldsymbol{M}.\ddot{\boldsymbol{U}} + \boldsymbol{C}.\dot{\boldsymbol{U}} + \boldsymbol{K}.\boldsymbol{U} = \boldsymbol{R}} \qquad (2.29)$$

with $\boldsymbol{M}$ as mass matrix, $\ddot{\boldsymbol{U}}$ as nodal acceleration vector obtained from the second time derivation of $\boldsymbol{U}$, $\boldsymbol{C}$ as damping matrix and $\dot{\boldsymbol{U}}$ as nodal velocity vector obtained from the first time derivation of $\boldsymbol{U}$. The solution of Equation (2.29) is given in Chapter 6.

More detailed information on the derivation of the FEM equations is available in the specialized literature, e.g., (Bathe, 2002), (Hughes, 1987)(Zienkiewicz, Taylor, & Zhu, 2005).

3 Solving Nonlinear Equations

3.1 Newton-Raphson Method for a Single Nonlinear Equation

The following nonlinear equation should be solved:

$$f(x) = 0 \qquad (3.1)$$

If x^* is the solution of (3.1) and an approximate solution is x_{i-1}, then a Taylor series expansion at $x = x_{i-1}$ can be written as:

$$f(x^*) = f(x_{i-1}) + f'(x_{i-1})(x^* - x_{i-1}) = 0 \qquad (3.2)$$

The high order terms of the Taylor series expansion are neglected. Rearranging Equation (3.2) for x^* results in:

$$f(x_{i-1}) + f'(x_{i-1})(x^* - x_{i-1}) = 0$$

$$f'(x_{i-1})(x^* - x_{i-1}) = -f(x_{i-1})$$

$$x^* - x_{i-1} = -\frac{f(x_{i-1})}{f'(x_{i-1})}$$

$$x^* = x_{i-1} - \frac{f(x_{i-1})}{f'(x_{i-1})} \qquad (3.3)$$

Equation (3.3) can now be written in an iterative scheme with $x^* = x_i$:

$$\boxed{x_i = x_{i-1} - \frac{f(x_{i-1})}{f'(x_{i-1})}} \qquad (3.4)$$

This equation represents the Newton-Raphson scheme for one nonlinear equation. The Newton-Raphson method is based on the calculation of tangents to the function $f(x)$. Therefore, the first derivation $f'(x)$ is calculated. This is graphically illustrated in Figure 3.1.

The iteration with the iteration counter (i) is aborted if $(x_i - x_{i-1})$ does not more changes within a selected numerical tolerance. Now x_i is the requested solution x^*.

For the reliability of the scheme the initial value of x must be close to x^*. Or more precisely, special conditions have to be maintained for convergence (Bathe, Finite Elemente Methoden, 2002). So in Figure 3.2 the solution x^* will not be found with the selected initial value x_{start} for example. The iteration scheme (3.4) will not converge here.

The scheme (3.4) was applied and implemented later within the governing parameter method (Bathe, Chaudhary, Dvorkin, & Kojic, 1984) for the search of the one unknown parameter p (see Section 4.2.2). The condition for convergence is maintained, because the initial value of p is always chosen from the last time (load) step. So the initial value of p is in the near vicinity of the requested root.

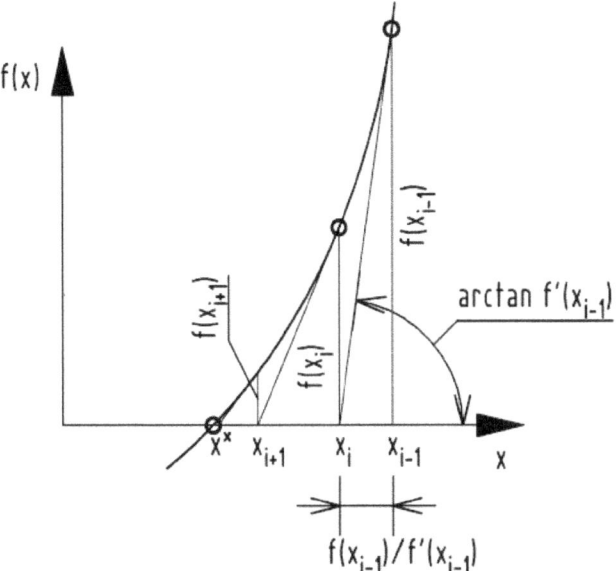

FIGURE 3.1. NEWTON-RAPHSON ITERATION ALGORITHM

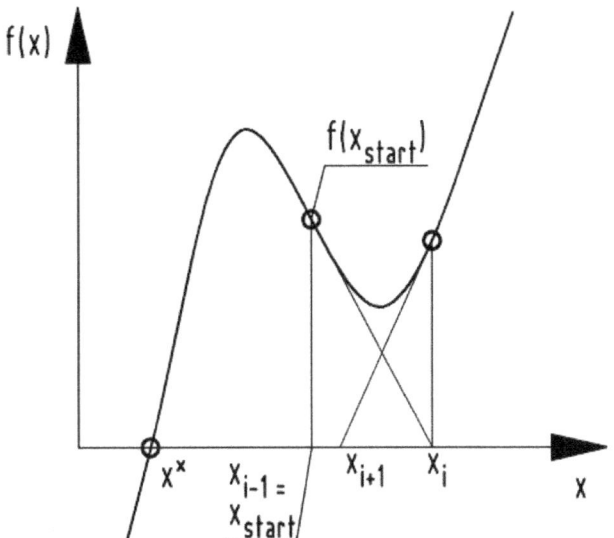

FIGURE 3.2. FAILURE OF NEWTON-RAPHSON ITERATION ALGORITHM FOR INAPPROPRIATE INITIAL VALUE X

3.2 Newton-Raphson Method for Systems of Nonlinear Equations

3.2.1 General Case

The Newton-Raphson method for one nonlinear equation can easily be assigned to a system of nonlinear equations. The displacements U at a nodal finite element point are used instead of the general displacement vector u at a material point, from now on. So for a system of nonlinear equations with the displacement vector U (instead of x), the problem (3.1) can be written as:

$$f(U) = 0 \qquad\qquad (3.5)$$

With the approximate initial solution $U^{(i-1)}$ in the i-th iteration follows analogous to (3.4):

$$U^{(i)} = U^{(i-1)} - \frac{f[U^{(i-1)}]}{\frac{\partial f[U^{(i-1)}]}{\partial U^{(i-1)}}} = U^{(i-1)} - \frac{f[U^{(i-1)}]}{K^{(i-1)}} = U^{(i-1)} - [K^{(i-1)}]^{-1} \cdot f[U^{(i-1)}] \qquad (3.6)$$

$K^{(i-1)} = \frac{\partial f[U^{(i-1)}]}{\partial U^{(i-1)}}$ is the stiffness matrix here. When U^* is the solution vector Equation (3.5) yields:

$$f(U^*) = 0 \qquad (3.7)$$

Equation (3.6) can be rearranged as:

$$U^{(i)} = U^{(i-1)} - [K^{(i-1)}]^{-1} \cdot f[U^{(i-1)}]$$

$$U^{(i)} - U^{(i-1)} = -[K^{(i-1)}]^{-1} \cdot f[U^{(i-1)}]$$

$$K^{(i-1)} \cdot (U^{(i)} - U^{(i-1)}) = - f[U^{(i-1)}]$$

$$f[U^{(i-1)}] + K^{(i-1)} \cdot (U^{(i)} - U^{(i-1)}) = 0$$

This result is analogous to writing a Taylor series expansion at $U = U^{(i-1)}$:

$$f(U^*) = f[U^{(i-1)}] + K^{(i-1)} \cdot (U^* - U^{(i-1)}) = 0 \qquad (3.8)$$

Here the high order terms of the Taylor series are also neglected. With approximated $U^* = U^{(i)}$ in the i-th iteration, the Taylor series (3.8) can be expressed as:

$$\boxed{f(U^{(i)}) = f[U^{(i-1)}] + K^{(i-1)} \cdot (U^{(i)} - U^{(i-1)}) = 0} \qquad (3.9)$$

This equals the rearranged Equation (3.6) and represents the Newton-Raphson iteration for the solution of nonlinear system of equations.

3.2.2   Special Case for Structural Problems

The initial values for $U^{(i-1)}$ have to lie near the solution U^*, as illustrated in Section 3.1. To account for this circumstance for time or load steps Δt the calculation is taken stepwise. It is assumed that the solution is known for the time t and that the solution for the time $t + \Delta t$ is sought after.

For a static calculation the external forces are subdivided into load steps Δt. The time denotes only the different values of the external forces in the load steps Δt here. In a dynamic calculation (or a static calculation with time dependent loads) the considered time must be subdivided into time steps Δt anyway. Here the time is a real variable. The stepwise notation with the upper left indices (t) for the last time (load) step and $(t + \Delta t)$ for the current time (load) step is included from here on.

The fundamental relation between the external forces R and the internal forces F in a finite element system is that the external forces must be equal to the internal forces:

$$^{t+\Delta t}F(U^*) = {}^{t+\Delta t}R(U^*)$$

$$^{t+\Delta t}F(U^*) - {}^{t+\Delta t}R(U^*) = 0 \qquad (3.10)$$

The internal forces in the current time step $(t + \Delta t)$ in the first iteration $i = 1$ can be expressed with the Taylor series expansion from the last time step (t):

$$^{t+\Delta t}F\big(U^{(1)}\big) = {}^{t}F\big({}^{t}U\big) + \frac{\partial\,{}^{t}F\big({}^{t}U\big)}{\partial\,{}^{t}U}\cdot\big({}^{t+\Delta t}U^{(1)} - {}^{t}U\big)$$

(3.11)

$$^{t+\Delta t}F\big(U^{(1)}\big) = {}^{t}F\big({}^{t}U\big) + {}^{t}K\cdot\big({}^{t+\Delta t}U^{(1)} - {}^{t}U\big)$$

Here the initial condition for the current time step $(t + \Delta t)$ at $i = 1$ is $^{t+\Delta t}U^{(i-1)} = {}^{t+\Delta t}U^{(0)} = {}^{t}U$. The increment of displacement can be written general as:

$$\Delta U^{(i)} = {}^{t+\Delta t}U^{(i)} - {}^{t+\Delta t}U^{(i-1)}$$

(3.12)

with approximated $U^{*} = {}^{t}U$ in the first iteration (3.10) can be expressed as:

$$^{t+\Delta t}R\big({}^{t}U\big) - \big[{}^{t}F\big({}^{t}U\big) + {}^{t}K\cdot\big({}^{t+\Delta t}U^{(1)} - {}^{t}U\big)\big] = 0$$

$$^{t+\Delta t}R\big({}^{t}U\big) - {}^{t}F\big({}^{t}U\big) = {}^{t}K\cdot\big({}^{t+\Delta t}U^{(1)} - {}^{t}U\big)$$

(3.13)

Writing (3.13) in iteration notation and substituting (3.12) in (3.13) results in:

$$\boxed{^{t+\Delta t}R - {}^{t+\Delta t}F^{(i-1)} = {}^{t+\Delta t}K\cdot\Delta U^{(i)}}$$

(3.14)

with the assumption that the external forces R are independent of the displacements. The internal forces F and the stiffness matrix K are dependent of the displacement. Hence, these variables will be updated in the current step $(t + \Delta t)$ and in every iteration (i), with respect to the displacements from the last iteration $(i - 1)$. The updated displacements are following from (3.12):

$$\boxed{^{t+\Delta t}U^{(i)} = {}^{t+\Delta t}U^{(i-1)} + \Delta U^{(i)}}$$

(3.15)

Equations (3.14) and (3.15) represent the Newton-Raphson method for multi-degree of freedom systems. The derivation of the Newton-Raphson method for the general case in (3.9) can also be conducted now.

Inserting (3.7) in (3.10) yields:

$$f(U^{*}) = {}^{t+\Delta t}R(U^{*}) - {}^{t+\Delta t}F(U^{*})$$

(3.16)

For stepwise calculation $f[U^{(i-1)}]$ in (3.9) can be written as:

$$^{t+\Delta t}f\big[U^{(i-1)}\big] = {}^{t+\Delta t}F\big[U^{(i-1)}\big] - {}^{t+\Delta t}R\big[U^{(i-1)}\big]$$

(3.17)

Then (3.9) can be expressed stepwise in:

$$^{t+\Delta t}f\big[U^{(i-1)}\big] + {}^{t+\Delta t}K^{(i-1)}\cdot\big({}^{t+\Delta t}U^{(i)} - {}^{t+\Delta t}U^{(i-1)}\big) = 0$$

$$^{t+\Delta t}K^{(i-1)}\cdot\big({}^{t+\Delta t}U^{(i)} - {}^{t+\Delta t}U^{(i-1)}\big) = {}^{t+\Delta t}F\big[U^{(i-1)}\big] - {}^{t+\Delta t}R\big[U^{(i-1)}\big]$$

(3.18)

(3.18) and (3.12) then yield (3.14).

The Newton-Raphson iterative scheme is summarized in Table 3.1. The table was adopted from (Kojic & Bathe, 2005). The specified convergence criteria are not implemented for this work. For simplicity only one convergence criterion in the form of the *Euclidean vector norm* is used:

$$\|\Delta U(i)\| \leq \varepsilon \qquad (3.19)$$

The Newton-Raphson scheme in Table 3.1 represents the so-called *full Newton-Raphson* iteration, because the stiffness matrix is computed within every iteration. This represents a large computational effort. It is also possible to modify the scheme using a stiffness matrix recalculated only at certain times. Then the scheme is called *modified Newton-Raphson* method. A special case of the modified Newton-Raphson iteration is to use the initial stiffness matrix $K^{(0)} = {}^tK$:

$$\boxed{{}^{t+\Delta t}R - {}^{t+\Delta t}F^{(i-1)} = {}^tK . \Delta U^{(i)}} \qquad (3.20)$$

Equation (3.20) will be mentioned later in the context of the HHT-alpha method (Hilber, Hughes, & Taylor, 1977).

Step 1	Initialization for current time step Δt
	$i = 0,$ ${}^{t+\Delta t}F^{(0)} = {}^tF, {}^{t+\Delta t}K^{(0)} = {}^tK, {}^{t+\Delta t}U^{(0)} = {}^tU$
Step 2	Iteration i
	$i = i + 1$ ${}^{t+\Delta t}R - {}^{t+\Delta t}F^{(i-1)} = {}^{t+\Delta t}K^{(i-1)} . \Delta U^{(i)}$ ${}^{t+\Delta t}U^{(i)} = {}^{t+\Delta t}U^{(i-1)} + \Delta U^{(i)}$
Step 3	Check for convergence
	a) Force criterion: $\left\| {}^{t+\Delta t}R - {}^{t+\Delta t}F^{(i)} \right\| \leq \varepsilon_F \left\| {}^{t+\Delta t}R - {}^tF \right\|$ b) Displacement criterion: $\|\Delta U^{(i)}\| \leq \varepsilon_D \left\| {}^{t+\Delta t}U^{(i-1)} \right\|$ c) Energy criterion: $\Delta U^{(i)^T} . ({}^{t+\Delta t}R - {}^{t+\Delta t}F^{(i)}) \leq \varepsilon_E \Delta U^{(1)^T} . ({}^{t+\Delta t}R - {}^tF)$
Step 4	If convergence criteria are not satisfied, go to step 2; otherwise go to step 5
Step 5	Start iterations for next time step; go to step 1

TABLE 3.1. NEWTON-RAPHSON ITERATIVE SCHEME

4 GENERAL PLASTICITY

Theories for plastic material behavior are subdivided into micro mechanical and macro mechanical theories. Micromechanical theories investigate the plastic deformations on microscopic level and try to explain the plastic yielding in the conditions of crystals and grains. The macro mechanical theories describe the deformations phenomenologically. Macro mechanical theories are applied here. Therefore, material properties are determined on an experimental basis from macroscopic samples. From these samples the material characteristic can be described mathematically. This is why the macro mechanical theories are named mathematical theories. The treated material model is based upon isotropic material behavior. Hence, the material behavior is equal for all directions.

4.1 FUNDAMENTAL RELATIONS AND NOTIONS

4.1.1 ONE DIMENSIONAL CASE

In the following the plastic computation will be illustrated on a one dimensional rod. The curve in Figure 4.1a (Kojic & Bathe, 2005) points the fundamental relations in calculations with small strains. Between point A and point B the material behaves elastically. The elasticity modulus changes if the force is increased by the flow limit σ_f. This is dependent on stress to the tangent modulus E_T. If the material is unloaded after reaching point C, permanent plastic strain will remain. In point C the strain is composed of elastic and plastic strain. The total strain corresponds here:

$$e = e^E + e^P \qquad (4.1)$$

with:

$$e = \sigma/E \qquad (4.2)$$

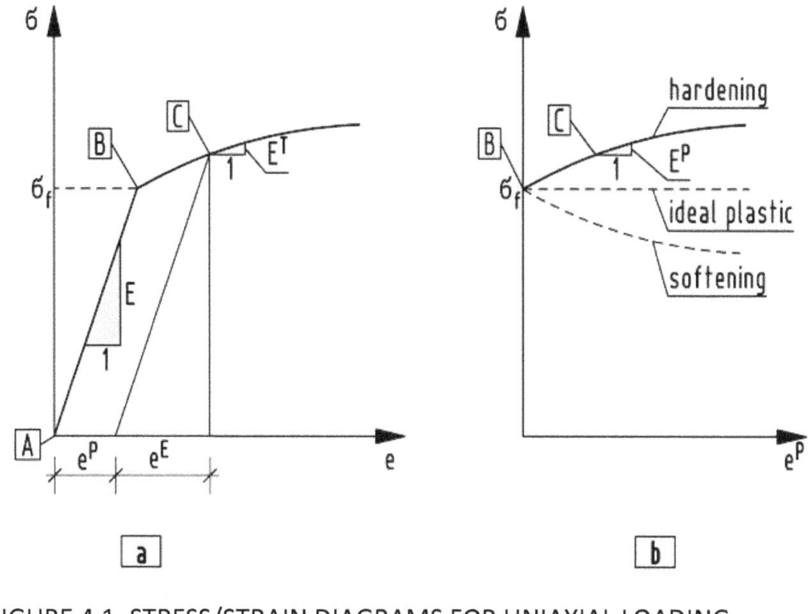

FIGURE 4.1. STRESS/STRAIN DIAGRAMS FOR UNIAXIAL LOADING

Figure 4.1b shows stress according to plastic strain e^p. From this it follows that the stress in the plastic region is only dependent on the plastic strains:

$$\sigma(e) - \sigma_f(e^E) = \sigma(e^P) \tag{4.3}$$

After the rearrangement of Equation (4.3), with $\sigma(e) - \sigma_f(e^E) - \sigma(e^P) = 0$, (4.3) can be written as a so-called yield condition:

$$f_y(\sigma, e^P) = 0 \tag{4.4}$$

With increasing plastic strain the stress also increases. This material property is also known as hardening. From the slope in point C the plastic modulus E^P can be determined. The stress in point B is also named *initial yield stress* σ_f. Furthermore, Figure 4.1b contains the additional possible cases of plastic behavior. In addition to *hardening*, there is the *ideal plastic strain*, where the stress with increasing plastic strain no more changes. Then there is also the *softening*, with reducing plastic strain with increasing stress.

4.1.2   GENERAL THREE DIMENSIONAL CASE

There is an initial stress for the one dimensional case at which the material flows and, therefore, the plastic deformation starts. This can now be set for a general three dimensional case analogous. Here we use the general stress tensor in index notation σ_{ij}. In connection with index notation, the summation convention is applied (see Appendix A2). Thereafter, all double indices in one term are added. Accordantly in Equation (4.4) the yield condition for the beginning flow is formulated as:

$$f_y(\sigma_{ij}) = 0 \tag{4.5}$$

at which f_y is denoted as the yield function. As long as the yield condition is not reached ($f_y \leq 0$) the material response is elastic. In the isotropic case, which is applied here, the material response is identical in all directions. However, the stresses are changing with the coordinate system. To avoid this, the three invariants of stress are introduced, which are independent of the used coordinate system.

So Equation (4.5) changes to:

$$f_y(I_1, I_2, I_3) = 0 \tag{4.6}$$

with:

$$I_1 = \sigma_{ii}$$

$$I_2 = \sigma_{11}\sigma_{22} + \sigma_{22}\sigma_{33} + \sigma_{33}\sigma_{11} - (\sigma_{12}\sigma_{21} + \sigma_{23}\sigma_{32} + \sigma_{13}\sigma_{31}) \tag{4.7}$$

$$I_3 = det(\sigma)$$

Experimental investigations show that, e.g., for metals, no volumetric strain occurs in the plastic region. For this reason, the computation of the first invariant can be neglected for metals. For metals only an alteration of the shape occurs, which can be expressed in the second invariant. Furthermore, the third invariant can also be neglected for metals. This plastic material response is named isochoric or volume preserving. However, for the material models of soil, experimental confirmation offered volume and shape alterations in the plastic region. Hence, for soils the first and second invariant of the stress tensor is important. The change of volume can be expressed in the first invariant as follows:

$$\sigma_m = \frac{1}{3} I_1 \qquad (4.8)$$

Whereas the shape alteration is expressed in the stress deviator:

$$S_{ij} = \sigma_{ij} - \sigma_m \, \delta_{ij} \qquad (4.9)$$

δ_{ij} denotes the known Kronecker Delta function with $\delta_{ij} = 1$ for $i = j$ and $\delta_{ij} = 0$ for $i \neq j$. For the stress deviator S_{ij} invariants can be formed analogously to the general stress tensor σ_{ij}. Especial the second invariant of the stress deviator is important:

$$J_{2D} = \frac{1}{2} S_{ij} S_{ij} \qquad (4.10)$$

J_{2D} plays a role for soils as well as for metals. The yield functions are arranged according to the named invariants. Therefore, failure theories in the *principal stress space* are formed. With the *von Mises* hypothesis, which is applicable for metals, the elastic limit is exceeded when the shape alternation energy reaches a certain value. For soils other assumptions are suitable. The change of volume in the plastic region is also considered here. So for the Drucker-Prager model the following yield function was found according to the invariants:

$$f_{DP} = -\alpha I_1 + \sqrt{J_{2D}} - k = 0 \qquad (4.11)$$

whereas α and k are material constants.

4.1.3   Constitutive Three Dimensional Stress-Plastic Strain Relations

Next to the named yield condition and yield function a flow rule must also be arranged. Such a connection between the stress tensor and the plastic strain tensor is established.

At a homogeneous isotropic material the increments of plastic strain must be run coaxially to the direction of the stress tensor. This relationship was confirmed experimentally e.g. in (Pugh & Robinson, 1978) or (Graham, Noonan, & Lew, 1983). That is why the principal stress space and the principal strain space can be overlaid. For this combination the notion of the plastic potential $G(\sigma_{ij} = 0)$ is introduced, which connects the plastic strain increments with the according stress state.

The relations are given in Figure 4.2 and Figure 4.3 . In Figure 4.2a/b the yield surface is similar with the plastic potential. This is known as the associated flow rule, in contrast to the non-associated flow rule pictured in Figure 4.3 a/b. In the non-associated flow rule the stress state is tested on the yield surface. If the material is then in a plastic state, the tensor of plastic strain increments is normal to the plastic potential.

In Figure 4.2b the Drucker-Prager (Drucker & Prager, 1952) yield surface is illustrated. This is a special case of the associated flow rule. The case of the associated flow rule is considered and implemented in the later described generalized cap model. The simplified Figure 4.3b (ABAQUS® User's Manual, ABAQUS®/Standard User's Manual, Version 6.5, 2004) shows a special case of the non-associated flow rule instead. This material model is implemented in the commercial software ABAQUS®, which is used for the verification of the implemented material model here.

The described relationship between the increments of plastic strain and the stress tensor for the associated flow rule can be expressed in the following:

$$de_{ij}{}^P = d\lambda\, \frac{\partial f_y}{\partial \sigma_{ij}}$$

(4.12)

This equation represents the flow rule or the *normality principle*. Equation (4.12) shows that plastic strains with associated flow are perpendicular to the yield surface. The positive Scalar λ is a proportionality factor which has yet to be determined. In case of the non-associated flow, f_y in Equation (4.12) will be replaced by the plastic potential $G(\sigma_{ij} = 0)$.

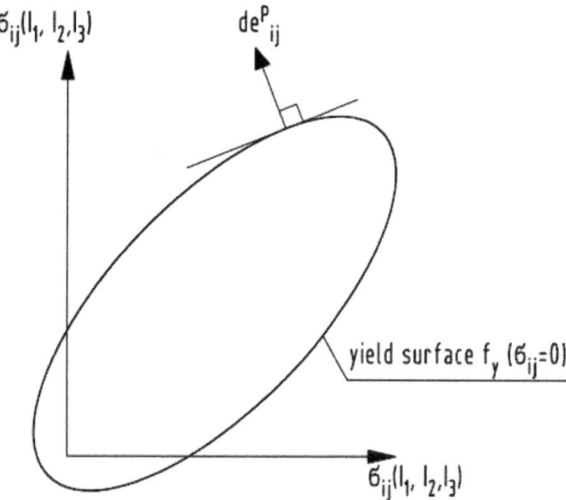

a general case with yield surface = plastic potential

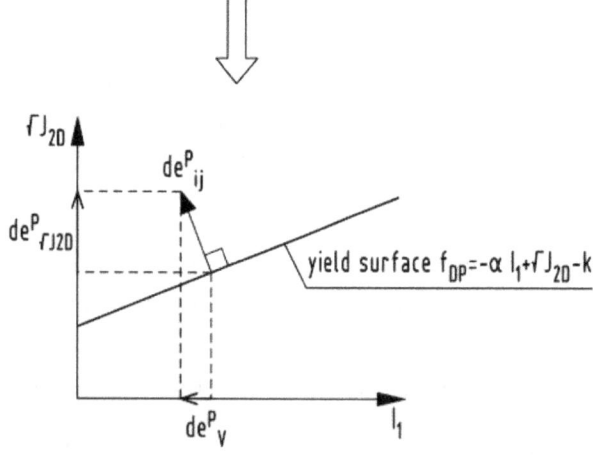

b special case drucker-prager yield surface with yield surface = plastic potential

FIGURE 4.2. YIELD SURFACES WITH EQUAL PLASTIC POTENTIAL

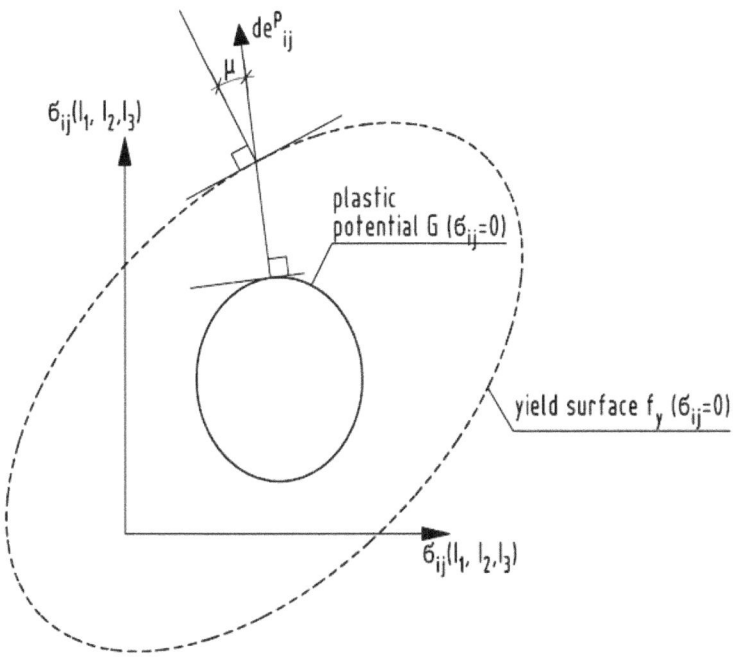

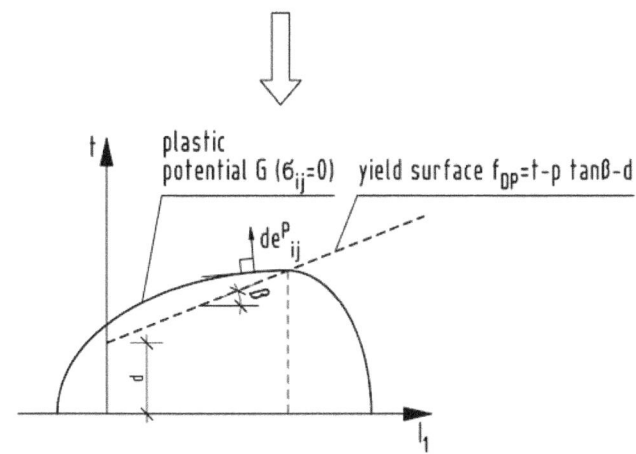

FIGURE 4.3. YIELD SURFACES WITH UNEQUAL PLASTIC POTENTIAL

4.1.4 GENERALIZED CAP MODEL

The model described here is based upon the Drucker-Prager model (Drucker & Prager, 1952). This plastic model predicts the material response under shear load, but cannot predict the plastic flow under hydrostatic compression. Drucker-Prager models lead to an oversized plastic volumetric strain. For soils under hydrostatic compression work hardening was established, so the volumetric strain must be limited. For this reason, the cap models were introduced. With the cap the volumetric plastic strain can be controlled. The *generalized cap model* described here was adopted from (DiMaggio & Sandler, 1971), (Sandler, DiMaggio, & Baladi, 1976), (Kojic, Slavkovic, Grujovic, & Zivkovic, 1995) and (Kojic & Bathe, 2005). The summary of the equations is specifically oriented at

(Kojic & Bathe, 2005). Figure 4.5 shows the circumstance of the implemented soil model. The elastic region is bounded by three surfaces in the stress space: $f_1 = 0, f_c = 0$ and $f_T = 0$

The **failure surface f_1** characterizes the material under shear loading:

$$f_1 = \sqrt{J_{2D}} - k + A\, exp(-B_1\, I_1) - \alpha I_1 = 0 \tag{4.13}$$

The material constants k, A, B_1 and α can be observed experimentally, e.g. in (Desai & Siriwardane, Constitutive laws for engineering materials, 1984). The curve is fixed or not displaceable. If the material constant $A = 0$, the failure surface f_1 corresponds to the Drucker-Prager line (see Figure 4.5).

The **hardening cap f_c** changes the position under volumetric pressure:

$$f_c = (I_1 - L)^2 + R^2(J_{2D} - B^2) = 0 \tag{4.14}$$

The variable L defines the center of the ellipse and B the vertical semi axis. R is defined as the ratio between the semi axes:

$$R = \frac{X - L}{B} \tag{4.15}$$

The ratio R can depend of the start position L of the ellipse. But for simplicity R is chosen as the constant here. This is analogous to (Sandler & Rubin, 1979) or (ABAQUS® User's Manual, ABAQUS®/Standard User's Manual, Version 6.5, 2004). The position X of the cap depends on the volumetric plastic strain e_V^P.

The work hardening response is given as following (DiMaggio & Sandler, 1971):

$$X = -\frac{1}{D}ln\left(1 - \frac{e_V^P}{W}\right) + X_0 \tag{4.16}$$

Rearranged as:

$$e_V^P = W\,[1 - e^{[-D\,(X-X_0)]}] \tag{4.17}$$

The volumetric plastic strain rate decreases with increasing plastic deformation, so the cap surface hardens as a function of the volumetric plastic strain. W and D are material constants. W is the maximum possible volumetric plastic strain and D characterizes the changing volumetric strain rate, as illustrated in Figure 4.4.

For the sake of completeness the possible elastic stress space can be closed by the **tension cut-off f_T** (Sandler & Rubin, 1979):

$$f_T = I_1 - T = 0 \tag{4.18}$$

This characterizes the material failure under tensile stresses. To simplify matters, the stress deviators are set to zero when tension cut-off is triggered. The material then remains in the hydrostatic stress state $I_1 = T$.

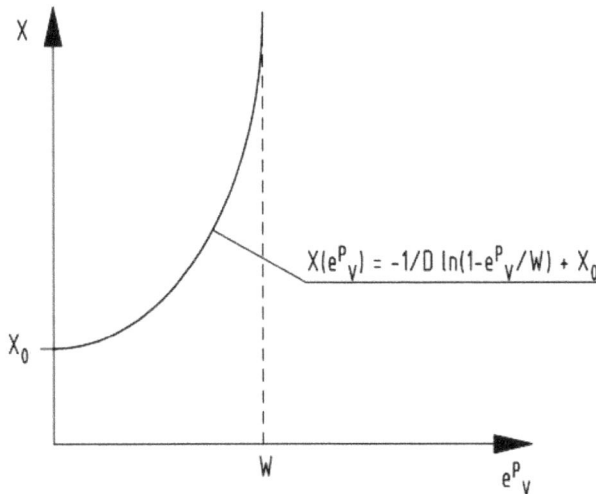

FIGURE 4.4. FUNCTION OF THE POSITION OF THE CAP ACCORDING TO VOLUMETRIC PLASTIC STRAIN

From a strict viewpoint it is not sufficient to explain hydrostatic tension as a criterion for tensile failure. For granular materials this can be appropriate, but for brittle rocks for example other tensile failure theories such as the maximum principal stress theory or William Warnke models must be applied (Katona, 1983), (Chen, 1982).

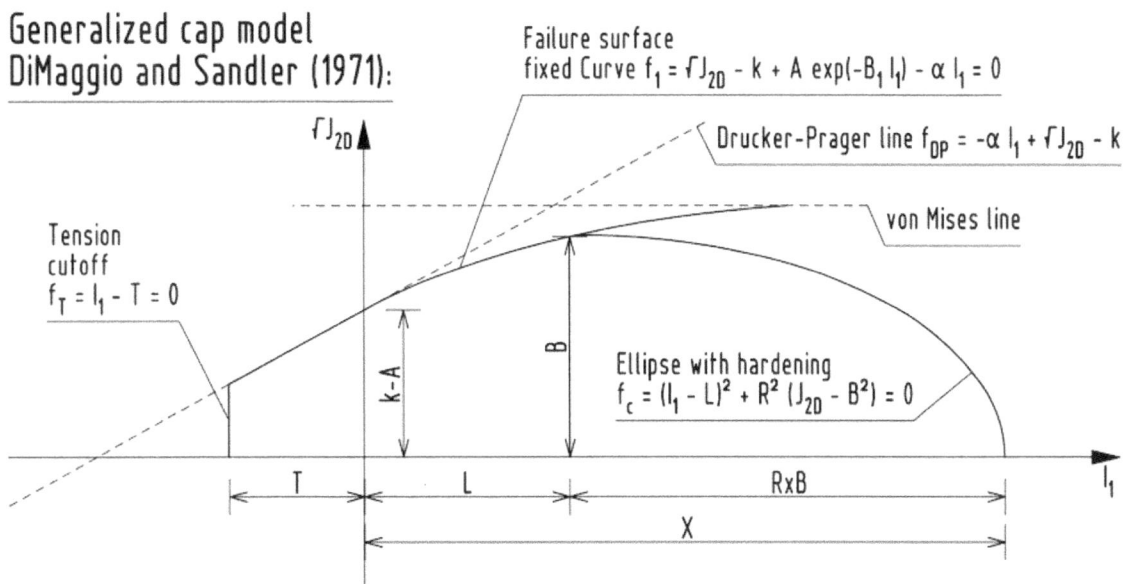

FIGURE 4.5. GENERALIZED CAP MODEL (DIMAGGIO & SANDLER, 1971)

4.2 GENERAL PROCEDURE FOR STRESS IMPLEMENTATION

4.2.1 RADIAL RETURN METHOD

The algorithm of the *radial return method* (Wilkins, 1964), (Krieg & Krieg, 1977) is explained here. The method can be subdivided into two steps. First, an elastic prediction of the stresses, with assumed $\Delta e^P = 0$ will be conducted. Second, if the predicted stress exceeds the yield surface, a correction of the stresses will be applied.

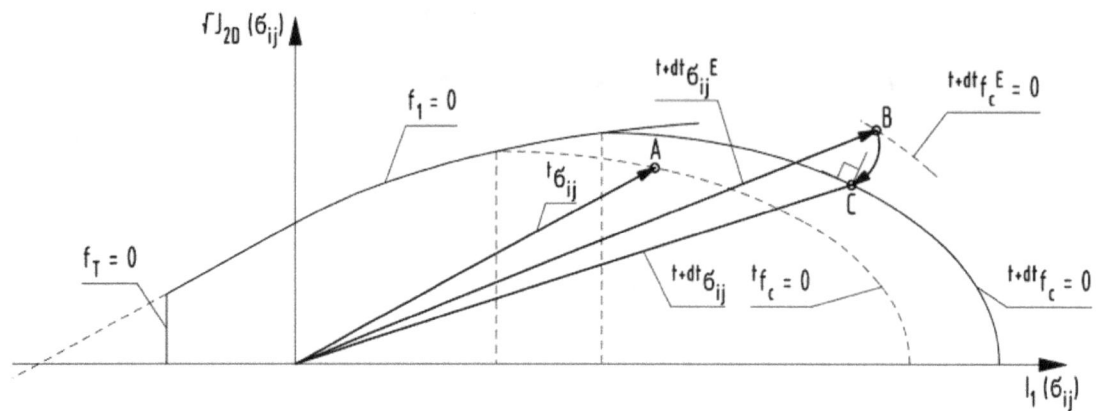

FIGURE 4.6. RADIAL RETURN METHOD FOR CAP MODEL

Figure 4.6 shows the circumstance geometrically for the *generalized cap model*. Point A is the stress solution to the time (t). Point B equates the elastic prediction of the stresses to the time $(t + \Delta t)$. The yield surface $^t f_c = 0$ is exceeded. Hence, in this step the deformation is plastic and a stress correction is applied to point C. Then the vector from the origin to point C is the stress solution to the time $(t + \Delta t)$. And because of the hardening, the cap has the new position $^{t+\Delta t} f_c = 0$.

This is briefly described mathematically as follows (Kojic, 2002):

1) Calculate the trial elastic state:

$$^{t+\Delta t} \sigma^E = C^E \left(^{t+\Delta t}\hat{e} - ^{t+\Delta t}\hat{e}^P \right) \tag{4.19}$$

with C^E as elasticity matrix, $^{t+\Delta t}\hat{e}$ as strain vector and $^{t+\Delta t}\hat{e}^P$ as plastic strain vector (see Appendix A3).

2) Calculate the yield function:

$$^{t+\Delta t} f_y^E = ^{t+\Delta t} f_y \left(^{t+\Delta t}\sigma^E, \, ^t\beta \right) \tag{4.20}$$

with the internal material variables $^t\beta$ from the previous time step. If there are no internal material variables, as in the case of perfect plasticity, the curve BC in Figure 4.6 is the closest point projection of $^{t+\Delta t}\sigma^E$ to the yield surface $^{t+\Delta t} f_y$ due to the application of Equation (4.12).

3) Check for yielding in the time step. If

$$^{t+\Delta t} f_y^E \leq ^t f_y$$

the complete deformation in time step is elastic and $^{t+\Delta t}\sigma^E$ is the solution. If

$$^{t+\Delta t} f_y^E > ^t f_y$$

the deformation in current time step is plastic.

4) In the case of plastic deformation the stress correction is now conducted as follows:

$$^{t+\Delta t}\sigma = ^{t+\Delta t}\sigma^E - C^E . \Delta\hat{e}^P \tag{4.21}$$

with $\Delta \hat{e}^P$ as plastic strain increment vector.

4.2.2 GOVERNING PARAMETER METHOD

The *governing parameter method* is a general concept for implicit stress implementation which is implemented here for the plastic calculations of the *generalized cap model*. The concept is used for example in (Bathe, Chaudhary, Dvorkin, & Kojic, 1984) for the "effective stress function algorithm". This algorithm was then generalized to the *governing parameter method* in (Kojic, 1996). The procedure is a generalization of the *radial return method* (see Section 4.2.1).

The fundamental characteristic of the *governing parameter method* is that the calculation of the unknown stresses and internal material variables is reduced to the evaluation of a single parameter. In an incremental analysis of a strain-driven problem the known quantities at the start of the time step are the stresses ${}^t\sigma$, the strains ${}^te$, the plastic strains ${}^te^P$, and the internal material variables ${}^t\beta$, with the left upper index (t) for the start of time step Δt. The unknowns are the stresses ${}^{t+\Delta t}\sigma$, the plastic strains ${}^{t+\Delta t}e^P$ and the internal variables ${}^{t+\Delta t}\beta$, with the left upper index $(t + \Delta t)$ for the end of time step Δt.

Table 4.1 was adopted from (Kojic, 2002). It shows the explained basic steps of the implicit stress implementation for the *governing parameter method*.

Known quantities:	${}^t\sigma,\ {}^te,\ {}^te^P,\ {}^t\beta,\ {}^{t+\Delta t}e$
Unknown quantities:	${}^{t+\Delta t}\sigma,\ {}^{t+\Delta t}e^P,\ {}^{t+\Delta t}\beta$
Step 1: Express all unknowns in terms of one unknown parameter p and known quantities	${}^{t+\Delta t}\sigma({}^t\sigma,\ {}^te,\ {}^te^P,\ {}^t\beta,\ {}^{t+\Delta t}e, p)$ ${}^{t+\Delta t}e^P({}^t\sigma,\ldots,p)$ (a) ${}^{t+\Delta t}\beta({}^t\sigma,\ldots,p)$
Step 2: Form a function $f(p)$ and solve the governing equation	$f(p) = 0$ (b)
Step 3: Substitute the solution ${}^{t+\Delta t}p$ of the governing equation in (b) to determine the unknowns in (a)	

TABLE 4.1. COMPUTATIONAL STEPS FOR THE GOVERNING PARAMETER METHOD

The function $f(p)$ was solved here with the Newton-Raphson method for a single nonlinear equation (see Section 3.1). The procedure enables the calculation of the elasto-plastic tangent matrix ${}^{t+\Delta t}C^{EP}$, as well. As pictured in Figure 4.1a, the tangent modulus E^T and the tangent matrix ${}^{t+\Delta t}C^{EP}$ can be determined with the differentiation of stresses according to strains:

$$
{}^{t+\Delta t}C_{ijrs}^{EP} = \frac{\partial\, {}^{t+\Delta t}\sigma_{ij}}{\partial\, {}^{t+\Delta t}e_{rs}}
\qquad\qquad (4.22)
$$

The strains depend on the governing parameter p. Therefore, (4.22) can be written (with respect to the chain rule) as:

$$^{t+\Delta t}C_{ijrs}^{EP} = \frac{\partial^{t+\Delta t}\sigma_{ij}}{\partial^{t+\Delta t}p}\frac{\partial^{t+\Delta t}p}{\partial^{t+\Delta t}e_{rs}} + \frac{\partial\sigma_{ij}}{\partial^{t+\Delta t}e_{rs}}\bigg|_{p=const} \qquad (4.23)$$

The derivatives $\dfrac{\partial^{t+\Delta t}p}{\partial^{t+\Delta t}e_{rs}}$ are obtained by differentiation of $f(p) = 0$:

$$\frac{\partial f}{\partial^{t+\Delta t}e_{ij}} =$$

$$\left(\frac{\partial f}{\partial^{t+\Delta t}\sigma_{rs}}\frac{\partial^{t+\Delta t}\sigma_{rs}}{\partial^{t+\Delta t}p} + \frac{\partial f}{\partial^{t+\Delta t}e_{rs}^{P}}\frac{\partial^{t+\Delta t}e_{rs}^{P}}{\partial^{t+\Delta t}p} + \frac{\partial f}{\partial^{t+\Delta t}\beta_{rs}}\frac{\partial^{t+\Delta t}\beta_{rs}}{\partial^{t+\Delta t}p}\right)\frac{\partial^{t+\Delta t}p}{\partial^{t+\Delta t}e_{ij}} + \frac{\partial f}{\partial^{t+\Delta t}e_{ij}}\bigg|_{p=const} = 0 \qquad (4.24)$$

$$\frac{\partial^{t+\Delta t}p}{\partial^{t+\Delta t}e_{ij}} = -\left(\frac{\partial f}{\partial^{t+\Delta t}\sigma_{rs}}\frac{\partial^{t+\Delta t}\sigma_{rs}}{\partial^{t+\Delta t}p} + \frac{\partial f}{\partial^{t+\Delta t}e_{rs}^{P}}\frac{\partial^{t+\Delta t}e_{rs}^{P}}{\partial^{t+\Delta t}p} + \frac{\partial f}{\partial^{t+\Delta t}\beta_{rs}}\frac{\partial^{t+\Delta t}\beta_{rs}}{\partial^{t+\Delta t}p}\right)^{-1}\frac{\partial f}{\partial^{t+\Delta t}e_{ij}}\bigg|_{p=const}$$

Here the governing parameter function f is equal to the yield functions (see 4.1.4). But in general it can also be another function.

5 PLASTICITY FOR THE GENERALIZED CAP MODEL

The fundamental equations and terms for the *generalized cap model* are given in Section 4.1.4. The implementation of the general statements in Chapter 4 will be conducted in this chapter.

The calculation of stresses and the elasto-plastic tangent matrix is necessary, as illustrated in Section 4.2. The correct calculation of stresses is fundamental for convergence. The complete calculation is executed stepwise. With respect to this circumstance it is noted that occurring errors in the stress calculation cannot be compensated through the iterative correction scheme. With increasing steps, errors in stress calculation increase until they reach an irreversible status and the equilibrium iterations do not converge.

Another reason for divergence can be a overly large time step. So in the case of divergence the time step Δt will usually be reduced. This is very conveniently implemented in the commercial program ABAQUS® for example. Here the time step is automatically reduced in the case of divergence for particular steps. In this work the time step will be reduced for all steps in the case of divergence. In divergence the first calculation is aborted. Then the time step is reduced. And with the reduced time step a second calculation is realized.

As a further important fact it is usual in soil mechanics to define compressive stresses and strains as positive. This is included in this work with respect to the soil mechanics notations.

As pictured in Figure 5.1, four yielding cases are possible. If the stress point is over the line f_1, *yielding on failure surface* occurs. If the stress point is right of the line $^{t+\Delta t}f_c = 0$ and under the line $f_1 = 0$ *cap yielding* is present. If the stress point is right of the line $^{t+\Delta t}f_c = 0$ and over the line $f_1 = 0$ we have *vertex yielding*. *Vertex yielding* can be seen as an addition of yielding on failure surface and cap yielding. Furthermore, in the case of tension stresses we have the *tension cutoff*, when the stress point is left of the line $f_T = 0$. In the following section these four cases are processed.

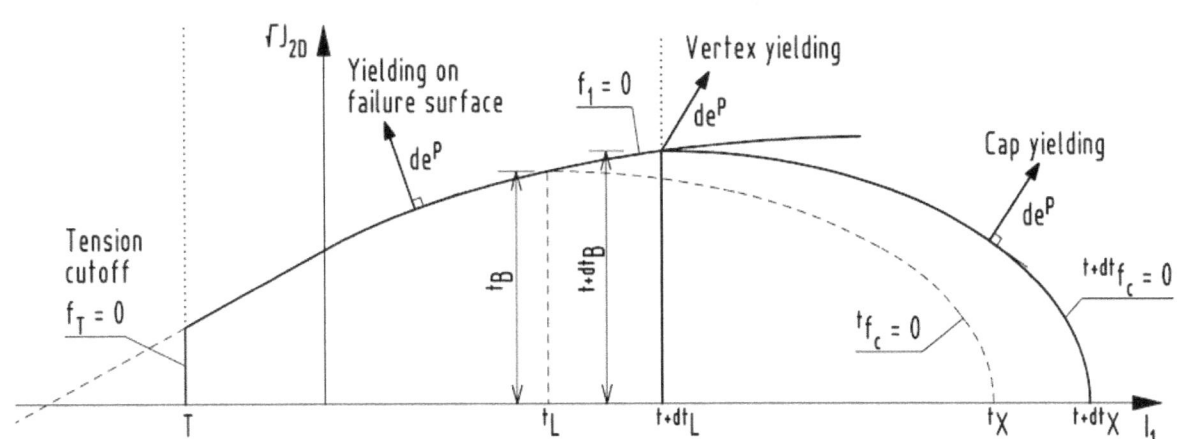

FIGURE 5.1. YIELDING SURFACES OF THE GENERALIZED CAP MODEL

5.1 Stress Implementation

Analogous to (Kojic & Bathe, 2005) the procedure of stress implementation is conducted here. The stress implementation procedure of (Kojic & Bathe, 2005) is expanded, so that all equations are derived and further some equations are adapted for special cases. The following sections are related to the different possible yield cases. For better readability the derivations for the numbered main equations are written in index notation, neglecting the notation for the current time step. The numbered main equations are written in matrix notation with regard to the current time step. For the stress implementation in the following sections the two-index notation is used.

5.1.1 Elastic Material Response

The elastic solutions of the stress deviator $^{t+\Delta t}\mathbf{S}^E$ and the mean stress $^{t+\Delta t}\sigma_m^E$ are determined first:

$$^{t+\Delta t}\mathbf{S}^E = 2\,G\,{}^{t+\Delta t}\mathbf{e}''$$

(5.1)

$$^{t+\Delta t}\sigma_m^E = c_m\,{}^{t+\Delta t}e''\quad no\ sum\ on\ m$$

(5.2)

with the shear modulus G: $G = 0.5\,E/(1+v)$ and the two known independent material constants: Young's modulus E and Poisson's ratio v. The value c_m is also dependent on E and v with: $c_m = E/(1-2\,v)$. The bulk modulus K can be expressed in c_m as: $K = \frac{1}{3}c_m$. Further:

$$^{t+\Delta t}\mathbf{e}'' = {}^{t+\Delta t}\mathbf{e}' - {}^{t}\mathbf{e}'^P$$

(5.3)

$$^{t+\Delta t}e_m'' = {}^{t+\Delta t}e_m - {}^{t}e_m^P$$

(5.4)

with $^{t}\mathbf{e}'^P$ as the deviator plastic strain vector and $^{t}e_m^P$ as the mean plastic strain. Both cases are related to the previous time step. For the application of (5.1) and (5.2) the bulk modulus K and the shear modulus G have to be independent of the stress state. In the next step the yielding check for the current time step Δt will be done. Therefore, the elastic invariants $^{t+\Delta t}I_1^E$ and $^{t+\Delta t}J_{2D}^E$ are calculated with the equations (4.7) and (4.10). These invariants are then substituted in the equations (4.13), (4.14) and (4.18) to get $^{t+\Delta t}f_1^E$, $^{t+\Delta t}f_c^E$ and $^{t+\Delta t}f_T^E$. Therefore, ^{t}L and ^{t}B from the last time step are used.

Elastic deformations in the current time step exist if $^{t+\Delta t}f_1^E \leq 0$, $^{t+\Delta t}f_c^E \leq 0$ and $I_1^E > T$, otherwise the deformation in the current time step is plastic.

5.1.2 Yielding on Failure Surface

Yielding on failure surface is present if $^{t+\Delta t}f_1^E \leq 0$ and $3\,{}^{t+\Delta t}\sigma_m^E \leq {}^{t}L$. The increments of mean and deviatoric plastic strain can be derived from (4.12) and (4.13):

$$\Delta e_{ij}^P = \Delta e_m^P\,\delta_{ij} + \Delta e_{ij}'^P = \Delta\lambda\,\frac{\partial f_y}{\partial\sigma_{ij}} = \Delta\lambda\,\frac{\partial\left(\sqrt{J_{2D}} - k + A\,e^{(-B_1\,I_1)} - \alpha\,I_1\right)}{\partial(\sigma_m\,\delta_{ij} - S_{ij})}$$

$$\Delta e_{ij}^P = \Delta \lambda \left. \frac{\partial \sqrt{J_{2D}}}{\partial S_{ij}} \right|_{1.\text{term}} + \Delta \lambda \left. \frac{\partial \left(A \, e^{(-B_1 \, I_1)} \right)}{\partial (\sigma_m \, \delta_{ij})} \right|_{2.\text{term}} + \Delta \lambda \left. \frac{\partial (-\alpha I_1)}{\partial (\sigma_m \, \delta_{ij})} \right|_{3.\text{term}} \qquad (5.5)$$

The first term of (5.5) yields the increment of deviatoric strain $\Delta e_{ij}^{\prime P}$. Applying the derivation formula $(\sqrt{x})' = \frac{1}{2\sqrt{x}}$, the chain rule and the product rule with (4.10) yields:

$$\Delta e_{ij}^{\prime P} = \Delta \lambda \frac{\partial \sqrt{J_{2D}}}{\partial S_{ij}} = \Delta \lambda \frac{\partial \sqrt{\frac{1}{2} S_{ij} S_{ij}}}{\partial S_{kl}} = \Delta \lambda \frac{1}{2 \sqrt{\frac{1}{2} S_{ij} S_{ij}}} \left(\frac{1}{2} \delta_{ijkl} S_{ij} + \frac{1}{2} S_{ij} \delta_{ijkl} \right) = \Delta \lambda \frac{1}{2 \sqrt{J_{2D}}} S_{kl}$$

In matrix notation for the current time step it follows:

$$\boxed{\Delta \boldsymbol{e}^{\prime P} = \Delta \lambda \frac{1}{2 \sqrt{J_{2D}}} \, {}^{t+\Delta t}\boldsymbol{S}} \qquad (5.6)$$

The second and third term of (5.5) yields the increment of mean strain. With $\Delta e_V^P = 3 \, \Delta e_m^P$ and $\sigma_m = \frac{1}{3} I_1$ follows for Δe_m^P:

$$3 \, \Delta e_m^P \delta_{ij} = \Delta \lambda \left(3 \, \delta_{ij} \frac{\partial \left(A \, e^{(-B_1 \, I_1)} \right)}{\partial I_1} + 3 \, \delta_{ij} \frac{\partial (-\alpha I_1)}{\partial I_1} \right)$$

$$3 \, \Delta e_m^P \delta_{ij} = \Delta \lambda \left(-B_1 \, 3 \, A \, e^{(-B_1 \, I_1)} \, \delta_{ij} - 3 \, \alpha \, \delta_{ij} \right)$$

$$\Delta e_m^P = \Delta \lambda \left(-B_1 \, A \, e^{(-B_1 \, I_1)} \, \delta_{ij} - \alpha \right)$$

In notation for the current time step, we get:

$$\boxed{\Delta e_m^P = \Delta \lambda \left(-B_1 \, A \, exp\left(-B_1 \, {}^{t+\Delta t}I_1 \right) - \alpha \right)} \qquad (5.7)$$

Rearranged for $\Delta \lambda$:

$$\boxed{\Delta \lambda = \frac{\Delta e_m^P}{-B_1 \, A \, exp\left(-B_1 \, {}^{t+\Delta t}I_1 \right) - \alpha}} \qquad (5.8)$$

In this context the dilatancy for the yielding case *yielding on failure surface* will be mentioned here. Figure 5.1 shows that the projection of Δe^P on the I_1 axis is negative. That means that a volumetric increase under shear stress occurs. The mean stress ${}^{t+\Delta t}\sigma_m^E$ follows directly from (4.21) and (A.11):

$$\boxed{{}^{t+\Delta t}\sigma_m = {}^{t+\Delta t}\sigma_m^E - c_m \, \Delta e_m^P} \qquad (5.9)$$

Hence, follows:

$$\boxed{{}^{t+\Delta t}I_1 = 3 \, {}^{t+\Delta t}\sigma_m} \qquad (5.10)$$

Equation (4.21) can also be assigned analogously to the deviatoric stress S_{ij} with respect to (A.16):

$$S_{ij} = S_{ij}^E - 2 \, G \, \Delta e_{ij}^{\prime P}$$

With (5.6) follows:

$$S_{ij} = S_{ij}^E - 2 G \, \Delta\lambda \, \frac{1}{2\sqrt{J_{2D}}} \, S_{ij}$$

$$S_{ij}^E = S_{ij} + 2 G \, \Delta\lambda \, \frac{1}{2\sqrt{J_{2D}}}$$

$$S_{ij} = S_{ij} \left(1 + 2 G \, \Delta\lambda \, \frac{1}{2\sqrt{J_{2D}}} \right)$$

$$S_{ij} = \frac{S_{ij}^E}{\left(1 + G \, \Delta\lambda \, \frac{1}{\sqrt{J_{2D}}} \right)}$$

In matrix notation for the current time step:

$$^{t+\Delta t}S = \frac{^{t+\Delta t}S^E}{\left(1 + G \, \Delta\lambda \, \frac{1}{\sqrt{^{t+\Delta t}J_{2D}}} \right)} \qquad (5.11)$$

From (4.10) follows that $S_{ij} = J_{2D} \, 2 \, S_{ij}^{-1}$. Replacing $\boldsymbol{S}$ and $\boldsymbol{S^E}$ in (5.11) with this yields the derivation of $\sqrt{^{t+\Delta t}J_{2D}}$ in (5.11):

$$J_{2D} 2 \, S_{ij}^{-1} = \frac{J_{2D}^E \, 2 \, S_{ij}^{E\,-1}}{\left(1 + G \, \Delta\lambda \, \frac{1}{\sqrt{J_{2D}}} \right)}$$

$$J_{2D} \, S_{ij}^{-1} = \frac{J_{2D}^E \, S_{ij}^{E\,-1}}{\left(1 + G \, \Delta\lambda \, \frac{1}{\sqrt{J_{2D}}} \right)} \Rightarrow multiply: S_{jk} \, S_{jk}^E$$

$$J_{2D} \, \delta_{ik} \, S_{jk}^E = \frac{J_{2D}^E \, \delta_{ik} \, S_{jk}}{\left(1 + G \, \Delta\lambda \, \frac{1}{\sqrt{J_{2D}}} \right)} \Rightarrow with \ (5.11) \, replace \ S_{jk} \ on \ the \ right \ hand \ side$$

$$J_{2D} \, S_{ji}^E = \frac{J_{2D}^E \, S_{ji}^E}{\left(1 + G \, \Delta\lambda \, \frac{1}{\sqrt{J_{2D}}} \right)^2} \Rightarrow multiply: S_{ik}^{E\,-1}$$

$$J_{2D} = \frac{J_{2D}^E}{\left(1 + G \, \Delta\lambda \, \frac{1}{\sqrt{J_{2D}}} \right)^2} \Rightarrow square \ root \ of \ all \ terms$$

$$\sqrt{J_{2D}} = \frac{\sqrt{J_{2D}^E}}{\left(1 + G\,\Delta\lambda\,\frac{1}{\sqrt{J_{2D}}}\right)}$$

$$\sqrt{J_{2D}^E} = \sqrt{J_{2D}}\left(1 + G\,\Delta\lambda\,\frac{1}{\sqrt{J_{2D}}}\right) = \sqrt{J_{2D}} + G\,\Delta\lambda$$

$$\sqrt{J_{2D}} = \sqrt{J_{2D}^E} - G\,\Delta$$

Written in notation for the current time step:

$$\boxed{\sqrt{^{t+\Delta t}J_{2D}} = \sqrt{^{t+\Delta t}J_{2D}^E} - G\,\Delta\lambda} \qquad\qquad (5.12)$$

The governing function $f(p)$ relates to (4.13). The yield condition (4.13) must be satisfied at the end of the time step. In notation for the current time step this is given as:

$$\boxed{^{t+\Delta t}f_1 = \sqrt{^{t+\Delta t}J_{2D}} - k + A\,exp\left(-B_1\,^{t+\Delta t}I_1\right) - \alpha\,^{t+\Delta t}I_1 = 0} \qquad\qquad (5.13)$$

The governing parameter was chosen as Δe_m^P. So the governing function is $^{t+\Delta t}f_1(\Delta e_m^P)$. The backtracking of the variables in (5.13) gives the computational steps for the *yielding on failure surface*. Therefore, the above given functions are nested, so that the only unknown is Δe_m^P. This is listed in Table 5.1.

Here, the nonlinear equation $^{t+\Delta t}f_1(\Delta e_m^P) = 0$ was solved with the Newton-Raphson method for one nonlinear equation (see Section 3.1). Furthermore, it was implemented that for *yielding on failure surface* the cap size decreases (dilatancy). This is done with the calculation of the cap position L (see Figure 5.1). From (4.15) follows for the current time step:

$$\boxed{^{t+\Delta t}X = R\,^{t+\Delta t}B + {}^{t+\Delta t}L} \qquad\qquad (5.14)$$

With (5.23):

$$\boxed{f\left(^{t+\Delta t}L\right) = {}^{t+\Delta t}X - R\left(k - A\,exp\left(-B_1\,^{t+\Delta t}L\right) + \alpha\,^{t+\Delta t}L\right) - {}^{t+\Delta t}L = 0} \qquad\qquad (5.15)$$

The variable $^{t+\Delta t}X$ is given by (4.16). A rearrangement for $^{t+\Delta t}L$ is not possible. Hence, this is also a nonlinear equation which must be solved numerically. So the Newton-Raphson method for one nonlinear equation (see Section 3.1) is applied also. Therefore, $f\left(^{t+\Delta t}L\right)$ as (5.15) is needed and further $f'\left(^{t+\Delta t}L\right)$ is given as:

$$\boxed{f'\left(^{t+\Delta t}L\right) = -R\left[\alpha + A\,B_1\,exp\left(-B_1\,^{t+\Delta t}L\right)\right] - 1 = 0} \qquad\qquad (5.16)$$

For some rock materials other assumptions are applicable. Here, the cap position remains unchanged (Chen & Mizuno, 1990).

1.	**With the independent variable Δe_m^P calculate:**

$^{t+\Delta t}\sigma_m$ from (5.9)

with $^{t+\Delta t}\sigma_m$ calculate $^{t+\Delta t}I_1$ from (5.10)

with $^{t+\Delta t}I_1$ calculate $\Delta\lambda$ from (5.8)

with $\Delta\lambda$ and $^{t+\Delta t}S^E$ from (5.1) and $\sqrt{^{t+\Delta t}J_{2D}^E}$ from (4.10) calculate $\sqrt{^{t+\Delta t}J_{2D}}$ from (5.12)

2.	**With $\sqrt{^{t+\Delta t}J_{2D}(\Delta e_m^P)}$ and $^{t+\Delta t}I_1(\Delta e_m^P)$ iterate on (5.13) until convergence is reached:**

$^{t+\Delta t}f_1 \leq \varepsilon$

3.	**Finally:**

With $\sqrt{^{t+\Delta t}J_{2D}}$ and $^{t+\Delta t}S^E$ from (5.1) calculate $^{t+\Delta t}S$ from (5.11)

With $^{t+\Delta t}S$ and $\sqrt{^{t+\Delta t}J_{2D}}$ calculate $\Delta e'^P$ from (5.6)

TABLE 5.1. ITERATIVE STEPS FOR STRESS INTEGRATION OF YIELDING ON FAILURE SURFACE

5.1.3 CAP YIELDING

Cap yielding occurs if $^{t+\Delta t}f_c^E > 0, (3\ ^{t+\Delta t}\sigma_m^E) >\ ^{t}L$ and $^{t+\Delta t}f_1^E \leq 0$. In the same way as for *yielding on failure surface* will be proceeded here. The increments of mean and deviatoric plastic strain can be derived from (4.12) and (4.14):

$$\Delta e_{ij}^P = \Delta e_m^P\ \delta_{ij} + \Delta e_{ij}'^P = \Delta\lambda_c\ \frac{\partial f_y}{\partial\sigma_{ij}} = \Delta\lambda_c\ \frac{\partial[(I_1 - L)^2 + R^2\ (J_{2D} - B^2)]}{\partial(\sigma_m\ \delta_{ij} + S_{ij})}$$

$$\Delta e_{ij}^P = \Delta\lambda_c\ \frac{\partial(I_1 - L)^2}{\partial(\sigma_m\ \delta_{ij})}\bigg|_{1.term} + \Delta\lambda_c\ \frac{\partial[R^2\ (J_{2D} - B^2)]}{\partial S_{ij}}\bigg|_{2.term} \qquad (5.17)$$

The first term of (5.17) yields the increment of mean strain. With $\Delta e_V^P = 3\ \Delta e_m^P$, $\sigma_m = \frac{1}{3}\ I_1$ and the product rule follows:

$$3\ \Delta e_m^P\ \delta_{ij} = \Delta\lambda_c\ \frac{\partial(I_1 - L)^2}{\partial(\sigma_m\ \delta_{ij})} = \Delta\lambda_c\ 3\ \frac{\partial(I_1 - L)^2}{\partial I_1}\ \delta_{ij} = \Delta\lambda_c\ 2\ (I_1 - L)\ 3\ \delta_{ij}$$

$$\Delta e_m^P = \Delta\lambda_c\ 2\ (3\ \sigma_m - L)$$

Written in notation for the current time step:

$$\boxed{\Delta e_m^P = \Delta\lambda_c\ 2\ (3\ ^{t+\Delta t}\sigma_m -\ ^{t+\Delta t}L)} \qquad (5.18)$$

Rearranged for $\Delta\lambda_c$:

$$\Delta\lambda_c = \frac{\Delta e_m^P}{2\,(3\,^{t+\Delta t}\sigma_m - \,^{t+\Delta t}L)} \qquad (5.19)$$

The second term of (5.17) yields the increment of deviatoric strain. Applying the product rule and (4.10) yields:

$$\Delta e_{ij}'^P = \Delta\lambda_c\,\frac{\partial[R^2\,(J_{2D} - B^2)]}{\partial\,S_{ij}} = \Delta\lambda_c\,R^2\,\frac{\partial\,(J_{2D} - B^2)}{\partial\,S_{ij}} = \Delta\lambda_c\,R^2\,\frac{\partial\,J_{2D}}{\partial\,S_{ij}} = \Delta\lambda_c\,R^2\,\frac{\partial\,(\frac{1}{2}S_{ij}\,S_{ij})}{\partial\,S_{kl}}$$

$$\Delta e_{ij}'^P = \Delta\lambda_c\,R^2\left(\frac{1}{2}\,\delta_{ijkl}\,S_{ij} + \frac{1}{2}\,S_{ij}\,\delta_{ijkl}\right) = \Delta\lambda_c\,R^2\,S_{kl}$$

In matrix notation for the current time step, we get:

$$\Delta\boldsymbol{e}'^P = \Delta\lambda_c\,R^2\,{}^{t+\Delta t}\boldsymbol{S} \qquad (5.20)$$

Equation (4.21) is again be assigned to the deviatoric stress S_{ij} with respect to (A.16):

$$S_{ij} = S_{ij}^E - 2\,G\,\Delta e_{ij}'^P$$

With (5.20) it follows:

$$S_{ij} = S_{ij}^E - 2\,G\,\Delta\lambda_c\,R^2\,S_{ij}$$

$$S_{ij}^E = S_{ij} + 2\,G\,\Delta\lambda_c\,R^2\,S_{ij} = S_{ij}\,(1 + 2\,G\,\Delta\lambda_c\,R^2)$$

$$S_{ij} = \frac{S_{ij}^E}{(1 + 2\,G\,\Delta\lambda_c\,R^2)}$$

Written in matrix notation for the current time step:

$$^{t+\Delta t}\boldsymbol{S} = \frac{^{t+\Delta t}\boldsymbol{S}^E}{(1 + 2\,G\,\Delta\lambda_c\,R^2)} \qquad (5.21)$$

Again with (4.10) as $S_{ij} = J_{2D}\,2\,S_{ij}^{-1}$ and replacing $\boldsymbol{S}$ and $\boldsymbol{S}^E$ in (5.21) this yields the derivation of J_{2D}:

$$J_{2D}\,2\,S_{ij}^{-1} = \frac{J_{2D}^E\,2\,S_{ij}^{E\,-1}}{(1 + 2\,G\,\Delta\lambda_c\,R^2)}$$

$$J_{2D}\,S_{ij}^{-1} = \frac{J_{2D}^E\,S_{ij}^{E\,-1}}{(1 + 2\,G\,\Delta\lambda_c\,R^2)} \Rightarrow multiply:\,S_{jk}\,S_{jk}^E$$

$$J_{2D}\,\delta_{ik}\,S_{jk}^E = \frac{J_{2D}^E\,\delta_{ik}\,S_{jk}}{(1 + 2\,G\,\Delta\lambda_c\,R^2)} \Rightarrow with\,(5.21)\,replace\,S_{jk}\,on\,the\,right\,hand\,side$$

$$J_{2D}\,S_{ji}^E = \frac{J_{2D}^E\,S_{ji}^E}{(1 + 2\,G\,\Delta\lambda_c\,R^2)^2} \Rightarrow multiply:\,S_{ik}^{E\,-1}$$

$$J_{2D} = \frac{J_{2D}^E}{(1 + 2\,G\,\Delta\lambda_c\,R^2)^2}$$

In notation for the current time step it follows:

$$^{t+\Delta t}J_{2D} = \frac{^{t+\Delta t}J_{2D}^E}{(1 \,+\, 2\,G\,\Delta\lambda_c\,R^2)^2} \tag{5.22}$$

From Figure 5.1 and (4.13) follows the vertical half axis of the cap ellipse. Equation (4.13) is arranged for $\sqrt{J_{2D}} = B$ and $I_1 = L$:

$$\sqrt{J_{2D}} - k + A\,exp(-B_1\,I_1) - \alpha\,I_1 = 0$$

$$B - k + A\,exp(-B_1\,L) - \alpha\,L = 0$$

$$B = k - A\,exp(-B_1\,L) + \alpha\,L$$

Written in notation for the current time step:

$$^{t+\Delta t}B = k - A\,exp\left(-B_1\,{}^{t+\Delta t}L\right) + \alpha\,{}^{t+\Delta t}L \tag{5.23}$$

To calculate the plastic volumetric strain e_V^P (4.17) is applied. With use of notation for current time step:

$$^{t+\Delta t}e_V^P = W\left[1 - e^{\left(-D\,({}^{t+\Delta t}X - X_0)\right)}\right] \tag{5.24}$$

The initial position of the cap X_0 can be calculated from (5.14) and (5.23) with $^{t+\Delta t}L = {}^t L$. Furthermore, Equation (A.14) provides the context to the mean strain:

$$^{t+\Delta t}e_m^P = \frac{1}{3}\,{}^{t+\Delta t}e_V^P \tag{5.25}$$

The increment of mean plastic strain Δe_m^P is defined by:

$$\Delta e_m^P = {}^{t+\Delta t}e_m^P - {}^t e_m^P \tag{5.26}$$

Here $^t e_m^P$ is the mean strain from the last time step. The governing function $f(p)$ relates now to (4.14). The yield condition (4.14) must be satisfied at the end of the time step. This is in notation for the current time step given as:

$$^{t+\Delta t}f_c = \left({}^{t+\Delta t}I_1 - {}^{t+\Delta t}L\right)^2 + R^2\left({}^{t+\Delta t}J_{2D} - {}^{t+\Delta t}B^2\right) = 0 \tag{5.27}$$

The governing parameter was chosen as $^{t+\Delta t}L$. So the governing function is $^{t+\Delta t}f_c({}^{t+\Delta t}L)$. The backtracking of the variables in (5.27) gives the computational steps for the *cap yielding*. Therefore, the given functions are nested, so that the only unknown is $^{t+\Delta t}L$. This is listed in Table 5.2.

1.	**With the independent variable $^{t+\Delta t}L$ calculate:**
	$^{t+\Delta t}B$ from (5.23)
	with $^{t+\Delta t}B$ calculate $^{t+\Delta t}X$ from (5.14)
	with $^{t+\Delta t}X$ calculate $^{t+\Delta t}e_V^P$ from (5.24)
	with $^{t+\Delta t}e_V^P$ calculate $^{t+\Delta t}e_m^P$ from (5.25)
	with $^{t+\Delta t}e_m^P$ calculate Δe_m^P from (5.26)
	with Δe_m^P calculate $^{t+\Delta t}\sigma_m$ from (5.9)
	with $^{t+\Delta t}\sigma_m$ and Δe_m^P calculate $\Delta\lambda_c$ from (5.19)
	with $\Delta\lambda_c$ and $\sqrt{^{t+\Delta t}J_{2D}^E}$ from (4.10) calculate $^{t+\Delta t}J_{2D}$ from (5.22)

2.	**With $\sqrt{^{t+\Delta t}J_{2D}\left(^{t+\Delta t}L\right)}$ and $^{t+\Delta t}I_1\left(^{t+\Delta t}L\right)$ iterate on (5.27) until convergence is reached:**
	$^{t+\Delta t}f_c \leq \varepsilon$

3.	**Finally:**
	With $^{t+\Delta t}S^E$ from (5.1) and $\Delta\lambda_c$ calculate $^{t+\Delta t}S$ from (5.21)
	With $^{t+\Delta t}S$ and $\Delta\lambda_c$ calculate $\Delta e'^P$ from (5.20)

TABLE 5.2. ITERATIVE STEPS FOR STRESS INTEGRATION OF CAP YIELDING

The nonlinear equation $^{t+\Delta t}f_c\left(^{t+\Delta t}L\right) = 0$ was solved also with the Newton-Raphson method for one nonlinear equation (see Section 3.1) here.

5.1.4 VERTEX YIELDING

Vertex yielding occurs if $\left(3\ ^{t+\Delta t}\sigma_m^E\right) > \ ^{t}L$ and $^{t+\Delta t}f_1^E > 0$. The procedure is the same as for *yielding on failure surface* and *cap yielding*. *Yielding on failure surface* and *cap yielding* must be implicated for *vertex yielding*. So the increments of plastic strain from *yielding on failure surface* and *cap yielding* are added from (5.6) and (5.20):

$$\Delta e_{ij}'^P = \Delta\lambda_F \frac{1}{2\sqrt{J_{2D}}}\ ^{t+\Delta t}S + \Delta\lambda_c R^2\ ^{t+\Delta t}S$$

$$\Delta e_{ij}'^P = \left(\Delta\lambda_F \frac{1}{2\sqrt{J_{2D}}} + \Delta\lambda_c R^2\right)^{t+\Delta t}S = \Delta\lambda_V\ ^{t+\Delta t}S \qquad (5.28)$$

The stress deviator $^{t+\Delta t}S$ can be determined again (see Sections 5.1.2 and 5.1.3) from (4.21) and (A.16):

$$S_{ij} = S_{ij}^E - 2\,G\,\Delta e'^P_{ij}$$

With (5.28) follows:

$$S_{ij} = S_{ij}^E - 2\,G\,\Delta\lambda_V\,S_{ij}$$

$$S_{ij}^E = S_{ij} + 2\,G\,\Delta\lambda_V\,S_{ij}$$

$$S_{ij} = \frac{S_{ij}^E}{(1 + 2\,G\,\Delta\lambda_V)}$$

In matrix notation for the current time step, we get:

$$\boxed{^{t+\Delta t}S = \frac{^{t+\Delta t}S^E}{(1 + 2\,G\,\Delta\lambda_V)}} \qquad (5.29)$$

From (4.10) follows that $S_{ij} = J_{2D}\,2\,S_{ij}^{-1}$. Replacing S and S^E in (5.29) with this yields the derivation of $\sqrt{^{t+\Delta t}J_{2D}}$:

$$J_{2D}\,2\,S_{ij}^{-1} = \frac{J_{2D}^E\,2\,S_{ij}^{E\,-1}}{(1 + 2\,G\,\Delta\lambda_V)}$$

$$J_{2D}\,S_{ij}^{-1} = \frac{J_{2D}^E\,S_{ij}^{E\,-1}}{(1 + 2\,G\,\Delta\lambda_V)} \Rightarrow multiply:\ S_{jk}\,S_{jk}^E$$

$$J_{2D}\,\delta_{ik}\,S_{jk}^E = \frac{J_{2D}^E\,\delta_{ik}\,S_{jk}}{(1 + 2\,G\,\Delta\lambda_V)} \Rightarrow replace\ S_{jk}\ on\ the\ right\ hand\ side$$

$$J_{2D}\,S_{ji}^E = \frac{J_{2D}^E\,S_{ji}^E}{(1 + 2\,G\,\Delta\lambda_V)^2} \Rightarrow multiply:\ S_{ik}^{E\,-1}$$

$$J_{2D} = \frac{J_{2D}^E}{(1 + 2\,G\,\Delta\lambda_V)^2} \Rightarrow square\ root\ of\ all\ terms$$

$$\sqrt{J_{2D}} = \frac{\sqrt{J_{2D}^E}}{(1 + 2\,G\,\Delta\lambda_V)}$$

Written in notation for the current time step:

$$\boxed{\sqrt{^{t+\Delta t}J_{2D}} = \frac{\sqrt{^{t+\Delta t}J_{2D}^E}}{(1 + 2\,G\,\Delta\lambda_V)}} \qquad (5.30)$$

Now the positive scalar $\Delta\lambda_V$ is calculated from (5.30). With the conclusion that $\sqrt{^{t+\Delta t}J_{2D}} = {}^{t+\Delta t}B$ at the vertex follows from (5.30):

$$B = \frac{\sqrt{J_{2D}^E}}{(1 + 2\,G\,\Delta\lambda_V)}$$

$$1 + 2\,G\,\Delta\lambda_V = \frac{\sqrt{J_{2D}^E}}{B}$$

$$\Delta\lambda_V = \frac{\frac{\sqrt{J_{2D}^E}}{B} - 1}{2\,G}$$

In notation for the current time step:

$$\Delta\lambda_V = \frac{\frac{\sqrt{^{t+\Delta t}J_{2D}^E}}{^{t+\Delta t}B} - 1}{2\,G} \tag{5.31}$$

From Figure 5.1 follows:

$$^{t+\Delta t}I_1 = {}^{t+\Delta t}L \tag{5.32}$$

The stress point for *vertex yielding,* at the end of the current step, should lie on the intersection of the cap and the failure surface. The failure surface is not displaceable. Hence, only the position of the cap for *vertex yielding* has to be determined. The increment of volumetric plastic strain Δe_m^P follows from (5.9) and (5.32) with the conclusion that $\sigma_V^E = I_1^E = 3\,\sigma_m^E$:

$$\sigma_m = \sigma_m^E - c_m\,\Delta e_m^P$$

$$\sigma_V = \sigma_V^E - c_m\,\Delta e_V^P$$

$$\Delta e_V^P = \frac{(\sigma_V^E - \sigma_V)}{c_m} \Rightarrow \sigma_V^E = I_1^E \text{ and } \sigma_V = I_1 = L$$

$$\Delta e_V^P = \frac{(I_1^E - L)}{c_m}$$

In notation for current time step:

$$\Delta e_V^P = \frac{(^{t+\Delta t}I_1^E - {}^{t+\Delta t}L)}{c_m} \tag{5.33}$$

Finally the governing function $f(p)$ relates now to (4.17). With the use of (5.33) and $e_V^P = {}^t e_V^P + \Delta e_V^P$, the Equation (4.17) is written as:

$$^t e_V^P + \Delta e_V^P = W[1 - e^{(-D\,(X-X_0)}]$$

$$^t e_V^P + \frac{(I_1^E - L)}{c_m} = W[1 - e^{(-D\,(X-X_0)}]$$

$$f(L) = {}^{t}e_{V}^{P} + \frac{(I_{1}^{E} - L)}{c_{m}} - W\left[1 - e^{[-D\,(X - X_{0})]}\right] = 0$$

In notation for the current time step:

$${}^{t + \Delta t}f_{V}({}^{t + \Delta t}L) = {}^{t}e_{V}^{P} + \frac{({}^{t + \Delta t}I_{1}^{E} - {}^{t + \Delta t}L)}{c_{m}} - W\left[1 - e^{[-D\,({}^{t + \Delta t}X - X_{0})]}\right] = 0 \qquad (5.34)$$

The governing parameter was chosen as ${}^{t + \Delta t}L$. So the governing function is ${}^{t + \Delta t}f_{V}({}^{t + \Delta t}L)$. The backtracking of the variables in (5.34) gives the computational steps for vertex *yielding*. Therefore, the given functions are nested again, so that the only unknown is ${}^{t + \Delta t}L$. This is listed in Table 5.3.

The nonlinear equation ${}^{t + \Delta t}f_{V}({}^{t + \Delta t}L) = 0$ was solved also with the Newton-Raphson method for one nonlinear equation (see Section 3.1).

In (Kojic & Bathe, 2005) vertex yielding is subdivided into case b) which is given above and case a) with: $(3\,{}^{t + \Delta t}\sigma_{m}^{E}) = {}^{t + \Delta t}I_{1}^{E} = {}^{t}L$ and ${}^{t + \Delta t}f_{1}^{E} > 0$. The case a) is ignored here, because $(3\,{}^{t + \Delta t}\sigma_{m}^{E}) = {}^{t + \Delta t}I_{1}^{E} = {}^{t}L$ does not occur in practice (when not any numerical tolerances are specified).

1.	**With the independent variable ${}^{t + \Delta t}L$ calculate:**
	${}^{t + \Delta t}B$ from (5.23) and ${}^{t + \Delta t}I_{1}^{E} = 3\,{}^{t + \Delta t}\sigma_{m}^{E}$ from (5.2) with ${}^{t + \Delta t}B$ calculate ${}^{t + \Delta t}X$ from (5.14)
2.	**With ${}^{t + \Delta t}I_{1}^{E}$ and ${}^{t + \Delta t}X({}^{t + \Delta t}L)$ iterate on (5.34) until convergence is reached:**
	${}^{t + \Delta t}f_{V} \leq \varepsilon$
3.	**Finally:**
	With ${}^{t + \Delta t}I_{1}^{E}$ and ${}^{t + \Delta t}L$ calculate Δe_{V}^{P} from (5.33) With ${}^{t + \Delta t}S^{E}$ from (5.1) calculate $\sqrt{{}^{t + \Delta t}J_{2D}^{E}}$ from (4.10) With $\sqrt{{}^{t + \Delta t}J_{2D}^{E}}$ and ${}^{t + \Delta t}B$ calculate $\Delta\lambda_{V}$ from (5.31) With $\Delta\lambda_{V}$ and $\sqrt{{}^{t + \Delta t}J_{2D}^{E}}$ calculate $\sqrt{{}^{t + \Delta t}J_{2D}}$ from (5.30) With $\Delta\lambda_{V}$ and ${}^{t + \Delta t}S^{E}$ calculate ${}^{t + \Delta t}S$ from (5.29) With $\Delta\lambda_{V}$ and ${}^{t + \Delta t}S$ calculate $\Delta e'^{P}$ from (5.28)

TABLE 5.3. ITERATIVE STEPS FOR STRESS INTEGRATION OF VERTEX YIELDING

5.1.5 PRACTICAL CALCULATION OF THE GOVERNING PARAMETER IN THE YIELDING CASES

As mentioned the governing function $f(p)$ was solved with the Newton-Raphson method. However, the positioning of the function $f(p)$ is necessary first. The nesting of the different functions for every iteration (as pointed in Table 5.1, Table 5.2 and Table 5.3) to $f(p)$ needs a large computational effort. To reduce the calculation time, the functions $f(p)$ are calculated and expanded with a computer algebra program here. The functions $f(p)$ and $f'(p)$ are comparatively short for the case of vertex yielding. Therefore, they are given exemplarily here.

For *vertex yielding* the governing function $^{t+\Delta t}f_V(^{t+\Delta t}L)$ is given as:

$$^{t+\Delta t}f_V(^{t+\Delta t}L) = \left(-1 + e^{D\left(A\,R\,e^{-B1\,^{t+\Delta t}L} - k\,R - ^{t+\Delta t}L\,(1+\alpha\,R)+X_0\right)}\right) W + {}^t\hat{e}_1^P + {}^t\hat{e}_2^P +$$

$$^t\hat{e}_3^P + \frac{^{t+\Delta t}L - 2\,^{t+\Delta t}L\,v + E\left({}^t\hat{e}_1^P + {}^t\hat{e}_2^P + {}^t\hat{e}_3^P - ^{t+\Delta t}\hat{e}_1^P - ^{t+\Delta t}\hat{e}_2^P - ^{t+\Delta t}\hat{e}_3^P\right)}{c_m\,(-1+2\,v)}$$

with the Young's modulus E and the Poisson's ratio v, and the strains ${}^t\hat{e}_i^P$ and $^{t+\Delta t}\hat{e}_i^P$ in one index notation according to (A.5). Furthermore, the derivation $^{t+\Delta t}f_V'(^{t+\Delta t}L)$ for the Newton-Raphson scheme is given as:

$$^{t+\Delta t}f_V'(^{t+\Delta t}L) =$$

$$-\frac{1}{cm} - D\,e^{D\left(A\,R\,e^{-B1\,^{t+\Delta t}L} - k\,R - ^{t+\Delta t}L\,(1+\alpha\,R)+X_0\right)}(1 + \alpha\,R + A\,B_1\,R\,e^{-B1\,L})\,W$$

5.1.6 CALCULATION OF TOTAL PLASTIC STRAINS AND TOTAL STRESS

The increments of mean plastic strain Δe_m^P and deviatoric plastic strain $\Delta e'^P$ are calculated in Sections 5.1.2-5.1.4. Now the total plastic strain will be calculated. With regard to (A.17) the total plastic strain increment is given as:

$$\boxed{\Delta e^P = \Delta e_m^P\,I + \Delta e'^P} \tag{5.35}$$

with I as Identity matrix. The total plastic strain is then derived as:

$$\boxed{e^P = {}^t e^P + \Delta e^P} \tag{5.36}$$

The total plastic strain increment $\Delta\hat{e}^P$ in one index notation with regard to (A.5) is written as:

$$\boxed{\Delta\hat{e}^{P^T} = [\Delta e_{11}^P, \Delta e_{22}^P, \Delta e_{33}^P, 2\,\Delta e_{12}^P, 2\,\Delta e_{23}^P, 2\,\Delta e_{13}^P]} \tag{5.37}$$

Finally, the total stress $^{t+\Delta t}\sigma$ is calculated with (4.21).

5.2 TANGENT MATRICES

For better readability in the following sections the one index notation is used. This is done to avoid a four dimensional tensor notation for the tangent matrix C^{EP}. The derivation of the tangent matrices is related to the general concept of Section 4.2.2. So the stress in Equation (4.22) is subdivided into the mean stress and deviatoric stress. Then the tangent matrix, analogous to (4.22), can be written as:

$$
\begin{aligned}
{}^{t+\Delta t}C_{ij}^{EP} &= \frac{\partial^{t+\Delta t}S_i}{\partial^{t+\Delta t}e_j} + \frac{\partial^{t+\Delta t}\sigma_m}{\partial^{t+\Delta t}e_j} \qquad for\ i = 1,2,3; j = 1\dots6 \\[2em]
{}^{t+\Delta t}C_{ij}^{EP} &= \frac{\partial^{t+\Delta t}S_i}{\partial^{t+\Delta t}e_j} \qquad\qquad\quad for\ i = 4,5,6; j = 1\dots6
\end{aligned}
\tag{5.38}
$$

For the three yield cases the derivations in (5.38) can now be calculated. The tangent matrices are obtained by skillful derivation of the stresses with respect to the strains. The comma convention is used for conciseness in the following sections (see Appendix A2).

5.2.1 YIELDING ON FAILURE SURFACE

For conciseness the denominator in (5.11) is called D_λ here:

$$
D_\lambda = (1 + G\,\Delta\lambda\,\frac{1}{\sqrt{{}^{t+\Delta t}J_{2D}}})
\tag{5.39}
$$

Equation (5.11) is then written as:

$$
S_i = \frac{S_i^E(e_i)}{D_\lambda(e_i)}
$$

With regard to the quotient rule $\frac{\partial S_i}{\partial e_j} = S_{i,j}$ can be derived as:

$$
S_{i,j} = \frac{S_{i,j}^E D_\lambda - D_{\lambda,j} S_i^E}{D_\lambda^2} \Rightarrow with\ S_i^E = S_i D_\lambda
$$

$$
S_{i,j} = \frac{S_{i,j}^E D_\lambda - D_{\lambda,j} S_i D_\lambda}{D_\lambda^2}
$$

$$
S_{i,j} = D_\lambda \frac{S_{i,j}^E - D_{\lambda,j} S_i}{D_\lambda^2}
$$

$$
S_{i,j} = \frac{S_{i,j}^E - D_{\lambda,j} S_i}{D_\lambda}
$$

In notation for the current time step:

$$
{}^{t+\Delta t}S_{i,j} = \frac{{}^{t+\Delta t}S_{i,j}^E - D_{\lambda,j}\,{}^{t+\Delta t}S_i}{D_\lambda}
\tag{5.40}
$$

The matrix ${}^{t+\Delta t}S_{i,j}^E$ follows from (5.1) written in index notation:

$$
S_{i,j}^E = 2\,G\,e_{i,j}''
$$

For conciseness p_{ij} is introduced with:

$$p_{ij} = \begin{bmatrix} 1 & 1 & 1 \\ 1 & 1 & 1 \\ 1 & 1 & 1 \end{bmatrix} \qquad (5.41)$$

Then $e_{i,j}'' = \frac{\partial e_i''}{\partial e_j}$ can be derived as:

$$\frac{\partial e_i''}{\partial e_j} = \frac{\partial(e_i' - {}^t e_i'^P)}{\partial e_j} = \frac{\partial e_i'}{\partial e_j} \Rightarrow replace\ e_i'\ with\ (A.17)$$

$$\frac{\partial e_i''}{\partial e_j} = \frac{\partial(e_{\underline{i}}\, q_{\underline{i}} - e_m\, p_i)}{\partial e_j} \qquad no\ sum\ on\ \underline{i}\ (see\ Appendix\ A4),$$

$and\ with\ q_i\ from\ (A.16)\ and\ p_i\ from\ (A.15)$

This is subdivided for the indices 1, 2, 3 and 4, 5, 6:

$$\frac{\partial e_i''}{\partial e_j} = \frac{\partial e_i}{\partial e_j} - \frac{1}{3}\frac{\partial\, p_i(e_1 + e_2 + e_3)}{\partial e_j} = \delta_{ij} - \frac{1}{3}\, p_{ij} \quad for\ i,j = 1,2,3$$

$$\frac{\partial e_i''}{\partial e_j} = \frac{\partial \frac{1}{2} e_i}{\partial e_j} = \frac{1}{2}\, \delta_{ij} \qquad\qquad for\ i,j = 4,5,6$$

Finally, ${}^{t+\Delta t}S_{i,j}^E$ is then given as:

$$\begin{aligned} {}^{t+\Delta t}S_{i,j}^E &= 2\,G\left(\delta_{ij} - \frac{1}{3}\, p_{ij}\right) \quad for\ i,j = 1,2,3 \\[2mm] {}^{t+\Delta t}S_{i,j}^E &= G\,\delta_{ij} \qquad\qquad\quad for\ i,j = 3,4,5 \end{aligned} \qquad (5.42)$$

The derivation $D_{\lambda,j}$ in (5.40) is obtained by differentiation of (5.39) with regard to the quotient rule:

$$D_{\lambda,j} = G\left(\frac{\Delta\lambda}{\sqrt{J_{2D}}}\right)_{,j} = G\,\frac{\Delta\lambda_{,j}\sqrt{J_{2D}} - \Delta\lambda\left(\sqrt{J_{2D}}\right)_{,j}}{J_{2D}} \qquad (5.43)$$

where $\left(\sqrt{J_{2D}}\right)_{,j}$ with regard to (5.12) is given as:

$$\left(\sqrt{J_{2D}}\right)_{,j} = \left(\sqrt{J_{2D}^E}\right)_{,j} - G\,\Delta\lambda_{,j} \qquad (5.44)$$

with the application of product and chain rule $\left(\sqrt{J_{2D}^E}\right)_{,j}$ is derived as:

$for\ i = 1,2,3; j = 1 \dots 6:$

$$\left(\sqrt{J_{2D}^E}\right)_{,j} = \left(\sqrt{\frac{1}{2} S_i^E S_i^E}\right)_{,j} = \frac{1}{2\sqrt{\frac{1}{2} S_i^E S_i^E}} \frac{1}{2}(S_{i,j}^E S_i^E + S_i^E S_{i,j}^E) = \frac{S_i^E S_{i,j}^E}{2\sqrt{J_{2D}^E}}$$

(5.45)

$for\ i = 4,5,6; j = 1 \dots 6:$

$$\left(\sqrt{J_{2D}^E}\right)_{,j} = \left(\sqrt{S_i^E S_i^E}\right)_{,j} = \frac{1}{2\sqrt{S_i^E S_i^E}}(S_{i,j}^E S_i^E + S_i^E S_{i,j}^E) = \frac{S_i^E S_{i,j}^E}{\sqrt{J_{2D}^E}}$$

For $S_{i,j}^E$ in (5.45) Equation (5.42) can be replaced:

$$\left(\sqrt{J_{2D}^E}\right)_{,j} = \frac{S_i^E G \left(\delta_{ij} - \frac{1}{3} p_{ij}\right)}{\sqrt{J_{2D}^E}} = \frac{S_j^E G}{\sqrt{J_{2D}^E}} \quad for\ i = 1,2,3; j = 1 \dots 6$$

$$\left(\sqrt{J_{2D}^E}\right)_{,j} = \frac{S_i^E G\ \delta_{ij}}{\sqrt{J_{2D}^E}} = \frac{S_j^E G}{\sqrt{J_{2D}^E}} \quad for\ i = 4,5,6; j = 1 \dots 6$$

Here the summation over the index (i) of $S_i^E G \left(\delta_{ij} - \frac{1}{3} p_{ij}\right) = S_j^E$. So $\left(\sqrt{J_{2D}^E}\right)_{,j}$ is written as:

$$\left(\sqrt{J_{2D}^E}\right)_{,j} = G\ \frac{S_j^E}{\sqrt{J_{2D}^E}}$$

(5.46)

With (5.44) and (5.46) the Equation (5.43) can be rearranged to:

$$D_{\lambda,j} = G\ \frac{\Delta\lambda_{,j} \sqrt{J_{2D}} - \Delta\lambda \left(G\ \frac{S_j^E}{\sqrt{J_{2D}^E}} - G\ \Delta\lambda_{,j}\right)}{J_{2D}} = \frac{G\ \Delta\lambda_{,j} \sqrt{J_{2D}} - G\ \Delta\lambda \left(G\ \frac{S_j^E}{\sqrt{J_{2D}^E}} - G\ \Delta\lambda_{,j}\right)}{J_{2D}}$$

$$D_{\lambda,j} = \frac{G\ \Delta\lambda_{,j} \sqrt{J_{2D}} - \Delta\lambda\ G^2\ \frac{S_j^E}{\sqrt{J_{2D}^E}} + \Delta\lambda\ G^2\ \Delta\lambda_{,j}}{J_{2D}} = \frac{G\ \Delta\lambda_{,j} \left(\sqrt{J_{2D}} + \Delta\lambda\ G\right) - \Delta\lambda\ G^2\ \frac{S_j^E}{\sqrt{J_{2D}^E}}}{J_{2D}}$$

$$D_{\lambda,j} = G\ \Delta\lambda_{,j} \left(\sqrt{J_{2D}} + \Delta\lambda\ G\right) \frac{1}{J_{2D}} - \Delta\lambda\ G^2\ \frac{S_j^E}{\sqrt{J_{2D}^E}} \frac{1}{J_{2D}}$$

$$D_{\lambda,j} = G\ \Delta\lambda_{,j} \left(\frac{1}{\sqrt{J_{2D}}} + \Delta\lambda\ G\ \frac{1}{J_{2D}}\right) - \Delta\lambda\ G^2\ \frac{1}{J_{2D}}\ \frac{S_j^E}{\sqrt{J_{2D}^E}}$$

Written in notation for current time step:

$$D_{\lambda,j} = G\,\Delta\lambda_j\left(\frac{1}{\sqrt{^{t+\Delta t}J_{2D}}} + \Delta\lambda\,G\,\frac{1}{^{t+\Delta t}J_{2D}}\right) - \Delta\lambda\,G^2\,\frac{1}{^{t+\Delta t}J_{2D}}\,\frac{S_j^E}{\sqrt{^{t+\Delta t}J_{2D}^E}} \qquad (5.47)$$

The differentiation $\Delta\lambda_{,j}$ in (5.47) can be obtained from (5.8):

$$\Delta\lambda_{,j} = \left(-\frac{\Delta e_m^P(e_j)}{B_1\,A\,(e_j)e^{[-B_1\,I_1(e_j)]} + \alpha}\right)_{,j} = \left(-\frac{\Delta e_m^P(e_j)}{c_0(e_j)}\right)_{,j} \Rightarrow apply\ quotient\ rule$$

$$\Delta\lambda_{,j} = -\frac{\Delta e_{m,j}^P\,c_0 - \Delta e_m^P\left[B_1\,A\,e^{[-B_1\,I_1]}\right]_{,j}}{c_0{}^2} \Rightarrow apply\ chain\ rule$$

$$\Delta\lambda_{,j} = \frac{\Delta\lambda\,B_1^2\,A\,I_{1,j}\,e^{[-B_1\,I_1]}}{c_0} - \frac{\Delta e_{m,j}^P}{c_0} \qquad (5.48)$$

where $I_{1,j}$ follows from (5.10) and (5.2):

$$I_{1,j} = 3\,\sigma_{m,j} \qquad (5.49)$$

with $\sigma_{m,j}$ from (5.9):

$$\sigma_{m,j} = \sigma_{m,j}^E - c_m\,\Delta e_{m,j}^P \Rightarrow replace\ \sigma_m^E\ with\ (5.2)$$

$$\sigma_{m,j} = c_m\,e_{m,j}'' - c_m\,\Delta e_{m,j}^P = c_m\,e_{m,j} - c_m\,\Delta e_{m,j}^P$$

$$\sigma_{m,j} = c_m\frac{1}{3}\left(e_{1,j} + e_{2,j} + e_{3,j}\right) - c_m\,\Delta e_{m,j}^P$$

$$\sigma_{m,j} = c_m\frac{1}{3}\,p_j - c_m\,\Delta e_{m,j}^P$$

with p_j from (A.18). In notation for the current time step $\sigma_{m,j}$ is then written as:

$$^{t+\Delta t}\sigma_{m,j} = c_m\frac{1}{3}\,p_j - c_m\,\Delta e_{m,j}^P \qquad (5.50)$$

Now in (5.48) replace (5.49) and (5.50):

$$\Delta\lambda_{,j} = \frac{\Delta\lambda\,B_1^2\,A\,e^{[-B_1\,I_1]}\left(c_m\,p_j - 3\,c_m\,\Delta e_{m,j}^P\right)}{c_0} - \frac{\Delta e_{m,j}^P}{c_0}$$

$$\Delta\lambda_{,j} = \frac{\Delta\lambda\,B_1^2\,A\,e^{[-B_1\,I_1]}\,c_m\,p_j - 3\,\Delta\lambda\,B_1^2\,A\,e^{[-B_1\,I_1]}\,c_m\,\Delta e_{m,j}^P - \Delta e_{m,j}^P}{c_0}$$

$$\Rightarrow \Delta\lambda\,B_1^2\,A\,e^{[-B_1\,I_1]}\,c_m = a_0$$

$$\Delta\lambda_{,j} = \frac{a_0\, p_j - \Delta e^P_{m,j}(3\, a_0 + 1)}{c_0}$$

$$\Delta\lambda_{,j} = \frac{a_0\, p_j}{c_0} - \Delta e^P_{m,j}\frac{(3\, a_0 + 1)}{c_0}$$

for conciseness the above equation is written in the following:

$$\boxed{\lambda_{,j} = d_j - \Delta e^P_{m,j}\, d_0} \tag{5.51}$$

where:

$$\boxed{\begin{aligned}
d_j &= \frac{a_0\, p_j}{c_0}\\[1em]
d_0 &= \frac{(3\, a_0 + 1)}{c_0}\\[1em]
a_0 &= \Delta\lambda\, B_1^2\, A\, e^{[-B_1\ ^{t+\Delta t}I_1]}\, c_m\\[0.5em]
c_0 &= B_1\, A\, (e_j)e^{[-B_1\ ^{t+\Delta t}I_1]} + \alpha
\end{aligned}} \tag{5.52}$$

Finally, implicit differentiation $\left[F(x, y(x)) = 0, y' = F_{,x}/F_{,y}\right]$ of Equation (5.13) yields $\Delta e^P_{m,j}$:

$$f_1\left(e_j, \Delta e^P_m\right) = 0$$

$$\boxed{\Delta e^P_{m,j} = -\frac{f_{1,j}}{f_{1,\Delta e^P_m}}} \tag{5.53}$$

Note that now for $f_{1,j}$ the mean plastic strain Δe^P_m is a constant now:

$$f_{1,j} = \left(\sqrt{J_{2D}} - k + A\, exp(-B_1\, I_1) - \alpha\, I_1\right)_{,j}$$

$$f_{1,j} = (\sqrt{J_{2D}})_{,j} + \left(A\, exp(-B_1\, I_1)\right)_{,j} - \alpha\, I_{1,j}$$

$$f_{1,j} = G\left(\frac{S^E_j}{\sqrt{J^E_{2D}}} - \Delta\lambda_{,j}\right) - A\, B_1\, c_m\, p_j\, e^{(-B_1\, I_1)} - \alpha\, c_m\, p_j$$

$$f_{1,j} = G\left(\frac{S^E_j}{\sqrt{J^E_{2D}}} - d_j\right) - c_m\, p_j(A\, B_1\, e^{(-B_1\, I_1)} + \alpha)$$

$$f_{1,j} = G\left(\frac{S^E_j}{\sqrt{J^E_{2D}}} - d_j\right) - c_m\, p_j\, c_0$$

Written in notation for the current time step:

$$\boxed{f_{1,j} = G\left(\frac{^{t+\Delta t}S_j^E}{\sqrt{^{t+\Delta t}J_{2D}^E}} - d_j\right) - c_m\, p_j\, c_0}$$

(5.54)

The differentiation of $f_{1,\Delta e_m^P}$ can also be obtained from (5.13):

$$f_{1,\Delta e_m^P} = \left(\sqrt{J_{2D}} - k + A\,exp(-B_1\,I_1) - \alpha\,I_1\right)_{,\Delta e_m^P}$$

$$f_{1,\Delta e_m^P} = \left(\sqrt{J_{2D}}\right)_{,\Delta e_m^P} + \left(A\,exp(-B_1\,I_1)\right)_{,\Delta e_m^P} - \alpha\,I_{1,\Delta e_m^P}$$

with (5.12) for $\sqrt{J_{2D}}$ and (5.10) for I_1:

$$f_{1,\Delta e_m^P} = \left(\sqrt{J_{2D}^E} - G\,\Delta\lambda\right)_{,\Delta e_m^P} + \left(A\,exp(-B_1\,I_1)\right)_{,\Delta e_m^P} - \alpha\,I_{1,\Delta e_m^P}$$

$$f_{1,\Delta e_m^P} = \left(\sqrt{J_{2D}^E}\right)_{,\Delta e_m^P} - G\,\Delta\lambda_{,\Delta e_m^P} - B_1\,A\,I_{1,\Delta e_m^P}\,exp(-B_1\,I_1) - \alpha\,I_{1,\Delta e_m^P}$$

$$f_{1,\Delta e_m^P} = \left(\sqrt{J_{2D}^E}\right)_{,\Delta e_m^P} - G\,\Delta\lambda_{,\Delta e_m^P} - I_{1,\Delta e_m^P}\left(B_1\,A\,exp(-B_1\,3\,\sigma_m) + \alpha\right)$$

$\Rightarrow$ with c_0 from (5.52)

$$f_{1,\Delta e_m^P} = \left(\sqrt{J_{2D}^E}\right)_{,\Delta e_m^P} - G\,\Delta\lambda_{,\Delta e_m^P} - I_{1,\Delta e_m^P}\,c_0$$

(5.55)

where in (5.55) $\left(\sqrt{J_{2D}^E}\right)_{,\Delta e_m^P}$ is derived as:

$$\left(\sqrt{J_{2D}^E}\right)_{,\Delta e_m^P} = \left(\sqrt{\frac{1}{2}S_i^E S_i^E}\right)_{,\Delta e_m^P} = \frac{1}{2\sqrt{\frac{1}{2}S_i^E S_i^E}}\frac{1}{2}\left(S_{i,\Delta e_m^P}^E S_i^E + S_i^E S_{i,\Delta e_m^P}^E\right) = \frac{S_i^E S_{i,\Delta e_m^P}^E}{2\sqrt{J_{2D}^E}}$$

$$\left(\sqrt{J_{2D}^E}\right)_{,\Delta e_m^P} = \frac{S_i^E S_{i,\Delta e_m^P}^E}{2\sqrt{J_{2D}^E}} = \frac{S_i^E(2\,G\,e_i'')_{,\Delta e_m^P}}{2\sqrt{J_{2D}^E}} = \frac{G\,S_i^E}{\sqrt{J_{2D}^E}}\,e_{i,\Delta e_m^P}'' = \frac{G\,S_i^E}{\sqrt{J_{2D}^E}}\frac{\partial(e_i' - {}^t e_i'^P)}{\partial\Delta e_m^P}$$

$$\left(\sqrt{J_{2D}^E}\right)_{,\Delta e_m^P} = \frac{G\,S_i^E}{\sqrt{J_{2D}^E}}\frac{\partial e_i'}{\partial\Delta e_m^P} = \frac{G\,S_i^E}{\sqrt{J_{2D}^E}}\frac{\partial(e_{\underline{i}}\,q_{\underline{i}} - e_m\,p_i)}{\partial\Delta e_m^P} = \frac{G\,S_i^E}{\sqrt{J_{2D}^E}}\frac{\partial e_m\,p_i}{\partial\Delta e_m^P}$$

$$\left(\sqrt{J_{2D}^E}\right)_{,\Delta e_m^P} = 0$$

(5.56)

further in (5.55) $I_{1,\Delta e_m^P}$ follows from (5.10) and (5.2):

$$I_{1,\Delta e_m^P} = 3\,\sigma_{m,\Delta e_m^P}$$

(5.57)

with $\sigma_{m,\Delta e_m^P}$ from (5.9):

$$\sigma_{m,\Delta e_m^P} = \sigma_{m,\Delta e_m^P}^E - c_m\,\Delta e_{m,\Delta e_m^P}^P \Rightarrow replace\ \sigma_m^E\ with\ (5.2)$$

$$\sigma_{m,\Delta e_m^P} = c_m\,e_{m,\Delta e_m^P}'' - c_m\,\Delta e_{m,\Delta e_m^P}^P = -c_m \qquad (5.58)$$

In the end $\Delta\lambda_{,\Delta e_m^P}$ in (5.55) is derived as:

$$\Delta\lambda_{,\Delta e_m^P} = \left(-\frac{\Delta e_m^P(e_j)}{B_1\,A\,(e_j)e^{[-B_1\,I_1(e_j)]}+\alpha}\right)_{,\Delta e_m^P}$$

$$\Delta\lambda_{,\Delta e_m^P} = \left(-\frac{\Delta e_m^P(e_j)}{c_0(e_j)}\right)_{,\Delta e_m^P} \Rightarrow apply\ quotient\ rule$$

$$\Delta\lambda_{,\Delta e_m^P} = -\frac{\Delta e_{m,\Delta e_m^P}^P\,c_0 - \Delta e_m^P\left[B_1\,A\,e^{[-B_1\,I_1]}\right]_{,\Delta e_m^P}}{c_0^{\,2}} \Rightarrow apply\ chain\ rule$$

$$\Delta\lambda_{,\Delta e_m^P} = -\frac{c_0 + \Delta e_m^P\,B_1^2\,I_{1,\Delta e_m^P}\,A\,e^{[-B_1\,I_1]}}{c_0^{\,2}} \Rightarrow replace\ I_{1,\Delta e_m^P}$$

$$\Delta\lambda_{,\Delta e_m^P} = -\frac{c_0 - \Delta e_m^P\,B_1^2\,3\,c_m\,A\,e^{[-B_1\,I_1]}}{c_0^{\,2}} \qquad (5.59)$$

Now we can replace (5.56), (5.57),(5.58) and (5.59) in (5.55):

$$\boxed{f_{1,\Delta e_m^P} = G\left(\frac{c_0 - \Delta e_m^P\,B_1^2\,3\,c_m\,A\,e^{[-B_1\,^{t+\Delta t}I_1]}}{c_0^{\,2}}\right) + 3\,c_m\,c_0} \qquad (5.60)$$

When the plastic strain increment Δe_m^P (as governing parameter), the strain vector $^{t+\Delta t}\hat{e}$ and the plastic strain vector from last time step $^t\hat{e}^P$ are known, the calculation of the tangent matrix $^{t+\Delta t}C_{ij}^{EP}$ for the current iteration follows from the calculation scheme in Table 5.4.

calculate $^{t+\Delta t}C_{ij}^{EP}$ for yielding on failure surface in the following order:

- matrix $^{t+\Delta t}e$ from vector $^{t+\Delta t}\hat{e}$ with (A.5)
- $^{t+\Delta t}e_m$ from (A.10)
- $^{t+\Delta t}\boldsymbol{e}'$ from (A.17)
- matrix $^{t}e^P$ from vector $^{t}\hat{e}^P$ with (A.5)
- $^{t}e_m^P$ from (A.10)
- $^{t+\Delta t}\boldsymbol{e}^{P\prime}$ from (A.17)
- $^{t+\Delta t}\sigma_m^E$ from (5.2)
- $^{t+\Delta t}\boldsymbol{S}^E$ from (5.1)
- $^{t+\Delta t}J_{2D}^E$ from (4.10)
- $^{t+\Delta t}\sigma_m$ from (5.9)
- $^{t+\Delta t}I_1$ from (5.10)
- $\Delta\lambda$ from (5.8)
- a_0, c_0, d_j and d_0 from (5.52)
- $\sqrt{^{t+\Delta t}J_{2D}}$ from (5.12)
- $^{t+\Delta t}S_i^E$ from (A.21) and $^{t+\Delta t}\boldsymbol{S}^E$
- $^{t+\Delta t}J_{2D}$ by squaring $\sqrt{^{t+\Delta t}J_{2D}}$
- $^{t+\Delta t}\boldsymbol{S}$ from (5.11)
- $f_{1,j}$ from (5.54)
- $f_{1,\Delta e_m^P}$ from (5.60)
- $\Delta e_{m,j}^P$ from (5.53)
- $\lambda_{,j}$ from (5.51)
- D_λ from (5.39)
- $D_{\lambda,j}$ from (5.47)
- $^{t+\Delta t}S_i$ from (A.21) and $^{t+\Delta t}\boldsymbol{S}$
- $^{t+\Delta t}S_{i,j}^E$ from (5.42)
- $^{t+\Delta t}S_{i,j}$ from (5.40)
- $^{t+\Delta t}\sigma_{m,j}$ from (5.50)
- $^{t+\Delta t}C_{ij}^{EP}$ from (5.38)

TABLE 5.4. CALCULATION OF THE TANGENT MATRIX FOR YIELDING ON FAILURE SURFACE

5.2.2 CAP YIELDING

For conciseness the denominator in (5.21) is called D_C here:

$$D_C = 1 + 2\,G\,\Delta\lambda_c\,R^2 \qquad\qquad (5.61)$$

Equation (5.21) is then written as:

$$S_i = \frac{S_i^E(e_i)}{D_C(e_i)}$$

Analogous to Section 5.2.1 $^{t+\Delta t}S_{i,j}$ is with D_C instead of D_λ written as:

$$^{t+\Delta t}S_{i,j} = \frac{^{t+\Delta t}S_{i,j}^E - D_{C,j}\,^{t+\Delta t}S_i}{D_C} \qquad\qquad (5.62)$$

with $^{t+\Delta t}S_{i,j}^E$ given by (5.42) and $D_{C,j}$ derived from (5.61) as:

$$D_{C,j} = 2\,G\,\Delta\lambda_{c,j}\,R^2 \qquad\qquad (5.63)$$

The derivation of $\Delta e_{m,j}^P$ can be obtained from (4.17). The governing parameter is $^{t+\Delta t}L(e_j)$, with L as position of the cap (see Figure 5.1). So with respect to the chain rule $\Delta e_{m,j}^P$ is given as:

$$\Delta e_{m,j}^P = \frac{\partial \Delta e_m^P}{\partial X}\frac{\partial X}{\partial L}\frac{\partial L}{\partial e_j} \qquad\qquad (5.64)$$

with $\Delta e_{m,X}^P$ from (4.17):

$$\frac{\partial \Delta e_m^P}{\partial X} = \frac{1}{3}\Delta e_{V,X}^P = \frac{1}{3}\,D\,W\,e^{-D\,(^{t+\Delta t}X - X_0)} \qquad\qquad (5.65)$$

and $X_{,L}$ from (5.14):

$$X_{,L} = R\,B_{,L} + 1 \qquad\qquad (5.66)$$

where $B_{,L}$ is derived from (5.23):

$$B_{,L} = B_1\,A\,exp\!\left(-B_1\,^{t+\Delta t}L\right) + \alpha \qquad\qquad (5.67)$$

The differentiation $\Delta\lambda_{c,j}$ in (5.63) can be obtained from (5.19):

$$\Delta\lambda_{c,j} = \left(\frac{\Delta e_m^P}{2\,(3\,\sigma_m - L)}\right)_{,j} \Rightarrow apply\ quotient\ rule$$

$$\Delta\lambda_{c,j} = \frac{\Delta e_{m,j}^P\,2\,(3\,\sigma_m - L) - \Delta e_m^P\,2\,(3\,\sigma_{m,j} - L_{,j})}{2^2\,(3\,\sigma_m - L)^2} \Rightarrow replace\ \frac{\Delta e_m^P}{2\,(3\,\sigma_m - L)} = \Delta\lambda_c$$

$$\Delta\lambda_{c,j} = \frac{\Delta e_{m,j}^P - \Delta\lambda_c\,2\,(3\,\sigma_{m,j} - L_{,j})}{2\,(3\,\sigma_m - L)} \Rightarrow with\ \sigma_{m,j}\ from\ (5.50)$$

$$\Delta\lambda_{c,j} = \frac{\Delta e_{m,j}^P - \Delta\lambda_c\,2\,\left(3\,(c_m\frac{1}{3}\,p_j - c_m\,\Delta e_{m,j}^P) - L_{,j}\right)}{2\,(3\,\sigma_m - L)} \Rightarrow expand\ numerator$$

$$\lambda_{c,j} = \frac{\Delta e_{m,j}^P - \Delta\lambda_c\,2\,\left(c_m\,p_j - c_m\,3\,\Delta e_{m,j}^P - L_{,j}\right)}{2\,(3\,\sigma_m - L)}$$

$$\lambda_{c,j} = \frac{\Delta e_{m,j}^P - \Delta\lambda_c\,2\,c_m\,p_j + \Delta\lambda_c\,c_m\,6\,\Delta e_{m,j}^P + 2\,\Delta\lambda_c\,L_{,j}}{2\,(3\,\sigma_m - L)}$$

$$\lambda_{c,j} = \frac{\Delta e_{m,j}^P + \Delta\lambda_c\,c_m\,6\,\Delta e_{m,j}^P - \Delta\lambda_c\,2\,c_m\,p_j + 2\,\Delta\lambda_c\,L_{,j}}{2\,(3\,\sigma_m - L)}$$

$$\lambda_{c,j} = \frac{\Delta e_{m,j}^P\,(1 + \Delta\lambda_c\,c_m\,6) + 2\,\Delta\lambda_c\,L_{,j}}{2\,(3\,\sigma_m - L)} - \frac{\Delta\lambda_c}{(3\,\sigma_m - L)}\,c_m\,p_j \Rightarrow with\ \Delta e_{m,j}^P\ from\ (5.64)$$

$$\lambda_{c,j} = \frac{\Delta e_{m,X}^P\,X_{,L}\,L_{,j}\,(1 + \Delta\lambda_c\,c_m\,6) + 2\,\Delta\lambda_c\,L_{,j}}{2\,(3\,\sigma_m - L)} - \frac{\Delta\lambda_c}{(3\,\sigma_m - L)}\,c_m\,p_j$$

$$\lambda_{c,j} = L_{,j}\frac{\Delta e_{m,X}^P\,X_{,L}\,(1 + \Delta\lambda_c\,c_m\,3) + 2\,\Delta\lambda_c}{2\,(3\,\sigma_m - L)} - \frac{\Delta\lambda_c}{(3\,\sigma_m - L)}\,c_m\,p_j$$

for conciseness written in the following:

$$\boxed{\lambda_{c,j} = q_0\,L_{,j} - q_j} \tag{5.68}$$

where:

$$\boxed{\begin{aligned}
q_0 &= \frac{\Delta e_{m,X}^P\,X_{,L}\,(1 + \Delta\lambda_c\,c_m\,3) + 2\,\Delta\lambda_c}{2\,(3\,\sigma_m - L)}\\[2em]
q_j &= \frac{\Delta\lambda_c}{(3\,\sigma_m - L)}\,c_m\,p_j
\end{aligned}} \tag{5.69}$$

Finally, implicit differentiation $[F(x, y(x)) = 0, y' = F_x/F_y]$ of Equation (5.27) yields $L_{,j}$:

$$f_c(e_j, L) = 0$$

$$\boxed{{}^{t+\Delta t}L_{,j} = -\frac{f_{c,j}}{f_{c,L}}}$$

(5.70)

Note that now for $f_{c,j}$ in (5.70), the position ${}^{t+\Delta t}L$ of the cap is a constant now:

$$f_{c,j} = \left[(I_1(e_j) - L)^2\right]_{,j} + \left[R^2(J_{2D}(e_j) - B^2)\right]_{,j} \Rightarrow apply\ chain\ rule$$

$$f_{c,j} = 2\,I_{1,j}\,(I_1 - L) + R^2\,J_{2D,j} \Rightarrow with\ I_{1,j}\ from\ (5.49)\ and\ (5.50)$$

$$f_{c,j} = 2\left(c_m\,p_j - 3\,c_m\,\Delta e_{m,j}^P\right)(I_1 - L) + R^2\,J_{2D,j}$$

$$\Rightarrow with\ \Delta e_{m,j}^P = 0\ because\ L\ is\ a\ constant$$

$$f_{c,j} = 2\,c_m\,p_j\,(I_1 - L) + R^2\,J_{2D,j}$$

(5.71)

For the differentiation of $J_{2D,j}$ in (5.71) the differentiation $J_{2D,j}^E$ is necessary. It can be obtained analogous to (5.46) with:

$$J_{2D,j}^E = \left(\frac{1}{2}\,S_i^E S_i^E\right)_{,j} = \frac{1}{2}(S_{i,j}^E\,S_i^E + S_i^E\,S_{i,j}^E) = S_i^E\,S_{i,j}^E \quad for\ i = 1,2,3$$

$$J_{2D,j}^E = \left(S_i^E S_i^E\right)_{,j} = (S_{i,j}^E\,S_i^E + S_i^E\,S_{i,j}^E) = 2\,S_i^E\,S_{i,j}^E \quad for\ i = 4,5,6$$

(5.72)

For $S_{i,j}^E$ in (5.72) Equation (5.42) can be replaced with:

$$J_{2D,j}^E = S_i^E\,2\,G\left(\delta_{ij} - \frac{1}{3}\,p_{ij}\right) = 2\,S_j^E\,G \quad for\ i = 1,2,3$$

$$J_{2D,j}^E = 2\,S_i^E\,G\,\delta_{ij} = 2\,S_j^E\,G \quad\quad for\ i = 4,5,6$$

Here the summation over the index (i) of $S_i^E\,G\left(\delta_{ij} - \frac{1}{3}\,p_{ij}\right) = S_j^E$. So $J_{2D,j}^E$ is written as:

$$J_{2D,j}^E = 2\,S_j^E\,G$$

(5.73)

Now $J_{2D,j}$ in (5.71) can be derived from (5.22):

$$J_{2D,j} = \left[\frac{J_{2D}^E}{(1 + 2\,G\,\Delta\lambda_c\,R^2)^2}\right]_{,j} = \left[\frac{J_{2D}^E}{D_C^2}\right]_{,j} \Rightarrow apply\ quotient\ rule$$

$$J_{2D,j} = \frac{J_{2D,j}^E\,D_C^2 - \left(D_C^2\right)_{,j}\,J_{2D}^E}{(D_C^2)^2} \Rightarrow apply\ chain\ rule\ for\ \left(D_C^2\right)_{,j}$$

$$J_{2D,j} = \frac{J_{2D,j}^E D_C{}^2 - 2 D_C D_{C,j} J_{2D}^E}{(D_C{}^2)^2} \Rightarrow with\ J_{2D,j}^E\ from\ (5.73)\ and\ D_{C,j}\ from\ (5.63)$$

$$J_{2D,j} = \frac{2\ G\ S_j^E\ D_C{}^2 - 4\ D_C\ G\ \Delta\lambda_{c,j}\ R^2\ J_{2D}^E}{(D_C{}^2)^2} \Rightarrow with\ \Delta\lambda_{c,j}\ from\ (5.68)$$

$$J_{2D,j} = \frac{2\ G\ S_j^E\ - 4\ D_C\ G\ (q_0\ L_{,j} - q_j)\ R^2\ J_{2D}}{D_C{}^2}$$

$$J_{2D,j} = \frac{2\ G\ S_j^E\ + J_{2D}\ R^2\ 4\ D_C\ G\ q_j - J_{2D}\ R^2 4\ D_C\ G\ q_0\ L_{,j}}{D_C{}^2}$$

$$J_{2D,j} = \frac{2\ G}{D_C{}^2}\left(S_j^E\ + J_{2D}\ R^2\ 2\ D_C\ q_j\right) - \frac{J_{2D}\ R^2 4\ G\ q_0}{D_C}\ L_{,j}$$

For conciseness this is written as:

$$\boxed{{}^{t+\Delta t}J_{2D,j} = \bar{q}_j - \bar{q}_0\ L_{,j}} \tag{5.74}$$

where:

$$\boxed{\begin{aligned}\bar{q}_j &= \frac{2\ G}{D_C{}^2}\left({}^{t+\Delta t}S_j^E\ + {}^{t+\Delta t}J_{2D}\ R^2\ 2\ D_C\ q_j\right) \\[2mm] \bar{q}_0 &= \frac{{}^{t+\Delta t}J_{2D}\ R^2 4\ G\ q_0}{D_C}\end{aligned}} \tag{5.75}$$

When we replace (5.74) in (5.71), with regard to ${}^{t+\Delta t}L$ as constant, $f_{c,j}$ is written as:

$$\boxed{f_{c,j} = 2\ c_m\ p_j\ \left({}^{t+\Delta t}I_1 - {}^{t+\Delta t}L\right) + R^2 \bar{q}_j} \tag{5.76}$$

The differentiation of $f_{c,L}$ in (5.70) is also obtained from (5.27) with respect to ${}^{t+\Delta t}L$:

$$f_{c,L} = [(I_1 - L)^2]_{,L} + [R^2(J_{2D} - B^2)]_{,L} \Rightarrow apply\ chain\ rule$$

$$f_{c,L} = 2\ (I_1 - L)\ (I_{1,L} - 1) + (R^2\ J_{2D} - R^2 B^2)_{,L}$$

$$f_{c,L} = 2\ (I_1 - L)\ (3\ \sigma_{m,L} - 1) + R^2\ J_{2D,L} - R^2\ 2\ B\ B_{,L} \tag{5.77}$$

where $\sigma_{m,L}$ is derived from (5.9) and (4.17):

$$\sigma_{m,L} = \sigma_m^E - c_m\ \Delta e_m^P(L) \Rightarrow with\ chain\ rule\ and\ 3\ \Delta e_m^P = \Delta e_V^P\ from\ (4.17)$$

$$\sigma_{m,L} = -c_m\ \Delta e_{m,X}^P\ X_{,L} \tag{5.78}$$

and $J_{2D,L}$ from (5.74):

$$J_{2D,L} = -\bar{q}_0 \tag{5.79}$$

Replacing (5.78) and (5.79) in (5.77) yields:

$$\boxed{f_{c,L} = -2\left({}^{t+\Delta t}I_1 - {}^{t+\Delta t}L\right)\left(3\,c_m\,\Delta e^P_{m,X}\,X_{,L} + 1\right) - R^2\,\bar{q}_0 - R^2\,2\,{}^{t+\Delta t}B\,{}^{t+\Delta t}B_{,L}} \tag{5.80}$$

where $\Delta e^P_{m,X}, X_{,L}$ and ${}^{t+\Delta t}B_{,L}$ are given by (5.65), (5.66) and (5.67).

When the position of the cap ${}^{t+\Delta t}L$ (as governing parameter), the strain vector ${}^{t+\Delta t}\hat{e}$ and the plastic strain vector from last time step ${}^{t}\hat{e}^P$ are known, the tangent matrix ${}^{t+\Delta t}C^{EP}_{ij}$ for the current iteration is calculated as given in Table 5.5.

calculate $^{t+\Delta t}C_{ij}^{EP}$ for cap yielding in the following order:

- matrix $^{t+\Delta t}e$ from vector $^{t+\Delta t}\hat{e}$ with (A.5)
- $^{t+\Delta t}e_m$ from (A.10) and $^{t+\Delta t}e'$ from (A.17)
- matrix $^{t}e^P$ from vector $^{t}\hat{e}^P$ with (A.5)
- $^{t}e_m^P$ from (A.10)
- $^{t+\Delta t}e^{P\prime}$ from (A.17)
- $^{t+\Delta t}\sigma_m^E$ from (5.2)
- $^{t+\Delta t}S^E$ from (5.1)
- $^{t+\Delta t}B$ from (5.23)
- $^{t+\Delta t}X$ from (5.14)
- $^{t+\Delta t}e_V^P$ from (5.24)
- $^{t+\Delta t}e_m^P$ from (5.25)
- $^{t+\Delta t}\sigma_m$ from (5.9)
- $^{t+\Delta t}I_1$ from (5.10)
- $\Delta\lambda_c$ from (5.19)
- $\Delta e_{m,X}^P$ from (5.65), $B_{,L}$ from (5.67) and $X_{,L}$ from (5.66)
- D_C from (5.61)
- $^{t+\Delta t}J_{2D}^E$ from (4.10)
- $^{t+\Delta t}J_{2D}$ from (5.22)
- q_0 and q_j from (5.69)
- $\bar{q}_j$ and $\bar{\bar{q}}_j$ from (5.75)
- $f_{c,j}$ from (5.76)
- $f_{c,L}$ from (5.80)
- $^{t+\Delta t}L_{,j}$ from (5.70)
- $^{t+\Delta t}S$ from (5.21) and $^{t+\Delta t}S_i$ from (A.21) and $^{t+\Delta t}S$
- $\lambda_{c,j}$ from (5.68)
- $D_{C,j}$ from (5.63)
- $^{t+\Delta t}S_{i,j}$ from (5.62)
- $\Delta e_{m,j}^P$ from (5.64)
- $^{t+\Delta t}\sigma_{m,j}$ from (5.50)
- $^{t+\Delta t}C_{ij}^{EP}$ from (5.38)

TABLE 5.5. CALCULATION OF THE TANGENT MATRIX FOR CAP YIELDING

5.2.3 VERTEX YIELDING

Following the procedure of the two previous sections, for conciseness the denominator in (5.29) is called D_C here:

$$\boxed{D_V = 1 + 2\,G\,\Delta\lambda_V} \qquad\qquad (5.81)$$

Equation (5.29) is then written as:

$$S_i = \frac{S_i^E(e_i)}{D_V(e_i)}$$

Analogous to Section 5.2.1 $^{t+\Delta t}S_{i,j}$ is, with D_V instead of D_λ, written as:

$$\boxed{^{t+\Delta t}S_{i,j} = \frac{^{t+\Delta t}S_{i,j}^E - D_{V,j}\,^{t+\Delta t}S_i}{D_V}} \qquad\qquad (5.82)$$

with $^{t+\Delta t}S_{i,j}^E$ given by (5.42) and $D_{V,j}$ derived from (5.81) as:

$$\boxed{D_{V,j} = 2\,G\,\Delta\lambda_{V,j}} \qquad\qquad (5.83)$$

The requested differentiation $\Delta\lambda_{V,j}$ can be obtained from (5.31):

$$\Delta\lambda_{V,j} = \left[\frac{\frac{\sqrt{J_{2D}^E}}{B} - 1}{2\,G}\right]_{,j} = \left[\frac{\sqrt{J_{2D}^E}}{2\,G\,B}\right]_{,j} \Rightarrow apply\ quotient\ rule$$

$$\Delta\lambda_{V,j} = \frac{\left(\sqrt{J_{2D}^E}\right)_{,j}2\,G\,B - \sqrt{J_{2D}^E}\,2\,G\,B_{,j}}{4\,G^2\,B^2}$$

$$\Delta\lambda_{V,j} = \frac{\left(\sqrt{J_{2D}^E}\right)_{,j} - \sqrt{J_{2D}^E}\,B_{,j}}{2\,G\,B^2}$$

$\left(\sqrt{J_{2D}^E}\right)_{,j}$ follows from (5.46) and $B_{,j}$ is given by $B_{,j} = B_{,L}\,L_{,j}$ with respect to the chain rule. Furthermore, $B_{,L}$ is defined in (5.67). So $\Delta\lambda_{V,j}$ is given as:

$$\Delta\lambda_{V,j} = \frac{G\,\dfrac{S_j^E}{\sqrt{J_{2D}^E}} - \sqrt{J_{2D}^E}\,\left(B_1\,A\,exp\!\left(-B_1\,^{t+\Delta t}L\right) + \alpha\right)L_{,j}}{2\,G\,B^2}$$

$$\Delta\lambda_{V,j} = \frac{S_j^E}{\sqrt{J_{2D}^E}\,2\,B^2} - \frac{\sqrt{J_{2D}^E}\,\left(B_1\,A\,exp\!\left(-B_1\,^{t+\Delta t}L\right) + \alpha\right)}{2\,G\,B^2}\,L_{,j}$$

for conciseness written as:

$$\boxed{\Delta\lambda_{v,j} = q_j - q_0\, L_{,j}} \tag{5.84}$$

with:

$$\boxed{\begin{aligned} q_j &= \frac{S_j^E}{\sqrt{J_{2D}^E}\, 2\, B^2} \\[2em] q_0 &= \frac{\sqrt{J_{2D}^E}\, \left(B_1\, A\, exp\left(-B_1\, {}^{t+\Delta t}L\right) + \alpha\right)}{2\, G\, B^2} \end{aligned}} \tag{5.85}$$

Now, the implicit differentiation $\left[F(x, y(x)) = 0, y' = F_x/F_y\right]$ of Equation (5.34) yields $L_{,j}$:

$$f_V(e_j, L) = 0$$

$$\boxed{{}^{t+\Delta t}L_{,j} = -\frac{f_{V,j}}{f_{V,L}}} \tag{5.86}$$

Again, for $f_{c,j}$ in (5.86) the position ${}^{t+\Delta t}L$ of the cap is a constant now:

$$f_{V,j} = \left[{}^t e_V^P + \frac{(I_1^E - L)}{c_m} - W\left[1 - e^{[-D\,(X-X_0)]}\right] \right]_{,j}$$

$$f_{V,j} = \left[\frac{(I_1^E - L)}{c_m}\right]_{,j} - W\left[1 - e^{[-D\,(X-X_0)]}\right]_{,j} \Rightarrow X\ depends\ on\ L,\ so\ X_{,j} = 0$$

$$f_{V,j} = \frac{I_{1,j}^E}{c_m} + W\,D\,X_j\,e^{[-D\,(X-X_0)]} = \frac{I_{1,j}^E}{c_m} \tag{5.87}$$

where $I_{1,j}^E$ follows from (4.8) and (5.2):

$$I_{1,j}^E = 3\,\sigma_{m,j}^E = 3\,c_m\,e_{m,j}'' = 3\,c_m\,e_{m,j} = 3\,c_m\,\frac{1}{3}\left(e_{1,j} + e_{2,j} + e_{3,j}\right) = c_m\,p_j \tag{5.88}$$

with p_j defined in (A.18). So (5.87) is given as:

$$\boxed{f_{V,j} = p_j} \tag{5.89}$$

The differentiation $f_{V,L}$ is obtained in the following:

$$f_{V,L} = \left[{}^t e_V^P + \frac{(I_1^E - L)}{c_m} - W\left[1 - e^{[-D\,(X-X_0)]}\right] \right]_{,L}$$

$$f_{V,L} = \left[\frac{(I_1^E - L)}{c_m}\right]_{,L} - W\left[1 - e^{[-D\,(X-X_0)]}\right]_{,L} \Rightarrow apply\ chain\ rule$$

$$f_{V,L} = -\frac{1}{c_m} + W\, D\, X_{,L}\, e^{[-D\,(X-X_0)]}$$

$X_{,L}$ follows from (5.66). Hence, $f_{V,L}$ is given as:

$$f_{V,L} = -\frac{1}{c_m} + W\, D\, (R\,^{t+\Delta t}B_{,L} + 1)\, e^{[-D\,(^{t+\Delta t}X-X_0)]} \tag{5.90}$$

with $^{t+\Delta t}B_{,L}$ defined in (5.67).

To obtain the differentiation of the mean strain $^{t+\Delta t}\sigma_{m,j}$, which is given in (5.50), $\Delta e^P_{m,j}$ must be derived finally from (5.33):

$$\Delta e^P_{m,j} = \frac{1}{3}\,\Delta e^P_{V,j} = \frac{1}{3}\,\frac{(I^E_{1,j} - L_{,j})}{c_m} \Rightarrow replace\ I^E_{1,j}\ from\ (5.88)\ and\ L_{,j}\ from\ (5.86)$$

$$\Delta e^P_{m,j} = \frac{1}{3}\,\frac{\left(c_m\, p_j + \dfrac{f_{V,j}}{f_{V,L}}\right)}{c_m} = \frac{1}{3}\,\frac{\left(c_m\, p_j + \dfrac{p_j}{f_{V,L}}\right)}{c_m}$$

In abbreviated notation:

$$\Delta e^P_{m,j} = \frac{1}{3}\, p_j \left(1 + \frac{1}{c_m\, f_{V,L}}\right) \tag{5.91}$$

A calculation table is given analogous to the two previous sections. Therefore, when the position of the cap $^{t+\Delta t}L$ (as governing parameter), the strain vector $^{t+\Delta t}\hat{e}$ and the plastic strain vector from last time step $^{t}\hat{e}^P$ are known, the tangent matrix $^{t+\Delta t}C^{EP}_{ij}$ for the current iteration is calculated as in Table 5.6.

calculate $^{t+\Delta t}C_{ij}^{EP}$ for vertex yielding in the following order:
• matrix $^{t+\Delta t}e$ from vector $^{t+\Delta t}\hat{e}$ with (A.5)
• $^{t+\Delta t}e_m$ from (A.10)
• $^{t+\Delta t}\boldsymbol{e}'$ from (A.17)
• matrix $^{t}e^P$ from vector $^{t}\hat{e}^P$ with (A.5)
• $^{t}e_m^P$ from (A.10)
• $^{t+\Delta t}\boldsymbol{e}^{P\prime}$ from (A.17)
• $^{t+\Delta t}\sigma_m^E$ from (5.2)
• $^{t+\Delta t}\boldsymbol{S}^E$ from (5.1)
• $^{t+\Delta t}B$ from (5.23)
• $^{t+\Delta t}X$ from (5.14)
• $^{t+\Delta t}I_1^E$ from (4.8)
• Δe_V^P from (5.33)
• $\Delta e_m^P = \frac{1}{3}\Delta e_V^P$
• $B_{,L}$ from (5.67)
• $X_{,L}$ from (5.66)
• $\Delta\lambda_V$ from (5.31)
• $^{t+\Delta t}J_{2D}^E$ from (4.10)
• $^{t+\Delta t}S_i^E$ from (A.21) and $^{t+\Delta t}\boldsymbol{S}^E$
• q_0 and q_j from (5.85)
• D_V from (5.81)
• $^{t+\Delta t}\boldsymbol{S}$ from (5.29) and $^{t+\Delta t}S_i$ from (A.21) and $^{t+\Delta t}\boldsymbol{S}$
• $f_{V,j}$ from (5.89)
• $f_{V,L}$ from (5.90)
• $^{t+\Delta t}L_{,j}$ from (5.86)
• $\lambda_{V,j}$ from (5.84)
• $D_{V,j}$ from (5.83)
• $^{t+\Delta t}S_{i,j}$ from (5.82)
• $\Delta e_{m,j}^P$ from (5.91)
• $^{t+\Delta t}\sigma_{m,j}$ from (5.50)
• $^{t+\Delta t}C_{ij}^{EP}$ from (5.38)

TABLE 5.6. CALCULATION OF THE TANGENT MATRIX FOR VERTEX YIELDING

5.3　Incremental Calculation Scheme for Static Case

The following Table 5.7 shows a scheme for the evaluation of the stiffness matrix and the force vector. The scheme considers the incremental equilibrium iterations which are necessary for the evaluation of the displacements. The calculation tables, which are given Sections 5.1 and 5.2, are included. Furthermore, the Newton-Raphson scheme considered in Section 3.2.2 is applied here. Therefore, Table 5.7 is a global overview of the evaluation of the material nonlinear cap model.

The variables in the table are explained in Appendix A1. For the finite element evaluation the strain displacement transformation matrix B, the integration weight due to numerical integration W and the numerical integration point associated volume ΔV is contained. The left superscripts "t" and "$t + \Delta t$" denote the last and the current time step. If the iteration counter "i" in Loop B is equal to zero, this indicates the start of the current time step. The basics for the table are taken from (Kojic & Bathe, 2005). These basics are expanded and adopted for the cap model.

Loop A: Loop over all load steps

{

Load steps:

$$^{t+\Delta t}R = {}^{t}R + {}^{t+\Delta t}R$$

Initial value for $^{t+\Delta t}U^{(i)}$ to calculate flow limit:

$$^{t+\Delta t}U^{(0)} = {}^{t}U + {}^{t+\Delta t}K^{(i-1)^{-1}} \cdot ({}^{t+\Delta t}R - {}^{t+\Delta t}F^{(i-1)})$$

　　Loop B: Loop over all equilibrium iterations

　　{

　　Initial:

$$i = 1, {}^{t+\Delta t}F^{(i-1)} = 0, {}^{t+\Delta t}K^{(i-1)} = 0$$

　　　　Loop C: Loop over all finite elements and all integration points

　　　　{

　　　　Known:

$$^{t}e^{P}, {}^{t}L$$

　　　　Calculate:

$$^{t+\Delta t}e^{(i-1)} = B \cdot {}^{t+\Delta t}U^{(i-1)}$$

　　　　Check yielding:

$$\text{if } {}^{t+\Delta t}f_1^E \leq 0, {}^{t+\Delta t}f_c^E \leq 0 \text{ and } I_1^E \geq T \rightarrow elastic\ deformation$$

$$if \ {}^{t+\Delta t}f_1^E \leq 0 \ and \ 3 \ {}^{t+\Delta t}\sigma_m^E \leq \ {}^tL \rightarrow yielding \ on \ failure \ surface$$

$$if \ {}^{t+\Delta t}f_c^E > 0, \left(3 \ {}^{t+\Delta t}\sigma_m^E\right) > \ {}^tL \ and \ {}^{t+\Delta t}f_1^E \leq 0 \rightarrow cap \ yielding$$

$$if \left(3 \ {}^{t+\Delta t}\sigma_m^E\right) > \ {}^tL \ and \ {}^{t+\Delta t}f_1^E > 0 \rightarrow vertex \ yielding$$

$$if \ I_1^E < T \rightarrow tension \ cutoff$$

If yielding corresponds to elastic deformation:

$${}^{t+\Delta t}\boldsymbol{C}^{EP} = \boldsymbol{C}^E$$

$$\sigma = \boldsymbol{C}^E.\left({}^{t+\Delta t}\boldsymbol{e}^{(i-1)} - \ {}^t\boldsymbol{e}^P\right)$$

If yielding corresponds to yielding on failure surface:

Apply Table 5.1 to calculate $\Delta\boldsymbol{e}^P$

Apply Equation (4.21) to calculate ${}^{t+\Delta t}\sigma$

Apply Table 5.4 to calculate ${}^{t+\Delta t}\boldsymbol{C}^{EP}$

If yielding corresponds to cap yielding:

Apply Table 5.2 to calculate $\Delta\boldsymbol{e}^P$

Apply Equation (4.21) to calculate ${}^{t+\Delta t}\sigma$

Apply Table 5.5 to calculate ${}^{t+\Delta t}\boldsymbol{C}^{EP}$

If yielding corresponds to vertex yielding:

Apply Table 5.3 to calculate $\Delta\boldsymbol{e}^P$

Apply Equation (4.21) to calculate ${}^{t+\Delta t}\sigma$

Apply Table 5.6 to calculate ${}^{t+\Delta t}\boldsymbol{C}^{EP}$

If yielding corresponds to tension cutoff:

$${}^{t+\Delta t}\boldsymbol{C}^{EP} = \boldsymbol{0}$$

$$\sigma = \ {}^{t+\Delta t}\boldsymbol{C}^{EP}.\left({}^{t+\Delta t}\boldsymbol{e}^{(i-1)} - \ {}^t\boldsymbol{e}^P\right)$$

Calculate nodal forces:

$${}^{t+\Delta t}\boldsymbol{F}^{(i-1)} = \ {}^{t+\Delta t}\boldsymbol{F}^{(i-1)} + \boldsymbol{B}.\ {}^{t+\Delta t}\sigma W \ \Delta V$$

Calculate stiffness matrix:

$$^{t+\Delta t}K^{(i-1)} = {}^{t+\Delta t}K^{(i-1)} + B.{}^{t+\Delta t}C^{EP(i-1)}.B^T \ W \ \Delta V$$

} End of Loop C

Apply Newton– Raphson Scheme to calculate the increment of displacements:

$$\Delta U^{(i)} = {}^{t+\Delta t}K^{(i-1)^{-1}}.\left({}^{t+\Delta t}R - {}^{t+\Delta t}F^{(i-1)}\right)$$

$$^{t+\Delta t}U^{(i)} = {}^{t+\Delta t}U^{(i-1)} + \Delta U^{(i)}$$

Check convergence:

$$\left\|\Delta U^{(i)}\right\| < 10^{-12}$$

If the convergence criteria are satisfied, abort Loop B and go to Loop A.

$$i = max.\,iteration$$

Else:

$$i = i + 1$$

} End of Loop B

$$^{t}U = {}^{t+\Delta t}U^{(max.iteration)}$$

} End of Loop A

TABLE 5.7. INCREMENTAL STATIC CALCULATION SCHEME FOR MATERIAL NONLINEAR PROBLEMS

6 Time Integration for Finite Element Equations

In Section 2.4 the finite element equations were derived. This yield the equation of motion:

$$M.\ddot{U} + C.\dot{U} + K.U = R$$

(6.1)

with the inertia forces $M.\ddot{U}$ (the dot denotes a vector or matrix multiplication; see Appendix A2), the damping forces $C.\dot{U}$, the internal elastic forces $K.U$ as time dependent forces, and the external forces R which can be time dependent. Therefore, in dynamic calculations the equilibrium is considered at the time "t".

Equation (6.1) is a system of ordinary linear differential equations of second order. To solve (6.1) at any time "t" can be very expansive or may not be possible for practical examples. Hence, the solution of (6.1) is determined at discrete time stations with the time intervals Δt. That means, it is searched for equilibrium at discrete time points within the overall time interval. The considered time span T is subdivided in n equal time intervals. Hence, the time step is calculated to: $\Delta t = T/n$. The following integration schemes represent an approximated solution to the times $\Delta t, 2\Delta t, \dots, t + \Delta t, \dots T$.

The solution to the next time $(t + \Delta t)$ is calculated with the help of the solution of the previous time (t). Therefore, as initial condition the displacements, velocities and accelerations have to be known at the time $t = 0$. This approach is typically for all time integration methods.

Time integration methods are subdivided into *direct integration methods* and *methods with mode superposition*. Both groups of methods are closely related. The difference is that in *methods with mode superposition* the equation of motion is transformed into an effective form, to accelerate the solution of the equation system.

The *methods with mode superposition* are not further considered here. The solution with *direct integration methods* such as the *Newmark method* (Newmark, 1959) and the *Hilber-Hughes-Taylor-α method* (Hilber, Hughes, & Taylor, 1977) is explained in the following. Specifications for both methods are widespread. Hence, the linear case of the *Newmark method* and the *Hilber-Hughes-Taylor-α method (HHT-α method)* is only briefly cited.

The nonlinear description of the *HHT-α method*, which follows, is a new description based on the Crisfield formulation (Crisfield, 1997). The Crisfield formulation with modified Newton-Raphson iteration is extended for the full Newton-Raphson iteration (which is explained in Section 3.2.2) here.

6.1 Newmark Method

The group of the Newmark methods is the most popular method for time integration. Equation (6.1) is written for time steps with the time dependent quantities here as:

$$M.^{t+\Delta t}\ddot{U} + C.^{t+\Delta t}\dot{U} + K.^{t+\Delta t}U = {}^{t+\Delta t}R$$

(6.2)

The upper-left index denotes the current time step $(t + \Delta t)$ or the previous time step (t) (in the following equations). When the accelerations, velocities and displacements from the previous time step are known, the actual velocities and accelerations in the Newmark method can be determined with:

$$\boxed{{}^{t+\Delta t}\dot{U} = {}^{t}\dot{U} + \left[(1-\gamma)\ {}^{t}\ddot{U} + \gamma{}^{t+\Delta t}\ddot{U}\right]\Delta t} \qquad (6.3)$$

$$\boxed{{}^{t+\Delta t}U = {}^{t}U + {}^{t}\dot{U}\,\Delta t + \left[\left(\frac{1}{2}-\beta\right)\ {}^{t}\ddot{U} + \beta\ {}^{t+\Delta t}\ddot{U}\right]\Delta t^2} \qquad (6.4)$$

where the parameters β and γ are constants. Both control the integration accuracy and stability. If β is set to $\frac{1}{4}$ and γ is set to $\frac{1}{2}$ the equations yield to the trapezoid rule. The trapezoid rule is unconditionally stable and implicit.

The equations (6.3) and (6.4) can be rearranged for ${}^{t+\Delta t}\ddot{U}$ and ${}^{t+\Delta t}\dot{U}$ so that the only unknowns are the displacements ${}^{t+\Delta t}U$. These relations can be replaced in (6.2). Equation (6.2) is solved then for ${}^{t+\Delta t}U$. Detailed algorithms for this can be found in (Hughes, 1987) or (Bathe, Finite Elemente Methoden, 2002) for example.

6.2 HILBER-HUGHES-TAYLOR-α METHOD IN A LINEAR CONTEXT

Depending on the choice of the parameters β and γ in the Newmark method, numerical damping is introduced in the calculated system. This undesirable effect is avoided when the trapezoid rule is chosen.

The spatial finite element system approximates the lower eigenmodes better than the higher ones (Strang & Fix, 1973). Sometimes it is preferable to damp the higher eigenmodes, as in engineering problems, where generally only the low frequencies are of note. Therefore, in the Newmark method $\gamma > \frac{1}{2}$ has to be selected, but this involves numerical damping and a loss of accuracy of the evaluation (Wriggers, 2001). To overcome these unwanted effects, modifications of the Newmark method, such as the HHT-α method, are introduced.

In the HHT-α method a third parameter α is introduced into the Newmark method to control the numerical damping. Hence, the HHT-α method can be seen as a variant of the Newmark algorithm. According to (Hilber, Hughes, & Taylor, 1977) the equation of motion (6.2) for time steps is written as:

$$\boxed{\begin{aligned} &M.{}^{t+\Delta t}\ddot{U} + (1+\alpha)\,C.{}^{t+\Delta t}\dot{U} - \alpha C.\,{}^{t}\dot{U} + (1+\alpha)\,K.{}^{t+\Delta t}U - \alpha K.\,{}^{t}U \\ &= (1+\alpha)\,{}^{t+\Delta t}R - \alpha\,{}^{t}R \end{aligned}} \qquad (6.5)$$

Choosing α to zero reduces (6.5) to the Newmark method. For a linear system the parameter α, β and γ are chosen to:

$$-\frac{1}{3} \le \alpha \le 0, \beta = \frac{(1-\alpha)^2}{4}, \gamma = \frac{1-2\,\alpha}{2} \qquad (6.6)$$

This yields an unconditionally stable, second-order accurate scheme (Hughes, 1987).

A calculation algorithm for the HHT-α method is given in the following. The equations (6.3) and (6.4) from the Newmark method can be written for conciseness as:

$$^{t+\Delta t}U = {}^{t+\Delta t}\widetilde{U} + \beta \, \Delta t^2 \, {}^{t+\Delta t}\ddot{U} \tag{6.7}$$

$$^{t+\Delta t}\dot{U} = {}^{t+\Delta t}\dot{\widetilde{U}} + \gamma \Delta t \, {}^{t+\Delta t}\ddot{U} \tag{6.8}$$

where the predictor variables $^{t+\Delta t}\widetilde{U}$ and $^{t+\Delta t}\dot{\widetilde{U}}$ are given by:

$$^{t+\Delta t}\widetilde{U} = {}^{t}U + \Delta t \, {}^{t}\dot{U} + \Delta t^2 \left(\frac{1}{2} - \beta\right) {}^{t}\ddot{U} \tag{6.9}$$

$$^{t+\Delta t}\dot{\widetilde{U}} = {}^{t}\dot{U} + (1 - \gamma) \, \Delta t \, {}^{t}\ddot{U} \tag{6.10}$$

Rearranging (6.7) for $^{t+\Delta t}\ddot{U}$ yields:

$$^{t+\Delta t}\ddot{U} = \left({}^{t+\Delta t}U - {}^{t+\Delta t}\widetilde{U}\right)\frac{1}{\beta \, \Delta t^2} \tag{6.11}$$

Equation (6.11) is replaced in (6.8):

$$^{t+\Delta t}\dot{U} = {}^{t+\Delta t}\dot{\widetilde{U}} + \gamma \Delta t \left({}^{t+\Delta t}U - {}^{t+\Delta t}\widetilde{U}\right)\frac{1}{\beta \, \Delta t^2}$$

$$^{t+\Delta t}\dot{U} = {}^{t+\Delta t}\dot{\widetilde{U}} + \frac{\gamma}{\beta \, \Delta t} \left({}^{t+\Delta t}U - {}^{t+\Delta t}\widetilde{U}\right) \tag{6.12}$$

Inserting (6.11) and (6.12) in (6.5) yields:

$$M.\left({}^{t+\Delta t}U - {}^{t+\Delta t}\widetilde{U}\right)\frac{1}{\beta * \Delta t^2} + (1 + \alpha) \, C.\left[{}^{t+\Delta t}\dot{\widetilde{U}} + \frac{\gamma}{\beta * \Delta t}\left({}^{t+\Delta t}U - {}^{t+\Delta t}\widetilde{U}\right)\right]$$

$$- \alpha \, C. \, {}^{t}\dot{U} + (1 + \alpha) \, K. \, {}^{t+\Delta t}U - \alpha \, K. \, {}^{t}U = (1 + \alpha) \, {}^{t+\Delta t}R - \alpha \, {}^{t}R$$

$$\frac{1}{\beta * \Delta t^2} \, M. \, {}^{t+\Delta t}U - \frac{1}{\beta * \Delta t^2} \, M. \, {}^{t+\Delta t}\widetilde{U} + (1 + \alpha) \, C. \, {}^{t+\Delta t}\dot{\widetilde{U}} + (1 + \alpha) \, \frac{\gamma}{\beta * \Delta t} \, C. \, {}^{t+\Delta t}U$$

$$-(1 + \alpha) \, \frac{\gamma}{\beta * \Delta t} \, C. \, {}^{t+\Delta t}\widetilde{U} - \alpha \, C. \, {}^{t}\dot{U} + (1 + \alpha) \, K. \, {}^{t+\Delta t}U - \alpha \, K. \, {}^{t}U$$

$$= (1 + \alpha) \, {}^{t+\Delta t}R - \alpha \, {}^{t}R$$

multiplied with $\beta \, \Delta t^2$:

$$M.^{t+\Delta t}U - M.^{t+\Delta t}\widetilde{U} + (1+\alpha)\,\beta\,\Delta t^2\,C.^{t+\Delta t}\widetilde{U} + (1+\alpha)\,\gamma\Delta t\,C.^{t+\Delta t}U$$

$$-(1+\alpha)\,\gamma\Delta t\,C.^{t+\Delta t}\widetilde{U} - \alpha\beta\,\Delta t^2 C.^{t}\dot{U} + (1+\alpha)\,\beta\,\Delta t^2 K.^{t+\Delta t}U - \alpha\beta\,\Delta t^2 K.^{t}U$$

$$= (1+\alpha)\,\beta\,\Delta t^2\,{}^{t+\Delta t}R - \alpha\beta\,\Delta t^2\,{}^{t}R$$

$$M.^{t+\Delta t}U + (1+\alpha)\,\gamma\Delta t\,C.^{t+\Delta t}U + (1+\alpha)\,\beta\,\Delta t^2 K.^{t+\Delta t}U =$$

$$(1+\alpha)\,\beta\,\Delta t^{2\,t+\Delta t}R - \alpha\beta\,\Delta t^2\,{}^{t}R + M.^{t+\Delta t}\widetilde{U} - (1+\alpha)\,\beta\,\Delta t^2 C.^{t+\Delta t}\widetilde{U}$$

$$+(1+\alpha)\,\gamma\Delta t\,C.^{t+\Delta t}\widetilde{U} + \alpha\beta\,\Delta t^2 C.^{t}\dot{U} + \alpha\beta\,\Delta t^2 K.^{t}U$$

and written in short notation:

$$\boxed{K'.^{t+\Delta t}U = {}^{t+\Delta t}R' + (1+\alpha)\,\beta\,\Delta t^{2\,t+\Delta t}R - \alpha\beta\,\Delta t^2\,{}^{t}R} \qquad (6.13)$$

with:

$$\boxed{\begin{aligned} K' &= M + (1+\alpha)\,\gamma\Delta t\,C + (1+\alpha)\,\beta\,\Delta t^2 K \\[2mm] {}^{t+\Delta t}R' &= (M + (1+\alpha)\,\gamma\Delta t\,C).^{t+\Delta t}\widetilde{U} - (1+\alpha)\,\beta\,\Delta t^2 C.^{t+\Delta t}\widetilde{U} \\[2mm] &+ \alpha\beta\,\Delta t^2(C.^{t}\dot{U} + K.^{t}U) \end{aligned}} \qquad (6.14)$$

The equations (6.13) and (6.14) represent the HHT-α method in an implicit update equation form.

6.3 HILBER-HUGHES-TAYLOR-α METHOD IN A NONLINEAR CONTEXT

Originally the HHT-α method was formulated in a linear context. The nonlinear description of the *HHT-α method*, which is given here, is a new description based on the Crisfield formulation (Crisfield, 1997). The Crisfield formulation with modified Newton-Raphson iteration is extended for the full Newton-Raphson iteration (which is explained in Section 3.2.2).

6.3.1 NEW NONLINEAR HHT-α FORMULATION WITH FULL NEWTON-RAPHSON ITERATION

For the nonlinear derivation Equation (6.5) is given as (Crisfield, 1997):

$$^{t+\Delta t}\overline{g} = {}^{t+\Delta t}g^*(\alpha) + M.^{t+\Delta t}\ddot{U} = 0 \qquad (6.15)$$

with:

$$^{t+\Delta t}g^*(\alpha) = (1+\alpha)\left({}^{t+\Delta t}F - {}^{t+\Delta t}R + C.^{t+\Delta t}\dot{U}\right) - \alpha\left({}^{t}F - {}^{t}R + C.^{t}\dot{U}\right)$$

$$^{t+\Delta t}g^*(\alpha) = (1+\alpha)\left({}^{t+\Delta t}g + C.^{t+\Delta t}\dot{U}\right) - \alpha\left({}^{t}g + C.^{t}\dot{U}\right)$$

$$(6.16)$$

with $^{t+\Delta t}\overline{g}$ as dynamic residual, $^{t+\Delta t}g$ as static residual and ^{t}g as static residual from the previous time step. Now (6.3) and (6.4) are rearranged so that $^{t+\Delta t}U$ is the only unknown. First (6.4) is rearranged for $^{t+\Delta t}\ddot{U}$:

$$^{t+\Delta t}U = {}^{t}U + {}^{t}\dot{U}\,\Delta t + \left[\left(\frac{1}{2}-\beta\right){}^{t}\ddot{U} + \beta\,{}^{t+\Delta t}\ddot{U}\right]\Delta t^2$$

$$^{t+\Delta t}\ddot{U} = \frac{1}{\beta\,\Delta t^2}\left({}^{t+\Delta t}U - {}^{t}U - \Delta t\,{}^{t}\dot{U}\right) - \frac{1-2\beta}{2\beta}\,{}^{t}\ddot{U} \qquad (6.17)$$

And this is replaced in (6.3):

$$^{t+\Delta t}\dot{U} = {}^{t}\dot{U} + \left[(1-\gamma)\,{}^{t}\ddot{U} + \gamma\left\{\left({}^{t+\Delta t}U - {}^{t}U - \Delta t\,{}^{t}\dot{U}\right)\frac{1}{\beta\,\Delta t^2} - \frac{1-2\beta}{2\beta}\,{}^{t}\ddot{U}\right\}\right]\Delta t$$

$$^{t+\Delta t}\dot{U} = {}^{t}\dot{U} + \Delta t\,(1-\gamma)\,{}^{t}\ddot{U} + \frac{\gamma}{\beta\,\Delta t}\left({}^{t+\Delta t}U - {}^{t}U - \Delta t\,{}^{t}\dot{U}\right) - \Delta t\,\gamma\,\frac{1-2\beta}{2\beta}\,{}^{t}\ddot{U} \qquad (6.18)$$

Now the Taylor series expansion (3.11) is written with (3.12) as:

$$^{t+\Delta t}F^{(i)} = {}^{t}F + {}^{t}K.\Delta U^{(i)} \qquad (6.19)$$

$$^{t+\Delta t}U^{(i)} = {}^{t}U + \Delta U^{(i)} \qquad (6.20)$$

This equates to the modified Newton-Raphson (see Section 3.2.2) iteration scheme, where the values from the last time step are used for the complete equilibrium iteration "i", without updating these values in the iterations. When the derivation is continued with (6.19) and (6.20) this yields the Crisfield formulation for the nonlinear HHT-α method. But instead of the modified Newton-Raphson scheme, the full Newton-Raphson scheme is used now. So (6.19) and (6.20) are rewritten as:

$$^{t+\Delta t}F^{(i)} = {}^{t+\Delta t}F^{(i-1)} + {}^{t+\Delta t}K^{(i-1)}.\Delta U^{(i)} \qquad (6.21)$$

$$^{t+\Delta t}U^{(i)} = {}^{t+\Delta t}U^{(i-1)} + \Delta U^{(i)} \qquad (6.22)$$

The equations (6.17), (6.18), (6.21) and (6.22) are replaced now in (6.15) and (6.16):

$$^{t+\Delta t}\overline{g} = (1+\alpha)\left({}^{t+\Delta t}F^{(i-1)} + {}^{t+\Delta t}K^{(i-1)}.\Delta U^{(i)} - {}^{t+\Delta t}R\right.$$

$$+ C.\left[{}^{t}\dot{U} + \Delta t\,(1-\gamma)\,{}^{t}\ddot{U} + \frac{\gamma}{\beta\,\Delta t}\left({}^{t+\Delta t}U^{(i-1)} + \Delta U^{(i)} - {}^{t}U - \Delta t\,{}^{t}\dot{U}\right)\right.$$

$$\left.\left. - \Delta t\,\gamma\,\frac{1-2\beta}{2\beta}\,{}^{t}\ddot{U}\right]\right) \qquad (6.23)$$

$$- \alpha\left({}^{t}F - {}^{t}R + C.\,{}^{t}\dot{U}\right)$$

$$+ M.\left[\frac{1}{\beta\,\Delta t^2}\left({}^{t+\Delta t}U^{(i-1)} + \Delta U^{(i)} - {}^{t}U - \Delta t\,{}^{t}\dot{U}\right) - \frac{1-2\beta}{2\beta}\,{}^{t}\ddot{U}\right] = 0$$

The following equation in short notation is requested now:

$$\boxed{{}^{t+\Delta t}\Delta\overline{R}^{(i-1)} = {}^{t+\Delta t}\overline{K}^{(i-1)} \cdot \Delta U^{(i)}}$$

(6.24)

Therefore, (6.23) is rearranged for $\Delta U^{(i)}$. This yields the following equation (with regard to the commutative law for matrix and vector multiplications):

$$\Delta U^{(i)} = \left[{}^{t+\Delta t}\overline{K}^{(i-1)}\right]^{-1} \cdot {}^{t+\Delta t}\Delta\overline{R}^{(i-1)} =$$

$$\left[2\left(M + (1+\alpha)\Delta t\left(\gamma C + \beta\,\Delta t\,{}^{t+\Delta t}K^{(i-1)}\right)\right)\right]^{-1} \cdot$$

$$\left[-2\,M \cdot {}^{t+\Delta t}U^{(i-1)} + 2\,\Delta t\left(M \cdot {}^{t}\dot{U} - (1+\alpha)\,\gamma C \cdot {}^{t+\Delta t}U^{(i-1)}\right) + \right.$$

$$\Delta t^2\left((1-2\,\beta)\,M \cdot {}^{t}\ddot{U} + 2\,(1+\alpha)\,\beta\,{}^{t+\Delta t}R\right.$$

(6.25)

$$-2\,\beta\left\{{}^{t+\Delta t}F^{(i-1)} + C \cdot {}^{t}\dot{U} + \alpha\left({}^{t}R - {}^{t}F + {}^{t+\Delta t}F^{(i-1)}\right)\right\}$$

$$+2\,(1+\alpha)\,\gamma C \cdot {}^{t}\ddot{U}\right)$$

$$\left. C \cdot {}^{t}\ddot{U}\,(1+\alpha)\,(\gamma - 2\,\beta)\,\Delta t^3 + 2\,(M + (1+\alpha)\,\gamma\Delta t\,C) \cdot {}^{t}U\right]$$

${}^{t+\Delta t}\overline{K}^{(i-1)}$ is brought on the left hand side now and rearranged to the notation in (Crisfield, 1997):

$${}^{t+\Delta t}\overline{K}^{(i-1)} = 2\left(M + (1+\alpha)\Delta t\left(\gamma C + \beta\,\Delta t\,{}^{t+\Delta t}K^{(i-1)}\right)\right)$$

$${}^{t+\Delta t}\overline{K}^{(i-1)} = 2\left(M + (1+\alpha)\left(\Delta t\,\gamma C + \beta\,\Delta t^2\,{}^{t+\Delta t}K^{(i-1)}\right)\right) \Rightarrow exclude\ \beta\,\Delta t^2$$

$${}^{t+\Delta t}\overline{K}^{(i-1)} = 2\left(M + (1+\alpha)\,\beta\,\Delta t^2\left(\frac{1}{\beta\,\Delta t}\,\gamma C + {}^{t+\Delta t}K^{(i-1)}\right)\right) \Rightarrow exclude\ \beta\,\Delta t^2$$

(6.26)

$${}^{t+\Delta t}\overline{K}^{(i-1)} = 2\,\beta\,\Delta t^2\left(\frac{1}{\beta\,\Delta t^2}\,M + (1+\alpha)\left(\frac{1}{\beta\,\Delta t}\,\gamma C + {}^{t+\Delta t}K^{(i-1)}\right)\right)$$

The aim is to get a comparison to the notation from Crisfield. Hence, (6.24) is multiplied with $\frac{1}{2\,\beta\,\Delta t^2}$.

${}^{t+\Delta t}\Delta\overline{R}^{(i-1)}$ in (6.25) multiplied with $\frac{1}{2\,\beta\,\Delta t^2}$ yields:

$${}^{t+\Delta t}\Delta\overline{R}^{(i-1)} =$$

$$-\boldsymbol{M}.\,{}^{t}\ddot{\boldsymbol{U}} + {}^{t+\Delta t}\boldsymbol{R} - {}^{t+\Delta t}\boldsymbol{F}^{(i-1)} - \boldsymbol{C}.\,{}^{t}\dot{\boldsymbol{U}} - \alpha\,{}^{t}\boldsymbol{R} + \alpha\,{}^{t+\Delta t}\boldsymbol{R} + \alpha\,{}^{t}\boldsymbol{F} - \alpha\,{}^{t+\Delta t}\boldsymbol{F}^{(i-1)}$$

$$+\frac{1}{2\,\beta}\,\boldsymbol{M}.\,{}^{t}\ddot{\boldsymbol{U}} + \frac{\gamma}{\beta}\,\boldsymbol{C}.\,{}^{t}\dot{\boldsymbol{U}} + \alpha\frac{\gamma}{\beta}\,\boldsymbol{C}.\,{}^{t}\dot{\boldsymbol{U}} + \frac{1}{\beta\,\Delta t^2}\,\boldsymbol{M}.\,{}^{t}\boldsymbol{U} - \frac{1}{\beta\,\Delta t^2}\,\boldsymbol{M}.\,{}^{t+\Delta t}\boldsymbol{U}^{(i-1)}$$

$$+\frac{1}{\beta\,\Delta t}\,\boldsymbol{M}.\,{}^{t}\dot{\boldsymbol{U}} \qquad\qquad\qquad\qquad\qquad\qquad\qquad\qquad\qquad (6.27)$$

$$+\frac{\gamma}{\beta\,\Delta t}\,\boldsymbol{C}.\,{}^{t}\boldsymbol{U} - \frac{\gamma}{\beta\,\Delta t}\,\boldsymbol{C}.\,{}^{t+\Delta t}\boldsymbol{U}^{(i-1)} + \alpha\frac{\gamma}{\beta\,\Delta t}\,\boldsymbol{C}.\,{}^{t}\boldsymbol{U} - \alpha\frac{\gamma}{\beta\,\Delta t}\,\boldsymbol{C}.\,{}^{t+\Delta t}\boldsymbol{U}^{(i-1)}$$

$$-\Delta t\,\boldsymbol{C}.\,{}^{t}\ddot{\boldsymbol{U}}$$

$$-\alpha\,\Delta t\,\boldsymbol{C}.\,{}^{t}\ddot{\boldsymbol{U}} + \Delta t\frac{\gamma}{2\,\beta}\,\boldsymbol{C}.\,{}^{t}\ddot{\boldsymbol{U}} + \alpha\,\Delta t\frac{\gamma}{2\,\beta}\,\boldsymbol{C}.\,{}^{t}\ddot{\boldsymbol{U}}$$

Equation (6.27) is subdivided into several terms:

$${}^{t+\Delta t}\Delta\overline{R}^{(i-1)} =$$

$${}^{t+\Delta t}\boldsymbol{R} - {}^{t+\Delta t}\boldsymbol{F}^{(i-1)} + \alpha\,{}^{t+\Delta t}\boldsymbol{R} - \alpha\,{}^{t+\Delta t}\boldsymbol{F}^{(i-1)} \qquad\qquad\qquad term\ (6.27)\text{-}1$$

$$-\alpha\,{}^{t}\boldsymbol{R} + \alpha\,{}^{t}\boldsymbol{F} \qquad\qquad\qquad\qquad\qquad\qquad\qquad\qquad term\ (6.27)\text{-}2$$

$$-\boldsymbol{M}.\,{}^{t}\ddot{\boldsymbol{U}} + \frac{1}{2\,\beta}\,\boldsymbol{M}.\,{}^{t}\ddot{\boldsymbol{U}} + \frac{1}{\beta\,\Delta t^2}\,\boldsymbol{M}.\,{}^{t}\boldsymbol{U} - \frac{1}{\beta\,\Delta t^2}\,\boldsymbol{M}.\,{}^{t+\Delta t}\boldsymbol{U}^{(i-1)} + \frac{1}{\beta\,\Delta t}\,\boldsymbol{M}.\,{}^{t}\dot{\boldsymbol{U}} \quad term\ (6.27)\text{-}3$$

$$-\boldsymbol{C}.\,{}^{t}\dot{\boldsymbol{U}} + \frac{\gamma}{\beta}\,\boldsymbol{C}.\,{}^{t}\dot{\boldsymbol{U}} + \alpha\frac{\gamma}{\beta}\,\boldsymbol{C}.\,{}^{t}\dot{\boldsymbol{U}} \qquad\qquad\qquad\qquad\qquad term\ (6.27)\text{-}4$$

$$+\frac{\gamma}{\beta\,\Delta t}\,\boldsymbol{C}.\,{}^{t}\boldsymbol{U} + \alpha\frac{\gamma}{\beta\,\Delta t}\,\boldsymbol{C}.\,{}^{t}\boldsymbol{U} - \frac{\gamma}{\beta\,\Delta t}\,\boldsymbol{C}.\,{}^{t+\Delta t}\boldsymbol{U}^{(i-1)} - \alpha\frac{\gamma}{\beta\,\Delta t}\,\boldsymbol{C}.\,{}^{t+\Delta t}\boldsymbol{U}^{(i-1)} \quad term\ (6.27)\text{-}5$$

$$-\Delta t\,\boldsymbol{C}.\,{}^{t}\ddot{\boldsymbol{U}} - \alpha\,\Delta t\,\boldsymbol{C}.\,{}^{t}\ddot{\boldsymbol{U}} + \Delta t\frac{\gamma}{2\,\beta}\,\boldsymbol{C}.\,{}^{t}\ddot{\boldsymbol{U}} + \alpha\,\Delta t\frac{\gamma}{2\,\beta}\,\boldsymbol{C}.\,{}^{t}\ddot{\boldsymbol{U}} \qquad term\ (6.27)\text{-}6$$

Term (6.27)-1:

$$(1+\alpha)\,\left({}^{t+\Delta t}\boldsymbol{R} - {}^{t+\Delta t}\boldsymbol{F}^{(i-1)}\right)$$

Term (6.27)-2:

$$-\alpha\,\left({}^{t}\boldsymbol{R} - {}^{t}\boldsymbol{F}\right)$$

Term (6.27)-3:

$$M.\left[- {}^{t}\ddot{U} + \frac{1}{2\beta}\ {}^{t}\ddot{U} + \frac{1}{\beta\,\Delta t^2}\ {}^{t}U - \frac{1}{\beta\,\Delta t^2}\ {}^{t+\Delta t}U^{(i-1)} + \frac{1}{\beta\,\Delta t}\ {}^{t}\dot{U}\right]$$

$$= M.\left[(\frac{1}{2\beta} - 1)\ {}^{t}\ddot{U} + \frac{1}{\beta\,\Delta t^2}\ {}^{t}U - \frac{1}{\beta\,\Delta t^2}\ {}^{t+\Delta t}U^{(i-1)} + \frac{1}{\beta\,\Delta t}\ {}^{t}\dot{U}\right]$$

$$= M.\left[\frac{1-2\beta}{2\beta}\ {}^{t}\ddot{U} + \frac{1}{\beta\,\Delta t^2}\ \left({}^{t}U - {}^{t+\Delta t}U^{(i-1)}\right) + \frac{1}{\beta\,\Delta t}\ {}^{t}\dot{U}\right]$$

$$= M.\left[\frac{1}{\beta\,\Delta t}\ {}^{t}\dot{U} + \frac{1-2\beta}{2\beta}\ {}^{t}\ddot{U}\right] - \frac{1}{\beta\,\Delta t^2}\ M.\left({}^{t+\Delta t}U^{(i-1)} - {}^{t}U\right)$$

Term (6.27)-4:

$$\left(-1 + \frac{\gamma}{\beta} + \alpha\,\frac{\gamma}{\beta}\right) C.\ {}^{t}\dot{U}$$

$$= \left(-1 + (1+\alpha)\,\frac{\gamma}{\beta}\right) C.\ {}^{t}\dot{U}$$

Term (6.27)-5:

$$\left(\frac{\gamma}{\beta\,\Delta t} + \alpha\,\frac{\gamma}{\beta\,\Delta t}\right) C.\ {}^{t}U - \left(\frac{\gamma}{\beta\,\Delta t} + \alpha\,\frac{\gamma}{\beta\,\Delta t}\right) C.\ {}^{t+\Delta t}U^{(i-1)}$$

$$= (1+\alpha)\,\frac{\gamma}{\beta\,\Delta t}\ C.\ {}^{t}U - (1+\alpha)\,\frac{\gamma}{\beta\,\Delta t}\ C.\ {}^{t+\Delta t}U^{(i-1)}$$

$$= (1+\alpha)\,\frac{\gamma}{\beta\,\Delta t}\ C.\left({}^{t}U - {}^{t+\Delta t}U^{(i-1)}\right)$$

$$= -(1+\alpha)\,\frac{\gamma}{\beta\,\Delta t}\ C.\left({}^{t+\Delta t}U^{(i-1)} - {}^{t}U\right)$$

Term (6.27)-6:

$$\left(-\Delta t - \alpha\,\Delta t + \Delta t\frac{\gamma}{2\beta} + \alpha\,\Delta t\frac{\gamma}{2\beta}\right) C.\ {}^{t}\ddot{U}$$

$$= \left(-1 - \alpha + \frac{\gamma}{2\beta} + \alpha\,\frac{\gamma}{2\beta}\right) \Delta t\ C.\ {}^{t}\ddot{U}$$

$$= \frac{-2\beta - \alpha 2\beta + \gamma + \alpha\gamma}{2\beta}\,\Delta t\ C.\ {}^{t}\ddot{U}$$

$$= \frac{(1+\alpha)(\gamma - 2\beta)}{2\beta}\,\Delta t\ C.\ {}^{t}\ddot{U}$$

The terms (6.27)-1 to (6.27)-6 from Equation (6.27) are summarized to one equation now:

$$
\begin{aligned}
{}^{t+\Delta t}\Delta\bar{R}^{(i-1)} = \\
(1+\alpha)\left({}^{t+\Delta t}R - {}^{t+\Delta t}F^{(i-1)}\right) - \alpha\left({}^{t}R - {}^{t}F\right) + M.\left(\frac{1}{\beta\,\Delta t}\,{}^{t}\dot{U} + \frac{1-2\beta}{2\beta}\,{}^{t}\ddot{U}\right) \\
\overbrace{-\frac{1}{\beta\,\Delta t^2}\,M.\left({}^{t+\Delta t}U^{(i-1)} - {}^{t}U\right)}^{additional} + \left(-1 + (1+\alpha)\frac{\gamma}{\beta}\right)C.\,{}^{t}\dot{U} \\
+\frac{(1+\alpha)(\gamma - 2\beta)}{2\beta}\Delta t\, C.\,{}^{t}\ddot{U} \\
\overbrace{-(1+\alpha)\frac{\gamma}{\beta\,\Delta t}\,C.\left({}^{t+\Delta t}U^{(i-1)} - {}^{t}U\right)}^{additional}
\end{aligned}
\tag{6.28}
$$

The denoted terms in (6.28) are additional to the Crisfield-formulation. The other terms relate to the formulation for the nonlinear HHT-α method given in (Crisfield, 1997). Multiplying (6.26) with $\frac{1}{2\,\beta\,\Delta t^2}$ yields:

$$
{}^{t+\Delta t}\bar{K}^{(i-1)} = \frac{1}{\beta\,\Delta t^2}\,M + (1+\alpha)\left(\frac{1}{\beta\,\Delta t}\,\gamma C + {}^{t+\Delta t}K^{(i-1)}\right)
\tag{6.29}
$$

The equations (6.28) and (6.29) with ${}^{t+\Delta t}\Delta\bar{R}^{(i-1)} = {}^{t+\Delta t}\bar{K}^{(i-1)}.\Delta U^{(i)}$ derived in (6.24) describe a nonlinear variant of the HHT-α method with full Newton-Raphson iteration.

6.3.2 Derivation of the Trapezoid Rule from the Given HHT-α Formulation

The trapezoid rule is calculated from (6.28) and (6.29) by setting: $\alpha = 0, \beta = \frac{1}{4}$ and $\gamma = \frac{1}{2}$. This is directed to verify the given derivation from (6.28) and (6.29). For (6.28) follows then:

$$
{}^{t+\Delta t}\Delta\bar{R}^{(i-1)} = {}^{t+\Delta t}R - {}^{t+\Delta t}F^{(i-1)} + M.\left(\frac{1}{\frac{1}{4}\,\Delta t}\,{}^{t}\dot{U} + \frac{1 - 2\frac{1}{4}}{2\frac{1}{4}}\,{}^{t}\ddot{U}\right)
$$

$$
-\frac{1}{\frac{1}{4}\,\Delta t^2}\,M.\left({}^{t+\Delta t}U^{(i-1)} - {}^{t}U\right) + \left(-1 + \frac{\frac{1}{2}}{\frac{1}{4}}\right)C.\,{}^{t}\dot{U} + \frac{\left(\frac{1}{2} - 2\frac{1}{4}\right)}{2\frac{1}{4}}\Delta t\, C.\,{}^{t}\ddot{U}
$$

$$
-\frac{\frac{1}{2}}{\frac{1}{4}\,\Delta t}\,C.\left({}^{t+\Delta t}U^{(i-1)} - {}^{t}U\right)
$$

and expanded:

$$
{}^{t+\Delta t}\Delta\overline{\mathbf{R}}^{(i-1)} = {}^{t+\Delta t}\mathbf{R} - {}^{t+\Delta t}\mathbf{F}^{(i-1)} - \mathbf{M}.\left(\frac{4}{\Delta t^2}\left({}^{t+\Delta t}\mathbf{U}^{(i-1)} - {}^{t}\mathbf{U}\right) - \frac{4}{\Delta t}\,{}^{t}\dot{\mathbf{U}} - {}^{t}\ddot{\mathbf{U}}\right)
$$
$$
- \mathbf{C}.\left(\frac{2}{\Delta t}\left({}^{t+\Delta t}\mathbf{U}^{(i-1)} - {}^{t}\mathbf{U}\right) - {}^{t}\dot{\mathbf{U}}\right)
$$

(6.30)

The same applied for (6.29):

$$
{}^{t+\Delta t}\overline{\mathbf{K}}^{(i-1)} = {}^{t+\Delta t}\mathbf{K}^{(i-1)} + \frac{4}{\Delta t^2}\,\mathbf{M} + \frac{2}{\Delta t}\,\mathbf{C}
$$

(6.31)

The equations (6.30) and (6.31) with ${}^{t+\Delta t}\Delta\overline{\mathbf{R}}^{(i-1)} = {}^{t+\Delta t}\overline{\mathbf{K}}^{(i-1)}.\Delta\mathbf{U}^{(i)}$ derived in (6.24) describe the trapezoid rule with full Newton-Raphson iteration. The same notation of the trapezoid rule can be found in, e.g., (Bathe, 2002).

6.3.3   REARRANGEMENT OF THE GIVEN HHT-α FORMULATION FOR THE IMPLEMENTATION

The HHT-α formulation given in (6.28) and (6.29) is rearranged here. The aim is to obtain a notation similar to the linear context of the HHT-α method given in (6.13) and (6.14). For this purpose (6.24) is multiplied with $\beta\,\Delta t^2$. So that ${}^{t+\Delta t}\overline{\mathbf{K}}^{(i-1)}$ is given as:

$$
{}^{t+\Delta t}\overline{\mathbf{K}}^{(i-1)} = \mathbf{M} + (1+\alpha)\,\beta\,\Delta t^2\,{}^{t+\Delta t}\mathbf{K}^{(i-1)} + (1+\alpha)\,\Delta t\,\gamma\mathbf{C}
$$

(6.32)

This is the same notation as in (6.14). Only the stiffness matrix is updated every iteration.

A similar rearrangement is done for ${}^{t+\Delta t}\Delta\overline{\mathbf{R}}^{(i-1)}$ in the following. Equation (6.28) is subdivided into several terms. Then terms are rearranged and multiplied with $\beta\,\Delta t^2$ (partially with coloring for better readability):

$$
{}^{t+\Delta t}\Delta\overline{\mathbf{R}}^{(i-1)} =
$$

$$
(1+\alpha)\left({}^{t+\Delta t}\mathbf{R} - {}^{t+\Delta t}\mathbf{F}^{(i-1)}\right) - \alpha\left({}^{t}\mathbf{R} - {}^{t}\mathbf{F}\right) \qquad\qquad\qquad \textit{term (6.28)-1}
$$

$$
+\mathbf{M}.\left[\frac{1}{\beta\,\Delta t}\,{}^{t}\dot{\mathbf{U}} + \frac{1-2\beta}{2\beta}\,{}^{t}\ddot{\mathbf{U}}\right] - \frac{1}{\beta\,\Delta t^2}\,\mathbf{M}.\left({}^{t+\Delta t}\mathbf{U}^{(i-1)} - {}^{t}\mathbf{U}\right) \qquad \textit{term (6.28)-2}
$$

$$
+\left(-1 + (1+\alpha)\,\frac{\gamma}{\beta}\right)\mathbf{C}.\,{}^{t}\dot{\mathbf{U}} \qquad\qquad\qquad\qquad\qquad \textit{term (6.28)-3}
$$

$$
+\frac{(1+\alpha)(\gamma-2\beta)}{2\beta}\,\Delta t\,\mathbf{C}.\,{}^{t}\ddot{\mathbf{U}} \qquad\qquad\qquad\qquad\qquad \textit{term (6.28)-4}
$$

$$
-(1+\alpha)\,\frac{\gamma}{\beta\,\Delta t}\,\mathbf{C}.\left({}^{t+\Delta t}\mathbf{U}^{(i-1)} - {}^{t}\mathbf{U}\right) \qquad\qquad\qquad\qquad \textit{term (6.28)-5}
$$

Term (6.28)-1 with $\beta \, \Delta t^2$:

$$\beta \, \Delta t^2 \left[(1 + \alpha) \left({}^{t+\Delta t}\boldsymbol{R} - {}^{t+\Delta t}\boldsymbol{F}^{(i-1)} \right) - \alpha \left({}^{t}\boldsymbol{R} - {}^{t}\boldsymbol{F} \right) \right]$$

$$= \alpha \beta \, \Delta t^2 \; {}^{t}\boldsymbol{F} + (1 + \alpha) \, \beta \, \Delta t^2 \left({}^{t+\Delta t}\boldsymbol{R} - {}^{t+\Delta t}\boldsymbol{F}^{(i-1)} \right) - \alpha \beta \, \Delta t^2 \; {}^{t}\boldsymbol{R}$$

Term (6.28)-2 with $\beta \, \Delta t^2$:

$$\beta \, \Delta t^2 \left[+\boldsymbol{M}. \left[\frac{1}{\beta \, \Delta t} \; {}^{t}\dot{\boldsymbol{U}} + \frac{1 - 2\beta}{2\beta} \; {}^{t}\ddot{\boldsymbol{U}} \right] - \frac{1}{\beta \, \Delta t^2} \, \boldsymbol{M}. \left({}^{t+\Delta t}\boldsymbol{U}^{(i-1)} - {}^{t}\boldsymbol{U} \right) \right]$$

$$= \boldsymbol{M}. \left[\Delta t \; {}^{t}\dot{\boldsymbol{U}} + \beta \, \Delta t^2 \left(\frac{1}{2\beta} - 1 \right) \; {}^{t}\ddot{\boldsymbol{U}} - \left({}^{t+\Delta t}\boldsymbol{U}^{(i-1)} - {}^{t}\boldsymbol{U} \right) \right]$$

$$= \boldsymbol{M}. \left[{}^{t}\boldsymbol{U} + \Delta t \; {}^{t}\dot{\boldsymbol{U}} + \Delta t^2 \left(\frac{1}{2} - \beta \right) \; {}^{t}\ddot{\boldsymbol{U}} \right] - \boldsymbol{M}. {}^{t+\Delta t}\boldsymbol{U}^{(i-1)} \Rightarrow with \ (6.9)$$

$$= \boldsymbol{M}. {}^{t+\Delta t}\tilde{\boldsymbol{U}} - \boldsymbol{M}. {}^{t+\Delta t}\boldsymbol{U}^{(i-1)}$$

Term (6.28)-3:

$$\left(-1 + (1 + \alpha) \, \frac{\gamma}{\beta} \right) \boldsymbol{C}. \; {}^{t}\dot{\boldsymbol{U}}$$

$$= \left(\frac{\gamma}{\beta} + \alpha \frac{\gamma}{\beta} - 1 - \alpha + \alpha \right) \boldsymbol{C}. \; {}^{t}\dot{\boldsymbol{U}}$$

$$= \boldsymbol{C}. \; {}^{t}\dot{\boldsymbol{U}} \left(\frac{\gamma}{\beta} + \alpha \frac{\gamma}{\beta} - 1 - \alpha \right) + \alpha \boldsymbol{C}. \; {}^{t}\dot{\boldsymbol{U}}$$

$$= \boldsymbol{C}. \; {}^{t}\dot{\boldsymbol{U}} \left(\frac{\gamma}{\beta} (1 + \alpha) - (1 + \alpha) \right) + \alpha \boldsymbol{C}. \; {}^{t}\dot{\boldsymbol{U}}$$

$$= (1 + \alpha) \, \frac{\gamma}{\beta} \, \boldsymbol{C}. \; {}^{t}\dot{\boldsymbol{U}} - (1 + \alpha) \, \boldsymbol{C}. \; {}^{t}\dot{\boldsymbol{U}} + \alpha \boldsymbol{C}. \; {}^{t}\dot{\boldsymbol{U}}$$

Term (6.28)-4:

$$\frac{(1 + \alpha)(\gamma - 2\beta)}{2\beta} \Delta t \, \boldsymbol{C}. \; {}^{t}\ddot{\boldsymbol{U}}$$

$$= \Delta t \, (1 + \alpha) \, (\frac{\gamma}{2\beta} - 1) \, \boldsymbol{C}. \; {}^{t}\ddot{\boldsymbol{U}}$$

$$= \Delta t \, (1 + \alpha) \, (\frac{\gamma}{2\beta} - \gamma - 1 + \gamma) \, \boldsymbol{C}. \; {}^{t}\ddot{\boldsymbol{U}}$$

$$= \Delta t \, (1 + \alpha) \left(\frac{\gamma}{\beta} \left(\frac{1}{2} - \beta \right) - (1 - \gamma) \right) \boldsymbol{C}. \; {}^{t}\ddot{\boldsymbol{U}}$$

$$= \Delta t \, \boldsymbol{C}. \; {}^{t}\ddot{\boldsymbol{U}} \left((1 + \alpha) \, \frac{\gamma}{\beta} \left(\frac{1}{2} - \beta \right) - (1 - \gamma) \, (1 + \alpha) \right)$$

$$= \Delta t \, (1 + \alpha) \, \frac{\gamma}{\beta} \left(\frac{1}{2} - \beta \right) \, C. \; {}^{t}\ddot{U} - \Delta t \, (1 - \gamma) \, (1 + \alpha) \, C. \; {}^{t}\ddot{U}$$

Term (6.28)-5:

$$-(1 + \alpha) \, \frac{\gamma}{\beta \, \Delta t} \, C. \left({}^{t+\Delta t}U^{(i-1)} - {}^{t}U \right)$$

$$= (1 + \alpha) \, \frac{\gamma}{\beta \, \Delta t} \, C. \; {}^{t}U - (1 + \alpha) \, \frac{\gamma}{\beta \, \Delta t} C. \; {}^{t+\Delta t}U^{(i-1)}$$

The terms (6.28)-3 until (6.28)-5 are now summarized to a single term:

$$(1 + \alpha) \, \frac{\gamma}{\beta} \, C. \; {}^{t}\dot{U} - (1 + \alpha) \, C. \; {}^{t}\dot{U} + \alpha C. \; {}^{t}\dot{U}$$

$$+ \Delta t \, (1 + \alpha) \, \frac{\gamma}{\beta} \left(\frac{1}{2} - \beta \right) \, C. \; {}^{t}\ddot{U} - \Delta t \, (1 - \gamma) \, (1 + \alpha) \, C. \; {}^{t}\ddot{U}$$

$$+ (1 + \alpha) \, \frac{\gamma}{\beta \, \Delta t} \, C. \; {}^{t}U - (1 + \alpha) \, \frac{\gamma}{\beta \, \Delta t} C. \; {}^{t+\Delta t}U^{(i-1)}$$

and rearranged to:

$$(1 + \alpha) \, \frac{\gamma}{\beta \, \Delta t} \, C. \; {}^{t}U + (1 + \alpha) \, \frac{\gamma}{\beta} \, C. \; {}^{t}\dot{U} + \Delta t \, (1 + \alpha) \, \frac{\gamma}{\beta} \left(\frac{1}{2} - \beta \right) \, C. \; {}^{t}\ddot{U}$$

$$-(1 + \alpha) \, C. \; {}^{t}\dot{U} - \Delta t \, (1 - \gamma) \, (1 + \alpha) \, C. \; {}^{t}\ddot{U} + \alpha C. \; {}^{t}\dot{U} - (1 + \alpha) \, \frac{\gamma}{\beta \, \Delta t} C. \; {}^{t+\Delta t}U^{(i-1)}$$

and further without color:

$$C. \left[(1 + \alpha) \, \frac{\gamma}{\beta \, \Delta t} \; {}^{t}U + (1 + \alpha) \, \frac{\gamma}{\beta} \; {}^{t}\dot{U} + \Delta t \, (1 + \alpha) \, \frac{\gamma}{\beta} \left(\frac{1}{2} - \beta \right) \; {}^{t}\ddot{U} \right]$$

$$-(1 + \alpha) \, C. \left[{}^{t}\dot{U} + \Delta t \, (1 - \gamma) \; {}^{t}\ddot{U} \right] + \alpha C. \; {}^{t}\dot{U} - (1 + \alpha) \, \frac{\gamma}{\beta \, \Delta t} C. \; {}^{t+\Delta t}U^{(i-1)}$$

with excluded $\frac{\gamma}{\beta \, \Delta t}$ in the first row:

$$(1 + \alpha) \, \frac{\gamma}{\beta \, \Delta t} \, C. \left[{}^{t}U + \Delta t \; {}^{t}\dot{U} + \Delta t^2 \left(\frac{1}{2} - \beta \right) \; {}^{t}\ddot{U} \right]$$

$$-(1 + \alpha) \, C. \left[{}^{t}\dot{U} + \Delta t \, (1 - \gamma) \; {}^{t}\ddot{U} \right] + \alpha C. \; {}^{t}\dot{U} - (1 + \alpha) \, \frac{\gamma}{\beta \, \Delta t} C. \; {}^{t+\Delta t}U^{(i-1)}$$

and multiplied with $\beta \, \Delta t^2$:

$$(1 + \alpha) \, \gamma \Delta t \, C. \left[{}^{t}U + \Delta t \; {}^{t}\dot{U} + \Delta t^2 \left(\frac{1}{2} - \beta \right) \; {}^{t}\ddot{U} \right]$$

$$-(1 + \alpha) \, \beta \, \Delta t^2 \, C. \left[{}^{t}\dot{U} + \Delta t \, (1 - \gamma) \; {}^{t}\ddot{U} \right] + \alpha \beta \, \Delta t^2 C. \; {}^{t}\dot{U} - (1 + \alpha) \, \gamma \Delta t \, C. \; {}^{t+\Delta t}U^{(i-1)}$$

Now, the equations (6.9) and (6.10) are replaced:

$$(1 + \alpha)\,\gamma \Delta t\,C.^{t+\Delta t}\widetilde{U} - (1 + \alpha)\,\beta\,\Delta t^2\,C.^{t+\Delta t}\widetilde{U} + \alpha\beta\,\Delta t^2 C.^{t}\dot{U}$$

$$-(1 + \alpha)\,\gamma \Delta t\,C.^{t+\Delta t}U^{(i-1)}$$

All terms [(6.28)-1 until (6.28)-5] are summarized to one equation for $^{t+\Delta t}\Delta\overline{R}^{(i-1)}$ now:

$$^{t+\Delta t}\Delta\overline{R}^{(i-1)} = \alpha\beta\,\Delta t^2\,{}^{t}F + (1 + \alpha)\,\beta\,\Delta t^2\left(^{t+\Delta t}R - {}^{t+\Delta t}F^{(i-1)}\right) - \alpha\beta\,\Delta t^2\,{}^{t}R$$

$$+M.^{t+\Delta t}\widetilde{U} - M.^{t+\Delta t}U^{(i-1)}$$

$$(1 + \alpha)\,\gamma \Delta t\,C.^{t+\Delta t}\widetilde{U}$$

$$-(1 + \alpha)\,\beta\,\Delta t^2\,C.^{t+\Delta t}\widetilde{U} + \alpha\beta\,\Delta t^2 C.^{t}\dot{U} - (1 + \alpha)\,\gamma \Delta t\,C.^{t+\Delta t}U^{(i-1)}$$

rearranged to:

$$^{t+\Delta t}\Delta\overline{R}^{(i-1)} =$$

$$(M + (1 + \alpha)\,\gamma \Delta t\,C).^{t+\Delta t}\widetilde{U} - (1 + \alpha)\,\beta\,\Delta t^2\,C.^{t+\Delta t}\widetilde{U} + \alpha\beta\,\Delta t^2(C.^{t}\dot{U} + {}^{t}F)$$

$$\overbrace{+(1 + \alpha)\,\beta\,\Delta t^2\left(^{t+\Delta t}R - {}^{t+\Delta t}F^{(i-1)}\right) - \alpha\beta\,\Delta t^2\,{}^{t}R}^{additional}$$

$$\overbrace{-M.^{t+\Delta t}U^{(i-1)}}^{additional}$$

$$\overbrace{-(1 + \alpha)\,\gamma \Delta t\,C.^{t+\Delta t}U^{(i-1)}}^{additional} \qquad (6.33)$$

The denoted terms in (6.33) are additional to the linear notation of $^{t+\Delta t}\Delta\overline{R}^{(i-1)}$, which is given in (6.14). The first additional part relates to the term:

$$(1 + \alpha)\,\beta\,\Delta t^{2\,t+\Delta t}R - \alpha\beta\,\Delta t^2\,{}^{t}R$$

in (6.13) accordingly to the nonlinear context. The stiffness matrix ^{t}F relates to the same as in the linear notation only with updated stiffness matrix ($^{t}F = {}^{t}K.\,^{t}U$).

When $\Delta U^{(i)}$ is calculated from (6.32) and (6.33) with (6.24), the displacements $^{t+\Delta t}U^{(i)}$ are updated with (6.22). At the end of the time step the accelerations and velocities can be updated with (6.11) and (6.12) :

$$^{t+\Delta t}\ddot{U} = \left(^{t+\Delta t}U^{(max.i)} - {}^{t+\Delta t}\widetilde{U}\right)\frac{1}{\beta\,\Delta t^2} \qquad (6.34)$$

$$\boxed{{}^{t+\Delta t}\dot{U} = {}^{t+\Delta t}\widetilde{\dot{U}} + \frac{\gamma}{\beta\,\Delta t}\left({}^{t+\Delta t}U^{(max.i)} - {}^{t+\Delta t}\widetilde{U}\right)}$$

(6.35)

where the index $(max.i)$ means that equilibrium is reached. The variables ${}^{t+\Delta t}\widetilde{U}$ and ${}^{t+\Delta t}\widetilde{\dot{U}}$ are given by (6.9) and (6.10).

6.4   INCREMENTAL CALCULATION SCHEME FOR DYNAMIC CASE

The following Table 6.1 shows a scheme for the evaluation of ${}^{t+\Delta t}\overline{K}^{(i-1)}$ and ${}^{t+\Delta t}\Delta\overline{R}^{(i-1)}$ for the dynamic case. Table 6.1 is an extension of Table 5.7.

Table 6.1 takes into consideration the fact that the external loads R can be time dependent. Hence, external loads from the last time ${}^{t}R$ step are contained. Further simplifications in Table 6.1 are possible if loads are not time dependent (${}^{t}R = {}^{t+\Delta t}R$).

For the nonlinear HHT-α method Equation (6.6) is also used where α is chosen as $\alpha = -0.05$ (Hibbitt & Karlsson, 25-29 June, 1979) and (Hibbitt & Karlsson, Nov. 1979). Setting α to zero yields the Newmark method in an implicit scheme.

For an incremental calculation scheme the equations (6.32), (6.33), (6.34) and (6.35) are further summarized in Table 6.1 with the use of the following integration constants:

$$\boxed{\begin{aligned}
a_0 &= \frac{1}{\beta\,\Delta t^2} \\[2mm]
a_1 &= \left(\frac{1}{2} - \beta\right)\Delta t^2 \\[2mm]
a_2 &= \Delta t\,(1 - \gamma) \\[2mm]
a_3 &= \gamma\,\Delta t \\[2mm]
a_4 &= \beta\,\Delta t^2\,\alpha \\[2mm]
a_5 &= (1 + \alpha)\,\beta\,\Delta t^2 \\[2mm]
a_6 &= \beta\,\Delta t^2 \\[2mm]
a_7 &= (1 + \alpha)\,a_3
\end{aligned}}$$

(6.36)

Table 6.1 is implemented in the used program system as given here. A robust and efficient algorithm which combines plastic calculations in time domain is given by the table.

Loop A: Loop over all time steps

{

Time steps:

$$^{t+\Delta t}R = constant\ loads + variable\ loads$$

$$^{t+\Delta t}\widetilde{U} = \ ^tU + \Delta t\ ^t\dot{U} + a_1\ ^t\ddot{U}$$

$$^{t+\Delta t}\widetilde{\dot{U}} = \ ^t\dot{U} + a_2\ ^t\ddot{U}$$

Initial value for $^{t+\Delta t}U^{(i)}$ *to calculate flow limit:*

$$^{t+\Delta t}U^{(0)} = \ ^tU + {}^{t+\Delta t}\overline{K}^{(i-1)}.\ ^{t+\Delta t}\Delta\overline{R}^{(i-1)}$$

Loop B: Loop over all equilibrium iterations

{

Initial:

$$i = 1,\ ^{t+\Delta t}F^{(i-1)} = 0,\ ^{t+\Delta t}K^{(i-1)} = 0$$

Loop C: Loop over all finite elements and all integration points

{

$^{t+\Delta t}K^{(i-1)}$ *and* $^{t+\Delta t}F^{(i-1)}$ *are determined as in Table 5.7*

} End of Loop C

Determine $^{t+\Delta t}\overline{K}^{(i-1)}$ *and* $^{t+\Delta t}\Delta\overline{R}^{(i-1)}$

$$^{t+\Delta t}\overline{K}^{(i-1)} = \ M + a_5\ ^{t+\Delta t}K^{(i-1)} + a_7\ C$$

$$^{t+\Delta t}\Delta\overline{R}^{(i-1)} = (M + a_7\ C).\ ^{t+\Delta t}\widetilde{U} - a_5\ C.\ ^{t+\Delta t}\widetilde{\dot{U}} + a_4\left(C.\ ^t\dot{U} + \ ^tF\right)$$

$$+a_5\left(^{t+\Delta t}R - \ ^{t+\Delta t}F^{(i-1)}\right) - a_4\ ^tR - M.\ ^{t+\Delta t}U^{(i-1)} - a_7\ C.\ ^{t+\Delta t}U^{(i-1)}$$

Apply Newton– Raphson Scheme to calculate the increment of displacements:

$$\Delta U^{(i)} = \ ^{t+\Delta t}\overline{K}^{(i-1)-1}.\ ^{t+\Delta t}\Delta\overline{R}^{(i-1)}$$

$$^{t+\Delta t}U^{(i)} = \ ^{t+\Delta t}U^{(i-1)} + \Delta U^{(i)}$$

Check convergence:

$$\left\|\Delta U^{(i)}\right\| < 10^{-12}$$

If the convergence criteria are satisfied, abort Loop B and go to Loop A.

$$i = max.\,iteration$$

Else:

$$i\ =\ i + 1$$

} End of Loop B

Update displacements, accelerations, velocities and loads

$${}^{t}U\ =\ {}^{t+\Delta t}U^{(max.iteration)}$$

$${}^{t}\ddot{U} = a_0 \left({}^{t}U - {}^{t+\Delta t}\widetilde{U} \right)$$

$${}^{t}\dot{U}\ =\ {}^{t+\Delta t}\widetilde{\dot{U}}\ + a_3\ {}^{t}U$$

$${}^{t}F = {}^{t+\Delta t}F^{(i-1)}$$

$${}^{t}R = {}^{t+\Delta t}R$$

} End of Loop A

TABLE 6.1. INCREMENTAL DYNAMIC CALCULATION SCHEME FOR MATERIAL NONLINEAR PROBLEMS

7 SCALED BOUNDARY FINITE ELEMENT METHOD

Introduction: Infinite or semi-infinite mediums have to be analyzed in many physical domains. Difficulties occur in a complete analysis while considering the dynamic response of these unbounded domains. The dynamic response is specifically related to wave propagations in an elastic half space. Half space means that one part of the domain is bounded and the other part of the domain is infinite. Problems of wave propagations in infinite domains can be solved with the *scaled boundary finite element method (SBFEM)*. First proceedings with basic ideas in this topic were made by (Silvester, Lowther, Carpenter, & Wyatt, 1977) , (Thatcher, 1978), (Dasgupta, 1982). The SBFEM was originally formulated under the name *consistent infinitesimal finite element cell method* by (Wolf & Song, 1996).

Soil-structure interactions are analyzed in this work as a specific case of the wave propagation problems. Time dependent excitations of the structure due to wind, traffic or earthquakes are damped by the soil.

Advantages of the SBFEM and comparison with other methods: Modeling a structure with the FEM is easy and widely investigated, but the modeling of the unbounded medium soil presents a problem. A special problem of the FEM is to include the radiation condition at infinity. The radiation condition ensures that no energy from infinity is absorbed by the considered domain.

The finite element method cannot represent the radiation condition exactly. Here reflections occur at the artificial boundaries. Some other calculation methods, such as the boundary element method (BEM) have been developed to solve this problem (see Section 1.2.2). However, for the BEM the so-called *fundamental solution* is needed. This fundamental solution does not exist for all domains. Furthermore, the occurring system matrices in the BEM are non-symmetric and fully populated.

The SBFEM can represent the radiation condition, needs no fundamental solution and the system matrices are symmetric. The system matrices in the FEM are also symmetric. Hence, a coupling of the FEM with the SBFEM is possible to combine the advantages of both methods.

7.1 FUNDAMENTALS OF THE SCALED BOUNDARY FINITE ELEMENT METHOD

The approach of modeling is pictured in Figure 7.1. The structure and the near-field are discretized with the FEM. Both parts can contain nonlinear behavior. In this work the near-field contains the nonlinear behavior. The structure/soil interface can model specific behavior, as friction or contact, between structure and soil. This is not considered in this work. Moreover, the near-field/far-field interface transfers the dynamic interactions to the infinite far-field. In the backwards case incident waves from earthquakes or underground explosions can be transferred from the far-field to the structure. The far-field can only contain linear behavior. It is also possible to abandon the near-field, but in this case for adequate accuracy a strong boundary condition has to be maintained.

The boundary condition on the near-field/far-field interface relates to an interaction force/displacement relationship. With changing displacement the interactions force changes. This is also known as stiffness relationship. In time domain the interaction force and the displacement to a time t are dependent on the load history. To yield the interaction force R in time domain the following convolution integral is given (Wolf & Song, 1996):

$$R(t) = \int_0^t M^\infty(t - \sigma)\, \ddot{U}(\sigma)d\sigma \qquad\qquad (7.1)$$

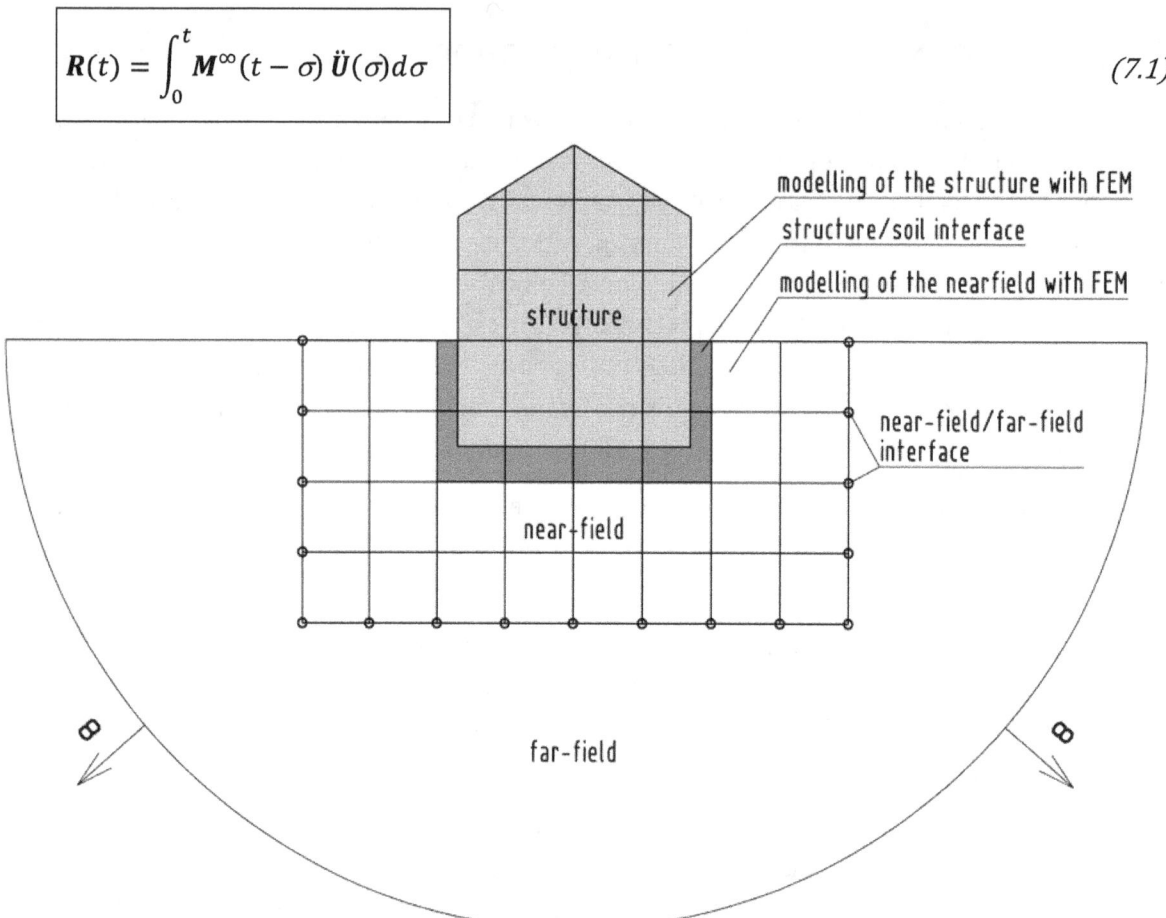

FIGURE 7.1. SOIL STRUCTRURE INTERACTION MODELING WITH COUPLED FEM/SBFEM APPROACH

In this convolution integral the integration operator yields with the functions of the acceleration unit impulse response matrix $M^\infty(t - \sigma)$ and the acceleration $\ddot{U}(\sigma)$ the function of the interaction force $R(t)$. The aim of the SBFEM in the time domain is to determine $M^\infty(t - \sigma)$.

For the derivation of the acceleration unit impulse response matrix a similar fictitious boundary is introduced, as pictured in Figure 7.2. The location of the internal boundary (near-field/far-field interface) and the fictitious external boundary is defined by length r_i and the length r_e from the so-called scaling center "O". For the derivation the area between the two boundaries is filled with finite elements. Then the limit of the finite element cell width $r_e - r_i$ towards zero is performed analytically. The postulation of equilibrium and compatibility for the finite elements yields with a similarity transformation to the unit impulse response matrix. The unit impulse response matrix is then expressed as a function of the mass matrix and stiffness matrix of the finite elements. The piecewise analytical derivation shows that the SBFEM can be seen as a semi-analytical method. In radial direction from the scaling center "O" the solution is performed analytically and in the other directions the calculation is performed numerically.

This is only a short introduction to the topic. A detailed description of the derivation of the unit impulse response matrix is given in (Wolf & Song, 1996) or (Wolf, 2003).

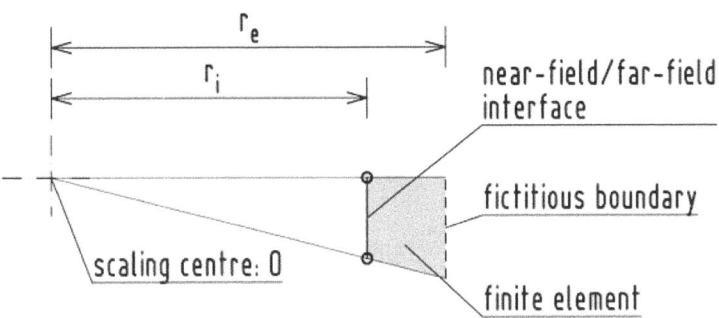

FIGURE 7.2. DERIVATION OF ONE SBFEM ELEMENT

7.2 FEM/SBFEM COUPLING

Here, a short overview of FEM/SBFEM coupling is given. The implementation of the unit impulse response matrix is not the focus of this work. Here, the already implemented calculation of the unit impulse response matrix in the form of the program system *SIMILAR* (see (Wolf & Song, 1996)) is used. As mentioned, the modeling of the structure and the near-field is performed by the FEM and the modeling of the far-field is performed by the SBFEM.

When FEM and SBFEM are coupled, the entities of the matrices in (6.1) have to be sorted into near-field and the far-field part of the matrix:

$$\begin{bmatrix} M_{nn} & M_{nf} \\ M_{fn} & M_{ff} \end{bmatrix} \cdot \ddot{U} + \begin{bmatrix} C_{nn} & C_{nf} \\ C_{fn} & C_{ff} \end{bmatrix} \cdot \dot{U} + \begin{bmatrix} K_{nn} & K_{nf} \\ K_{fn} & K_{ff} \end{bmatrix} \cdot U = \begin{bmatrix} R_{nn} \\ R_{ff} \end{bmatrix} \tag{7.2}$$

The index nn represents nodes at the near-field and ff represents nodes at the far-field. Coupled near-field/far-field nodes are denoted by the index nf or fn. The forces at the near-field/far-field interface $R(t)$ are given by (7.1). To solve the convolution integral in (7.1) a piecewise constant approximation of M^∞ is assumed:

$$M^\infty(t) = \begin{cases} M_0^\infty & t \in (0; \Delta t) \\ M_1^\infty & t \in (\Delta t; 2\Delta t) \\ \quad \cdot \\ \quad \cdot \\ \quad \cdot \\ M_n^\infty & t \in ([n-1]\Delta t; n\,\Delta t) \end{cases} \tag{7.3}$$

With (7.3) the convolution integral (7.1) can be written in the discrete form as:

$$R(t) = \sum_{j=1}^{n} M_{n-j}^\infty \int_{(j-1)\Delta t}^{j\,\Delta t} \ddot{U}(\sigma)d\sigma = \sum_{j=1}^{n} M_{n-j}^\infty (\ddot{U}_j - \ddot{U}_{j-1}) \tag{7.4}$$

When the α-parameter of the HHT-α method from Section 6.2 is introduced, and the unknown acceleration vector $\ddot{U}_n$ for the time step n is separated, the interaction force $R(t)$ is calculated with:

$$R(t) = \alpha\,\Delta t\,M_0^\infty\,\ddot{U}_n + \sum_{j=1}^{n} M_{n-j}^\infty (\ddot{U}_j - \ddot{U}_{j-1}) = \alpha\,\Delta t\,M_0^\infty\,\ddot{U}_n + \hat{R} \tag{7.5}$$

$\widehat{R}$ are the loads on the near-field/far-field interface which occur by the infinite domain. Now the coupling of FEM and SBFEM is done by adding (7.5) to (7.2) at the far-field nodes:

$$\begin{bmatrix} M_{nn} & M_{nf} \\ M_{fn} & M_{ff} + \alpha\,\Delta t\,M_0^\infty \end{bmatrix} \cdot \ddot{U} + \begin{bmatrix} C_{nn} & C_{nf} \\ C_{fn} & C_{ff} \end{bmatrix} \cdot \dot{U} + \begin{bmatrix} K_{nn} & K_{nf} \\ K_{fn} & K_{ff} \end{bmatrix} \cdot U = \begin{bmatrix} R_{nn} \\ R_{ff} - \widehat{R} \end{bmatrix} \qquad (7.6)$$

For a long simulation time the calculation of (7.2) needs a large computational effort. A faster algorithm is given by (Lehmann, 2007). An approximation of M_{n-j}^∞ in time is suggested here. The change of the entries of M_{n-j}^∞ is then approximated by a linear function from a certain time step.

7.3   INCREMENTAL CALCULATION SCHEME FOR DYNAMIC CASE WITH INCLUDED SBFEM

The calculation scheme from Table 6.1 is extended here for a coupled FEM/SBFEM model.

Initial calculation:

$$M = M + \begin{bmatrix} M_{nn} & M_{nf} \\ M_{fn} & M_{ff} + \alpha\,\Delta t\,M_0^\infty \end{bmatrix} \cdot {}^t\ddot{U}$$

Loop A: Loop over all time steps

{

Time steps:

$${}^{t+\Delta t}R = constant\ loads + variable\ loads$$

$${}^{t+\Delta t}\widehat{R} = \sum_{j=1}^{n} M_{n-j}^\infty \left({}^{t+\Delta t}\ddot{U}_j - {}^{t+\Delta t}\ddot{U}_{j-1} \right)$$

$${}^{t+\Delta t}R = \begin{bmatrix} {}^{t+\Delta t}R_{nn} \\ {}^{t+\Delta t}R_{ff} - {}^{t+\Delta t}\widehat{R} \end{bmatrix}$$

...same calculations as given in Table 6.1

} End of Loop A

TABLE 7.1. INCREMENTAL DYNAMIC CALCULATION SCHEME FOR MATERIAL NONLINEAR PROBLEMS WITH INCLUDED SBFEM

With the calculation scheme of Table 7.1 it is possible to simulate elasto-plastic soil-structure interaction with included wave radiation. The scheme presents a new approach due to the different included calculation methods. Table 7.1 incorporates Table 6.1 and Table 5.7. Table 7.1 includes the SBFEM, Table 6.1 the dynamic effects and Table 5.7 the elasto-plastic material calculation. The examples of Part II are calculated with Table 7.1.

II APPLICATION

8 Introduction to The Example Calculations

The examples of Part II are constrained to the calculation of shallow foundations. This shows the basic use of the elasto-plastic FEM/SBFEM method combined here with the extended HHT-α procedure.

The modeling of other geotechnical construction elements, such as piles or retaining walls, is more complicated. This requires additional special calculation procedures, such as contact and friction, which are not available here.

For the implementation a program system is employed which was developed at the "*Institute of Applied Mechanics of the Technical University of Braunschweig*". This program system consists of different calculation parts for specific problems.

Here, for the calculation of the influence matrix the contained program SIMILAR (Wolf & Song, 1996) is used. The program system provided the means for an elastic FEM calculation (Clasen, 2008) of 3D elements.

One aim of this work is the extension of the linear FEM calculation to an elasto-plastic FEM calculation for 3D elements. This is done with the implementation of the calculation schemes of Table 5.7, Table 6.1 and Table 7.1 with the included formulas for 3D FEM elements into this program system.

8.1 Verification With Commercial FEM Software ABAQUS® (2004)

8.1.1 Derivation of the Conversion Equations

The verification of the implemented program code is done with the commercial program system ABAQUS® (ABAQUS® User's Manual, ABAQUS®/Standard User's Manual, Version 6.5, 2004). The cap model in ABAQUS® is slightly different from the cap model given in Chapter 5. Hence, a comparison between the two models is given here. In Figure 8.1 the two models are pictured.

The horizontal and vertical axes have to be converted. From the ABAQUS® manual (ABAQUS® User's Manual, ABAQUS®/Standard User's Manual, Version 6.5, 2004) the following is given for p and t:

$$t = \frac{1}{2} q \left[1 + \frac{1}{K} - \left(1 - \frac{1}{K} \right) \left(\frac{r}{q} \right)^3 \right] \tag{8.1}$$

$$p = -\frac{1}{3} \sigma_{ii} \tag{8.2}$$

with K as shape factor for the yield surface (a circular yield surface in principal stress space, as in the implemented cap model, is obtained with $K = 1$), q as Mises equivalent stress and r as third stress invariant (see ABAQUS® manual).

Conversion from $\sqrt{J_{2D}}$ to t:

If $K = 1$ (see ABAQUS® manual) Equation (8.1) changes to:

$$t = q \tag{8.3}$$

with q as Mises equivalent stress:

$$q = \sqrt{\frac{3}{2} S_{ij} S_{ij}} \qquad (8.4)$$

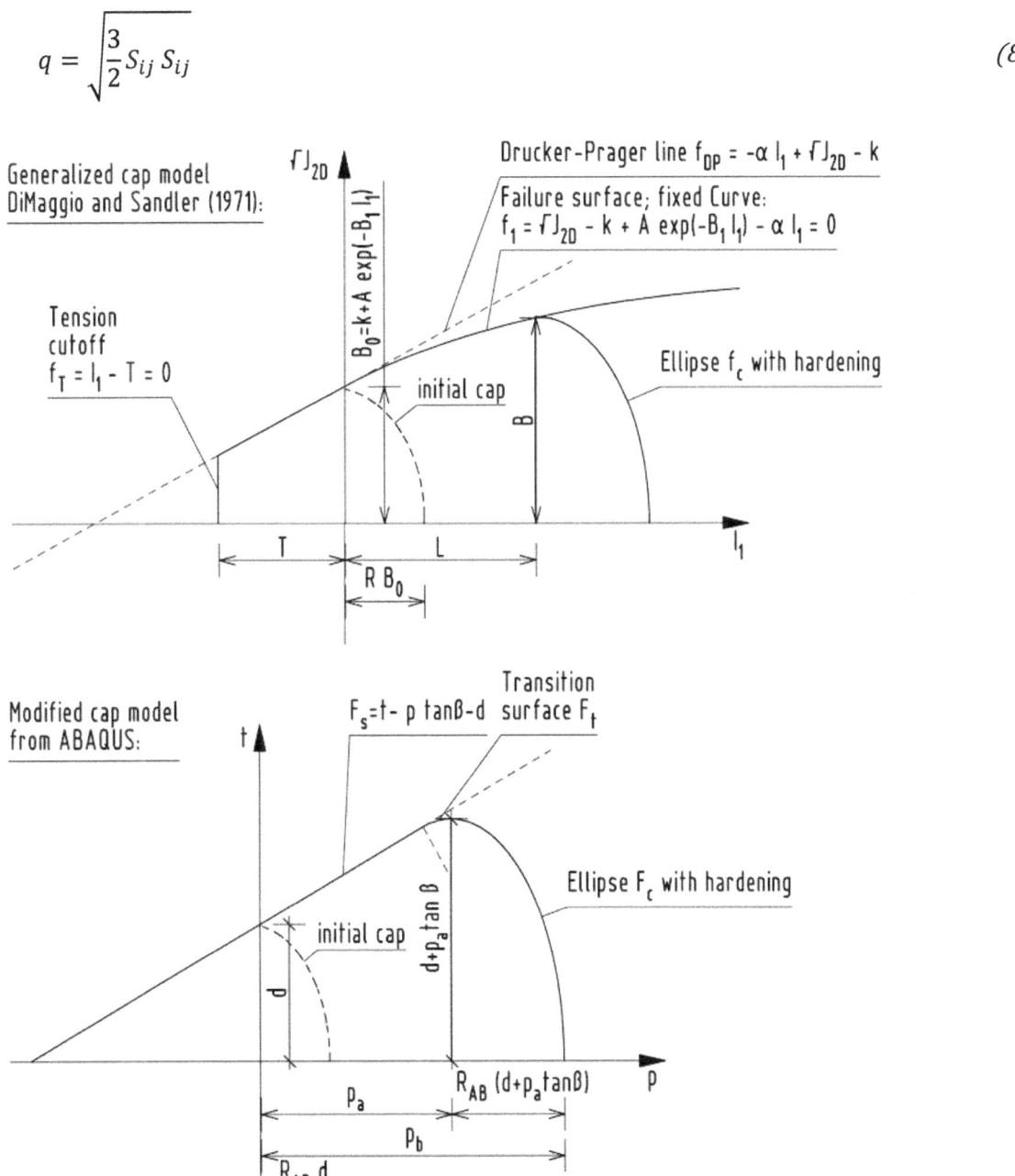

FIGURE 8.1. COMPARISON OF THE ABAQUS® CAP MODEL WITH THE GENRALIZED CAP MODEL

If we rearrange (8.4) and (4.10) which contains $\sqrt{J_{2D}}$ the following relation is given:

$$\sqrt{S_{ij} S_{ij}} = \frac{q}{\sqrt{\frac{3}{2}}} = \frac{\sqrt{J_{2D}}}{\sqrt{\frac{1}{2}}} \Rightarrow q = \sqrt{J_{2D}} \sqrt{\frac{\frac{3}{2}}{\frac{1}{2}}}$$

$$q = t = \sqrt{J_{2D}}\sqrt{3} \qquad\qquad (8.5)$$

Conversion from I_1 to p:

From (8.2) and (4.7) follows:

$$p = -\frac{1}{3}\,I_1 \qquad\qquad (8.6)$$

With (8.5) and (8.6) all conversions to the ABAQUS® cap model can be applied.

Setting the material constant A in (4.13) to zero yields the Drucker-Prager line in (4.11). Figure 8.1 shows that the failure surface in ABAQUS® is then analogous to the *generalized cap model* from (DiMaggio & Sandler, 1971):

$$F_s = t - p\,tan\,\beta - d \Rightarrow f_1 = f_{DP} = \sqrt{J_{2D}} - \alpha I_1 - k \qquad\qquad (8.7)$$

The material constant d follows then from (8.5):

$$d = B_0\,\sqrt{3} \qquad\qquad (8.8)$$

with B_0 as initial position of the cap on the vertical $\sqrt{J_{2D}}$ axis (see Figure 8.1).

And for the ratio between the semi axes of the ellipse R_{AB} in ABAQUS® follows from (8.6):

$$\frac{1}{3}\,R\,B_0 = R_{AB}\,d$$

$$R_{AB} = R\,\frac{B_0}{3\,d} \qquad\qquad (8.9)$$

8.1.2 COMPARISON OF THE SOLUTIONS ON THE FAILURE SURFACE

With (8.8) and (8.9) an analogous yield surface (if A = 0) for the failure surface in ABAQUS® can be obtained from the generalized cap model.

Nevertheless, the solution in Abaqus® will be different to the generalized cap model in the case of *yielding on the failure surface*. This is explained in the context of the associated and non-associated flow rule. As mentioned in Section 4.1.3 the generalized cap model has an associated flow rule and the modified cap model in ABAQUS® has a non-associated flow rule.

8.1.3 COMPARISON OF THE SOLUTIONS OF CAP YIELDING AND VERTEX YIELDING

For the cases of *cap yielding* and *vertex yielding* a very good approximation to the results from ABAQUS® is obtained. In ABAQUS® the cap hardening can be entered piecewise in the form of a stress/strain table. The table data are obtained from (4.16) with regard to (8.6):

$$p = \frac{X}{3} = \frac{-\frac{1}{D}ln\left(1 - \frac{e_V^P}{W}\right) + X_0}{3} \qquad\qquad (8.10)$$

This is graphically represented in Figure 8.2:

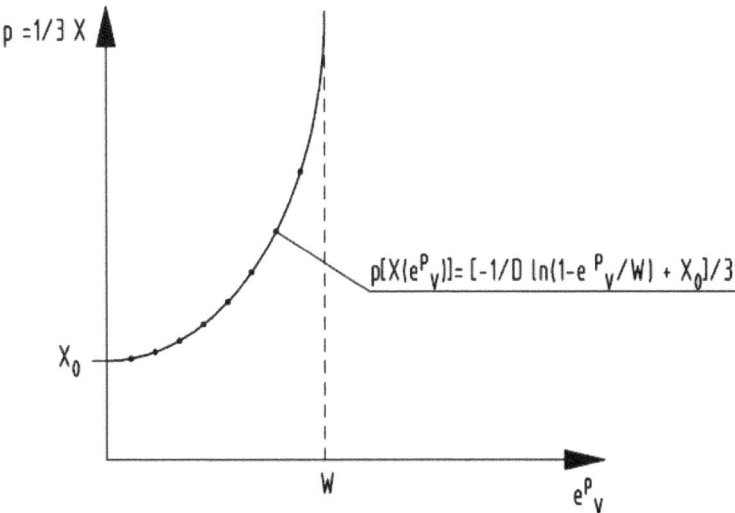

FIGURE 8.2. FUNCTION OF CAP HARDENING

Using (8.10) the data can be entered as discrete values (see Table 9.1).

8.2 EXPLANATORY NOTES TO THE GIVEN EXAMPLES

All calculations are only conducted on theoretical basis. The material properties are extracted from examples in (DiMaggio & Sandler, 1971) or (Desai & Siriwardane, 1984). Except for the density in the Examples 1-3, all material properties are realistic because they are determined experimentally. An unrealistic high density is used in the verification Examples 1-3 to clarify the oscillation behavior. The density in the practical Example 4 relates to the realistic values.

The magnitude of the building ground deformations depends on mechanical properties of the soil and the *current state* of the soil. The *current state* depends on the history of the soil deformation previous to the considered load application. The *current state* can be considered as a *disturbed state* with respect to a defined initial state (Desai, The disturbated state concept, 2001). If two soil samples with the same material properties but different current states are subjected to the same loading, the deformation of the soil samples will be different (see Chapter 12).

Therefore, the loads have to be applied time dependently in their occurring order in dynamic building ground calculations. Nevertheless, this fact is neglected in the Examples 1 to 3 in order to verify the given calculation method. Only the dynamic calculation of Example 4 includes the order of applied loads.

The FE-discretization of the Examples 2 to 4 is very coarse. The results show only the applicability of the given algorithms.

Due to the above mentioned reasons, the Examples 1 to 3 are purely of academic nature and cannot be transferred to real problems.

9 VERIFICATION EXAMPLE 1, ONE ELEMENT

This example is created in order to verify the developed hybrid calculation method. The example is adopted from (Kojic & Bathe, 2005) and (DiMaggio & Sandler, 1971). The same results should be obtained here for the static calculation. The numerical results are verified with experimental results from (DiMaggio & Sandler, 1971). The original U.S. units are converted to SI units here.

9.1 GEOMETRY, LOADING AND BOUNDARY CONDITIONS

The calculated element is pictured in Figure 9.1 with the following properties:

Dimensions: $x/y/z = 0,05 \, m$

Load: vertical unified distributed load with $p = 6895 \, kN/m^2$

Boundary conditions: only vertical displacement of node 5-8 possible

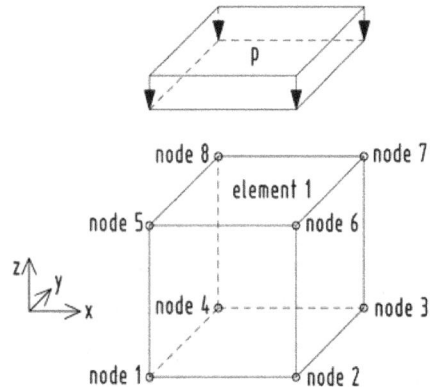

FIGURE 9.1. GEOMETRY OF EXAMPLE 1

9.2 MATERIAL

The following material constants are given (for description see Section 4.1.4):

$$E = 6,89 \, 10^5 \frac{kN}{m^2}; \; v = 0,25; \; \alpha = 0,05; \; k = 1724 \frac{kN}{m^2}; \; A = 1034 \frac{kN}{m^2}; \; B_1 = 0 \left(\frac{kN}{m^2}\right)^{-1};$$

$$D = 0,0001 \left(\frac{kN}{m^2}\right)^{-1}; W = 0,066; \; {}^0L = 0 \frac{kN}{m^2}; R = 2; T = -6,89 \, 10^5 \frac{kN}{m^2}$$

A very high density is chosen to clarify the oscillation behavior: $\rho = 2,77 \, 10^7 \frac{kg}{m^3}$

B_0 follows from (5.23) with $B_0 = 689 \frac{kN}{m^2}$

9.3 MATERIAL PARAMETERS FOR ABAQUS®

In order to perform a simulation with ABAQUS® these material parameters have to be used.

Elastic parameters:

$$E = 6,89 \, 10^5 \frac{kN}{m^2}$$

$$v = 0,25$$

Plastic parameters in ABAQUS® with description (the conversion equations are given in Section 8.1.1):

Material Cohesion: $d = B_0 \sqrt{3} = 689 \sqrt{3} = 1193 \frac{kN}{m^2}$

Angle of Friction: $\beta = ArcTan\left(\frac{\alpha\sqrt{3}}{\frac{1}{3}}\right) = 14{,}56°$

Cap Eccentricity: $R_{AB} = R\frac{B_0}{3\,d} = 2\frac{689}{3\,1193} = 0{,}385$

Initial Yield Surface Position: $0{,}0 \frac{kN}{m^2}$

Transition Surface Rod: $\alpha = 0{,}0$

Flow Stress Ratio: $K = 1$

The cap hardening in ABAQUS® is determined with Equation (8.10):

p	e_V^P
[kN/m²]	[-]
460	0,00
1023	0,01
1698	0,02
2539	0,03
3655	0,04
5321	0,05
8685	0,06
22730	0,066

TABLE 9.1. INPUT VALUES FOR CAP HARDENING IN ABAQUS®

For dynamic calculations the density is set to: $\rho = 2{,}77\ 10^7 \frac{kg}{m^3}$

9.4 RESULTS

All results relate to the vertical values of the displacements, stresses and strains of the upper nodes (displacements) or upper gauss points (stress and strain) of the element (see Figure 9.1).

9.4.1 STATIC CALCULATION

Load steps instead of time steps are applied for the static calculation. For this purpose the element is loaded and unloaded in different load step partitions (10 or 20 linear load increases until the maximum load is reached and 10 linear load decreases until the load is zero).

In Figure 9.2 (illustrated is only the loading and not the unloading) the comparison to results, gained by ABAQUS® simulation is conducted for a load step-displacement diagram and in Figure 9.3 for a strain-stress diagram. Figure 9.3 furthermore contains the results from (Kojic & Bathe, 2005) and the experimental results from (DiMaggio & Sandler, 1971) given as pointed plots.

As pictured in Figure 9.3, the material behaves elastically until a stress of approximately 1000 kN/m² is reached. After this, the stiffness slopes down and the material deforms disproportionately. The used cap model implies isotropic hardening under volumetric pressure. This hardening is visible by an increasing slope at a plastic strain between approximately 0,01 and 0,065. The maximum magnitude of the volumetric plastic strain is given by the material constant $W = 0,066$. If the load is increased to more than the maximum volumetric plastic strain, the material behaves in turn elastically.

The plastic strain after the unloading is given in Figure 9.3 to approximately 0,055. The hysteretic material behavior at the end of the unloading is already visible in the static calculation.

It is recognizable that the numerical calculations (including the *generalized cap model*) conform to the experimental results for loading and unloading. All models predict the hysteretic material behavior under cyclic loading. In the loading part of the *generalized cap model* the material first behaves elastic, then with plastic flow according to *cap yielding* and then with plastic flow according to *vertex yielding*. The unloading part proceeds with elastic unloading and finally with *yielding on failure surface*.

The results of the simulation with ABAQUS® and the generalized cap model are close because *cap yielding* and *vertex yielding* occurs here (see Section 8.1.3). Deviations result from different behavior of yielding on failure surface (see Section 8.1.2) at the end of the unloading, and from the discrete tabular values of the cap hardening in ABAQUS® (see Section 8.1.3). The deviations to the example in (Kojic & Bathe, 2005) result from the modification of Equation (4.17) where the initial position of the cap X_0 is included now.

The hysteretic material behavior under cyclic loading is investigated more closely for dynamic calculations in the following sections.

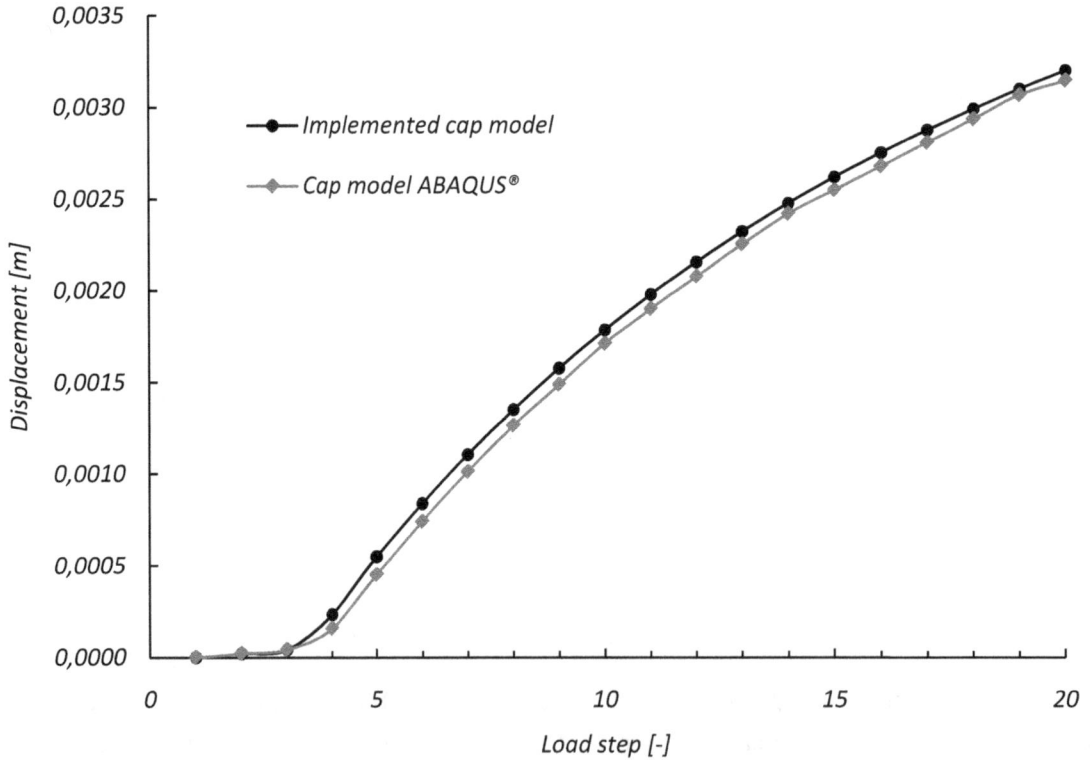

FIGURE 9.2. EXAMPLE 1; LOAD STEP/DISPLACEMENT DIAGRAM; CALCULATED AS STATIC FEM SIMULATION

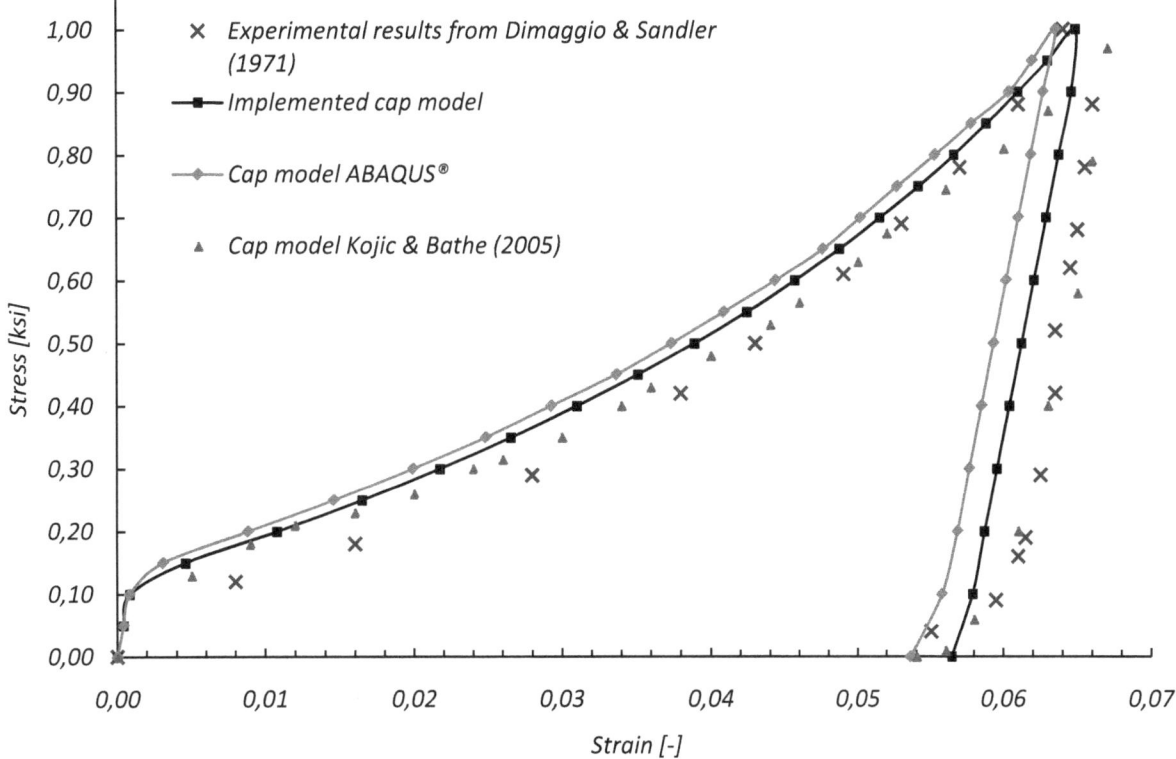

FIGURE 9.3. EXAMPLE 1; STRAIN/STRESS DIAGRAM; CALCULATED AS STATIC FEM SIMULATION

9.4.2   DYNAMIC CALCULATION WITH PURE FEM MODEL

The time step is chosen as $\Delta t = 0,02\ s$ for dynamic calculation with the pure FEM model; 500 time steps are calculated and the trapezoid rule with $\beta = \frac{1}{4}$ and $\gamma = \frac{1}{2}$ is applied. For the dynamic calculation, the load is applied in its full magnitude at $t_0 = 0$ to generate a clearly visible oscillation behavior.

In order to include additional damping, *Rayleigh damping* is used here. The damping matrix C is calculated from the mass matrix M and the stiffness matrix K with the *Rayleigh damping coefficients* α_R and β_R as follows:

$$C = \alpha_R\ M + \beta_R\ K \qquad\qquad (9.1)$$

The *Rayleigh damping coefficients* α_R and β_R are calculated analogous to Example 9.9 in (Bathe, Finite Elemente Methoden, 2002). So with the approach of 10% damping the *Rayleigh damping coefficients* are calculated to: $\alpha_R = 1,38264$ and $\beta_R = 0,00706271$.

A comparison of the *generalized cap model* and ABAQUS® without Rayleigh damping is given in Figure 9.4 for a time step/displacement diagram:

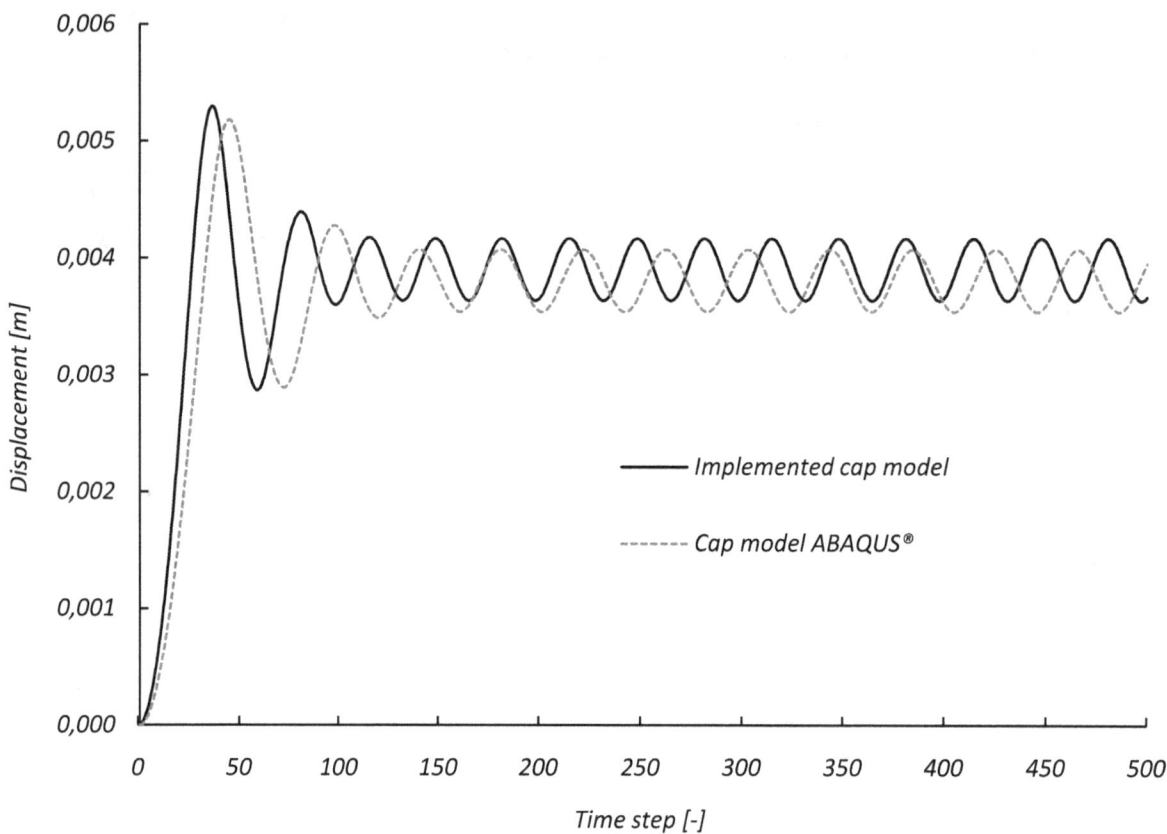

FIGURE 9.4. EXAMPLE 1; TIME STEP/DISPLACEMENT DIAGRAM; WITHOUT RAYLEIGH DAMPING; CALCULATED AS DYNAMIC FEM SIMULATION WITH PURE FEM MODEL

Figure 9.4 shows that the material contains a damping by itself in the form of the plastic energy dissipation. What means, the model includes theoretically the transformation of internal friction into thermal energy.

The system shows hysteretic damping due to plastic deformation until 100 time steps. Thereafter it oscillates elastically without a degradation of energy.

Because of the dynamic load the deformation is approximately 20% (0,0039/0,0032) greater than in the static case (see Figure 9.2).

A comparison of the *generalized cap model* and ABAQUS® with Rayleigh damping for a time step/displacement diagram is given in Figure 9.5. A good agreement between the two models for the dynamic calculation is achieved here, as well.

The hysteretic material behavior is pictured in Figure 9.6 for a strain/stress diagram and in Figure 9.7 for a plastic strain/stress diagram. Rayleigh damping is not included here and the data also relate to the 500 time steps.

Figure 9.4 shows the displacement curves which are associated to Figure 9.7.

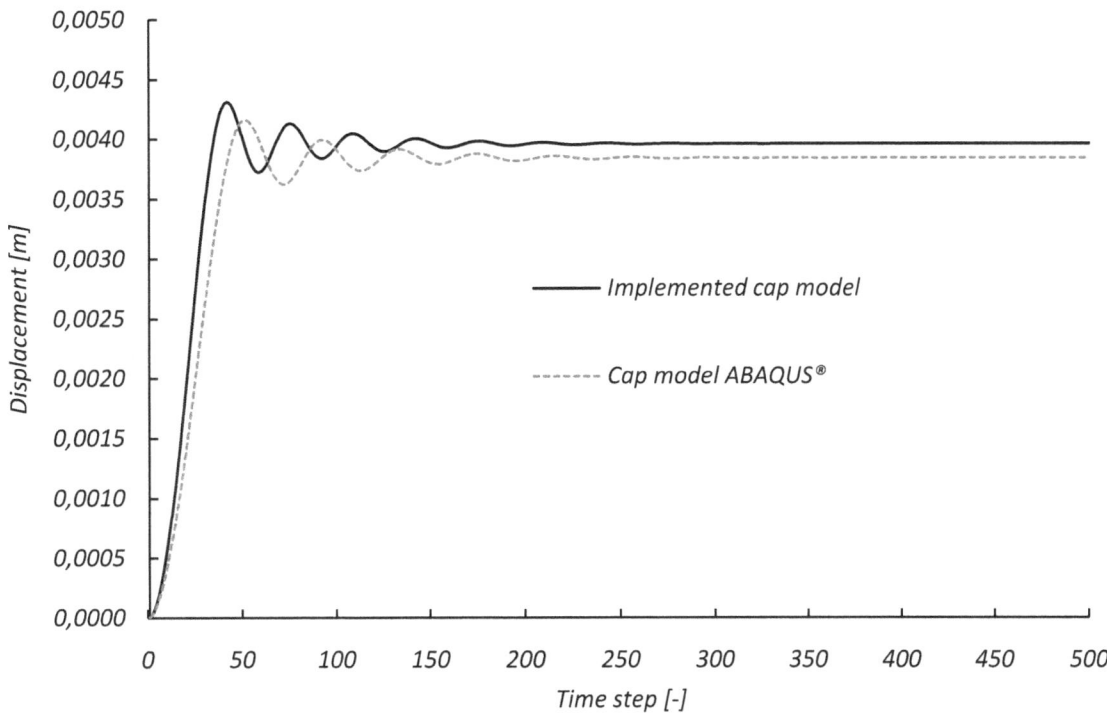

FIGURE 9.5. EXAMPLE 1; TIME STEP/DISPLACEMENT DIAGRAM; WITH RAYLEIGH DAMPING; CALCULATED AS DYNAMIC FEM SIMULATION WITH PURE FEM MODEL

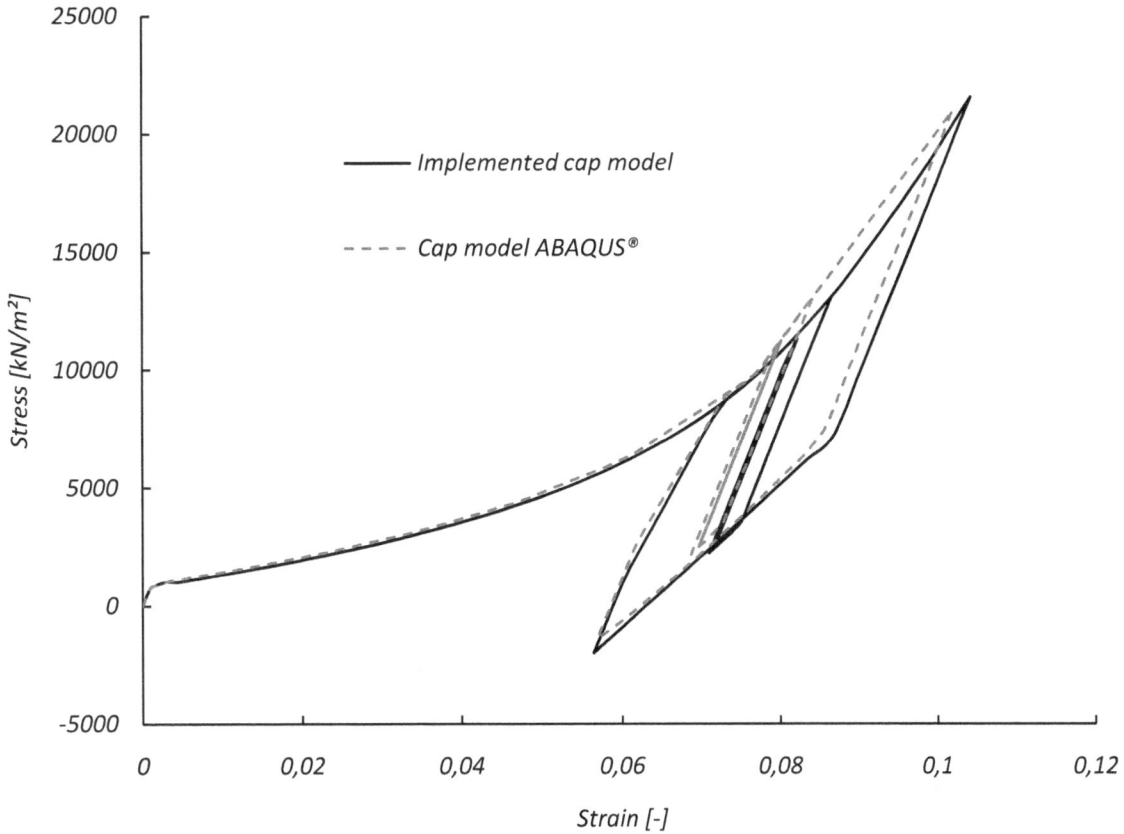

FIGURE 9.6. EXAMPLE 1; STRAIN/STRESS DIAGRAM; WITHOUT RAYLEIGH DAMPING; CALCULATED AS DYNAMIC FEM SIMULATION WITH PURE FEM MODEL

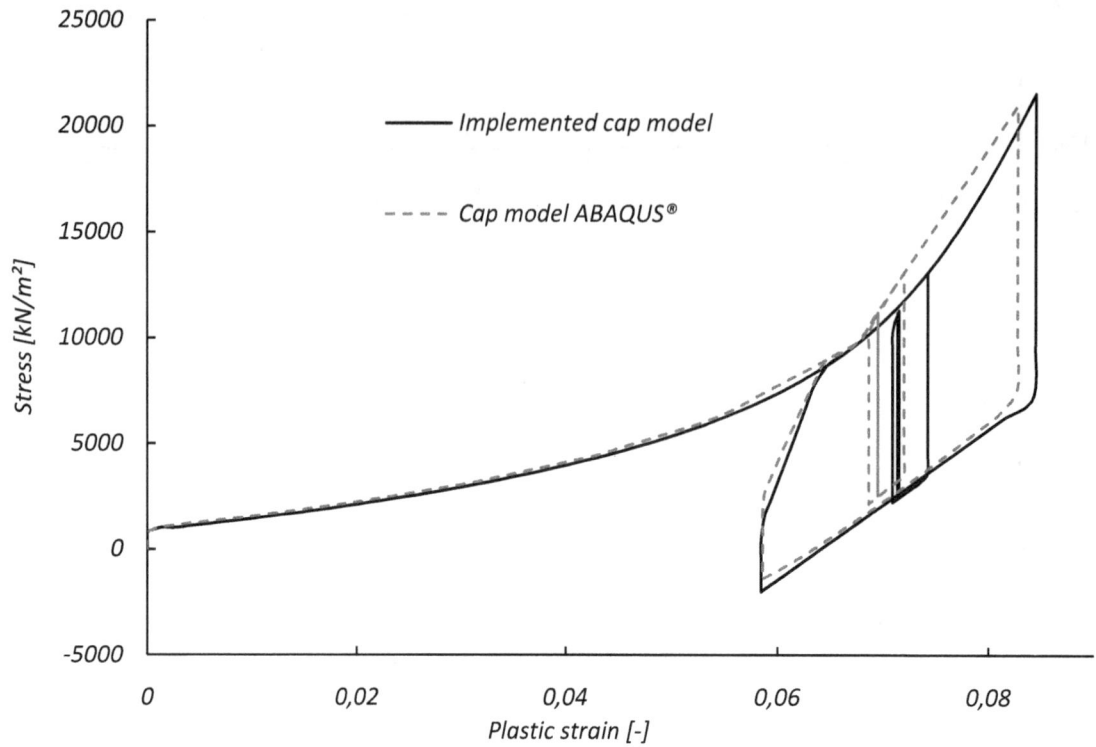

FIGURE 9.7. EXAMPLE 1; PLASTIC STRAIN/STRESS DIAGRAM; WITHOUT RAYLEIGH DAMPING; CALCULATED AS DYNAMIC FEM SIMULATION WITH PURE FEM MODEL

The enclosed area in Figure 9.6 and Figure 9.7 denotes the dissipated energy. When the elastic oscillation is reached, the values oscillate only on one line without enclosing an area. What means, no energy dissipation occurs in the elastic oscillation. The plastic energy dissipation is sketched in Figure 9.8:

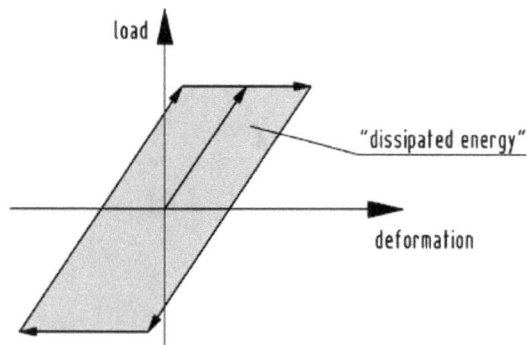

FIGURE 9.8. ENERGY DISSIPATION DUE TO PLASTIC DEFORMATION

The previous diagrams are calculated with the trapezoid rule. Figure 9.9 shows a comparison of the results calculated for the *generalized cap model* with the trapezoid rule ($\gamma = 0,5$ and $\beta = 0,25$) and the HHT-α method ($\alpha = -0,05$; $\gamma = \frac{1-2\,\alpha}{2} = 0,55$ and $\beta = \frac{(1-\alpha)^2}{4} = 0,276$).

In addition, a change of the Newmark parameters to $\gamma = 0,7$ and $\beta = 0,36$ was applied and pictured in Figure 9.9. This yields a numerical damping of the higher eigenmodes and includes a loss of accuracy, which results in a reduced amplitude (see Section 6.2).

In the trapezoid rule the acceleration is calculated as average acceleration from the time t and $t +$ Δt. A change of the Newmark parameters evaluates the acceleration higher or lower at the time $t + \Delta t$ dependent on the choice of γ and β. This results in a numerical damping, which not desired in many cases.

It is recognizable that the trapezoid rule and HHT-α method offer the same solution.

The advantage of the HHT-α method is the damping of the higher eigenmodes. In engineering practice are only the lower eigenmodes of interest. The higher eigenmodes will be quickly dissipated by the structure (Ludescher, 2003). Hence, an automatic included numerical damping of the higher eigenmodes simplifies the calculation.

Furthermore, the spatial FEM system approximates the lower eigenmodes much better than the higher ones (Bathe, 2002). For this reason, an incorporation of the higher eigenmodes can distort the solution, which can result in an inaccurate calculation.

In this simple example the damping of higher eigenmodes is not essential. But as mentioned above, the HHT-α method with FEM gives more accurate results because the higher eigenmodes are not incorporated (Bathe, 2002).

The damping of higher eigenmodes can be important, e.g., in soil-structure interaction with adjacent complicated structures.

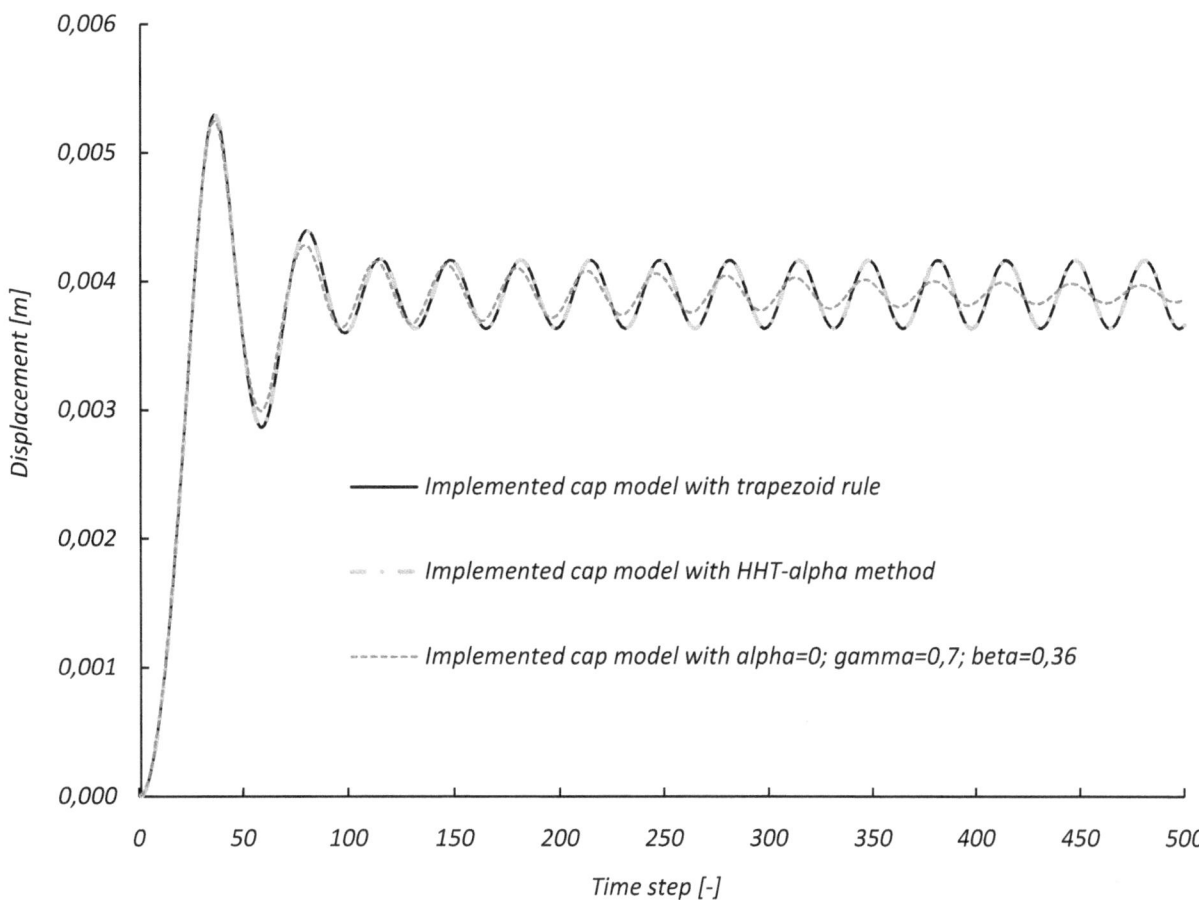

FIGURE 9.9. EXAMPLE 1; TIME STEP/DISPLACEMENT DIAGRAM; WITHOUT RAYLEIGH DAMPING; CALCULATED AS DYNAMIC FEM SIMULATION WITH PURE FEM MODEL AND WITH INCLUDED NUMERICAL DAMPING

9.4.3 Dynamic Calculation With Coupled FEM/SBFEM Model

The same input data as for the dynamic calculation with the pure FEM model are used here. The material data for the SBFEM far-field relate to the elastic values by:

$$E = 6{,}89 \; 10^5 \; \frac{kN}{m^2};$$

$$v = 0{,}25;$$

$$G = \frac{E}{2 \, (1 \, + \, v)} = \frac{6{,}89 \; 10^5}{2 \, (1 + 0{,}25)} = 275790 \; \frac{kN}{m^2}$$

For the coupling of the FEM with the SBFEM a single interface element is placed at the bottom side of the FEM element and the degrees of freedom for the vertical displacement are unfixed, as pictured in Figure 9.10. Accordingly to the 8 node brick element the interface element is to a 4 node element.

The calculation is performed with the HHT-α method ($\alpha = -0{,}05$; $\gamma = \frac{1-2\,\alpha}{2} = 0{,}55$ and $\beta = \frac{(1-\alpha)^2}{4} = 0{,}276$).

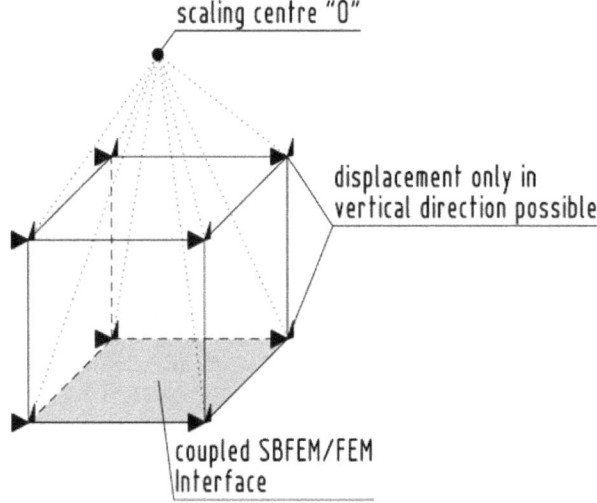

FIGURE 9.10. GEOMETRY OF COUPLED FEM/SBFEM ELEMENT FOR EXAMPLE 1

The results of the dynamic calculation with the pure FEM model (given in Figure 9.4 and Figure 9.5) are compared with the results of the coupled FEM/SBFEM model, as illustrated in Figure 9.11.

The incorporated wave propagation in the FEM/SBFEM element is visible in Figure 9.11, because no post-oscillation occurs. The SBFEM interface element enables wave propagation to infinity which results in an oscillation damping.

Furthermore, an additional damping (in the form of the Rayleigh damping applied here) can be included, as pictured in Figure 9.11.

The overall displacement of the coupled FEM/SBFEM element is greater than in the pure FEM element due to the elastic displacement of the bottom side of the coupled FEM/SBFEM element.

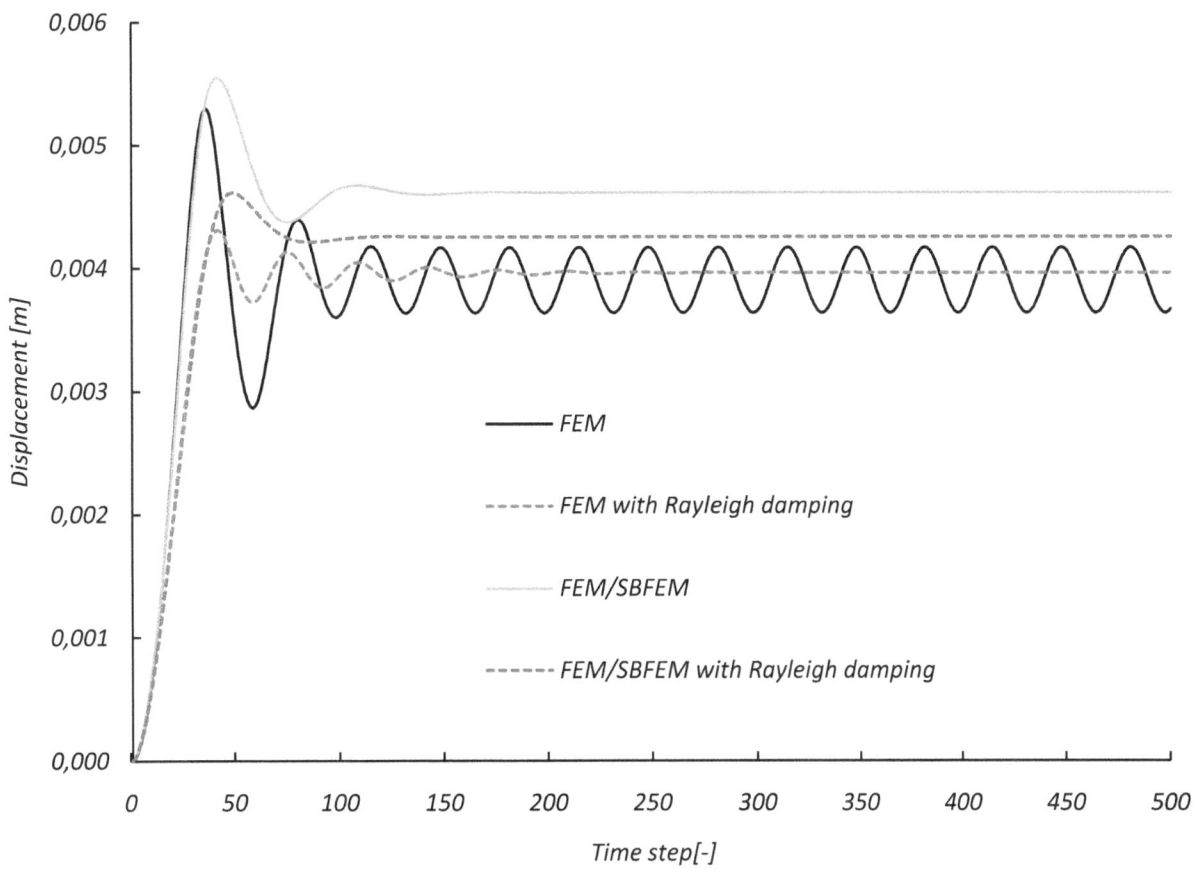

FIGURE 9.11. EXAMPLE 1; TIME STEP/DISPLACEMENT DIAGRAM; WITH AND WITHOUT RAYLEIGH DAMPING; CALCULATED AS DYNAMIC FEM SIMULATION WITH COUPLED FEM/SBFEM MODEL

The use of SBFEM interface elements yields an increase in accuracy for the solution, with the advantages of the HHT-alpha method. This example was used for the verification of the theory part. More complex examples are considered in the following chapters.

10 VERIFICATION EXAMPLE 2, STRIP FOUNDATION AS 2-D CALCULATION

A strip foundation with two different materials is calculated here as 2D-calculation. Due to the symmetry, only half of the strip foundation problem has to be modeled for the calculation. This is pictured in Figure 10.1. The geometry in this example is adopted from (Desai & Siriwardane, Constitutive laws for engineering materials, 1984) and the material is adopted from (DiMaggio & Sandler, 1971). The original U.S. units are converted to SI units.

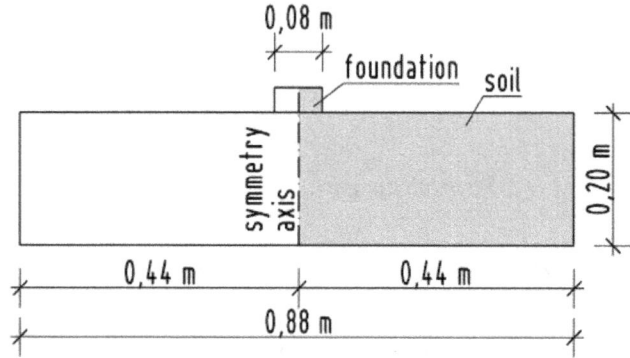

FIGURE 10.1. MODELLED STRIP FOUNDATION

10.1 GEOMETRY, LOADING AND BOUNDARY CONDITIONS

The discretized soil layer is pictured in Figure 10.2 with the following properties:

Dimensions: $x/y/z = 0{,}88/0{,}11/0{,}2\ m$

Foundation load: increasing load from $p_1 = 2068\ \frac{kN}{m^2}$ until shear failure (for static calculation) and $p_1 = 10342\frac{kN}{m^2}$ (for dynamic calculation)

Soil load: $p_2 = 2068\ kN/m^2$ (as coarse approach for self-weight of the soil)

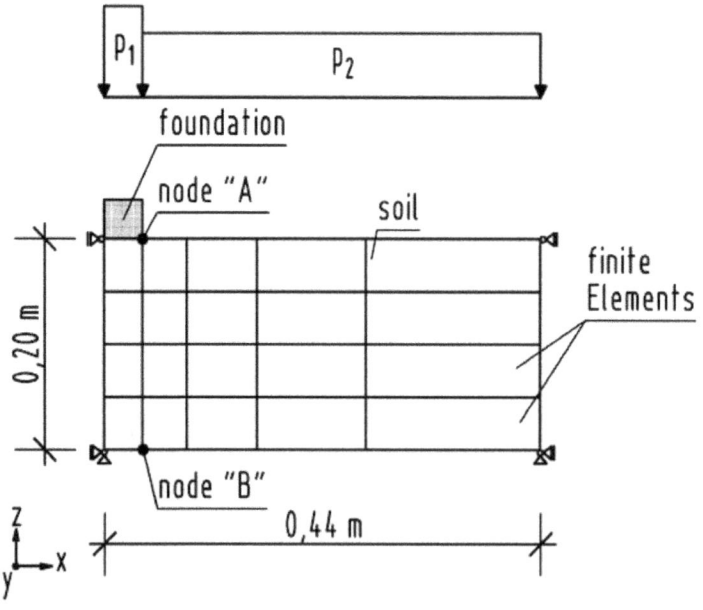

FIGURE 10.2. GEOMETRY OF EXAMPLE 2

10.2 MATERIAL

The same material properties for soil as chosen in Example 1 are applied. For the concrete foundation the following elastic values are assumed: $E = 2{,}07 \ 10^7 \frac{kN}{m^2}; \ v = 0{,}25$.

A very high density is chosen to clarify the oscillation behavior: $\rho = 2{,}77 \ 10^6 \ kg/m^3$

10.3 RESULTS

All results relate to the vertical component of the displacements in the node "A" (see Figure 10.2) if it is not otherwise denoted.

10.3.1 STATIC CALCULATION

The static calculation for the *generalized cap model* is done in 20 load steps.

Shear failure occurs at $22000 \ kN/m^2$ in the simulation with the implemented *generalized cap model,* and at $13000 \ kN/m^2$ in the simulation with ABAQUS®. This is pictured in Figure 10.3. The difference between the results is based on the application of the associated flow rule in the *generalized cap model* and the non-associated flow rule in ABAQUS® (see Sections 4.1.3 and 8.1.2). The shear failure in the *generalized cap model* is clearly recognizable in Figure 10.3. The displacement increases rapidly at approximately $20000 \ kN/m^2$. The coarse function of the *generalized cap model* results from the coarse FEM discretization.

Figure 10.4 shows the maximum displacement calculated with the *generalized cap model* to $0{,}002 \ m$. The soil on the right-hand side of the foundation already arches upward. The principle is illustrated in Figure 10.5, which was adopted from (Helwany, 2007). A typical settlement curve for local shear failure (Terzaghi, 1943) is given here. The settlement curve is characteristic for medium-dense sands and medium-stiff clays. This is analogous to the settlement curve of the *generalized cap model* in Figure 10.3.

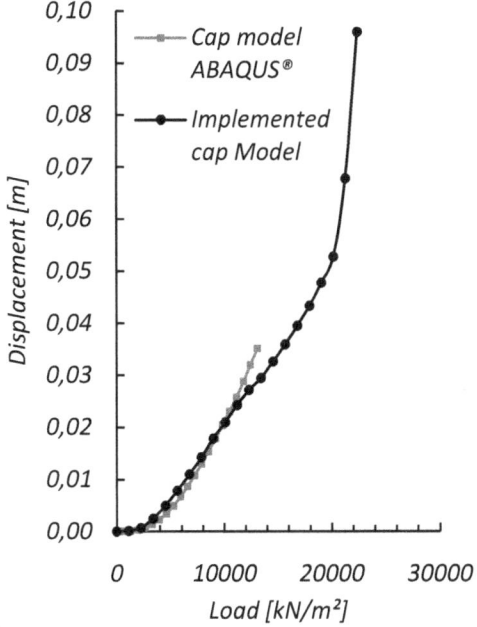

FIGURE 10.3. EXAMPLE 2; NODE "A" – BOTTOM SIDE OF THE FOOTING; LOAD/DISPLACEMENT DIAGRAM; CALCULATED AS STATIC FEM SIMULATION

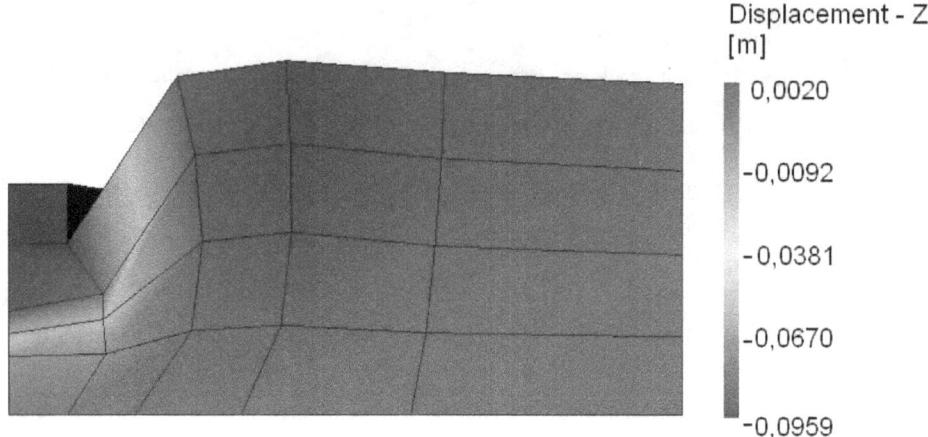

FIGURE 10.4. EXAMPLE 2; STATIC FEM SIMULATION; MAXIMUM DISPLACEMENT AT SHEAR FAILURE
CALCULATED WITH IMPLEMENTED CAP MODEL

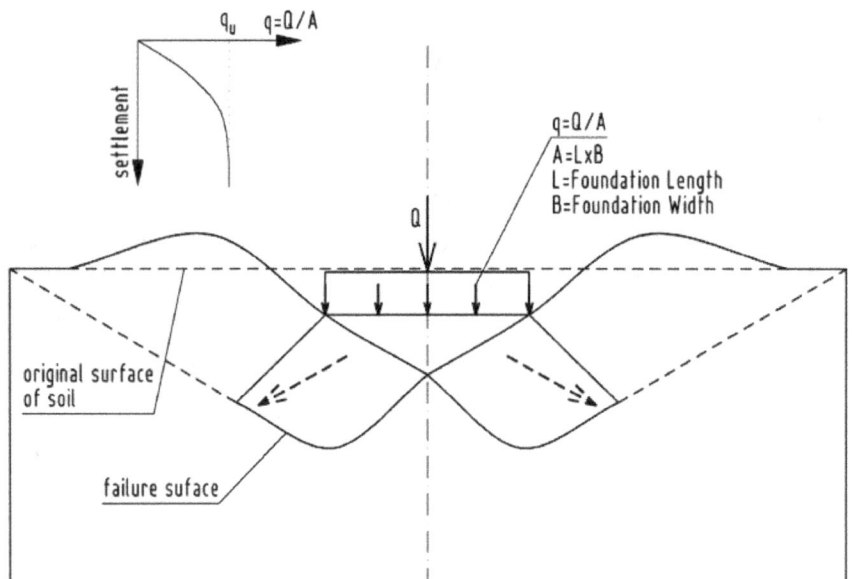

FIGURE 10.5. PRINCIPLE OF SHEAR FAILURE

10.3.2 DYNAMIC CALCULATION WITH PURE FEM MODEL

The time step is chosen as $\Delta t = 0,01\ s$ for the dynamic calculation with the pure FEM model and
500 time steps are calculated. The HHT-α method ($\alpha = -0,05$; $\gamma = \frac{1-2\,\alpha}{2} = 0,55$ and $\beta = \frac{(1-\alpha)^2}{4} =$
0,276) is applied and Rayleigh damping is not included in Example 2.

The results are displayed in Figure 10.6. Both analyses agree with each other. Differences result from
the associated flow rule of the *generalized cap model* and the non-associated flow rule of ABAQUS®
(see Sections 4.1.3 and 8.1.2), because slight yielding on failure surface occurs here.

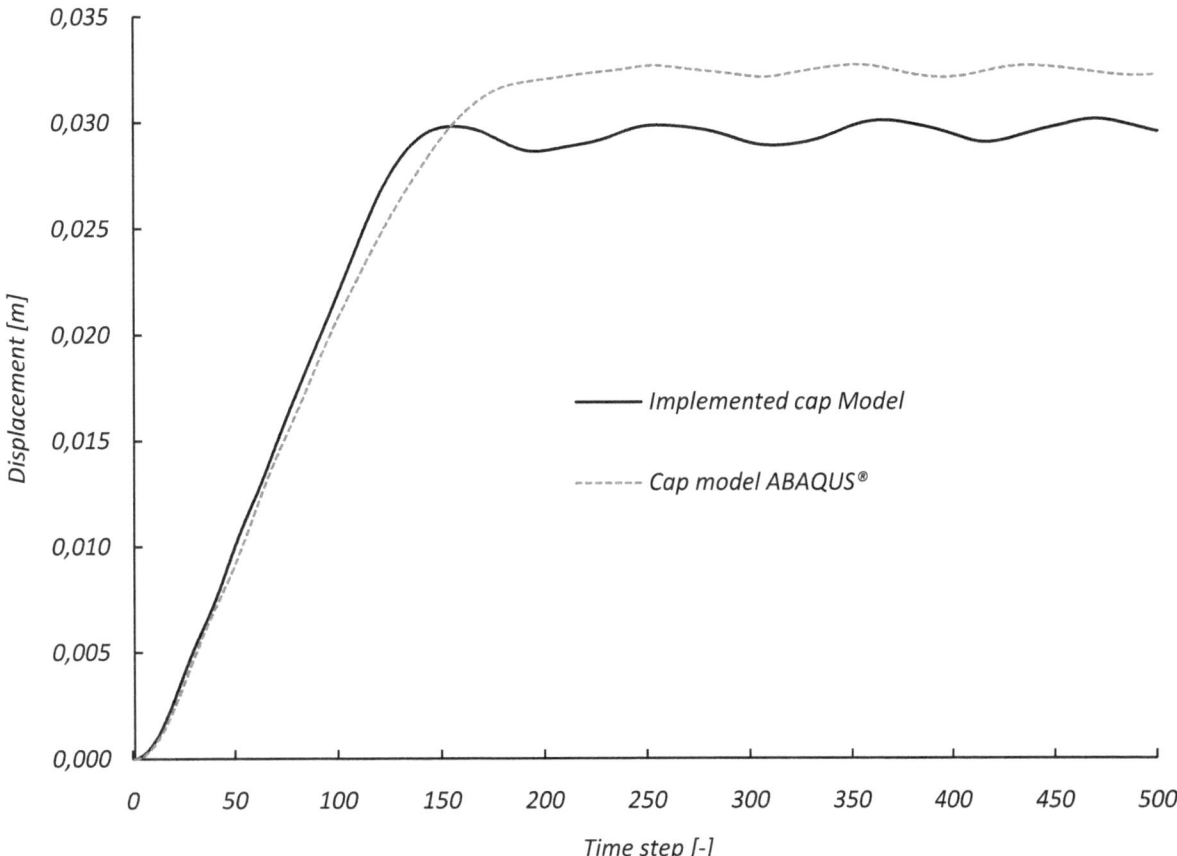

FIGURE 10.6. EXAMPLE 2; NODE "A" – BOTTOM SIDE OF THE FOOTING; TIME STEP/DISPLACEMENT DIAGRAM; CALCULATED AS DYNAMIC FEM SIMULATION WITH PURE FEM MODEL

10.3.3 DYNAMIC CALCULATION WITH COUPLED FEM/SBFEM MODEL

The same input data as for the dynamic calculation with pure FEM model are used here. The material data for the SBFEM far-field relate according to the elastic values with:

$$E = 6{,}89 \; 10^5 \; \frac{kN}{m^2};$$

$$v = 0{,}25;$$

$$G = \frac{E}{2 \, (1 \, + \, v)} = \frac{6{,}89 \; 10^5}{2 \, (1 + 0{,}25)} = 275790 \; \frac{kN}{m^2}$$

For the coupling of the FEM with the SBFEM at the bottom side and the right-hand side of the model interface elements (dashed lines) are arranged. And the related degrees of freedom for the displacement are unfixed, as pictured in Figure 10.7.

The calculation is conducted with the HHT-α method ($\alpha = -0{,}05$; $\gamma = \frac{1-2\,\alpha}{2} = 0{,}55$ and $\beta = \frac{(1-\alpha)^2}{4} = 0{,}276$) and Rayleigh damping is not included in Example 2.

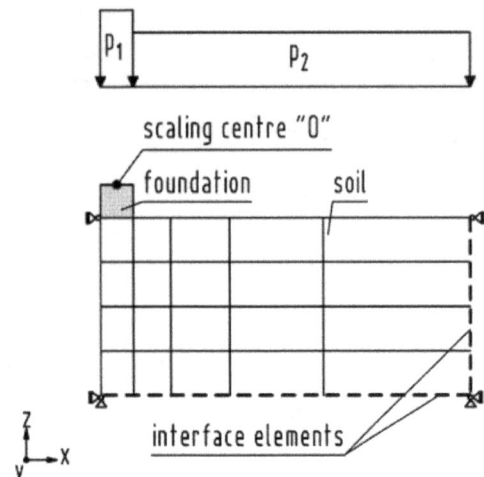

FIGURE 10.7. GEOMETRY OF COUPLED FEM/SBFEM MODEL FOR EXAMPLE 2

The results of the coupled FEM/SBFEM calculation are pictured in Figure 10.8 for node "A" (see Figure 10.2). The results from the dynamic calculation with the pure FEM (given in Figure 10.6) are compared with the results from the coupled FEM/SBFEM calculation.

As pictured in Figure 10.8, the displacement of the coupled FEM/SBFEM model is approximately 10% (0,032/0,029) greater than in the pure FEM model due to the elastic deformation of the bottom side of the model.

The oscillation of the coupled FEM/SBFEM model is damped due to the incorporated wave propagation to infinity (see Section 9.4.3).

For comparison, the linear-elastic solutions of the FEM model and of the coupled FEM/SBFEM model are given in Figure 10.8, as well.

The comparison shows that elasto-plastic deformation is a multiple greater than in the linear-elastic solution. That means in conclusion that the elasto-plastic calculation of soil in the near-field is essential (from the theoretical point of view; the numerical results are not verified with experimental results).

The analysis of node "B" can be interesting when an oscillation transmission to nearby buildings has to be included.

The time-step/displacement diagram for node "B" (see Figure 10.2) is illustrated in Figure 10.9. A comparison between the linear-elastic FEM/SBFEM calculation and the elasto-plastic FEM/SBFEM calculation is given here.

The bottom side of the discretized part behaves linear-elastic in the elasto-plastic FEM/SBFEM calculation and in the linear-elastic FEM/SBFEM calculation. Hence, the final displacement is equal in both calculations. However, the maximum amplitude in the elasto-plastic FEM/SBFEM model is approximately twice as large as in the linear-elastic FEM/SBFEM model.

This is based on the fact that Example 2 includes a large plastic deformation and a small near-field. The adjacent *Gauss point* to bode "B" (see Figure 10.2) shows plastic deformation.

For practical calculations, the near-field should be chosen so large that no (or negligible) plastic deformation occurs at the outer boundaries of the near-field, because the far-field includes only elastic deformations. However, this is not employed for the near-field of Example 2 (because this is only a verification example).

The elasto-plastic FEM/SBFEM calculation in Example 2 results in a very different oscillation transmission compared to the linear-elastic FEM/SBFEM calculation, as illustrated in Figure 10.2. The oscillation transmission is greater in the elasto-plastic FEM/SBFEM model.

This result is inaccurate.

Example 4 shows that a quite similar oscillation transmission can be obtained if a sufficient large near-field is used. In Example 4, the near-field is chosen so large so that no plastic deformation occurs at the outer boundaries.

Nevertheless, the result is interesting if a second structure is located in the domain of the plastic deformation of the near-field. The elasto-plastic oscillation transmission yields a greater loading to the second structure than the linear-elastic oscillation transmission if the second structure is located in the domain of the plastic deformation of the near-field.

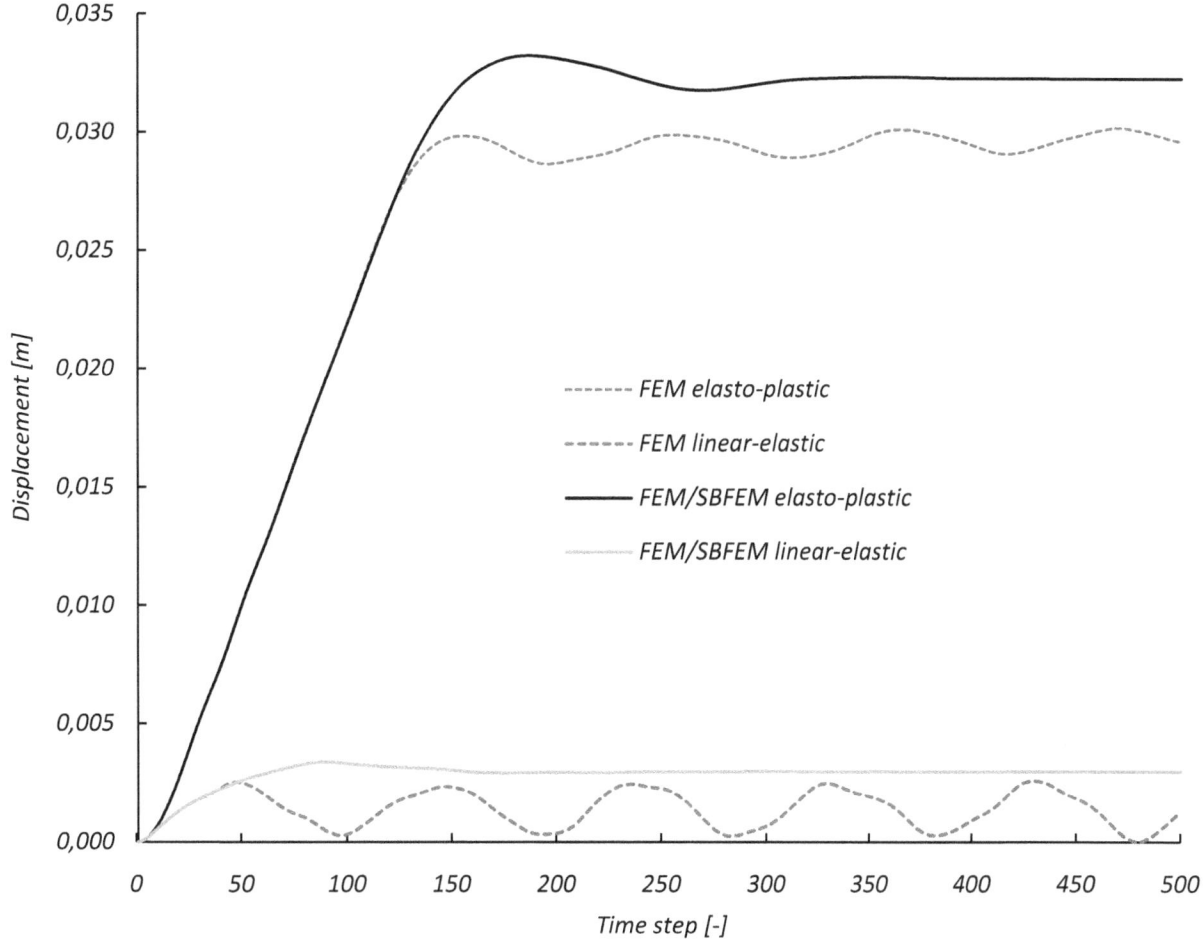

FIGURE 10.8. EXAMPLE 2; NODE "A" – BOTTOM SIDE OF THE FOOTING; TIME STEP/DISPLACEMENT DIAGRAM; CALCULATED AS DYNAMIC FEM SIMULATION WITH COUPLED FEM/SBFEM MODEL

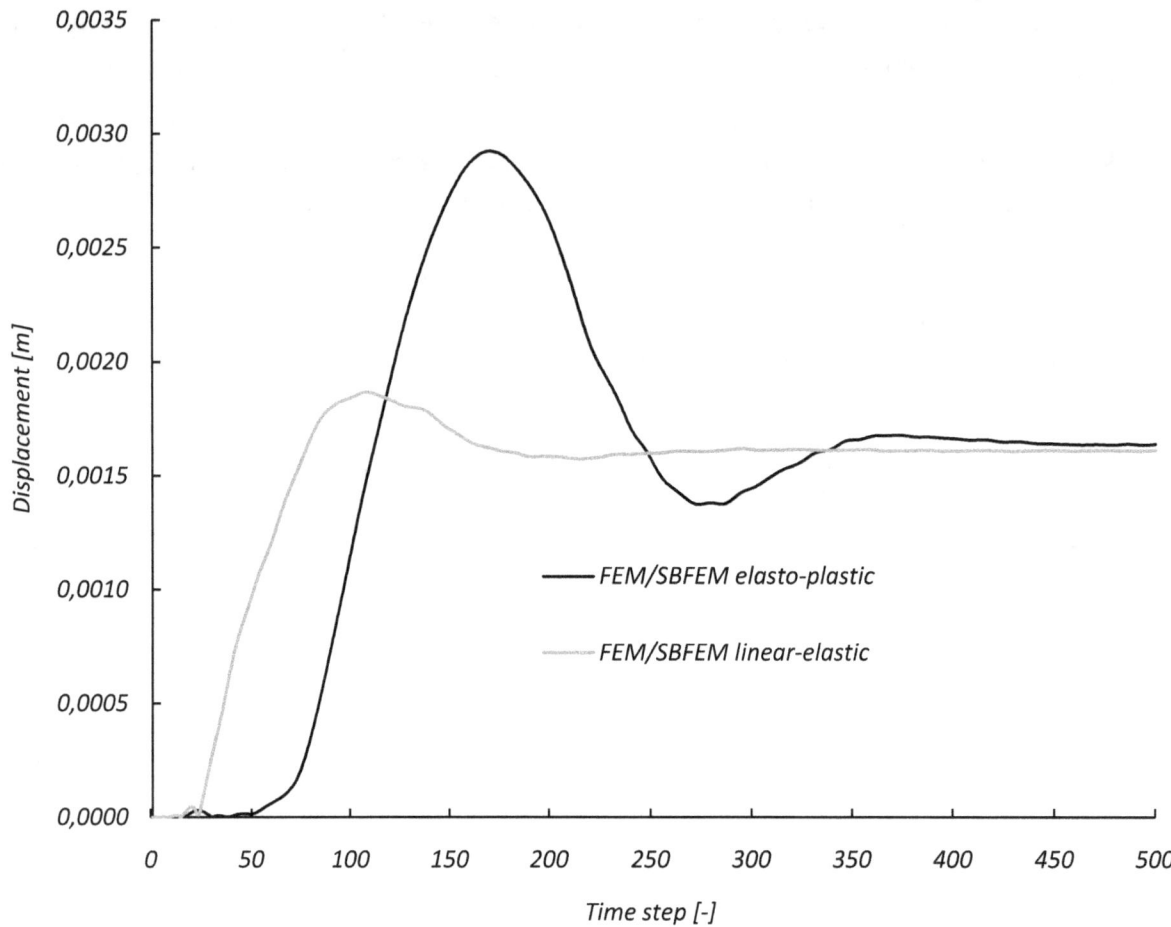

FIGURE 10.9. EXAMPLE 2; NODE "B" – BOTTOM SIDE OF THE DISCRETIZED PART; TIME STEP/DISPLACEMENT DIAGRAM; CALCULATED AS DYNAMIC FEM SIMULATION WITH COUPLED FEM/SBFEM MODEL

11 VERIFICATION EXAMPLE 3, SQUARE FOUNDATION AS 3-D CALCULATION

A square foundation is calculated here as 3-D calculation. The foundation is only modeled as a load. Therefore, only one material is used for the soil. Due to the symmetry only one quarter is analyzed, as pictured in Figure 11.1. This is applied for the layer of soil and for the foundation load to reduce the computational effort. The geometry in this example is adopted from (Helwany, 2007) and the material is adopted from (DiMaggio & Sandler, 1971). The original U.S. units are converted to SI units.

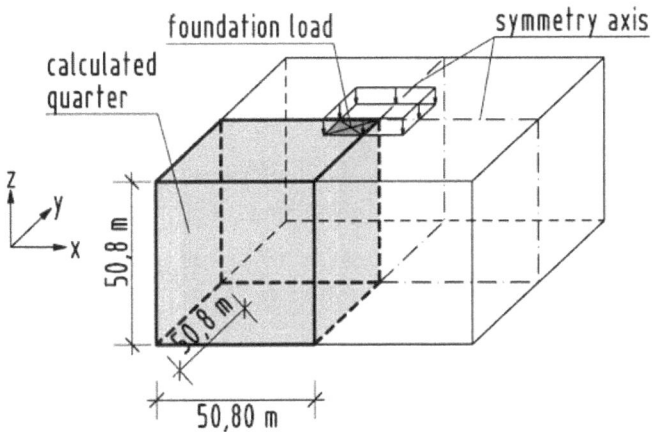

FIGURE 11.1. MODELING SQUARE FOUNDATIONS

11.1 GEOMETRY, LOADING AND BOUNDARY CONDITIONS

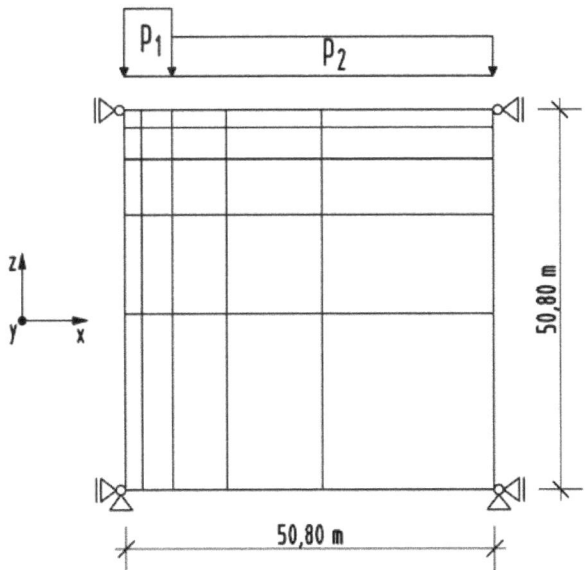

FIGURE 11.2. GEOMETRY OF EXAMPLE 3

The calculated soil layer is pictured in Figure 11.2 with the following properties:

Dimensions: $x/y/z = 50{,}8/50{,}8/50{,}8\ m\ (\cong 2000\ inch)$

Foundation load: increasing load from $p_1 = 3447\ \frac{kN}{m^2}$ until shear failure (for static calculation) and $p_1 = 10342\ \frac{kN}{m^2}$ (for dynamic calculation)

Soil load: $p_2 = 3447 \frac{kN}{m^2}$ (as coarse approach for self-weight of the soil)

11.2 MATERIAL

The same material for soil as in Example 1 is applied.

A very high density is chosen to clarify the oscillation behavior: $\rho = 2{,}77 \; 10^8 \; kg/m^3$

11.3 RESULTS

If it is not otherwise denoted, all results relate to the vertical component of the displacements in the node of the soil element under the foundation (node "A" in Figure 11.6).

11.3.1 STATIC CALCULATION

Shear failure occurs at $21000 \; kN/m^2$ in the simulation with implemented *generalized cap model* and in the simulation with ABAQUS® at $13000 \; kN/m^2$. This is pictured in Figure 11.3. The difference in the results is explained by the associated flow rule of the *generalized cap model* and non-associated flow rule of ABAQUS® (see Sections 4.1.3 and 8.1.2).

Notice: The displacement in this verification example is very large. A material-nonlinear-only type of analysis is used in this work. If close to reality results are required, a more complex nonlinear type of analysis with implicated large strains, rotations and displacements must be applied.

Figure 11.4 shows the maximum displacement of the *generalized cap model* at $21000 \; kN/m^2$.

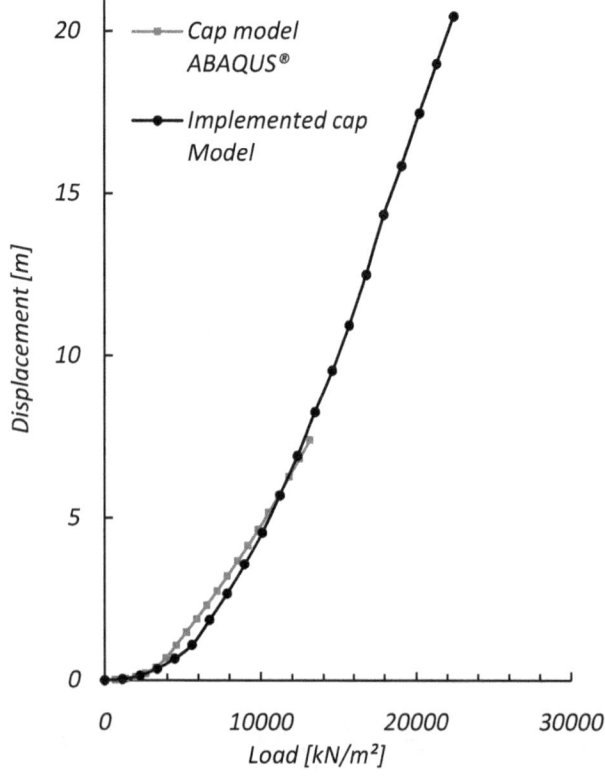

FIGURE 11.3. EXAMPLE 3; NODE "A" – BOTTOM SIDE OF THE FOOTING; LOAD/DISPLACEMENT DIAGRAM; CALCULATED AS STATIC FEM SIMULATION

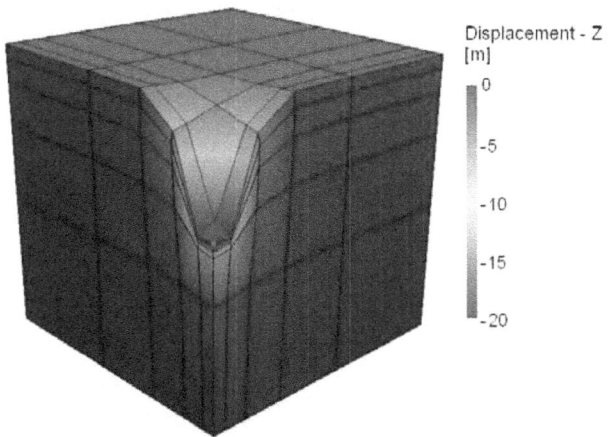

FIGURE 11.4. EXAMPLE 3; MAXIMUM DISPLACEMENT AT SHEAR FAILURE

11.3.2 Dynamic Calculation With Pure FEM Model

The time step is chosen as $\Delta t = 10\ s$ for the dynamic calculation with the pure FEM model and 1000 time steps are calculated. The HHT-α method ($\alpha = -0{,}05$; $\gamma = \frac{1-2\,\alpha}{2} = 0{,}55$ and $\beta = \frac{(1-\alpha)^2}{4} = 0{,}276$) is applied and Rayleigh damping is not included in Example 3.

The results are displayed in Figure 11.5. Differences result from the associated flow rule of the *generalized cap model* and non-associated flow rule of ABAQUS® (see Sections 4.1.3 and 8.1.2), because yielding on failure surface occurs here.

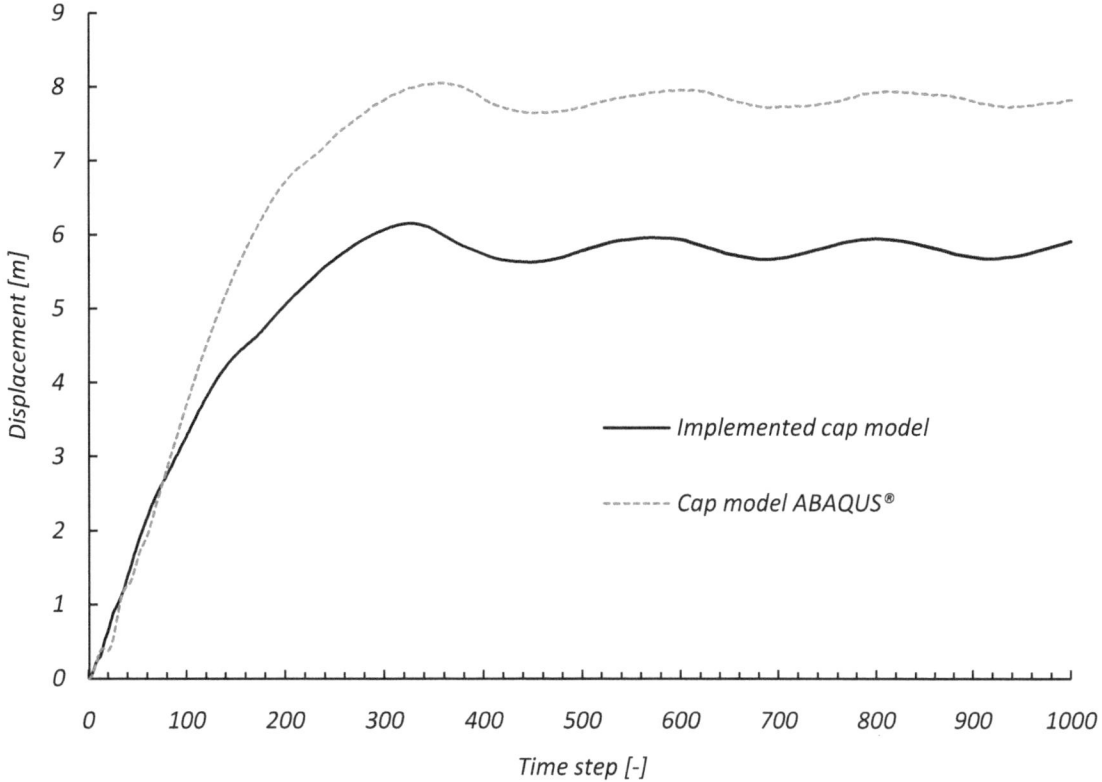

FIGURE 11.5. EXAMPLE 3; NODE "A" – BOTTOM SIDE OF THE FOOTING; TIME STEP/DISPLACEMENT DIAGRAM; CALCULATED AS DYNAMIC FEM SIMULATION WITH PURE FEM MODEL

Node "B" (see Figure 11.6) is analyzed for the same input data. The results are displayed in Figure 11.7. The node oscillates elastically at first, then at approximately 100 time steps the plastic deformation arrives at the node and the deformation increases rapidly.

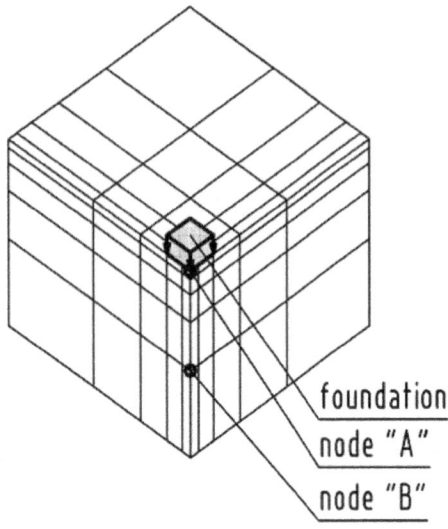

FIGURE 11.6. EXAMPLE 3; ISSUED NODE RESULTS

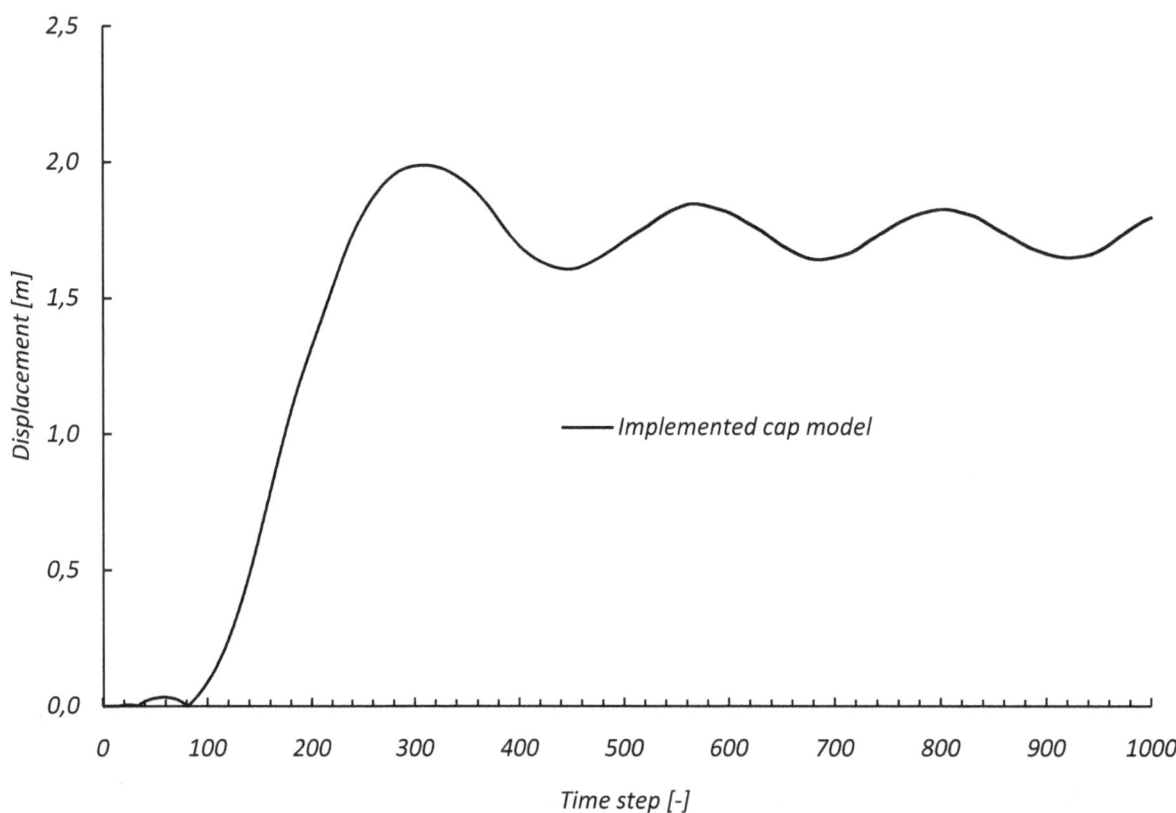

FIGURE 11.7. EXAMPLE 3; NODE "B"; TIME STEP/DISPLACEMENT DIAGRAM; CALCULATED AS DYNAMIC FEM SIMULATION WITH PURE FEM MODEL

11.3.3 DYNAMIC CALCULATION WITH COUPLED FEM/SBFEM MODEL

The same input data as for the dynamic calculation with pure FEM model are used here. The material data for the SBFEM far-field relate accordingly to the elastic values with:

$$E = 6{,}89 \ 10^5 \ \frac{kN}{m^2};$$

$$\nu = 0{,}25;$$

$$G = \frac{E}{2\,(1\,+\,\nu)} = \frac{6{,}89 \ 10^5}{2\,(1+0{,}25)} = 275790 \ \frac{kN}{m^2}$$

Interface elements (marked with a dashed line in Figure 11.1) are arranged at the bottom side and the outside of the soil layer for the coupling of the FEM with the SBFEM. The related degrees of freedom for the displacement are unfixed, as pictured in Figure 11.8. The calculation is conducted with the HHT-α method ($\alpha = -0{,}05$; $\gamma = \frac{1-2\,\alpha}{2} = 0{,}55$ and $\beta = \frac{(1-\alpha)^2}{4} = 0{,}276$) and Rayleigh damping is not included in Example 3.

The results of the calculation with the coupled FEM/SBFEM model are pictured in Figure 11.9. The results from the dynamic calculation with the pure FEM (given in Figure 11.5) are compared with the results from the coupled FEM/SBFEM calculation.

As illustrated in Examples 1 and 2 (see Section 9.4.3 and Section 10.3.3), the displacement in the dynamic FEM/SBFEM calculation is greater than in the dynamic calculation with the pure FEM and no post-oscillation occurs due to the included wave propagation to infinity.

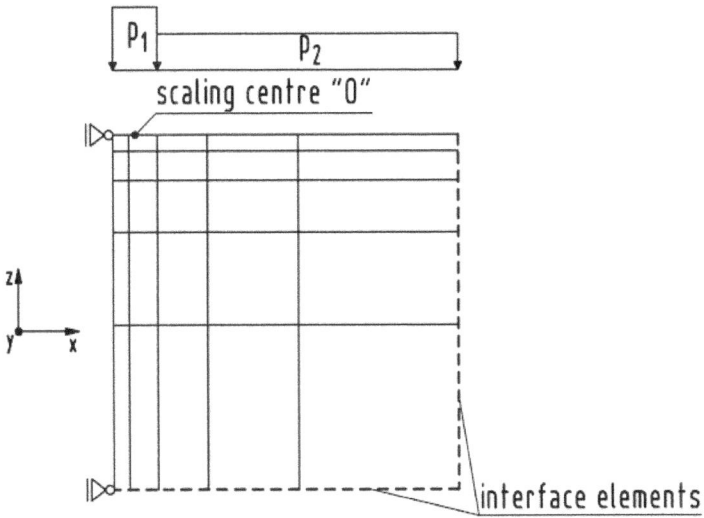

FIGURE 11.8. EXAMPLE 3; GEOMETRY OF COUPLED FEM/SBFEM MODEL FOR

For comparison, the linear-elastic solutions for the FEM model and the coupled FEM/SBFEM model are given in Figure 11.9, as well. The comparison shows that elasto-plastic deformation is a multiple greater than the linear-elastic solution (see also Section 10.3.3).

The chosen time step $\Delta t = 10$ is too large here for the linear-elastic calculation. As pictured in Figure 11.9 the oscillation increases more and more to the end of the time. A decreasing of the time step would improve the result to a smooth line (this was tested in an auxiliary calculation).

The time step for the linear-elastic calculation has to be smaller than for the elasto-plastic calculation in Example 3. This is founded in the additional hysteretic damping from the elasto-plastic material. The hysteretic damping suppresses the oscillations of the higher frequencies.

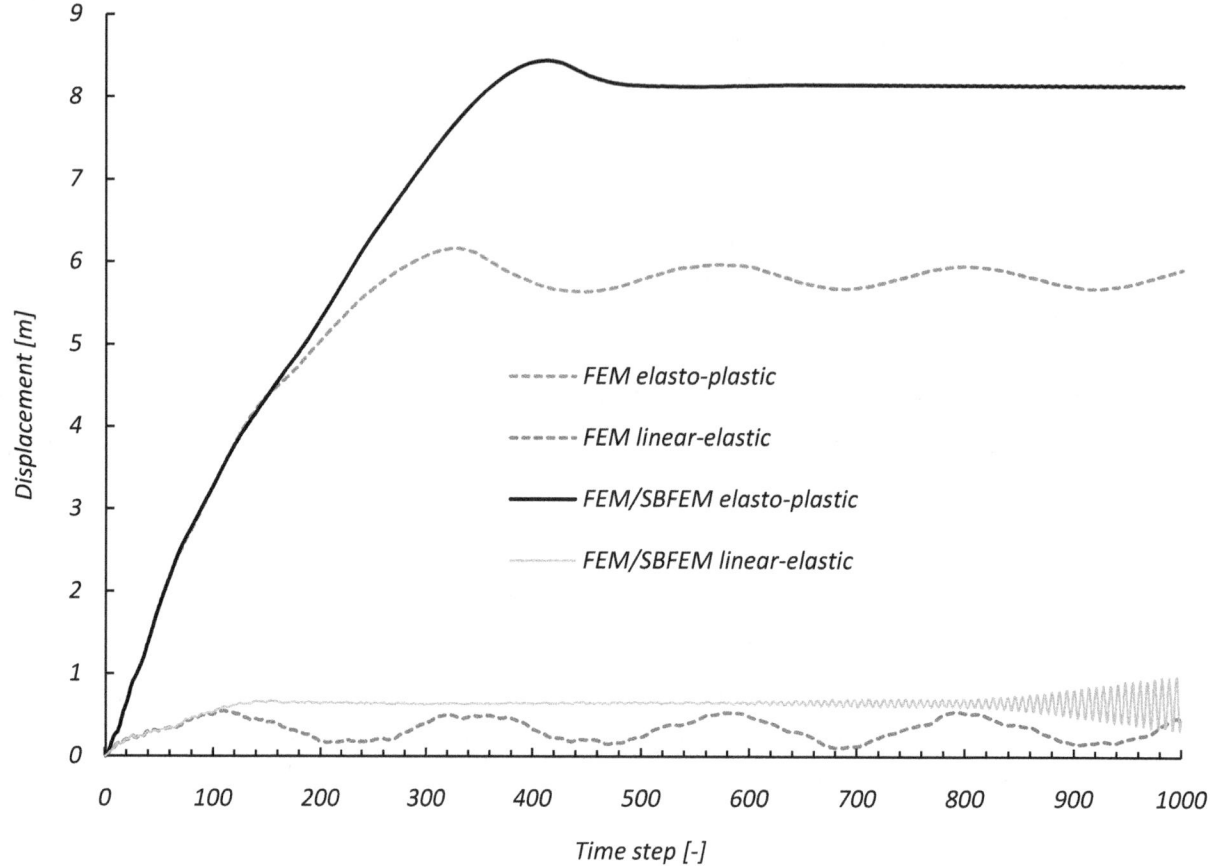

FIGURE 11.9. EXAMPLE 3; NODE "A" – BOTTOM SIDE OF THE FOOTING; TIME STEP/DISPLACEMENT DIAGRAM; CALCULATED AS DYNAMIC FEM SIMULATION WITH COUPLED FEM/SBFEM MODEL

The analogous comparison is pictured for node "B" (see Figure 11.6) in Figure 11.10. The results from the dynamic calculation with the pure FEM (given in Figure 11.7) are compared with the results from the coupled elasto-plastic FEM/SBFEM calculation and the coupled linear-elastic FEM/SBFEM calculation.

As in the dynamic calculation with the pure FEM model, the node oscillates elastically at first, then at approximately 100 time steps the wave propagation arrives at the node and the deformation increases rapidly.

The results are very different for the three calculations, as depicted in Figure 11.10.

In this case, the elasto-plastic oscillation transmission yields a greater loading to the second structure than the linear-elastic oscillation transmission.

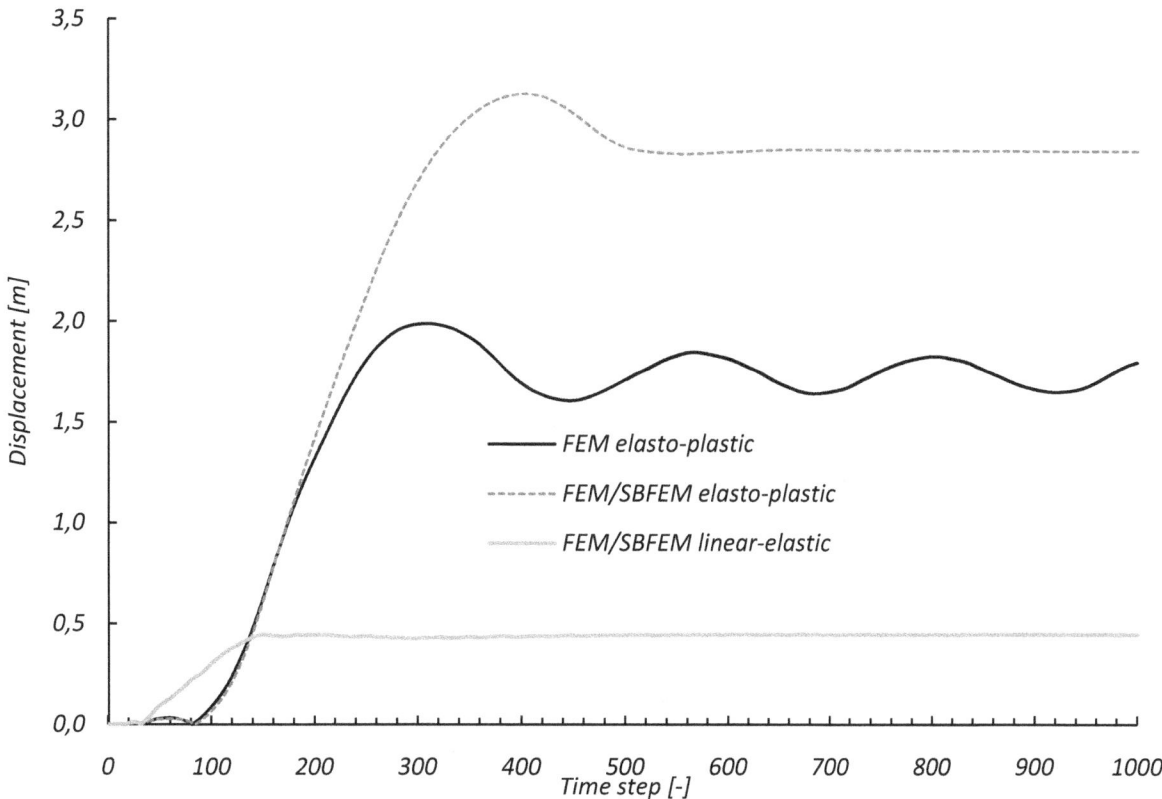

FIGURE 11.10. EXAMPLE 3; NODE "B"; TIME STEP/DISPLACEMENT DIAGRAM; CALCULATED AS DYNAMIC FEM SIMULATION WITH COUPLED FEM/SBFEM MODEL

12 PRACTICAL EXAMPLE 4, SETTLEMENT OF A BRIDGE FOOTING

Finally, a practical example of a bridge pier foundation for a railway bridge is calculated. The settlement of a bridge footing of a railway bridge is calculated as an application-oriented example.

The pier and the footing are generated as FEM mesh, while the superstructure is only applied as load. The FEM mesh of the discretized part of the soil is illustrated in Figure 12.3. The discretized part of the soil represents the near-field. The near-field is chosen so large that no (or negligible) plastic deformation occurs at the outer boundaries of the near-field, because the far-field includes only elastic deformations.

The magnitude of the building ground deformations depends on mechanical properties of the soil and the *current state* of the soil. The *current state* depends on the history of the soil deformation previous to the considered load application. The *current state* can be considered as a *disturbed state* with respect to a defined initial state (Desai, The disturbated state concept, 2001). If two soil samples with the same material properties but different current states are subjected to the same loading, the deformation of the soil samples will be different.

Hence, the different current states have to be determined firstly for the different loads in this example. For this reason the loads are applied successively. First, the soil is subjected to its self-weight, which results in *current state 1*. With *current state 1*, the soil is subjected to the self-weight of the bridge (concrete bridge), which results in *current state 2*. Finally, with *current state 2*, the soil is subjected to the traffic load (or train load).

In the previous dynamic calculations of the Examples 1-3, the loads are applied in its full magnitudes at $t_0 = 0$ and the loads do not vary over the time interval. In contrast, in this Example 4, all loads are applied time dependently in the dynamic calculations. The self-weight of soil and concrete are applied quasi-static due to a very slowly load increasing over the time (see Figure 12.14 and Figure 12.16). The traffic load is applied in its real occurring time, which is dependent on the design velocity. Therefore, only the traffic load causes dynamic effects in the form of oscillations.

Two material models are used here. The bridge pier and the footing are modeled with a linear-elastic material (with the linear-elastic material properties of concrete) and the adjacent soil is modeled with the implemented elasto-plastic cap model.

In Example 3, only one quarter of the entire square foundation and the soil is analyzed (see Figure 11.1). In Example 4, the entire model of the bridge pier, the footing and the soil section is calculated. The discretized part of Example 4 is pictured in Figure 12.3 and Figure 12.4.

The calculation of the entire model in Example 4 is used for comparison with the separated model in Example 3.

The calculation as entire model needs a large computational effort. It is also possible to analyze only one quarter of the model.

12.1 GEOMETRY

In Figure 12.1 the top view of the railway bridge is pictured, with the related longitudinal section 1-1. The railway bridge leads across a 4-lane road.

The cross-section of the superstructure is pictured in Figure 12.2. Figure 12.3 shows the lateral view of the meshed bridge pier, the footing and the adjacent soil. The soil is subdivided into 5 layers. Every soil layer is loaded with its self-weight on the top face of the elements.

Time dependent loads can only be entered as nodal forces in the used program system (http://www.infam.tu-braunschweig.de/). Hence, only nodal forces are used in Example 4.

These nodal forces are denoted as colored values in Figure 12.3 and Figure 12.4.

Due to the symmetry, only one quarter have to be considered for every soil layer. The blue denoted nodal forces from number 1 until number 25 in Figure 12.4 can be applied identically to all quarters. This can be used for all 5 soil layers, however, with different loads on top of each other.

Hence, 125 different nodal forces are calculated for the 5 soil layers (see Table 12.1). The magnitude of these 125 nodal forces is calculated from the influence areas (which are denoted in the lower-left quarter in Figure 12.4) and from the thickness of the soil layers.

The magnitude of the influence areas is given in Figure 12.4, as well.

The orange denoted self-weight of concrete is applied to the superstructure (orange nodal force 1) at the four outer corners on the upper side of the pier. For the pier (orange nodal force 2) and the footing (orange nodal force 3) this is used at the lower sides of these components. The loads are distributed at the four outer corners.

Finally, the traffic load of the train (green nodal force 1) acts on the middle of the pier distributed at two nodal forces.

The used boundary conditions for static and dynamic calculation are denoted in Figure 12.3. In the coupled FEM/SBFEM modal all boundary conditions are unfixed.

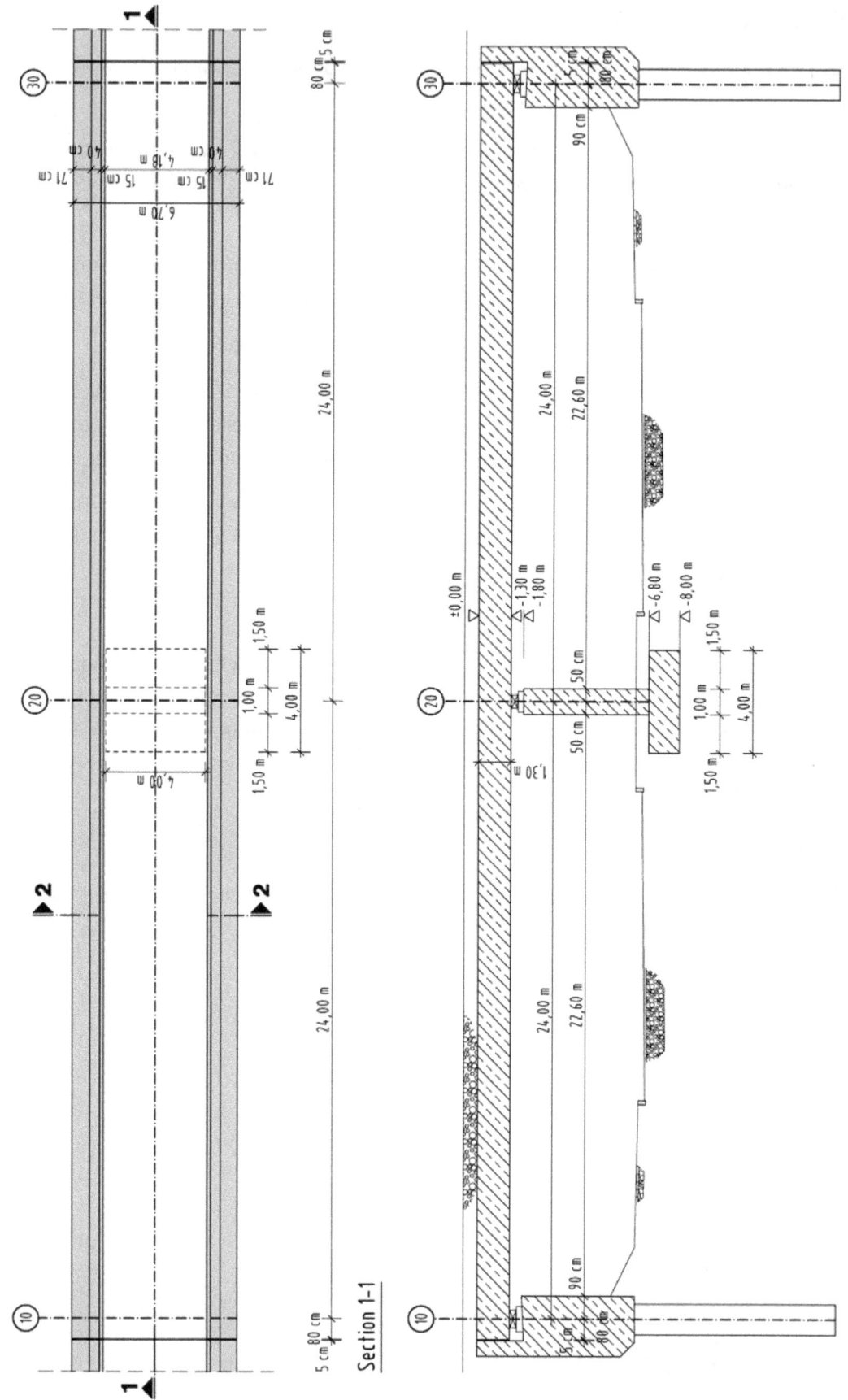

FIGURE 12.1. EXAMPLE 4; GEOMETRY; TOP VIEW OF THE RAILWAY BRIDGE WITH LONGITUDINAL SECTION 1-1

Section 2-2

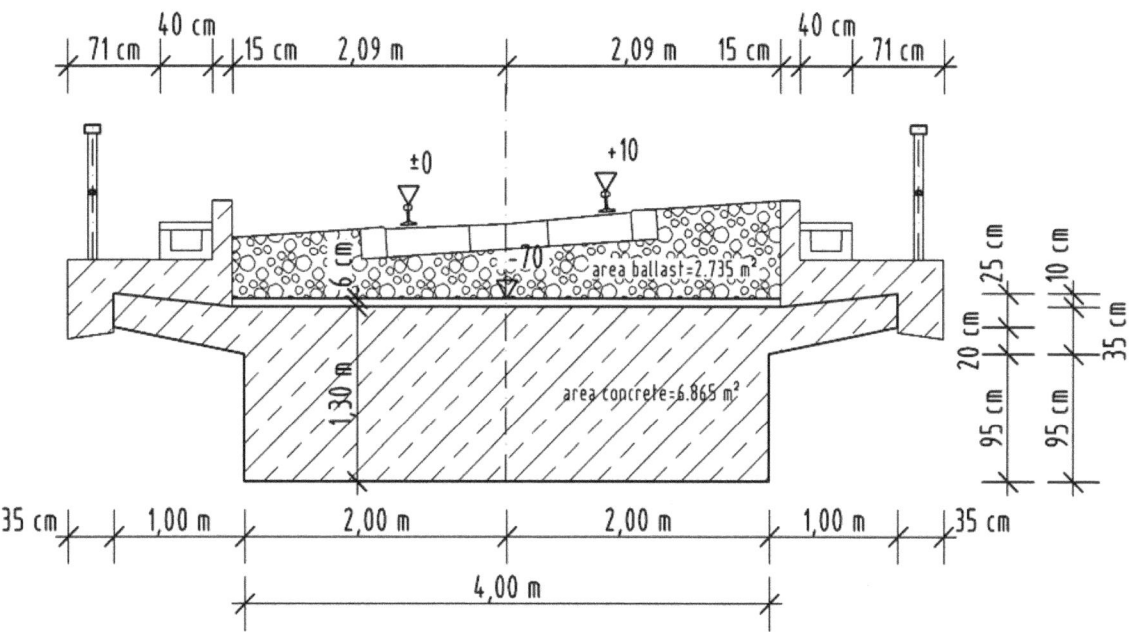

FIGURE 12.2. EXAMPLE 4; GEOMETRY; CROSS-SECTION OF THE SUPERSTRUCTURE

12.2 FEM-Mesh for Bridge Pier and Adjacent Soil

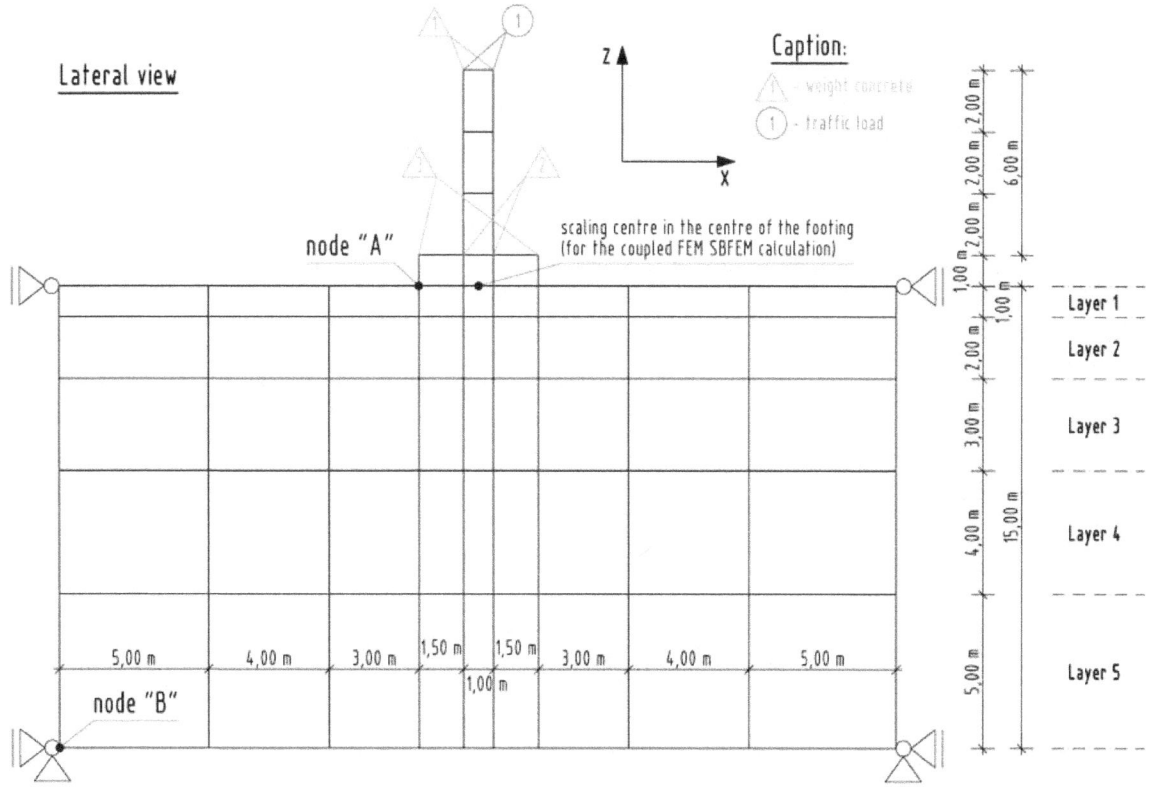

FIGURE 12.3. EXAMPLE 4; GEOMETRY; LATERAL VIEW TO THE FEM DISCRETIZATION OF THE MODEL

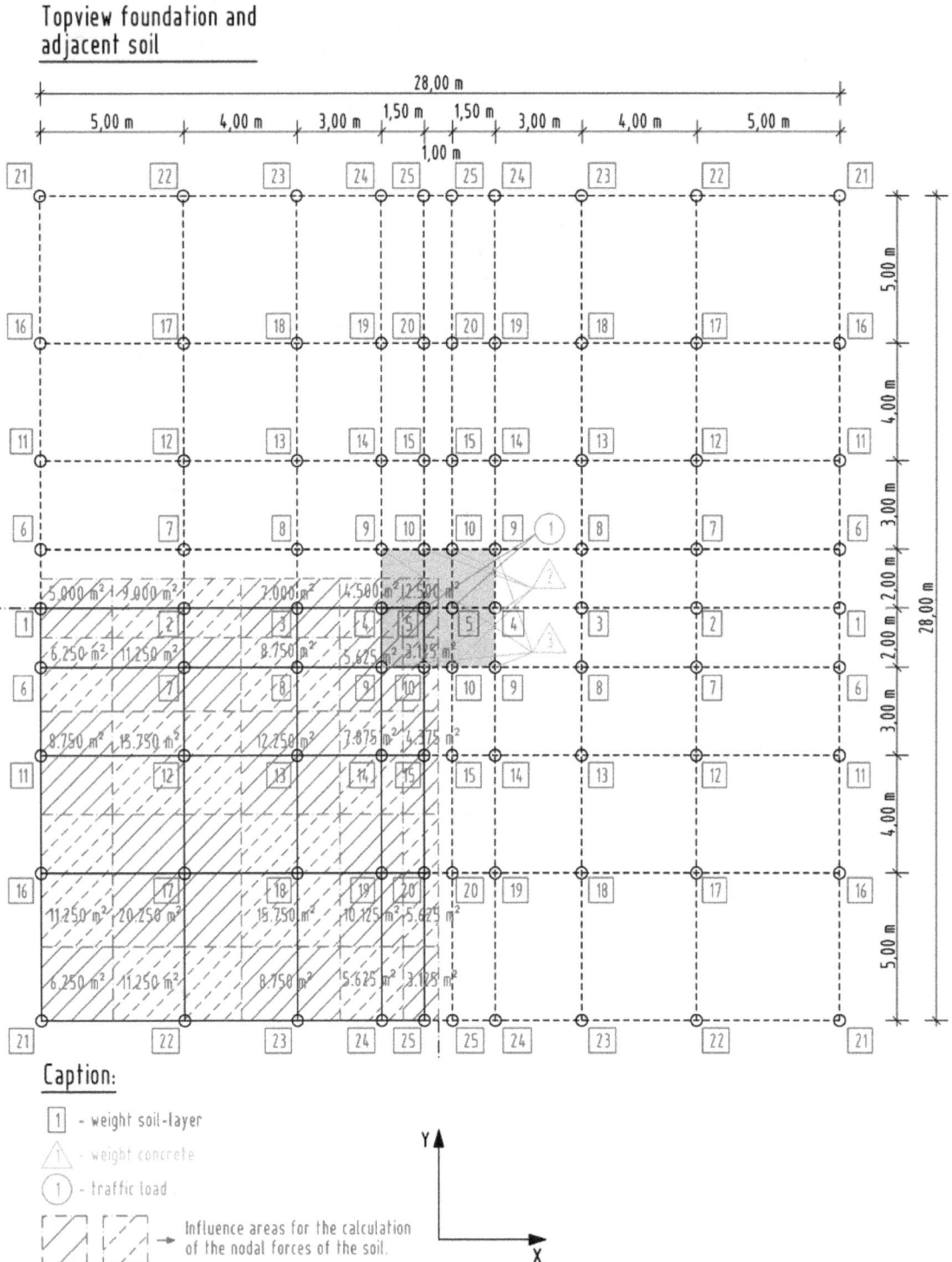

FIGURE 12.4. EXAMPLE 4; GEOMETRY; TOPVIEW OF THE FEM DISCRETIZATION OF THE MODEL WITH NODAL FORCES AND INFLUENCE AREAS FOR THE CALCULATION OF THE NODAL FORCES OF THE SOIL

12.3 MATERIAL

The material properties are chosen according to (Desai & Siriwardane, Constitutive laws for engineering materials, 1984). This soil relates to a sand/gravel mixture. The original U.S. units are converted to SI units:

$$E = 1{,}38\ 10^5\ \frac{kN}{m^2};\ v = 0{,}2;\ \alpha = 0{,}0;\ k = 179\ \frac{kN}{m^2}, A = 148\frac{kN}{m^2};\ B_1 = 0{,}003\ \left(\frac{kN}{m^2}\right)^{-1};$$

$$D = 4\ 10^{-5}\ \left(\frac{kN}{m^2}\right)^{-1};\ W = 0{,}035;\ {}^0L = 0{,}0\ \frac{kN}{m^2};\ R = 1{,}24;$$

$$T = -66\ \frac{kN}{m^2}\ (calculated\ from\ the\ values\ above)$$

Density of the soil: $\gamma = 18\frac{kN}{m^3}$; Density of the concrete $\gamma = 25\frac{kN}{m^3}$

12.4 LOADING

12.4.1 SELF-WEIGHT OF SOIL

The nodal forces for the self-weight of the soil are given in Table 12.1. The loads of the pavement are neglected in the calculation. The location of the nodal forces is given in Figure 12.4, where the soil loads are denoted in blue. The used density of the soil is given in Section 12.3.

	height	load
	[m]	[kN/m²]
layer 1	1	18
layer 2	2	36
layer 3	3	54
layer 4	4	72
layer 5	5	90

nodal force	layer 1	layer 2	layer 3	layer 4	layer 5	area
soillayer	[kN]	[kN]	[kN]	[kN]	[kN]	[m²]
1	90	180	270	360	450	5,000
2	162	324	486	648	810	9,000
3	126	252	378	504	630	7,000
4	81	162	243	324	405	4,500
5	45	90	135	180	225	2,500
6	113	225	338	450	563	6,250
7	203	405	608	810	1013	11,250
8	158	315	473	630	788	8,750
9	101	203	304	405	506	5,625
10	56	113	169	225	281	3,125
11	158	315	473	630	788	8,750
12	284	567	851	1134	1418	15,750
13	221	441	662	882	1103	12,250
14	142	284	425	567	709	7,875
15	79	158	236	315	394	4,375
16	203	405	608	810	1013	11,250
17	365	729	1094	1458	1823	20,250
18	284	567	851	1134	1418	15,750
19	182	365	547	729	911	10,125
20	101	203	304	405	506	5,625
21	113	225	338	450	563	6,250
22	203	405	608	810	1013	11,250
23	158	315	473	630	788	8,750
24	101	203	304	405	506	5,625
25	56	113	169	225	281	3,125
26	180	360	540	720	900	10
27	225	450	675	900	1125	12,5
28	315	630	945	1260	1575	17,5
29	405	810	1215	1620	2025	22,5
30	225	450	675	900	1125	12,5

TABLE 12.1. EXAMPLE 4; LOADING; NODAL FORCES OF SELF WEIGHT OF SOIL

12.4.2 SELF-WEIGHT OF CONCRETE

The nodal forces for the self-weight of concrete are given in Table 12.2. The location of the nodal forces is depicted in Figure 12.3 and Figure 12.4, where the concrete loads are denoted in orange.

The magnitude of the bearing load on the pier generated by the superstructure is calculated with (Schneider, 1996). The bearing load for a continuous beam with two fields and a uniformly distributed load is calculated as: $f = 1{,}25\,q\,l$; with f as bearing load at the bridge pier, q as uniformly distributed load and l as span. The used density of the concrete is given in Section 12.3.

superstructure:

	area	load
	[m²]	[kN/m]
self-weight	9,6	240

nodal force	lenght	table value	load
concrete	[m]	[-]	[kN]
1	24	1,25	7200
quartered self-weight 1			**1800**

pier:

	area	load
	[m²]	[kN/m]
self-weight	4	100

nodal force	lenght	load
	[m]	[kN]
self-weight 2	6	600
quartered self-weight 12		**150**

footing:

	area	load
	[m²]	[kN/m]
self-weight	16	400

nodal force	lenght	load
	[m]	[kN]
self-weight 3	1	400
quartered self-weight 3		**100**

TABLE 12.2. EXAMPLE 4; LOADING; NODAL FORCES OF SELF WEIGHT OF CONCRETE

12.4.3 TRAFFIC LOAD

The load model LM 71 from the *DIN-Fachbericht 101* (DIN Fachbericht 101, 2009) is applied as a traffic load. The load model is pictured in Figure 12.5.

LM 71:

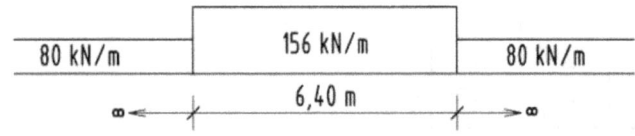

FIGURE 12.5. LOAD MODEL LM 71

The time dependent loads at the pier bearing are calculated with the help of influence lines. The influence line of a force relates to the elastic curve due to the conjugated displacement "-1" (Bochmann, 2001). This is sketched in Figure 12.6 for the pier bearing (bearing "B"). The bearing B is lowered by the magnitude of -1 here.

Influence line for bearing B:

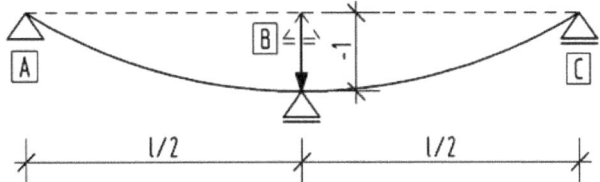

FIGURE 12.6. EXAMPLE 4; INFLUENCE LINE FOR THE PIER BEARING

First the moment diagram for the settlement "-1" of bearing B is determined. When the moment diagram is known, the elastic curve is determined from the following equation:

$$w'' = -\frac{M}{E\,I} \qquad (12.1)$$

with w'' as second derivation of the elastic curve, M as moment diagram, E as elastic modulus and I as moment of inertia. The double integration of $-\frac{M}{E\,I}$ yields the elastic curve. With the force method the moment diagram is calculated as following:

moment diagram for settlement -1 of bearing B:

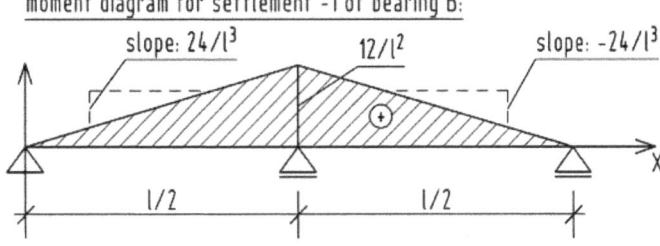

FIGURE 12.7. EXAMPLE 4; MOMENT DIAGRAM FOR THE SETTLEMENT "-1" OF BEARING B

The following is given if the moment diagram line is written as a function of x (with $x = 0 \ldots l$ and l as length of the superstructure):

$$f(x) = \begin{cases} \dfrac{24}{l^3}x & for\ 0 \leq x \leq \dfrac{l}{2} \\[2ex] -\dfrac{24}{l^3}x + \dfrac{24}{l^2} & for\ \dfrac{l}{2} < x \leq l \end{cases} \qquad (12.2)$$

The elastic curve $w(x)$ for $0 \leq x \leq \frac{l}{2}$ is then calculated with two times integration as:

$$w(x) = -x^3\frac{4}{l^3} + x^2\frac{12}{l^2} - x\frac{9}{l} + 1 \qquad for\ \frac{l}{2} < x \leq l \qquad (12.3)$$

The pier load B is calculated now with the integration of the elastic curve:

$$B = \int_a^b q(x)\, w(x)dx = q \int_a^b w(x)dx \qquad (12.4)$$

The circumstance is pictured in Figure 12.8 with the related upper and lower boundaries a and b. The traffic load q is a uniformly distributed load, therefore, not dependent on x.

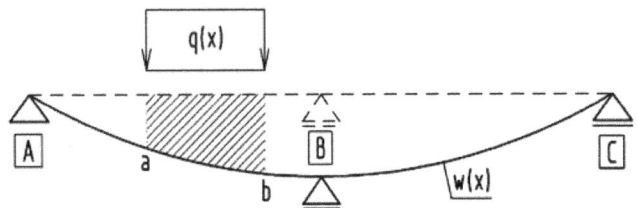

FIGURE 12.8. EXAMPLE 4; IMPLICATION OF A LINEAR DISTRIBUTED LOAD TO AN INFLUENCE LINE

Inserting (12.3) in (12.4) yields:

$$B = q \int_a^b \left(x^3 \frac{4}{l} - x\frac{3}{l}\right) dx = q \left. \left| \frac{x^4}{l} - \frac{3\,x^2}{2\,l} \right| \right._a^b \qquad for\ 0 \leq x \leq \frac{l}{2} \quad (12.5)$$

$$B = q \int_a^b \left(-x^3 \frac{4}{l^3} + x^2 \frac{12}{l^2} - x\frac{9}{l} + 1\right) dx$$

$$B = q \left. \left| -\frac{x^4}{l} - x^3 \frac{4}{l^2} - x^2 \frac{9}{2\,l} + x \right| \right._a^b \qquad for\ \frac{l}{2} < x \leq l \quad (12.6)$$

With help of the equations (12.5) and (12.6) the time dependent train load at the pier bearing can be calculated now. For the calculation the following input data (for the dynamic calculation with 2500 time steps in Section 12.5.2) are chosen:

q = 80   kN/m
$q_ü$ = 76   kN/m
$l_ü$ = 6,1   m
l = 48   m
v = 44,4   m/s
Δt = 0,1   s

The meaning of the variables is pictured in Figure 12.9. The velocity of the traffic load LM 71 is chosen as $v = 160\frac{km}{h} = 44,4\ \frac{m}{s}$ analogous to (DIN-Fachbericht 101, 2009).

The using of the equations (12.5) and (12.6) yields the values for the pier load B, which are given in Table 12.3. The load diagram in Figure 12.10 shows the developing of the pier load B due to the traffic load for the pure FEM model (for a total of 2500 time steps, see section 12.5.2).

The loads q and $q_ü$ (see Figure 12.9) are applied in the following order: first, q is applied to the superstructure; then, $q_ü$ is applied at bearing A when q reaches bearing C; finally, q scales down until it is zero at bearing C when the end of $q_ü$ reaches bearing C.

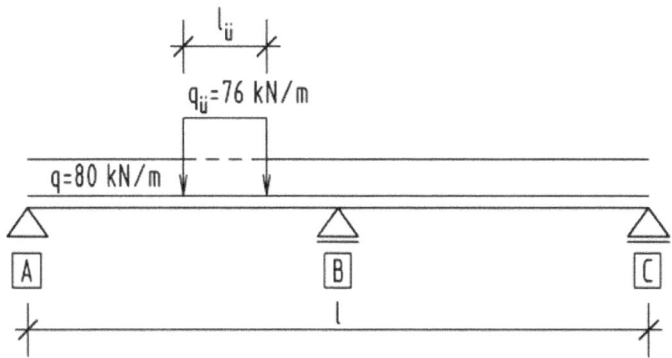

FIGURE 12.9. EXAMPLE 4; QUANTITIES OF THE LOAD MODEL LM 71

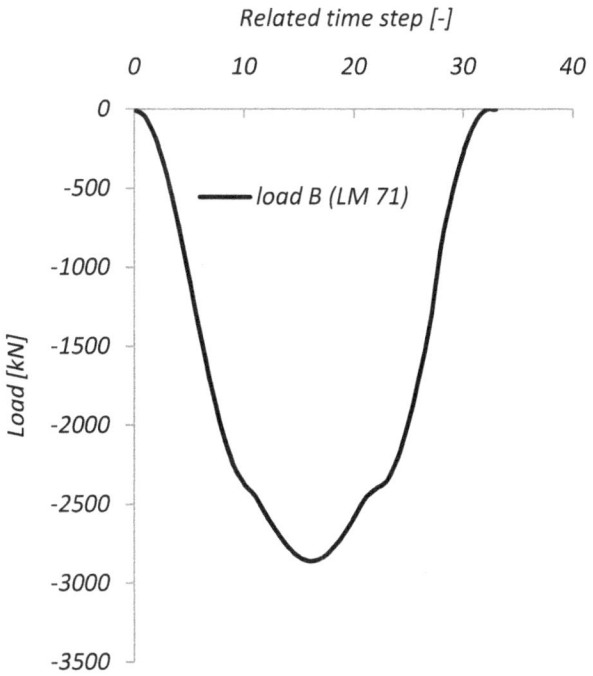

FIGURE 12.10. EXAMPLE 4; TIME DEPENDENT TRAFFIC LOAD AT BEARING "B" FOR DYNAMIC CALCULATION WITH PURE FEM MODEL

The traffic load is applied from time step 2000 (see Figure 12.14) in the dynamic calculation with the pure FEM model.

Therefore, the time step is denoted as a "related time step" in the load diagram Figure 12.10. The load (B/2) is given in Table 12.3 as a nodal force on the pier, as pictured in Figure 12.3 and Figure 12.4. Table 12.3 is applied in the dynamic calculation with the pure FEM model with a total of 2500 time steps (see Section 12.5.2).

The same input data are chosen for the dynamic calculation with the coupled FEM/SBFEM model. Only the time step is changed to 0,02 s for a total of 12500 time steps (see Section 12.5.3). The particular nodal forces are not depicted here. The calculation of the nodal forces for the coupled FEM/SBFEM model is conducted as explained above.

step	time	B	B/2
[-]	[s]	[kN]	[kN]
0	0,00	0	0
1	0,10	-49	-25
2	0,20	-193	-97
3	0,30	-422	-211
4	0,40	-718	-359
5	0,50	-1058	-529
6	0,60	-1412	-706
7	0,70	-1746	-873
8	0,80	-2030	-1015
9	0,90	-2243	-1121
10	1,00	-2369	-1184
11	1,10	-2447	-1223
12	1,20	-2565	-1282
13	1,30	-2678	-1339
14	1,40	-2771	-1385
15	1,50	-2834	-1417
16	1,60	-2860	-1430
17	1,70	-2842	-1421
18	1,80	-2784	-1392
19	1,90	-2696	-1348
20	2,00	-2586	-1293
21	2,10	-2464	-1232
22	2,20	-2401	-1201
23	2,30	-2351	-1175
24	2,40	-2207	-1103
25	2,50	-1978	-989
26	2,60	-1682	-841
27	2,70	-1342	-671
28	2,80	-850	-425
29	2,90	-533	-267
30	3,00	-275	-138
31	3,10	-96	-48
32	3,20	-8	-4
33	3,30	0	0

TABLE 12.3. EXAMPLE 4; TIME DEPENDENT NODAL FORCES OF THE TRAFFIC LOAD

12.5 RESULTS

All results relate to the vertical component of the displacements in the node "A" (see Figure 12.3) if it is not otherwise denoted.

12.5.1 STATIC CALCULATION

The static calculation is carried out in 15 load steps to document the developing of the displacements with increasing load. For the static calculation the maximum value of the traffic load with $B/2 = 1430\ kN$ is used (see Section 12.4.3).

The elasto-plastic displacement at the maximum load is pictured in Figure 12.11 with hundredfold magnification of the vertical displacement. The difference between the deepening under the foundation and the adjacent smooth surface characterizes the requested settlement of the bridge pier (approximately $0{,}017\ m$) due to the self-weight of the bridge and the traffic load. A similar result is obtained in the following dynamic calculations.

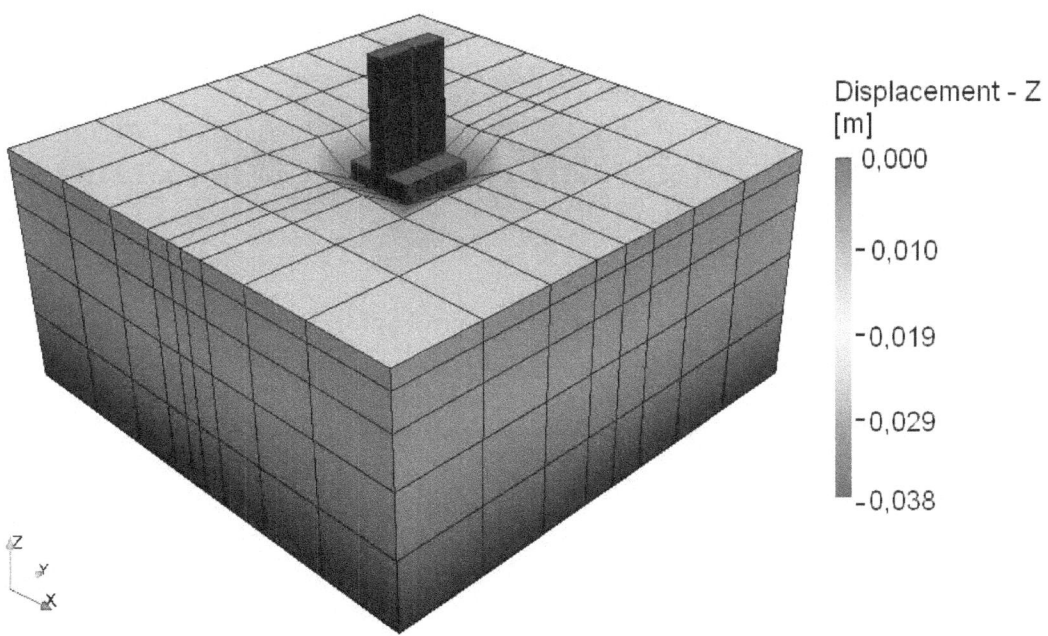

FIGURE 12.11. EXAMPLE 4; CALCULATED AS STATIC FEM SIMULATION; MAXIMUM DISPLACEMENT

The stress diagram of the first two invariants from Example 4 is given in Figure 12.12. The general type of the diagram is given in Figure 5.1. The developing of the stress point of the Gauss point 0 from element 3 (the element 3 is located adjacent to the footing) is given. Load step 1 is elastic. The green triangle denotes the position of the stress point at the elastic trial calculation of load step 2. The stress point visibly exceeds the blue dashed cap in load step 2. Hence, the deformation of the stress point in load step 2 is plastic. The purple crosses denote the equilibrium iterations of the stress point until the new position of the cap is found. The new cap position at the end of load step 2 is denoted as a continuous blue line.

The vertical displacement of the foundation is given in Figure 12.13 for elasto-plastic soil behavior and only linear-elastic soil behavior. As expected the elasto-plastic displacement is greater than the linear-elastic displacement.

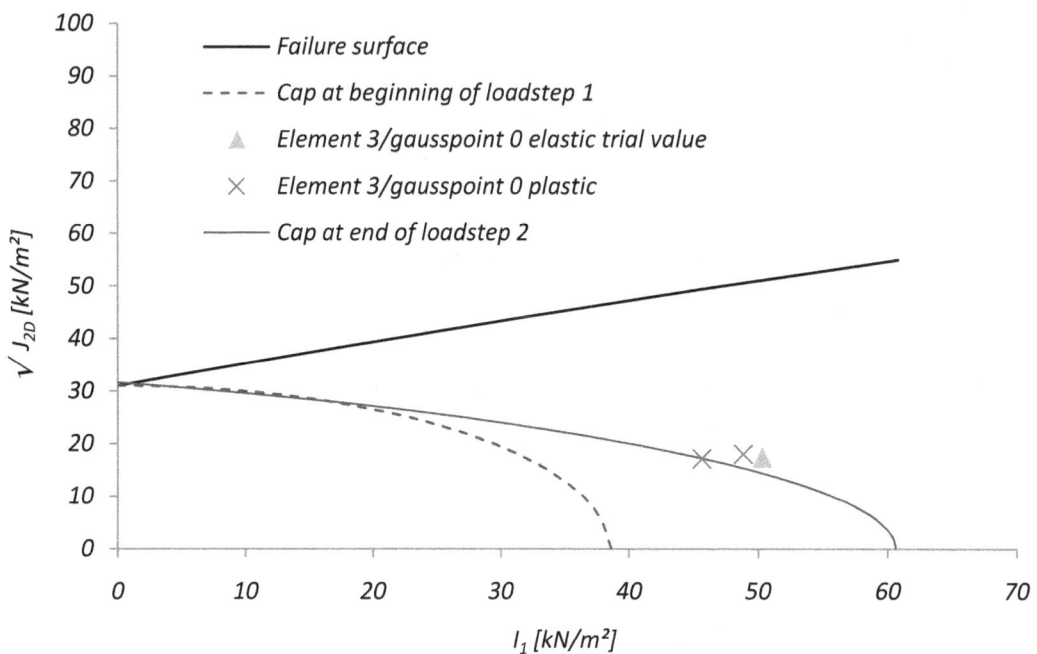

FIGURE 12.12. EXAMPLE 4; NODE "A" – BOTTOM SIDE OF THE FOOTING; CALCULATED AS STATIC FEM SIMULATION; EXAMPLARY ITERATIVE STRESS CALCULATION OF THE IMPLEMENTED CAP MODEL FOR TWO LOADSTEPS

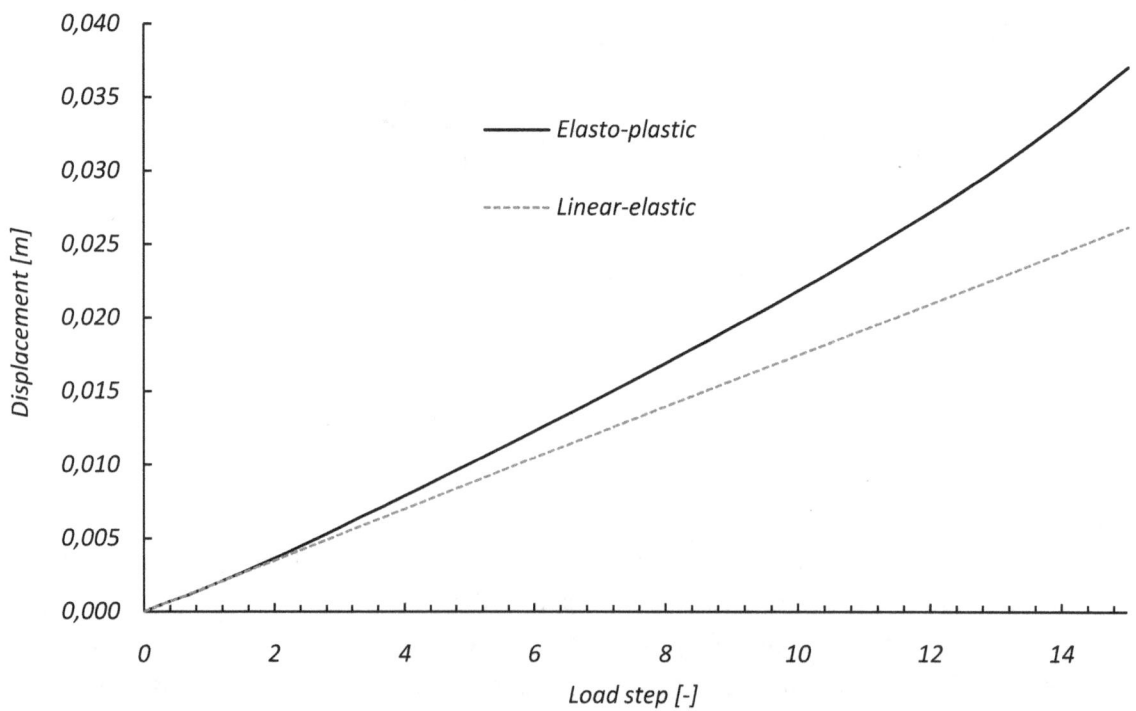

FIGURE 12.13. EXAMPLE 4; NODE "A" – BOTTOM SIDE OF THE FOOTING; LOAD STEP/DISPLACEMENT DIAGRAM; CALCULATED AS STATIC FEM SIMULATION

12.5.2 DYNAMIC CALCULATION WITH PURE FEM MODEL

The following input data are given:

Time:

$\Delta t = 0,1\ s$

$2500\ timesteps$

Overall simulated time: $0,1\ 2500 = 250\ s$

For the dynamic calculation with the pure FEM model, the soil density is chosen as $\rho = 1800\ \frac{kg}{m^3}$ and the concrete density is chosen as $\rho = 2500\ \frac{kg}{m^3}$.

Damping:

Rayleigh damping is not included in Example 4. Hysteretic material damping is automatically included due to plastic deformation (see Section 9.4.2).

Loads:

As described in the introduction of this chapter, the different current states (Desai, The disturbated state concept, 2001) of the soil have to be determined firstly for the different loads. For this reason the loads are applied successively. First, the soil is subjected to its self-weight, which results in *current state 1*. With *current state 1*, the soil is subjected to the self-weight of the bridge, which results in *current state 2*. Finally, with *current state 2*, the soil is subjected to the traffic load.

The loads from the self-weight are applied quasi-statically as they increase slowly, linearly over the time steps. This is visible in Figure 12.14 by a linear slow load increasing of the self-weight of the soil over 500 time steps (overall time $t = 0,1\ 500 = 50s$) and a linear slow increasing of the self-weight of concrete over 1500 time steps (overall time $t = 0,1\ 1500 = 150s$). The number of time steps was chosen as large as necessary for a quasi-static calculation of the self-weight. This is conducted in order to minimize the oscillations from the quasi-static loads (see Figure 12.15; 0–500 time steps for the self-weight of soil and 500–2000 time steps for the self-weight of concrete).

The traffic loads are applied dynamically to the pier (see Section 12.4.3). This is sketched in Figure 12.14. The traffic load acts only on approximately 30 time steps.

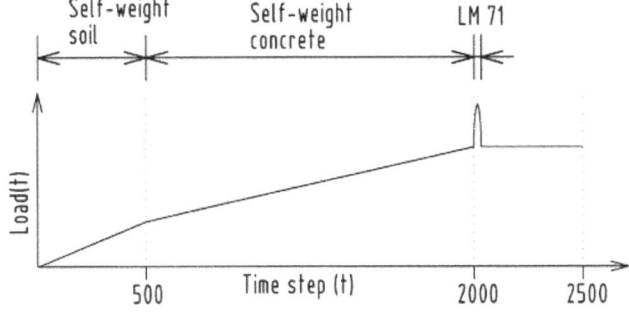

FIGURE 12.14. EXAMPLE 4; DYNAMIC CALCULATION WITH PURE FEM MODEL; APPLYING OF TIME DEPENDENT LOADS

A time step/displacement diagram is given in Figure 12.15. The plastic deformation due to the traffic load is well recognizable for the elasto-plastic calculation. For comparison the deformation for linear soil is given also in Figure 12.15. As expected, the dynamic calculation with the pure FEM model causes undesirable post-oscillations due to the dynamic traffic loads.

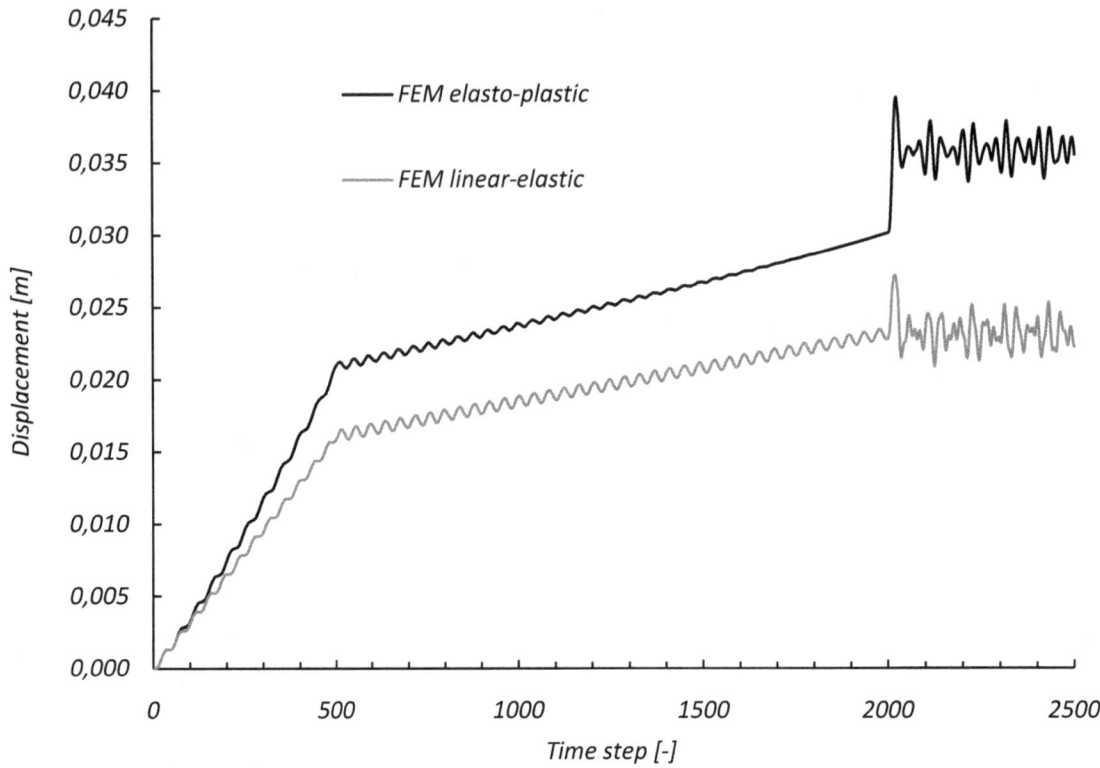

FIGURE 12.15. EXAMPLE 4; NODE "A" – BOTTOM SIDE OF THE FOOTING; TIME STEP/DISPLACEMENT DIAGRAM; CALCULATED AS DYNAMIC FEM SIMULATION WITH PURE FEM MODEL

12.5.3 DYNAMIC CALCULATION WITH COUPLED FEM/SBFEM MODEL

The location of the scaling center "O" is given in Figure 12.3. The following input data are given:

Time:

For convergence the time step must be reduced in the coupled FEM/SBFEM model (a criterion for the maximum magnitude of the time step Δt is given in, e.g., (Bathe, 2002)).

$\Delta t = 0,02 \, s$

$12500 \, timesteps$

Overall time: $0,02 \cdot 12500 = 250 \, s$

For the dynamic calculation the soil density is chosen as $\rho_s = 1800 \, \frac{kg}{m^3}$ and the concrete density is chosen as $\rho_c = 2500 \, \frac{kg}{m^3}$.

Damping:

Rayleigh damping is not included in Example 4. Hysteretic material damping is automatic included due to plastic deformation (see Section 9.4.2).

Loads:

As described in the introduction of this chapter, the different current states (Desai, The disturbated state concept, 2001) of the soil have to be determined firstly for the different loads. For this reason the loads are applied successively. First, the soil is subjected to its self-weight, which results in *current state 1*. With *current state 1*, the soil is subjected to the self-weight of the bridge, which results in *current state 2*. Finally, with *current state 2*, the soil is subjected to the traffic load.

The loads from the self-weight are applied quasi-statically as they increase slowly, linearly over the time steps. This is visible in Figure 12.16 by a linear slow load increasing the self-weight of the soil over 2500 time steps (overall time $t = 0,02\ 2500 = 50s$) and a linear slow increasing of the self-weight of concrete over 7500 time steps (overall time $t = 0,02\ 7500 = 150s$). The number of time steps was chosen as large as necessary for a quasi-static calculation.

The traffic loads are applied dynamically to the pier (see Section 12.4.3). This is sketched in Figure 12.16. The traffic load acts only on approximately 160 time steps.

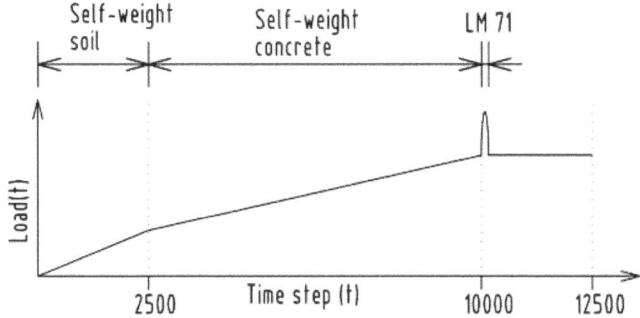

FIGURE 12.16. EXAMPLE 4; DYNAMIC CALCULATION WITH COUPLED FEM/SBFEM MODEL; APPLYING OF TIME DEPENDENT LOADS

The material data for the SBFEM far-field relate accordingly to the elastic values with:

$$E = 1,38\ 10^5\ \frac{kN}{m^2};$$

$$v = 0,25;$$

$$G = \frac{E}{2\ (1 + v)} = \frac{1,38\ 10^5}{2\ (1 + 0,25)} = 55158\ \frac{kN}{m^2}$$

Interface elements are arranged at the outer boundaries of the near-field to couple the FEM with the SBFEM.

The calculation is conducted with the HHT-α method ($\alpha = -0,05$; $\gamma = \frac{1-2\ \alpha}{2} = 0,55$ and $\beta = \frac{(1-\alpha)^2}{4} = 0,276$).

The time step displacement diagram for the coupled FEM/SBFEM model is pictured in Figure 12.17. The enlargement of the deformations due to the traffic load is given in Figure 12.18. As expected, the elasto-plastic calculation yields a larger deformation than the linear-elastic calculation. The deformation of the self-weight of soil in the coupled FEM/SBFEM model in Figure 12.17 is essentially larger than in the pure FEM model in Figure 12.15. This originates from the elastic deformation of the outer boundary of the discretized part.

However, the deformation through the self-weight of the soil represents only an initial condition for the further calculation (Desai, The disturbated state concept, 2001).

Only the results from the self-weight of the bridge and from the traffic are interesting for the practical interpretation. These results are illustrated in Figure 12.19 as difference displacements with an initial displacement of zero. The prior displacement of the self-weight of soil is not of interest. The time steps of the pure FEM calculation are scaled to the time steps of the coupled FEM/SBFEM calculation for a better comparison; this is applied to Figure 12.19 and Figure 12.20.

Settlements of 1,5 cm (due to the self-weight of concrete and the traffic load) are calculated with the coupled FEM/SBFEM model and in the pure FEM model, as pictured in Figure 12.19. This represents a normal magnitude for settlements in bridge construction.

However, a more precise comparison of the elasto-plastic pure FEM calculation with the coupled elasto-plastic FEM/SBFEM calculation shows significant differences between the particular loadings. The coupled FEM/SBFEM model shows a larger deformation due to the self-weight of the bridge and a smaller deformation due to the traffic load.

The larger deformation due to the self-weight of the bridge is founded in the elastic deformation of the discretized parts' outer boundary of the coupled FEM/SBFEM model. The smaller deformation due to the traffic load is founded in the included wave radiation of the FEM/SBFEM model.

The smaller deformation of the traffic load (coupled FEM/SBFEM model) is clearly pictured in Figure 12.20. Figure 12.20 shows difference displacements with an initial displacement of zero for a better comparison (as enlargement of the traffic loads). Here it is apparent that the traffic load deformation from the pure elasto-plastic FEM model (approximately 1 cm) is twice as large as in the coupled elasto-plastic FEM/SBFEM model (approximately 0,5 cm) during the vehicle crossing.

This fact results in an over-dimensioning of the structure for the pure elasto-plastic FEM model with respect to the higher safety factors for traffic loads. A larger plastic deformation of another soil would clarify this further still.

A further advantage of the coupled FEM/SBFEM model is visible in Figure 12.20. Wave reflections (visible by post-oscillations of the traffic in Figure 12.15, Figure 12.19 and Figure 12.20) do not occur in the coupled FEM/SBFEM model. This is important when oscillation transmissions to adjacent buildings have to be included.

Practical examples are domestic buildings in the immediate vicinity of urban railways and rail tracks, or road traffic ways and rail tracks near chip factories. Here, the chip production can be impossible due to overly large oscillations. The determination of realistic oscillation amplitudes is demanded in all named cases. This can in turn only be calculated with an appropriate soil model and included wave propagation.

With the determined "realistic" (from a theoretical point of view; the numerical results have to be verified by experimental studies) oscillation amplitudes, it may be possible to omit elaborate and cost-intensive vibration insulating.

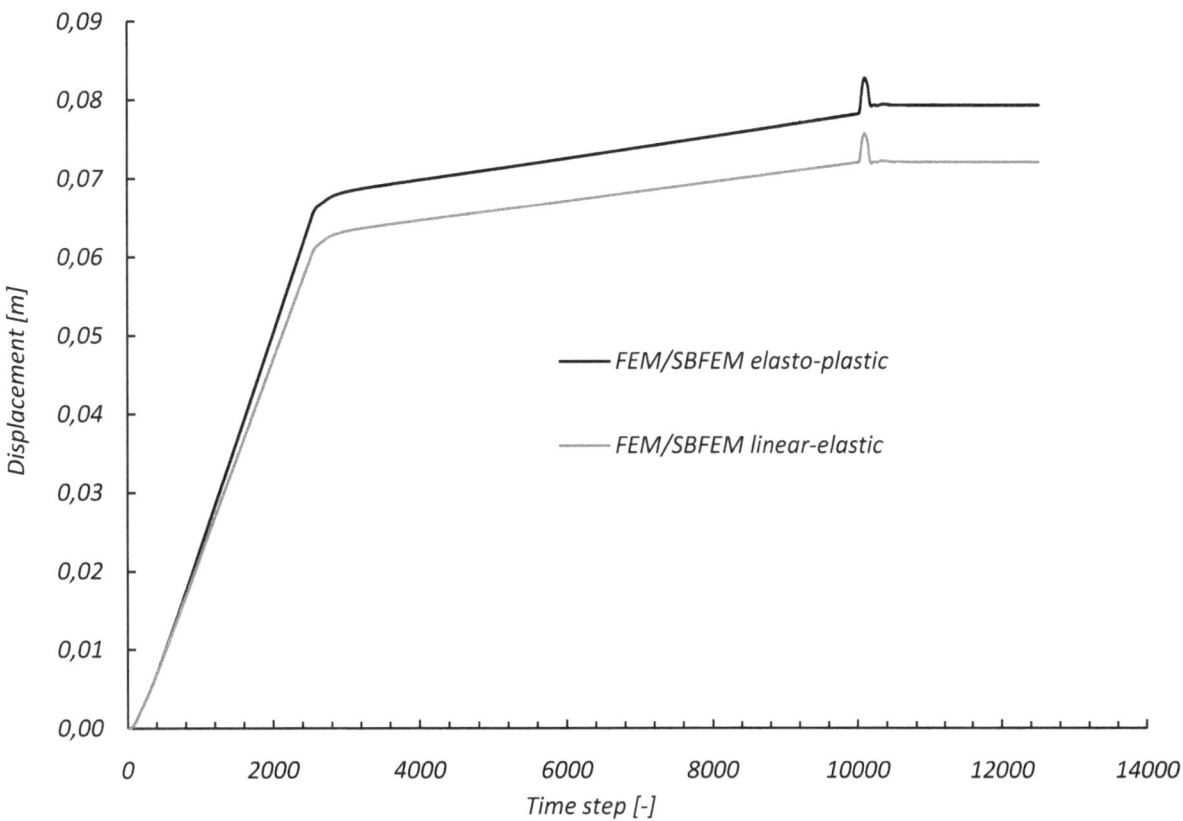

FIGURE 12.17. EXAMPLE 4; NODE "A" – BOTTOM SIDE OF THE FOOTING; TIME STEP/DISPLACEMENT DIAGRAM; CALCULATED AS DYNAMIC FEM SIMULATION WITH COUPLED FEM/SBFEM MODEL

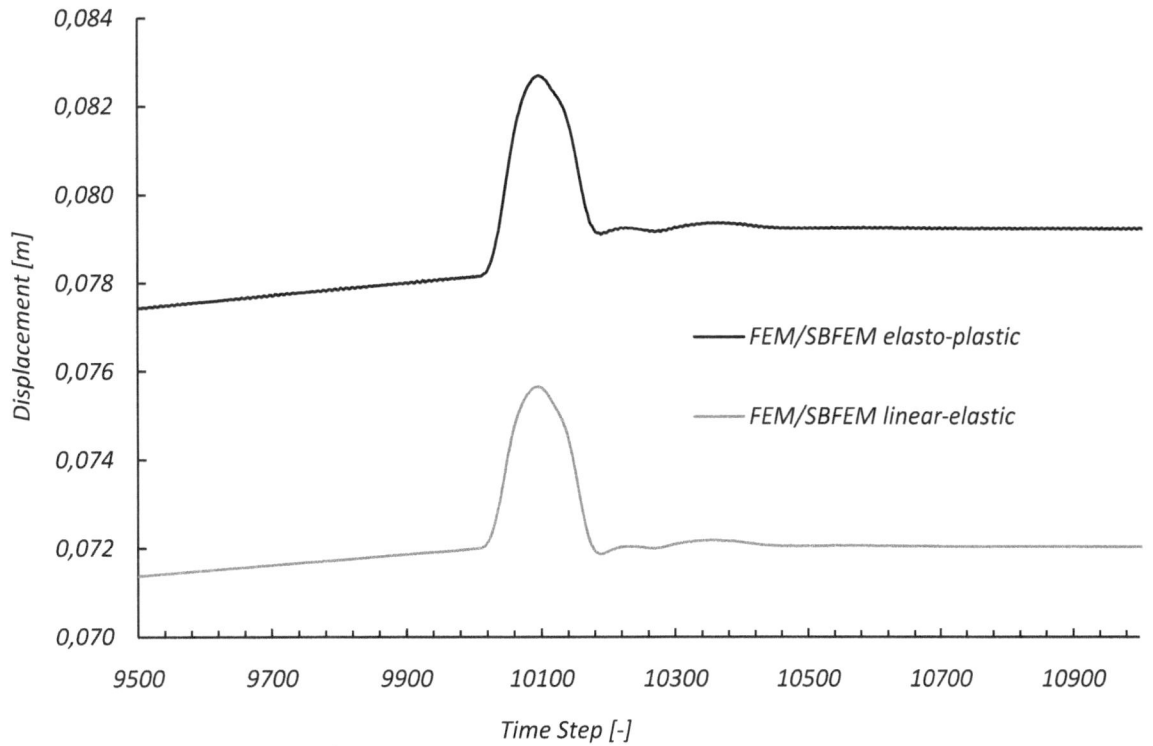

FIGURE 12.18. EXAMPLE 4; NODE "A" – BOTTOM SIDE OF THE FOOTING; TIME STEP/DISPLACEMENT DIAGRAM; CALCULATED AS DYNAMIC FEM SIMULATION WITH COUPLED FEM/SBFEM MODEL; ENLARGEMENT OF THE TRAFFIC LOAD OF FIGURE 12.17

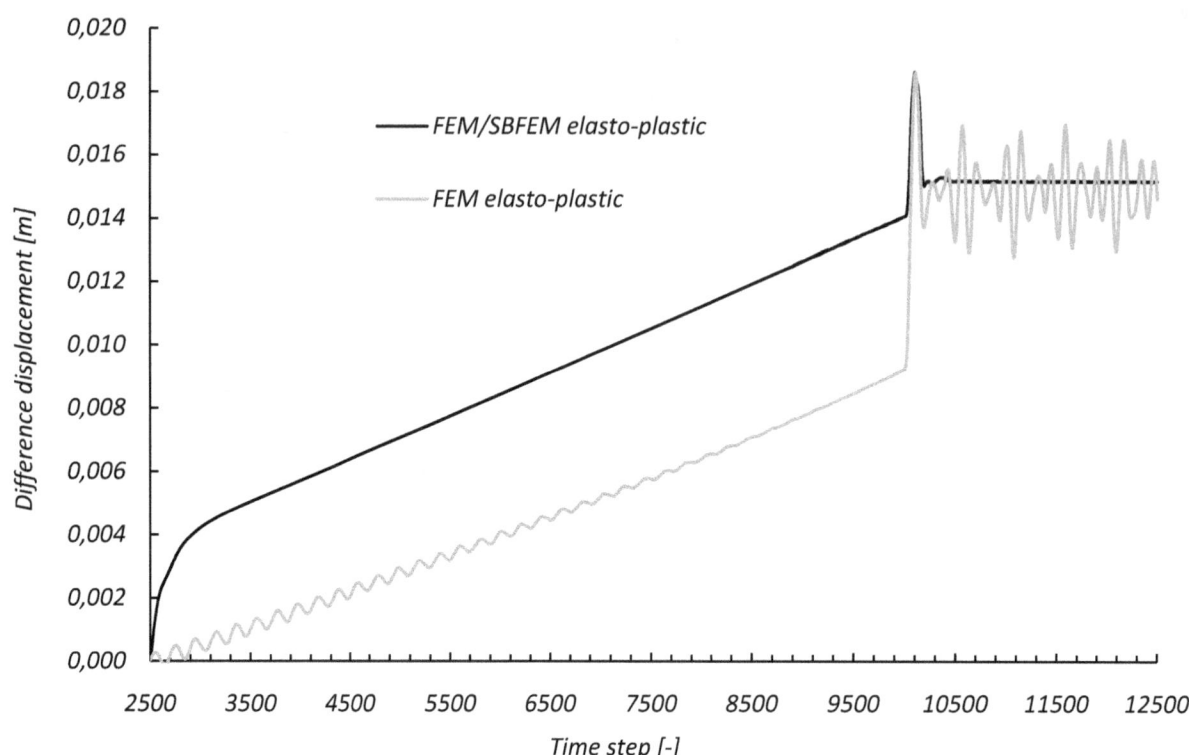

FIGURE 12.19. EXAMPLE 4; NODE "A" – BOTTOM SIDE OF THE FOOTING; TIME STEP/DISPLACEMENT DIAGRAM; CALCULATED AS DYNAMIC FEM SIMULATION WITH COUPLED FEM/SBFEM MODEL; COMPARISON OF THE DEFORMATIONS THROUGH SELF-WEIGHT OF CONCRETE AND TRAFFIC

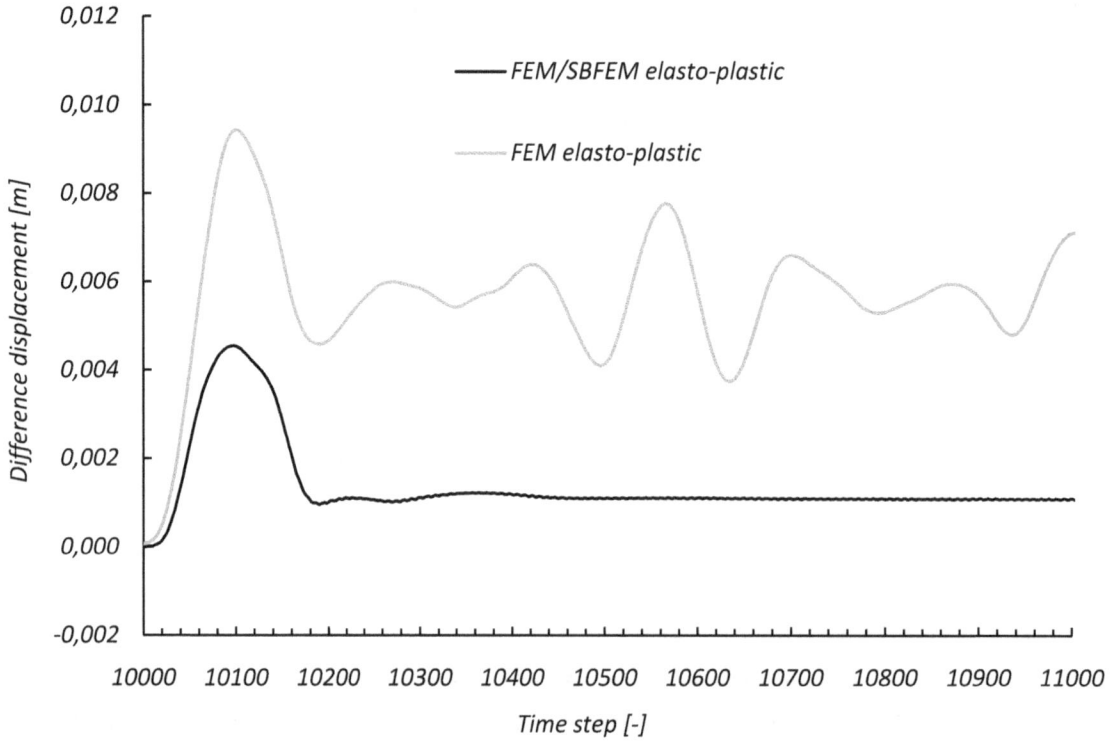

FIGURE 12.20. EXAMPLE 4; NODE "A" – BOTTOM SIDE OF THE FOOTING; TIME STEP/DISPLACEMENT DIAGRAM; CALCULATED AS DYNAMIC FEM SIMULATION WITH COUPLED FEM/SBFEM MODEL; COMPARISON OF THE TRAFFIC DEFORMATIONS

An oscillation transmission to nearby structures was already analyzed in the verification Examples 2 and 3 (see Sections 10.3.3 and 11.3.3). This is also applied for the traffic loads in this practical Example 4.

The time-step/displacement diagram (for the traffic load) of node "B" (see Figure 12.3) is illustrated in Figure 12.21. Figure 12.21 shows difference displacements in node "B" with an initial displacement of zero for a better comparison, as applied in Figure 12.20 for node "A". A comparison between the linear-elastic FEM/SBFEM calculation and the elasto-plastic FEM/SBFEM calculation is given here.

The maximum amplitudes in Figure 12.21 are similar (with a little difference) because the near-field is chosen so large that no plastic deformation occurs at the outer boundaries.

That means: the oscillation transmission of the linear-elastic FEM/SBFEM model is very similar compared to the elasto-plastic FEM/SBFEM model if node "B" is not in the domain of the plastic deformation of the near-field.

In contrast, Example 3 shows that a significant difference between the linear-elastic FEM/SBFEM and the elasto-plastic FEM/SBFEM exists if node "B" is in the domain of the plastic deformation of the near-field (see Figure 11.9 and Figure 11.10).

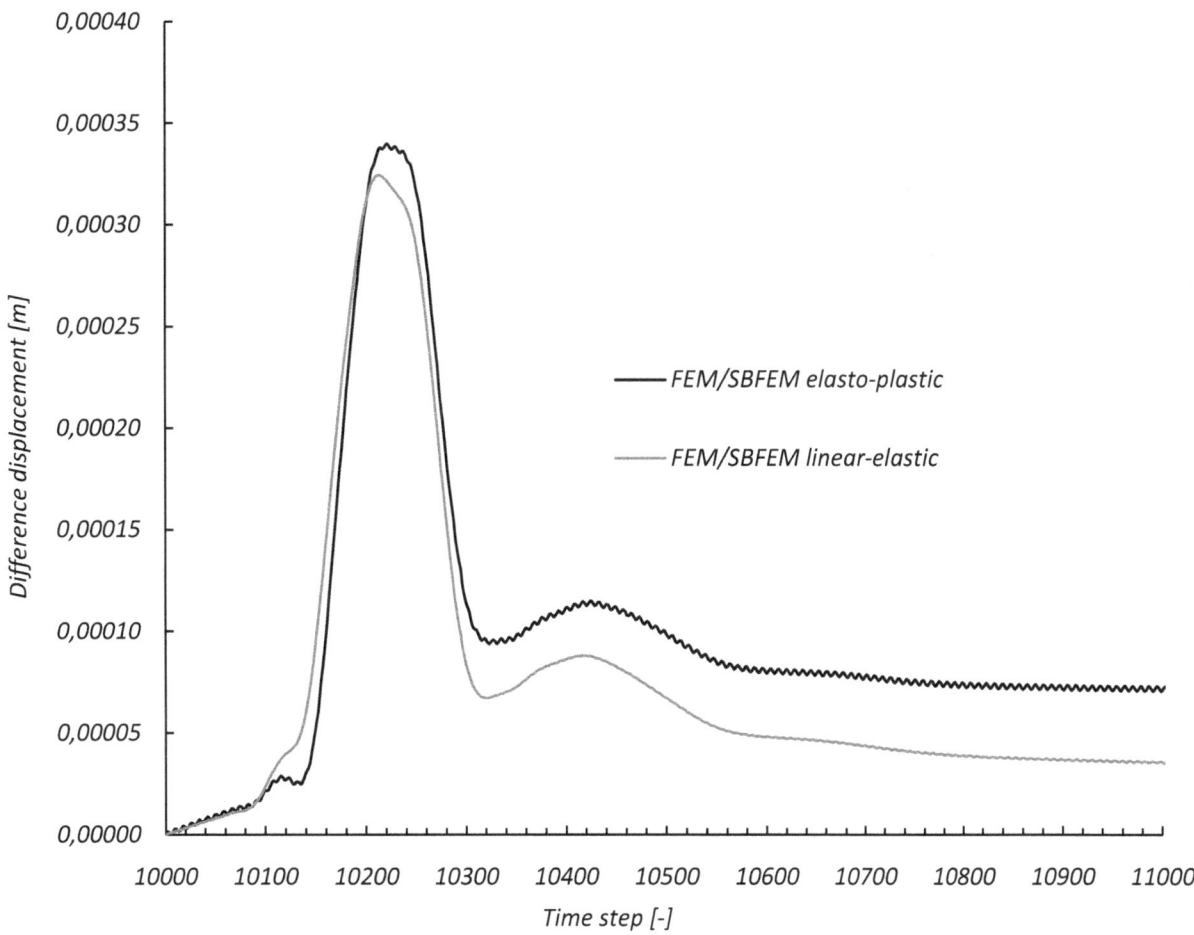

FIGURE 12.21. EXAMPLE 4; NODE "B" – BOTTOM SIDE OF THE DISCRETIZED PART; TIME STEP/DISPLACEMENT DIAGRAM; CALCULATED AS DYNAMIC FEM SIMULATION WITH COUPLED FEM/SBFEM MODEL; COMPARISON OF THE TRAFFIC DEFORMATIONS

13 FINAL REMARKS

13.1 SUMMARY

An *overall calculation scheme* was presented in this work. The *overall calculation scheme* includes the following calculation methods: FEM, Newton-Raphson method, an elasto-plastic material model in form of the cap model, the nonlinear HHT-α method und the SBFEM method. Accordingly to this, Part I of this work presents the theoretical basics of the particular methods. These methods are combined to an *overall calculation scheme*. Herewith, the *overall calculation scheme* contains all advantages of the particular methods. Application examples are calculated then, with the given *overall calculation scheme*, in Part II.

Part I:

The equations in Chapter 5 are based on a description from (Kojic & Bathe, 2005). However, the derivation of the equations from (Kojic & Bathe, 2005) was expanded here. So all equations are derived in detail and the relations among each other are given. Furthermore, equations are derived for the calculation of the constitutive matrix. These equations are sorted by the order of their application in tabular form (see Table 5.4, Table 5.5, Table 5.6).

Finally, a static overall calculation scheme was developed in Chapter 5. The relation to the elasto-plastic equations of the cap model was given here.

The static overall calculation scheme was then expanded for the dynamic calculation. A linear HHT-α method is implemented in the existent program system (http://www.infam.tu-braunschweig.de/). Therefore, the development of a nonlinear HHT-α method from the linear HHT-α method was expedient.

Only sparse information is given in the literature for the nonlinear HHT-α method. However, the search leads to a nonlinear HHT-α method with modified Newton-Raphson iteration (Crisfield, 1997). The equations of the cap model were derived for the full Newton-Raphson iteration. Hence, the extension of the nonlinear HHT-α method from (Crisfield, 1997) to a full Newton-Raphson iteration was expedient, as well. With it, the advantages of the full Newton-Raphson iteration can be used. Accordingly to this, the static overall calculation scheme from Section 5.3 was extended to a dynamic overall calculation scheme (see Section 6.4).

Finally, the dynamic overall calculation scheme has to be extended for the SBFEM (see Section 7.3) to include the wave propagation to infinity. Then, the dynamic overall calculation scheme with the coupled FEM/SBFEM was implemented into the existing program system (http://www.infam.tu-braunschweig.de/).

The arrangement of the equations of the cap model and of the overall calculation schemes is illustrated in detail. This can be used as a guideline for further implementations.

Part II:

After the formation of the theoretical basics in Part I, example calculations with the proposed calculation method are conducted in Part II. For this purpose, the Examples 1 to 3 are used to verify the given method and Example 4 is employed as practical example.

Notice to the examples: All results show primarily the applicability of the given algorithms. A transmission to real problems is only possible for Example 4 (see also section 8.2).

The comparison calculation in Example 1 shows a very good agreement (see Figure 9.3) of the implemented cap model with the results of the cap models from ABAQUS®, (DiMaggio & Sandler, 1971) und (Kojic & Bathe, 2005).

Good agreements with ABAQUS® are shown in the comparison of the calculations in Example 2 and 3, as well. Deviations are founded in the different yield surfaces for shear failure. The *yielding on failure surface* is associated in the implemented cap model and not associated in ABAQUS® (see Section 4.1.3).

The results of the elasto-plastic coupled FEM/SBFEM model were compared with the results of the linear-elastic coupled FEM/SBFEM model and the pure elasto-plastic FEM calculation in the examples.

The comparison shows significant differences between the different models. Hence, it can be concluded that the choice of the calculation model has a wide influence to the results. Herewith, the neglecting of the disadvantages of the pure FEM model and the linear-elastic FEM/SBFEM model can result in an inaccurate calculation.

As expected, the disadvantage of the pure elasto-plastic FEM calculation is the undesired wave reflection at the outer boundaries.

The linear-elastic calculation of the coupled FEM/SBFEM model does not include the plastic deformation of the subsoil. This results in too small deformations of the subsoil.

Furthermore, the oscillation transmission to nearby structures was considered. A calculation with the linear-elastic FEM/SBFEM model can be inaccurate if the nearby structure is located in the domain of the plastic deformation of the near-field. A significant difference between the results of the elasto-plastic and the linear-elastic FEM/SBFEM calculation was obtained here (see Section 11.3.3).

The calculation of the oscillation transmission to nearby structures with the pure elasto-plastic FEM model can be inaccurate, as well. Here, the results are distorted by the wave reflections.

The presented elasto-plastic FEM/SBFEM model compensates the named disadvantages of the other both methods due to the included elasto-plastic deformations and the wave propagation to infinity.

13.2 CONCLUSIONS

With the presented method it is possible to carry out "realistic" solid analysis of soil in time domain. The following influences are included: "realistic" deformation of the subsoil, dynamic effects and prevention of wave reflections at artificial boundaries. The word "realistic" is given in quotation marks because the numerical results of this work are not verified by experimental studies.

The solid analysis of soil was demonstrated with the help of example calculations for the section of shallow foundations. In principle the presented method can be applied to all other soil ground calculations, such as pile foundations or excavation pits. However, additional modifications, such as the use of interface elements at pile foundations, have to be conducted for this.

Plastic deformation of the near-field

The presented method includes in particular the plastic deformations of soil with simultaneous oscillation damping through wave propagation. The elasto-plastic deformation is only included in the near-field (see Chapter 7). This is sufficient because the soil in the far-field deforms elastically (in approximation). The location of the boundary between the domains with plastic deformation and elastic deformation has to be estimated with the help of the geometry and the loading. An approach for the adaptive coupling of the FEM/SBFEM interface with a plastic near-field is given in (Doherty & Deeks, 2005).

In conclusion it can be said that in oscillation investigations of the near-field and the structure an elasto-plastic calculation of the near-field cannot be ignored in general due to the great plastic deformations of soil (this is also recommended in many papers, e.g. (DGGT, 1991-2006)).

This fact can be clearly seen in the verification Examples 2 and 3, where the elasto-plastic deformations amount a multiple of the linear-elastic deformations (see Section 10.3.3 and Section 11.3.3). But also in the practically arranged Example 4, the elasto-plastic deformations are about 75% greater than the linear-elastic deformations, when the wave propagation is ignored. And with consideration of the wave propagation using the coupled FEM/SBFEM model of Chapter 7, the elasto-plastic deformations are about 25% greater than in the linear-elastic deformations. The magnitude of plastic deformation depends mainly on the properties of the soil. The soil of Example 4 deforms comparatively small due to its properties.

Damping phenomena

The presented method includes two damping phenomena. The first phenomenon is the damping through the wave propagation, which occurs automatically when a coupled FEM/SBFEM model is used. The second phenomenon is the hysteretic damping, which is included with elasto-plastic material. The hysteretic material damping occurs due to energy dissipation. Energy dissipation is characterized by the transmission of mechanical energy into thermal energy due to the inner material friction. The hysteretic material damping is automatically included with elasto-plastic material.

An advantage of the automatically included damping is that no damping values of the system have to be determined, because these damping values are generally not available or only difficult to find out.

However, an additional damping can be included if the automatic system damping of the presented method is not appropriate. This is shown in Example 1 where 10% damping are applied. Rayleigh constants are calculated from this 10% damping. Rayleigh damping was then applied with the calculated Rayleigh constants.

Nonlinear HHT-α method with full Newton-Raphson iteration

Furthermore, a nonlinear HHT-α method with a modified Newton-Raphson iteration from (Crisfield, 1997) was extended to a nonlinear HHT-α method with full Newton-Raphson iteration. The application of the full Newton-Raphson iteration is advantageous in certain situations due to better convergence; see e.g. (Bathe, Finite Elemente Methoden, 2002). This is appropriate if complex geometry or complex material behavior causes convergence problems. With it, a larger time step than in the modified Newton-Raphson iteration can be chosen, depending on the model.

Complexity of the presented method

The presented method is very complex and needs a large computational effort. This is a disadvantage mainly for the application in the engineering practice. But a further improvement of computer science will overcome this disadvantage. Moreover, improvements in the separate methods are continuously being made to reduce the computational effort; e.g. in (Lehmann, 2007).

13.3 APPLICATIONS OF THE PRESENTED METHOD

Dimensioning of constructional elements

The deformations between the elasto-plastic calculation and the linear-elastic calculation are different. This has an influence to the dimensioning of constructional elements which include elasto-plastic soil deformation. So, the foundation dimensioning of Example 4 is different for the elasto-plastic and linear-elastic calculation. The loading of the superstructure in Example 4 is also greater for the elasto-plastic settlement due to the greater foundation settlement in the elasto-plastic calculation.

Settlement calculations

The presented method includes elasto-plastic material behavior, dynamic loading and wave propagation. With it, a more accurate[2] settlement calculation than with the pure elasto-plastic FEM calculation or with the linear-elastic coupled FEM/SBFEM calculation is possible.

Earthquake calculations

If acceleration is applied to the outsides of the near-field, earthquake calculations can be conducted. With this loading the structure, which bounds at the near-field, can be calculated. The automatic hysteretic damping and the damping due to wave propagation is included. Earthquake calculations with a coupled linear-elastic FEM/SBFEM model are determined in, e.g., (Borsutzky, 2008).

13.4 OUTLOOK

Further developments of the presented method:

As a further development of the presented method a plastic deformation for the far-field is thinkable. For instance, an approach for a viscous boundary is given in (Wolf & Song, 1996). It could also be possible to define an accurate position of the boundary between the near-field and the far-field for standardized applications to reduce the computational effort.

Better convergence within the Newton-Raphson method:

If the equilibrium iterations did not converge it is generally sufficient to reduce the time or load step. The elasto-plastic calculation in time domain results in better convergence than the static elasto-plastic calculation. The reason is the amount of the mass matrix at the coefficient matrix, which increases when the time step is reduced.

In the presented method the loading or the accordant time is subdivided into linear load or time steps. This leads to divergence in some calculations. The divergence can be better suppressed if the time or load step is changed (if divergence occurs) variably over the whole calculation. For instance,

---

[2] The numerical results of this work are not verified by experimental studies

such a method is already implemented in the commercial program system ABAQUS®. However, ABAQUS® does not include a coupled FEM/SBFEM approach.

Further applications:

As mentioned in Chapter 9.4.2, the advantage of the HHT-α method is the damping of the higher eigenmodes. In engineering practice the lower eigenmodes are only of interest. The higher eigenmodes will be quickly dissipated by the structure (Ludescher, 2003).

It is difficult to determine appropriate damping values. The determination of accurate damping values is generally only possible by measurements at existing structures(Kramer, 2007), (Bathe, 2002). A further possibility is the transfer of existing damping values from similar structures to the model, which has to be calculated. Hence, an automatic included numerical damping of the higher eigenmodes simplifies the calculation.

Furthermore, the spatial FEM system approximates the lower eigenmodes much better than the higher ones (Bathe, 2002). For this reason, an incorporation of the higher eigenmodes can distort the solution, which can result in an inaccurate calculation. The HHT-α method with the FEM gives more accurate results because the higher eigenmodes are not incorporated (Bathe, 2002).

Due to these conclusions, it is interesting to analyze the oscillation behavior of the loaded structure more precisely. For this purpose, the presented elasto-plastic model with incorporated wave propagation and with the HHT-α method can be used. Hence, an example with a complex structure, e.g., a girder bridge or a high rise building, can be analyzed. The influences of the HHT-α method and of the wave propagation to this complex structure could be illustrated then.

An Approach for the adaptive coupling of the near-field/far-field interface is given in (Doherty & Deeks, 2005). This approach can be used for the further improving of the given method. With it, the elasto-plastic deformation, the wave radiation and the automatic adaption of the near-field/far-field interface are included. Herewith, computing time can be saved. Furthermore, the effort for the localization of the near-field/far-field interface is reduced.

Further investigations for applications such as earthquake loadings, excavation pits or pile foundations could be conducted with the presented method.

The presented algorithms are appropriate for the calculation of underground structures (such as tunnels and pipelines) without further modifications if friction between structure and adjacent soil can be neglected.

Moreover, oscillation transmissions from the considered structure to nearby buildings could be analyzed more precisely. This is interesting in particular if the nearby building is located in the domain of the plastic deformation of the near-field. The shield effect of a slotted wall (Dolling, 1970) could be analyzed in detail if a building is located in the domain of plastic deformation of the near-field (see Figure 13.1a).

A further application could be the analyzing of a sheet pile wall, which is driven in using a vibratory pile driver (see Figure 13.1b). A ram pile could be used instead of a sheet pile, as well.

Pile driving, adjacent to buildings, can lead to serious damages at these buildings (Mahutka & Grabe, 2005). Here, settlements occur without previous indications. These settlements are generally larger than in linear-elastic/dynamic calculations (Kramer, 2007). For these calculations, the presented method has to be adopted. So, e.g., interface elements have to be included between the sheet pile wall and the soil.

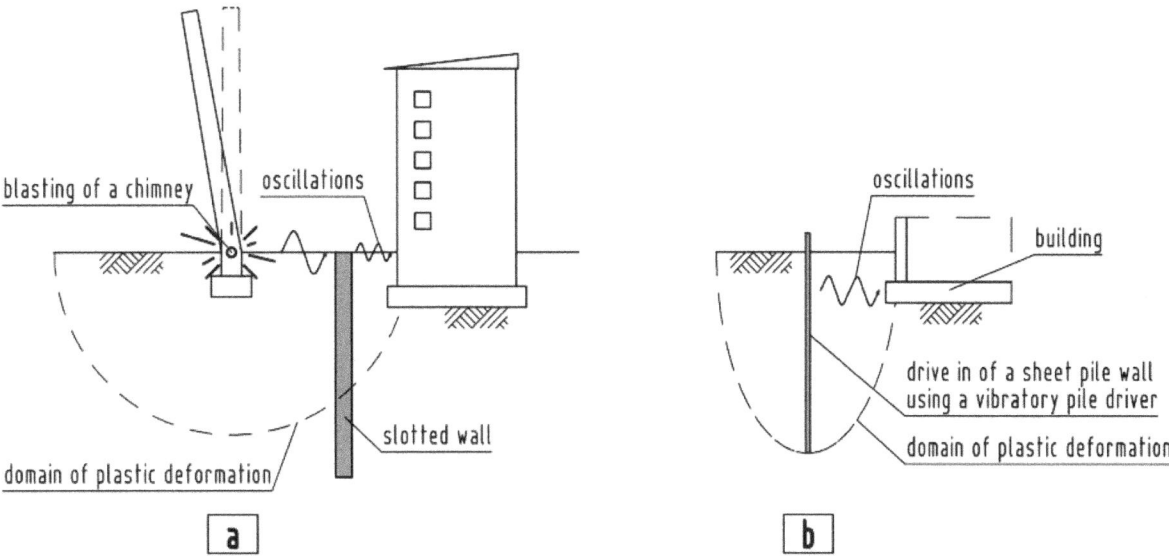

FIGURE 13.1. EXAMPLES FOR OSCILLATION TRANSMISSIONS TO ADJACENT BUILDINGS

The oscillation transmission from the considered structure to underground structures could be analyzed with the presented method, as well (see also Section 12.5.3). This is applied to structures, which are located in the domain of the plastic deformation of another structure. Examples would be the loading of a tunnel nearby to a footing (see Figure 13.2a) or the loading of a pipeline adjacent to a railway track (see Figure 13.2b).

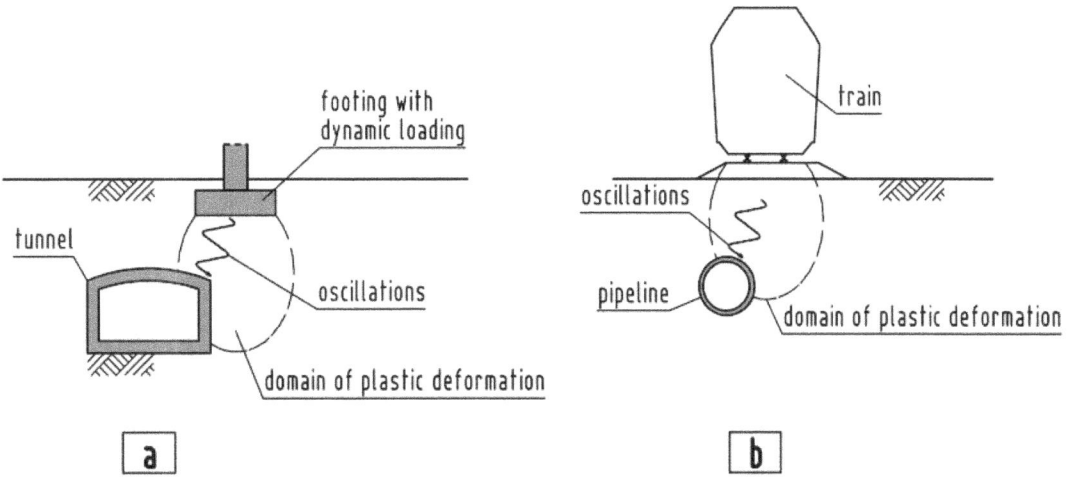

FIGURE 13.2. EXAMPLES FOR OSCILLATION TRANSMISSIONS TO UNDERGROUND STRUCTURES

14 BIBLIOGRAPHY

ABAQUS® User's Manual, ABAQUS®/Standard User's Manual, Version 6.5. (2004).

Abed, A. (2008). Dissertation: numerical modeling of expansive soil behavior. Stuttgart, Deutschland: Mitteilung - Institut für Geotechnik, Universität Stuttgart; 56.

Ang, A., & Newmark, N. (1963). Computation of underground structural response. *Technical report* . Urbana: DASA Report No. 1386.

Banerjee, P. (1994). *The Boundary Element Methods in Engineering.* London: McGraw-Hill.

Bathe, K. (2002). *Finite Elemente Methoden.* (P. Zimmermann, Übers.) Heidelberg: Springer.

Bathe, K., Chaudhary, A., Dvorkin, E., & Kojic, M. (1984). On the solution of nonlinear finite element equations. *Proc. Int. Conference on Computer Aided Analysis and Design of Concrete Structures I* (pp. 289-299). Swansea, U.K.: Pineridge Press.

Beskos, D. (1987). Boundary element methods in dynamic analysis. *Applied Mechanics Reviews* , Vol. 40, 1-23 .

Bettes, P. (1992). *Infinite Elements.* Sunderland, UK: Penshaw Press.

Bochmann, F. (2001). *Statik im Bauwesen, Band 1-3.* Berlin: Verlag Bauwesen.

Borsutzky, R. (2008). Seismic risk analysis of buried lifelines. *Dissertation* . Mechanik-Zentrum der Technischen Universität Braunschweig.

Brebbia, C., Telles, J., & Wrobel, L. (1984). *Boundary Element Techniques.* Berlin: Springer.

Chen, W. (1982). *Plasticity in reinforced concrete.* New York: McGraw-Hill.

Chen, W., & Mizuno, E. (1990). *Nonlinear Analysis in Soil Mechanics.* Amsterdam: Elsevier.

Clasen, D. (2008). *Numerische Untersuchung der akustischen Eigenschaften von trennenden und flankierenden Bauteilen.* Braunschweig: Mechanik-Zentrum der Technischen Universität Braunschweig.

Corliss, G. (1977). Which root does the bisection algorithm find? *19(2)*, 325-327.

Coulomb, C. (1776). Essai sur une application des regles des maximis et minimis a quelquels problemesde statique relatifs, a la architecture. *Mem. Acad. Roy. Div. Sav. , Vol. 7*, 343–387.

Crisfield, M. (1997). *Non-linear finite element analysis of solids and structures, Vol. 2 Advanced Topics.* John Wiley & Sons Ltd.

Crisfield, M. (1991). *Non-linear finite element analysis of solids and structures, Volume 1 Essentials.* Chichester: John Wiley & Sons.

Dasgupta, G. (1982). A finite element formulation for unbounded homogeneous media. *Journal of Applied Mechanics* , 136-140.

Dennis, J. J. (1976). A brief survey of convergence results for quasi-Newton methods. *SIAM-AMS Proceedings 9*, (pp. 185-200).

Desai, C. (2001). The disturbated state concept. *Mechanics of materials and interfaces* .

Desai, C., & Siriwardane, H. J. (1984). Constitutive laws for engineering materials. New Jersey: Prentice-Hall, Inc., Englewood Cliffs.

DGGT. (1991-2006). *Empfehlungen des Arbeitskreises "Numerik in der Geotechnik".* Deutsche Gesellschaft für Geotechnik, Arbeitskreis 1.6.

DiMaggio, F., & Sandler, I. (1971). Material model for granular soils. *Journal of the Engineering Mechanics Division* , 935-950.

DIN. (2009). *DIN-Fachbericht 101, Einwirkungen auf Brücken.* Berlin: Beuth Verlag GmbH.

Doherty, J., & Deeks, A. (2005). Adaptive coupling of the finite-element and scaled boundary finite-element methods for non-linear analysis of unbounded media. *Computers and Geotechnics 32 (2005) 436–444* .

Dolling, H.-J. (1970). Die Abschirmung von Erschütterungen durch Bodenschlitze. *Die Bautechnik 47* , Heft 5.

Drucker, D., & Prager, W. (1952). Soil mechanics and plastic analysis or limit design. *Q. Appl. Math. No. 2 , Vol. 10*, 157-164.

Duncan, J. M., & Chang, C. Y. (1970). Nonlinear analysis of stress and strain in soils. *Journal of the Soil Mechanics and Foundations Division, ASCE , 96(SM5)*, 1629-1653.

Estorff, O., & Firuziaan, M. (2000). Coupled bem/fem approach for nonlinear soil-structure interaction. *Engineering analysis with boundary elements , 24*, 715-725.

Estorff, O., & Kausel, E. (1989). Coupling of boundary and finite elements for soil-structure interaction problems. *Earthquake Engineering and Structural Dynamics* , (18), 1065-1075.

Gaul, L., & Fiedler, C. (1997). *Methode der Randelemente in Statik und Dynamik.* Wiesbaden: Friedrich Vieweg & Sohn.

Göhler, W., & Ralle, B. (1990). *Höhere Mathematik.* Leipzig: Deutscher Verlag für Grundstoffindustrie.

Graham, J., Noonan, M., & Lew, K. (1983). Yield states and stress-strain relationships in a natural plastic clay. *Canadian Geotechnical Journal, Vol. 20, No. 3* , 502-516.

Hackbusch, W., Schwarz, H., & Zeidler, E. (2003). *Taschenbuch der Mathematik, 2. Auflage.* Wiesbaden: Teubner Verlag.

Helwany, S. (2007). *Applied Soil Mechanics.* New Jersey: John Wiley & Sons.

Hibbitt, H., & Karlsson, B. (25-29 June, 1979). Analysis of pipe whip. *ASME Pressure Vessel and Piping Conference.* San Francisco.

Hibbitt, H., & Karlsson, B. (Nov. 1979). *Analysis of Pipe Whip, Report No. EPRI NP-1208.* Palo Alto: Electric Power Res. Inst.

Hilber, H., Hughes, T., & Taylor, R. (1977). Improved numerical dissipation for time integration algorithms. *Earthquake Engineering and Structural Dynamics* , 283-292.

Hughes, T. (1987). *The Finite Elemente Method.* New Jersey: Prentice Hall.

Katona, M. G. (1983). *Tension cutoff and parameter identification for the viscoplastic cap model.* Port Hueneme, CA 93043: Naval Civil Engineering Laboratory.

Kojic, M. (2002). Stress integration procedures for inelastic material models within the finite element method. *Appl. Mech. Reviews , Vol. 55, No. 4*, 389-414.

Kojic, M. (1996). The governing parameter method for implicit integration of viscoplastic constitutive relations for isotropic and orthotropic metals. *Computational Mechanics, Vol. 19* , 49-57.

Kojic, M., & Bathe, K. (2005). *Inelastic Analysis of Solids and Structures.* Berlin: Springer.

Kojic, M., Slavkovic, R., Grujovic, N., & Zivkovic, M. (1995). Implicit stress integration procedure for the generalized cap model in soil plasticity. In D. Owen, & E. Onate, *Computational Plasticity* (pp. 1809-1820). Swansea, U.K.: Pineridge Press.

Kramer, H. (2007). *Angewandte Baudynamik.* Berlin: Ernst & Sohn.

Krieg, R., & Krieg, D. (1977). Accuracies of numerical solution methods for the elastic-perfectly plastic model. *Journal of Pressure Vessel Technologiy 99 Nr.4* , pp. 510-515.

Lade, P. (1977). Elasto-plastic stress-strain theory for cohesionless soil with curved yield surfaces. *International Journal of Solids and Structures* , Vol. 13.

Lehmann, L. (2005). An effective finite element approach for soil structure analysis in the time-domain. *Structural Engineering and Mechanics* , 437-450.

Lehmann, L. (2007). Wave Propagation in Infinite Domains - With Applications to Structure Interaction. In *Volume 31 of Lecture Notes in Applied and Computational Mechanics.* Berlin, Wien, New York: Springer Verlag.

Lehmann, L., & Antes, H. (2001). Dynamic structure-soil-structure interaction applying the symmetric galerkin boundary element method (sgbem). *Mechanics Research Communications* , 297-304.

Ludescher, H. (2003). Berücksichtigung von dynamischen Verkehrslasten beim Tragsicherheitsnachweis von Straßenbrücken. *Dissertation , These Nr. 2894. EPFL.* Lausanne: Ecole Polytechnique Federale de Lausanne.

Lysmer, J. (1970). Lumped mass method for Rayleigh waves. *Bulletin of the Seismological Society of America* , Vol. 60, 89-104.

Lysmer, J., & Waas, G. (1972). Shear waves in plane infinite structures. *Journal of Engineering Mechanics Division* , Vol. 98, 85-105.

Mahutka, K.-P., & Grabe, J. (2005). Erschütterungs- und Sackungsprognose im Nahfeld von Rammarbeiten, Heft 80. *Pfahlsymposium* . Mitteilung des Institutes für Grundbau und Bodenmechanik der TU Braunschweig.

Matthies, H., & Strang, G. (1979). The solution of nonlinear finite element equations. *International Journal for Numerical methods in Engineering 14* , 1613-1626.

Muhs, H., & Weiß, K. (1972). Versuche über die Standsicherheit flach gegründeter Einzelfundamente in nichtbindigem Boden. *Mitteilungen der Deutschen Forschungsgesellschaft für Bodenmechanik an der Technischen Universität Berlin* , Heft 28, S.122.

Neto, E. d., Peric', D., & Owen, D. (2008). *Computational Methods for Plasticity.* Singapore: John Wiley & Sons Ltd.

Newmark, N. (1959). A method of computation for structural dynamics. *ASCE Journal of Engineering Mechanics Division* , 67-97.

Pugh, C., & Robinson, D. (1978). Some trends in constitutive equation model development für high temperature behaviour of fast-reactor structural alloys. *48*, 269-276.

Riks, E. (1979). An incremental approach to the solution of snapping and buckling problems. *International Journal of Solids and Structures 15* , 529-551.

Roscoe, K., & Burland, J. (1968). On the generalised stress-strain behaviour of wet clay. In J. Heyman, & F. Leckie, *Engineering Plasticity* (pp. 535-609). London: Cambridge University Press.

Roscoe, K., & Schofield, A. (1963). Mechanical behaviour of an idealized "wet" clay. *Proc. European Conf. on Soil Mechanics and Foundation Engineering, Vol. 1*, pp. 47-54. Wiesbaden.

Sandler, I., & Rubin, D. (1979). An algorithm and a modular subroutine for the cap model. *International Journal for Numerical and Analytical Methods in Geomechanics* , 173-186.

Sandler, I., DiMaggio, F., & Baladi, G. (1976). Generalized cap model for geological materials. *Journal of the Geotechnical Engineering Division* , 683-699.

Schade, H., & Neemann, K. (2006). *Tensoranalysis.* Berlin: Walter de Gruyter.

Schneider, K.-J. (1996). *Bautabellen für Ingenieure, 12. Auflage.* Düsseldorf: Werner-Verlag.

Silvester, P., Lowther, D., Carpenter, C., & Wyatt, E. (1977). Exterior finite elements for 2-dimensional field problesm with open boundaries. *Proceedings of the Institution of Electrical Engineers*, (pp. 1267-1270).

Simmer, K. (1994). *Grundbau Teil 1 und 2.* Stuttgard: Teubner.

Simo, J., & Hughes, T. (1998). *Computational Inelasticity.* New York: Springer Verlag.

Strang, G., & Fix, G. (1973). *An Analysis of the Finite Element Method.* Engelwood Cliffs: Prentice-Hall.

Terzaghi, K. (1943). *Theoretical Soil Mechanics.* New York: Wiley.

Thatcher, R. (1978). On the finite element method for unbounded media. *SIAM Journal of Numerical Analysis* , 466-477.

Türke, H. (1999). *Statik im Erdbau.* Berlin: Ernst & Sohn.

von Wolffersdorff, P.-A. (1996). A hypoplastic relation for granular materials with a predefined limit state surface. *Mechanics of Cohesive-Frictional Materials , Vol. 1*, 251–271.

Waas, G. (1972). Linear Two-Dimensional Analysis of Soil Dynamics Problems in Semi-Infinite Layered Media. *PhD dissertation* . Berkeley: University of California.

Wilkins, M. (1964). Calculation of elastic-plastic flow. In B. Alder, S. Fernback, & M. Rotenberg (Ed.). N.Y.: Academic Press.

Wolf, J. (1985). *Dynamic Soil-Structure Interaction.* N.Y.: Prentice Hall, Inc., Englewood Cliffs.

Wolf, J. (1988). *Soil-structure interaction analysis in time domain.* NJ.: Prentice-Hall, Inc., Engelwood Cliffs.

Wolf, J. (2003). *The Scaled Boundary Finite Element Method.* Chichester: John Wiley & Sons Ltd.

Wolf, J., & Song, C. (1996). *Finite Element Modelling of Unbounded Media.* Chichester: John Wiley & Sons Ltd.

Wriggers, P. (2001). *Nichtlineare Finite-Element-Methoden.* Berlin: Springer Verlag.

Zienkiewicz, O., & Taylor, R. (2005). *The Finite Element Method for Solids and Structural Mechanics* (Vol. 6). Butterworth-Heinemann.

Zienkiewicz, O., Taylor, R., & Zhu, J. (2005). *The Finite Element Method: Its Basis and Fundamentals* (Vol. 6). Butterworth-Heinemann.

III APPENDICES

A1 NOMENCLATURE

This appendix gives a list of the most commonly used symbols in the thesis. All symbols are also explained in the text when they appear for the first time.

1) Symbols:

A	area, surface or material constant for cap model
$\boldsymbol{B}$	strain displacement matrix [see Section 2.4]
B	vertical semi axis of the ellipse in cap model
B_1	material constant for cap model
$\boldsymbol{C}$	damping matrix
$\boldsymbol{C}^E$	elastic constitutive tangent matrix [see (A.7)]
$\boldsymbol{C}^{EP}$	elasto-plastic constitutive tangent matrix
D	material constant for cap model
$\boldsymbol{e}^E$	elastic strain tensor [see (A.5)]
$\boldsymbol{e}^P$	plastic strain tensor
$\boldsymbol{e}''$	trial elastic strain tensor
$\hat{\boldsymbol{e}}^E$	elastic strain vector [see (A.5)]
$\hat{\boldsymbol{e}}^P$	plastic strain vector
e_m	mean strain
e_V^P	plastic volumetric strain
E	Young's modulus
E^P	plastic modulus
$f(p)$	function of governing parameter p [see Section 4.2.2]
f_y	general yield function
f_1	yield function for yielding on failure surface
f_C	yield function for cap yielding
f_V	yield function for vertex yielding
$\boldsymbol{F}$	vector of internal forces
$\bar{\boldsymbol{g}}$	dynamic residual or dynamic out-of-balance forces [see Section 6.3.1]
$\boldsymbol{g}$	static residual or static out-of-balance forces [see Section 6.3.1]
G	shear modulus
$\boldsymbol{H}$	shape function matrix
i	iteration counter
$\boldsymbol{I}$	identity matrix
J_{2D}	second invariant of stress deviator
k	material constant for cap model

$\boldsymbol{K}$	stiffness matrix
$\bar{\boldsymbol{K}}$	stiffness matrix with included inertia terms
L	position of the center of the ellipse of cap model
$\boldsymbol{M}$	mass matrix
R	ratio between the semi axes of cap model
$\boldsymbol{R}$	vector of external forces
$\bar{\boldsymbol{R}}$	vector of external forces with included inertia terms
$\boldsymbol{S}$	stress deviator
$\boldsymbol{u}$	general displacement vector
$\boldsymbol{U}$	displacement vector at a finite element node
$\dot{\boldsymbol{U}}$	velocity vector at a finite element node
$\ddot{\boldsymbol{U}}$	acceleration vector at a finite element node
$\tilde{\boldsymbol{U}}$	nodal displacement vector as predictor [see Section 6.2]
$\dot{\tilde{\boldsymbol{U}}}$	nodal velocity vector as predictor [see Section 6.2]
W	material constant for cap model
X	position of the cap for cap model

2) Greek symbols:

α	material constant for cap model [in Chapters 4 and 5] or HHT-α constant [in Chapter 6]
$\boldsymbol{\beta}$	internal variables
β, γ	Newmark constants
δ_{ij}	Kronecker delta [see (A.1)]
$\Delta(\dots)$	increment in time step of the quantity (...)
λ	proportionality coefficient for stress-plastic strain relation
ν	Poisson's ratio
ρ	density
σ_m	mean stress
$\boldsymbol{\sigma}$	stress vector in Voigt notation [see (A.4)]
σ^E	trial elastic stress solution in time step

A2 MATHEMATICAL NOTATION

The used symbols should contain all necessary information, but in compact notation, so that the equations can easily be understood and written. Generally in this work a symbolic notation or an index notation was used.

In the symbolic notation bold symbols for vectors and matrices are used:

A, a - denotes a Scalar

$\boldsymbol{A}, \boldsymbol{a}$ - denotes a vector or a matrix

The same in index notation:

A, a - denotes a Scalar

A_i, a_i - denotes a vector

A_{ij}, a_{ij} - denotes a matrix

The multiplication of vectors and matrices in symbolic notation is denoted as:

$$\boldsymbol{C} = \boldsymbol{A}.\boldsymbol{B}$$

For the index notation the Einstein summation convention is applied. After this, all variables over the same indices in one term are added. For example:

$$\sigma_{ij}\, n_j = \sum_{j=1}^{3} \sigma_{ij}\, n_j$$

If the same indices in one term are underlined, they are not added:

$$a_i = b_{\underline{i}}\, c_{\underline{i}} \quad no\ sum\ on\ i$$

The Kronecker delta symbol is given as:

$$\boxed{\begin{array}{l} \delta_{ij} = 1 \ \ if \ \ i = j \\[4pt] \delta_{ij} = 0 \ \ if \ \ i \neq j \end{array}} \tag{A.1}$$

As denoted in Equation (A.1), equations of particular importance are framed in this work.

The inverse of a matrix $\boldsymbol{A}$ is denoted as $\boldsymbol{A}^{-1}$. Hence:

$$\delta_{ik} = A_{ij}\, A_{jk}^{-1} \ respectively\ \boldsymbol{I} = \boldsymbol{A}.\boldsymbol{A}^{-1}$$

with the Identity Matrix $\boldsymbol{I}$.

The Euclidean norm of a vector $\boldsymbol{a}$ is denoted as:

$$\|\boldsymbol{a}\| = \sqrt{(a_i\, a_i)} \tag{A.2}$$

For simplicity the iteration counter (i) in the time steps is not always used. In fact, the current time step $(t + \Delta t)$ corresponds to the state at iteration (i) and the previous time step (t) corresponds to the state at the iteration $(i - 1)$. For example:

$$^{t+\Delta t}e = {}^{t+\Delta t}e^{(i)}$$

If it is not otherwise denoted, the comma convention is used for abbreviations in partial differentiation. This is written as:

$$\frac{\partial a_i}{\partial x_j} = a_{i,j} \tag{A.3}$$

A3 ELASTIC CONSTITUTIVE RELATIONS

The indices 1,2,3 and x, y, z are used for the Cartesian components. Constitutive matrices with two indices are used here. So the stress and strain tensors σ and e are written in the *one index notation* (Voigt notation) as:

$$\sigma^T = [\sigma_1, \sigma_2, \sigma_3, \sigma_4, \sigma_5, \sigma_6] \tag{A.4}$$

with:

$$\sigma_1 = \sigma_{11}; \sigma_2 = \sigma_{22}; \sigma_3 = \sigma_{33};$$
$$\sigma_4 = \sigma_{12}; \sigma_5 = \sigma_{23}; \sigma_6 = \sigma_{31}$$

and:

$$\hat{e}^{E^T} = [e_1^E, e_2^E, e_3^E, e_4^E, e_5^E, e_6^E] \tag{A.5}$$

with:

$$e_1^E = e_{11}^E; e_2^E = e_{22}^E; e_3^E = e_{33}^E;$$
$$e_4^E = \gamma_{12}^E; e_2^E = \gamma_{23}^E; e_3^E = \gamma_{31}^E;$$

where the engineering strains are:

$$\gamma_{12}^E = 2\, e_{12}^E; \gamma_{23}^E = 2\, e_{23}^E; \gamma_{31}^E = 2\, e_{31}^E$$

The constitutive relation for an elastic isotropic material for the general three-dimensional case is given as:

$$\sigma = C^E . \hat{e}^E \tag{A.6}$$

With the elastic constitutive matrix C^E (unfilled cells are zero) defined as:

$$C^E = \frac{E\,(1-v)}{(1+v)(1-v)}
\begin{bmatrix}
1 & \frac{v}{1-v} & \frac{v}{1-v} & & & \\
\frac{v}{1-v} & 1 & \frac{v}{1-v} & & & \\
\frac{v}{1-v} & \frac{v}{1-v} & 1 & & & \\
& & & \frac{1-2v}{2\,(1-v)} & & \\
& & & & \frac{1-2v}{2\,(1-v)} & \\
& & & & & \frac{1-2v}{2\,(1-v)}
\end{bmatrix} \tag{A.7}$$

where E is the Young's modulus and v is the Poisson's ratio.

Further shear modulus G is given as:

$$G = \frac{E}{2\,(1 + v)}$$

(A.8)

And the mean stress σ_m and mean elastic strain e_m^E are defined as:

$$\sigma_m = \frac{\sigma_1 + \sigma_2 + \sigma_3}{3}$$

(A.9)

$$e_m^E = \frac{e_1^E + e_2^E + e_3^E}{3}$$

(A.10)

The mean stress σ_m can also be calculated as:

$$\sigma_m = c_m\, e_m^E \quad no\ sum\ on\ m$$

(A.11)

with:

$$c_m = \frac{E}{(1 - 2\,v)}$$

(A.12)

c_m can be related to the bulk modulus K as:

$$K = \frac{1}{3} c_m$$

(A.13)

The mean elastic strain e_m^E can also be related to the elastic volumetric strain e_V^E as:

$$e_m^E = \frac{1}{3}\, e_V^E$$

(A.14)

Two possibilities for calculation of deviatoric stress S_{ij} are defined as:

$$S_{ij} = \sigma_{ij} - \sigma_m\, \delta_{ij}$$

(A.15)

$$S_{ij} = 2\, G\, e'^E_{ij}$$

(A.16)

where the elastic deviatoric strains e'^E_{ij} is:

$$e'^E_{ij} = e_{ij}^E - e_m^E \quad if\ i = j$$

$$e'^E_{ij} = \frac{1}{2}\, \gamma_{ij}^E \quad\quad if\ i \neq j$$

(A.17)

S_{ij} and e'^E_{ij} can also be written in one index notation. Therefore, p_i and q_i are introduced:

$$p_i{}^T = [1,1,1,0,0,0]$$

(A.18)

$$q_i{}^T = [1, 1, 1, \frac{1}{2}, \frac{1}{2}, \frac{1}{2}] \tag{A.19}$$

Then S_{ij} and e'^E_{ij} with $e^E_i = $ (A. 5) are given as:

$$e'^E_i = e^E_{\underline{i}} \, q_{\underline{i}} - e^E_m \, p_i \quad no \; sum \; on \; \underline{i} \tag{A.20}$$

$$S_i = 2 \, G \, e'^E_i = [S^E_1, S^E_2, S^E_3, S^E_4, S^E_5, S^E_6]^T = [S^E_{11}, S^E_{22}, S^E_{33}, S^E_{12}, S^E_{23}, S^E_{31}]^T \tag{A.21}$$

www.ingramcontent.com/pod-product-compliance
Lightning Source LLC
Chambersburg PA
CBHW080803020726
47504CB00007B/1882